The Safe House

Nicci French

PENGUIN BOOKS

PENGUIN BOOKS

Published by the Penguin Group
Penguin Books Ltd, 80 Strand, London WC2R ORL, England
Penguin Putnam Inc., 375 Hudson Street, New York, New York 10014, USA
Penguin Books Australia Ltd, 250 Camberwell Road,
Camberwell, Victoria 3124, Australia
Penguin Books Canada Ltd, 10 Alcorn Avenue, Toronto, Ontario, Canada M4V 3B2
Penguin Books India (P) Ltd, 11 Community Centre,
Panchsheel Park, New Delhi – 110 017, India
Penguin Books (NZ) Ltd, Cnr Rosedale and Airborne Roads,
Albany, Auckland, New Zealand
Penguin Books (South Africa) (Pty) Ltd, 24 Sturdee Avenue,
Rosebank 2196, South Africa

Penguin Books Ltd, Registered Offices: 80 Strand, London WC2R ORL, England

www.penguin.com

First published by Michael Joseph 1998
Published in Penguin Books 1998

33

Set in Monotype Plantin Light
Typeset by Intype London Ltd
Printed in England by Clays Ltd, St Ives plc

To Pat and John

One

The door was the first thing. The door was open. The front door was never open, even in the wonderful heat of the previous summer that had been so like home, but there it was, teetering inwards, on a morning so cold that the moisture hanging in the air stung Mrs Ferrer's pocked cheeks. She pushed her gloved hand against the white painted surface, testing the evidence of her eyes.

'Mrs Mackenzie?'

Silence. Mrs Ferrer raised her voice and called for her employer once more and felt embarrassed as the words echoed, high and wavering, in the large hallway. She stepped inside and wiped her feet on the mat too many times, as she always did. She removed her gloves and clutched them in her left hand. There was a smell, now. It was heavy and sweet. It reminded her of something. The smell of a barnyard. No, inside. A barn maybe.

Each morning at eight-thirty precisely Mrs Ferrer would nod a good-morning at Mrs Mackenzie, click past her across the polished wood of the Mackenzies' hallway, turn right down the stairs into the basement, remove her coat, collect her vacuum cleaner from the utility room and spend an hour in an anaesthetized fog of noise. Up the large staircase at the front of the house, along the passageways on the first floor, the passageways on the second floor, then down the small back staircase. But where was Mrs

Mackenzie? Mrs Ferrer stood uncertainly by the door in her tightly buttoned porridge-meal-tweed coat, shifting her weight from one foot to another. She could hear a television. The television was never on. She carefully rubbed the sole of each shoe on the mat. She looked down. She had already done that, hadn't she?

'Mrs Mackenzie?'

She stepped off the mat on to the hard wood – beeswax, vinegar and paraffin. She walked across to the front room, which was never used for anything and hardly ever needed vacuuming, though she did it anyway. There was nobody, of course. The curtains were all closed, the light on. She walked across to the foot of the staircase to the other front room. She rested her hand on the newel, which was topped by an ornate carving like a beaked pineapple of dark wood. Afrormosia – linseed oil, it needed, boiled, not raw. There was nobody. She knew that the television was in the sitting room. She took a step forward, her hand brushing the wall as if for safety. A bookcase. Leather bindings, which required lanolin and neat's-foot in equal quantities. It was possible, she reflected, that whoever was watching television had not heard her call. And as for the door, perhaps something was being delivered, or the window cleaner may have left it open on his way in. Thus fortified she walked to the rear of the house and into the main sitting room. Very quickly, within a few seconds of entering the room, she had vomited profusely on to the carpet that she had vacuumed every weekday for eighteen months.

She leaned towards the ground, bent double, gasping. She felt in her coat pocket, found a tissue and wiped her mouth. She was surprised at herself, embarrassed almost. When she was a child, her uncle had led her through a slaughterhouse outside Fuenteobejuna and had smiled down at her as she refused to faint in the face of the blood and dismemberment and above all the steam rising from the cold stone floor. That was the smell she had remembered. It wasn't a barn at all.

There were splashes of blood across such a wide area, even on the ceiling, on the far wall, that Mr Mackenzie might have exploded. Mostly, though, it was in dark pools on his lap and on the sofa. There was so much of it. Could it be from just one man? What had made her sick, perhaps, was the ordinariness of his pyjamas, so English, even the top button done up. Mr Mackenzie's head now lolled back stupidly at an impossible angle. His neck was cut almost through and there was nothing to hold it up except the back of the sofa. She saw bone and sinew and the improbable spectacles, still uselessly over his eyes. The face was very white. And a horrible unexpected blue as well.

Mrs Ferrer knew where the phone was but had forgotten and had to look for it. She found it on a small table, on the other side of the room away from all the blood. She knew the number from a television programme. Nine nine nine. A female voice answered.

'*Hello. There has been a terrible murder.*'

'Excuse me?'

'*There has been a murder.*'

'It's all right. Calm down, don't cry. Can you speak English?'

'*Yes, yes. I am sorry. Mr Mackenzie is dead. Killed.*'

It was only when she had replaced the receiver that she thought of Mrs Mackenzie and walked upstairs. It took only a second for Mrs Ferrer to see what she had feared. Her employer was tied to her own bed. She seemed almost submerged in her blood, her nightie glossy with it against her gaunt body. Too thin, Mrs Ferrer had always thought privately. And the girl? She felt a weight in her chest as she walked up another flight of stairs. She pushed open the door of the one room in the house she wasn't allowed to clean. She could hardly see anything of the person tied to the bedstead. What had they done to her? Brown shiny tape around the face. Arms outstretched, wrists tied to the corners of the metal grille, thin streaks of red across the front of the nightgown.

Mrs Ferrer looked around Finn Mackenzie's bedroom. Bottles were scattered across the dresser and the floor. Photographs were torn and mutilated, faces gouged out. On one wall, a word she didn't understand was written in a smeary dark pink: piggies. She turned suddenly. There had been a sound from the bed. A gurgle. She ran forward. She touched the forehead, above the neat obscuring tape. It was warm. She heard a car outside and heavy footsteps in the hall. She ran down the stairs and saw men in uniform. One of them looked up at her.

'Alive,' Mrs Ferrer gasped. 'Alive.'

Two

I looked around me. This wasn't countryside. It was a
wasteland into which bits of countryside had been
dropped and then abandoned, a tree or a bush here and
there, a hedgerow stripped bare for winter, a sudden field,
stranded in the mud and marsh. I wanted a geographical
feature – a hill, a river – and I couldn't find one. I tugged
off a glove with my teeth to look at the map and let it fall
on to the slimy grass. The large sheet flapped wildly in
the wind until I concertinaed it into a wad and stared
at the pale brown contours and dotted red footpaths and
dashed red bridleways. I had followed the dotted red line
for miles but had failed to reach the sea wall that would
lead me back to the place where I had begun. I peered
into the distance. It was miles away, a thin twist of grey
against sky and water.

I looked at the map again, which seemed to disintegrate
under my gaze, an unbroken code of crosses and lines,
dots and dashes. I was going to be late for Elsie. I hate
being late. I'm never late. I'm always early, the one who's
kept waiting – standing crossly under the clock, sitting in
a café with a cooling cup of tea and a tic of impatience
under my right eye. I am never, not ever, late for Elsie.
This walk was meant to take exactly three and a half hours.

I twisted the map: I must have failed to see the fork in
the path. If I cut across to the left, along that thin black

line, I could cut off the headland of marsh and meet the sea wall just before it reached the hamlet where my car was parked. I shoved the map, now splitting at its folds, into my anorak pocket and picked up the glove. Its cold muddy fingers closed around my numbing ones. I started to walk. My calf muscles ached and my nose ran, snotty little dribbles down my stinging cheeks. The huge sky threatened rain.

Once, a dark-coloured bird, its long neck outstretched and its wings heavily batting the air, flew low past me, but otherwise I was quite alone in a landscape of grey-green marsh and grey-blue sea. Probably something rare and interesting, but I don't know the names of birds. Nor of trees, except obvious ones like weeping willows, and the plane trees that stand on every London street, sending out roots to undermine the houses. Nor of flowers, except obvious ones like buttercups and daisies, and the ones you buy from a florist on a Friday evening and stick in a vase for when friends come round: still-life roses, irises, chrysanthemums, carnations. But not the feeble plants that were scratching at my boots as I walked towards a small copse that didn't seem to be getting any nearer. Sometimes when I lived in London I would feel oppressed by all the billboards, shop signs, house numbers, street names, area codes, vans bearing legends 'Fresh Fish' or 'Friendly Movers', neon letters flashing on–off–on in the orange sky. Now I didn't have the words for anything at all.

I came to a barbed-wire fence which separated the marsh from what looked like something farmed. I held the wire firmly down with the ball of my thumb and swung one leg over.

'May I help you?' The voice sounded friendly. I turned

towards it, and a barbed prong embedded itself in the crotch of my jeans.

'Thanks, but I'm fine.' I managed to get my other leg over. He was a middle-aged bearded man, in a brown quilted jacket and green boots. He was smaller than me.

'I'm the farmer.'

'If I go straight across here, will I arrive at the road?'

'I own this field.'

'Well . . .'

'This is not a public right of way. You are trespassing. On my land.'

'Oh.'

'You have to go that way.' He pointed gravely. 'Then you'll come to a footpath.'

'Can't I just . . .?'

'No.'

He smiled at me, not unpleasantly. His shirt was wrongly buttoned at the neck.

'I thought of the countryside as something you were free to walk around in.'

'Do you see my wood over there?' he asked grimly. 'Boys from Lymne' – he pronounced it Lumney – 'started riding their pushbikes down the track through the wood. Then it was motorbikes. It terrified the cows and made the track impassable. Last spring, some people wandered across my neighbour's field with their dog and killed three of his lambs. And that's not with all the gates being left open.'

'I'm sorry about that but . . .'

'And Rod Wilson, just over there, he used to send calves over to Ostend. They started with the picketing of the port at Goldswan Green. Couple of months ago, Rod's

7

barn was burned down. It'll be somebody's house next. Then there's the Winterton and Thell Hunt.'

'All right, all right. You know what I'll do? I'll climb back over this gate and head in a huge circle around your land.'

'Do you come from London?'

'I did. I've bought Elm House on the other side of Lymne. *Lumney*. You know, the one without any elms.'

'They've finally managed to sell that, have they?'

'I came to the country to get away from stress.'

'Did you now. We always like visitors from London. I hope you'll come again.'

Friends had thought I was joking when I said I was going to work at the hospital in Stamford and live in the countryside. I've only ever lived in London – I grew up there, or at least in its trailing suburbs, went to university there, did my pre-med there, worked there. What about take-aways?, one had said. And, what about late-night films, twenty-four-hours shops, babysitters, M&S meals, chess partners?

Danny, though, when I'd summoned up the courage to tell him, had looked at me with eyes full of rage and hurt.

'What is it, Sam? Want to spend quality time with your kid on some fucking village green? Sunday lunch and planting bulbs?' Actually, I *had* imagined a few bulbs.

'Or,' Danny had continued, 'are you finally leaving me? Is that what this is all about, and is that why you never even bothered to tell me you were applying for a job in the sticks?'

I'd shrugged, cold and hostile in the knowledge that I was behaving badly.

'I didn't apply for it. *They* applied to *me*. And we don't live together, Danny, remember. You wanted your freedom.'

He'd given a kind of groan and said, 'Look, Sam, maybe the time has come . . .'

But I'd interrupted. I didn't want to hear him say we should live together at last and I didn't want to hear him say we should leave each other at last, although I knew that soon we would have to decide. I'd put one hand on his resistant shoulder. 'It's only an hour and a half away. You can come and visit me.'

'*Visit* you?'

'Stay with me.'

'Oh, I'll come and stay with you, my darling.' And he'd leaned forward, all dark hair and stubble and the smell of sawdust and sweat, and yanked me to him by the belt that was looped through my jeans. He'd unbuckled my belt and pulled me down on the lino of the kitchen, warm where a heating pipe ran underneath, his hands under my cropped head saving it from banging as we fell.

If I ran I might be in time for Elsie. On the sea wall the wind screamed and the sky was swallowed up by the water. My breath came in bursts. There was a bit of grit in my left shoe, pressing up under the ball of my foot, but I didn't want to stop. It was only her second day at school. The teacher will think I'm a bad mother. Houses: I see houses at last. Nineteen-thirties, red brick and square, a child's drawing of a home. Smoke curling perfectly, one–two–three puffs, out of the neat row of chimneys. And there was the car. I might be on time after all.

Elsie tipped from heel to toe, toe to heel. Her slick fair

hair swung as she moved. She was wearing a brown donkey jacket and a checked red and orange dress, and on her stocky legs she had pink spotty tights, which were wrinkled around her steadily pivoting ankles ('You told me I could choose my clothes and I want these,' she'd said truculently at breakfast). Her nose was red and her eyes were vacant.

'Am I late?' I hugged her unyielding bulk.

'Mungo was with me.'

I looked around the deserted playground.

'I can't see anyone.'

'Not now.'

That evening, after Elsie had gone to sleep, I felt lonely in my house by the sea. The dark outside was so very dark, the silence so eerily complete. I sat by the unmade fire with Anatoly on my lap, and his purr as I scratched behind his ears seemed to fill the room. I poked aimlessly around in the fridge, eating a lump of hardened cheese, half an apple, a chunk of nut-and-raisin milk chocolate. I rang up Danny but only got his stiff answering-machine voice and didn't leave a message.

I turned on the television for the evening news. A wealthy local couple had been brutally murdered, their throats cut. A picture of their formally smiling faces, his florid and plump, hers pale and thin and self-effacing, was followed by a view of their large red house from the end of a wide gravelled drive. Their teenage daughter was 'comfortable' in Stamford General. There was a blurry school photograph that must have been years old, a happy, roundly plump face, poor thing. A large police officer said something about unstinting efforts, a local politician expressed shock and outrage and called for measures.

Briefly, I wondered about the girl in hospital, her savaged future. Then the news switched to an obstacle in a peace process somewhere, and very quickly I forgot all about her.

Three

'After you.'

'No, after you.'

'For God's sake, pour it, you wally.'

They were four deep around the coffee machine, uniforms and suits fighting over the sugar and the milk jug. They were in a hurry. Seating in the generally unused conference room was restricted, and nobody wanted to be late for this one.

'It's a bit soon for a case conference, isn't it?'

'That's what the Super wants.'

'I'd say it's a bit soon.'

The conference room was in the new extension of Stamford Central police station, all Formica and strip lighting and the hum of the heating system. The head of the CID, Superintendent Bill Day, had called the meeting for 11.45 on the morning that the bodies had been discovered. Blinds were pulled up, revealing an office building opposite, whose mirrored windows reflected a bright winter sky. An overhead projector and a video recorder were pushed into the far corner. Plastic chairs were peeled from stacks against the wall and crammed around the long table.

Detective Inspector Frank 'Rupert' Baird edged his way through the ruck of officers – he towered over most of them – and took his seat at the end. He dumped some files on the table in front of him and looked at his watch, fingering his moustache reflectively. Bill Day and a senior uniformed man came into the room, which at once became silent, attentive. Day went and sat near Rupert Baird, but the uniformed man pointedly remained standing, just to one side of the door, leaning lightly back against the wall. Bill Day spoke first.

'Good morning, gentlemen,' he said. 'And ladies,' he added, catching the ironic eye of WPC MacAllister down at the far end of the table. 'We won't keep you long. This is just a preliminary meeting.' He paused, scanning the faces around the table. 'Look, lads. We need to get this one right. No pissing about.' There were nods of acknowledgement. 'I'd like to take the chance to introduce Chief Superintendent Anthony Cavan, who'll be new to most of you.'

The uniformed man by the door nodded at the heads turned towards him.

'Thanks, Bill,' he said. 'Good morning, everybody. I'm here for the press conference, but I wanted to put my head round the door, show some encouragement. Pretend I'm not here.'

'Yes,' said Bill Day, with a thin smile. 'I've asked Detective Inspector Baird to chair the meeting. Rupert?'

'Thank you, sir,' said Baird, and he shuffled some papers on the desk in front of him with a purposeful air. 'The point of this introductory meeting is to establish clarity right from the outset. Stamford CID is going to be under the spotlight. Let's not make fools of ourselves. Remember the Porter case.' Everybody knew the Porter case, if only by repute: the TV documentaries, the appeal, the books, the early retirements, reassignments. The atmosphere became noticeably chillier. 'I'll try to cover the ground as quickly as I can. Ask any questions. I want everybody to get all this straight.' He put his reading spectacles on and looked down at his notes. 'The bodies were found at about eight-thirty this morning. Thursday the eighteenth of January. The victims are Leopold Victor Mackenzie and his wife. Elizabeth. Mr Mackenzie was the chairman of Mackenzie & Carlow. They made medicines, drugs, that sort of thing. Their daughter, Fiona, was taken to Stamford General.'

'Will she live?'

'I haven't heard. We've got her in a fully secure room at the hospital with minimum access. Her own doctor insisted on it and we think he's right. A couple of PCs are standing by.'

'Has she said anything?'

'No. The emergency call was made by the family's Spanish cleaning lady, a Mrs Juana Ferrer, shortly after half-past eight. The scene was secured within ten minutes. Mrs Ferrers is downstairs at the moment.'

'Did she see anything?'

'Apparently not, she . . .'

Baird paused and looked up as the door opened. A middle-aged man with unbrushed hair and wire-framed spectacles stepped into the room. He was carrying a bulging briefcase and he was panting.

'Philip, thanks for stopping by,' said Baird. 'Could somebody give him a chair?'

'Haven't got time. I've just come from the house and I'm on my way to Farrow Street. I want to walk the bodies straight through. I can give you about one minute. Anyway, I don't think I'm much use to you here.'

'This is Dr Philip Kale, the Home Office pathologist,'

Baird explained to the meeting. 'What can you tell us?'

Dr Kale placed his bag on the floor and frowned.

'As you know, one of my responsibilities as a forensic pathologist is not to construct premature theories. But . . .' He began to count off his fingers, '. . . based on examination of the bodies at the scene, the two cases seem strikingly similar. Cause of death: anaemic anoxia, due to the incised wounds in the throats, which some of you have seen. Manner of death: their throats were cut with a blade, possibly non-serrated, of at least two centimetres in length. It could be anything from a Stanley knife to a carving knife. Mode of death: homicide.'

'Can you tell us the time of death?'

'Not with precision. You must understand that anything I say about this is very preliminary.' He paused for a moment. 'When I examined the bodies at the scene, hypostasis had commenced but was not fully developed. I would estimate that the deaths occurred more than two hours before they were found and not more than, say, five or six hours. Definitely not more than six.'

'The daughter couldn't have survived five hours with her throat cut, could she?'

Dr Kale paused for thought.

'I haven't seen her. Possibly not.'

'Anything else you can tell us? Anything about the murder?'

Dr Kale gave the smallest hint of a smile.

'The person who wielded the knife was using his or her right hand and has no disabling aversion to blood. And now I must go. The autopsies should be complete by mid afternoon. You'll have a report.'

There was a hum of conversation in the moments after

his departure, silenced by a rap of Baird's knuckles on the desk.

'Is there anything from the crime-scene people?'

There was a shaking of heads.

'I talked to the cleaning woman.'

It was Detective Chris Angeloglou who had spoken.

'Yes?'

'She said that the day before yesterday Mrs Mackenzie gave a party in the house. There were two hundred people there. Bad news. Sorry.'

'Christ.'

'Yes.'

'We'll just have to let them get on with it. We'll need a list of who was there.'

'I'm already on to it.'

'Good. We haven't found any signs of forced entry as yet. But it's early days. Anyway, you could open their front door with a credit card, a plastic ruler, anything. A cursory survey of the contents showed some rifling of drawers, cupboards. Lots of damage. Photographs torn and smashed.'

'Looking for something?'

'We'll leave the theories until we've gathered the information and collated it. I don't want officers looking for evidence to prove a theory. I want all the evidence. You can start thinking after that.' He looked down at his notes. 'What else is there? There was the writing on the wall, in Mrs Mackenzie's lipstick. "Piggies."'

'Manson,' said DC Angeloglou.

'What's that?'

'Isn't that what the Manson gang wrote on the wall in blood, when they killed all those people in California? "Death to Pigs." It's from a Beatles song.'

'All right, Chris. Look into it. Don't get carried away. It's probably a blind alley. So that's where we are now, which isn't anywhere much. I'm going to wind up in a moment. If you pop round to Christine afterwards, you can get a copy of the roster. The investigation is going to involve searching every inch of the house, knocking on doors in the area, talking to Mackenzie & whatever the company's called and interviewing people who were at the party. We've already got officers at the railway station and roadblocks on the Tyle road asking for witnesses. I hope we'll catch the bastard inside twenty-four hours. If we don't, I want a lot of information to fall back on. Any questions?'

'Did they have any enemies?'

'That's why we're having an inquiry.'

'Were there a lot of valuables in the house?'

'Go and find out. You're a policeman.'

'It may just be very simple, sir.'

Baird's bushy eyebrows rose to a forty-five degree angle. Everybody turned to Pam MacAllister down at the far end.

'Enlighten us WPC MacAllister.'

'If she survives, the daughter may be able to tell us.'

'Yes,' said Baird drily. 'Meanwhile, until she is fit to give a statement, we could pretend that we're policemen. Or policewomen. I will if you will.'

Pam McAllister reddened but said nothing.

'Right,' said Baird, grabbing his papers and standing. 'If you come across anything significant, see me. But don't waste my time.'

Four

'Wind up your window.'

'But I'm too hot.'

'It's freezing; we'll both get pneumonia. Wind it up.'

Elsie struggled sulkily with the handle. The window inched up and stopped.

'Can't.'

I leaned across her cross body. The car veered.

'Can we have my tape on? The worm tape.'

'Are you enjoying school?'

Silence.

'What did you do yesterday?'

'Dunno.'

'Tell me three things you did yesterday.'

'I played. And I played. And I played.'

'Who did you play with?' Brightly. Eagerly.

'Mungo. Can I have my tape?'

'The tape machine's broken. You shoved coins down it.'

'It's not fair. You promised.'

'I did not promise.'

'I'm telling of you.'

We'd been up three hours already, and it wasn't even nine o'clock. Elsie had slipped into my bed before six, scrambled up beside me, pulling the duvet off in the icy dawn, scratching my legs with her toenails, which I'd failed to cut, putting cold little feet against my back, butting her head under my arm, kissing me with a warm, wet, pursed mouth, peeling back my eyelids with her expert fingers, turning on the bedside light so that for a moment the room full of unpacked boxes and cases from which creased clothes spilled had disappeared in a dazzle of pain.

'Why can't you collect me?'

'I've got to work. Anyway, you like Linda.'

'I don't like her hair. Why do you have to work? Why can't Daddy work and you stay at home like other mummies?'

She doesn't have a daddy. Why does she say things like that?

'I'll come and get you as early as I can from Linda, I promise. I'll make you your supper.' I ignored the face she made at that. 'And I'll take you to school in the mornings. All right?' I tried to think of something cheerful. 'Elsie, why don't we play our game? What's in the house?'

'Don't know.'

'You *do* know. What's in the kitchen?'

Elsie closed her eyes and wrinkled her brow with the effort.

'A yellow ball.'

'Brilliant. What's in the bath?'

'A packet of Coco Pops.'

'Fantastic. And what's in Elsie's bed?'

But I'd lost her. Elsie was staring out of the window. She pointed at a low, slatey cloud. I turned on the radio. ' . . . freezing weather . . . high winds . . . north-easterlies'. Did that mean *from* the north-east or *towards* the north-east? What did it matter? I turned the knob: crackles, jazz, crackles, stupid discussion, crackles. I switched it off and focused on the landscape, such as it was. Was it for this I'd left London? Flat, furrowed, grey, wet, with an occasional industrial-looking barn made of aluminium or breeze-block. Not a good place to hide.

When I was trying to make up my mind about the Stamford job, I made a list. On one side I'd listed the PROS, the other the CONS. I love lists – every day at work I make long ones, with priorities asterisked in a different colour. I feel in control of my life once I've reduced it to a half-sheet of A4, and I love crossing off the things I've done, neatly. Sometimes I even put at the top of the list a few neatly crossed-out tasks I've already completed, as a way of getting some momentum which I hope will get me through the things I haven't done.

What had the pros been? Something like this:

> *Countryside*
> *Bigger house*
> *More time to spend with Elsie*
> *Job that I've always wanted*
> *More money*
> *Time to finish the trauma project*
> *Walks*
> *Pet for Elsie (?)*
> *Smaller school*
> *Work out relationship with Danny*
> *Adventure and change*
> *More time* (this was asterisked several times since it engulfed all the other reasons)
> On the con side it simply said:
> *Leave London.*

I grew up in the suburbs and through my teenage years I

only ever wanted to get to the centre, the hub, the bull's eye. I used to go shopping in Oxford Street with my mother when I was little and she was still choosing my clothes (demure circle skirts, polo-neck tops, neat jeans, navy sandals with nibbly little buckles, sensible coats with brass buttons, thick ribbed tights that never stayed up properly, and 'Oh, look at you, you're getting so tall,' my mother would say as she tried to force my gangly body into clothes for dainty girls). I'd sit at the top of the double-decker bus and stare at the crowds, the dirt, the chaos, the wild-haired youths swinging down the pavements, couples kissing on the corners, the hot bright shops, the disorder of it all, the terror and the delight. I always said I was going to be a doctor and move into the centre of London. While Roberta was dressing her dolls and carrying them around, clutched to her chest, cooing, I was amputating them. I was going to be a doctor because no one that I knew was a doctor, and because half of my class at school wanted to be nurses and because my mother raised her eyebrows and shrugged every time I told her my ambition.

London to me meant tiredness, early-morning starts, traffic jams, jaunty radio stations every notch along the dial, dirt in my clothes, dog shit on the pavements; meant I was called 'doctor' by men who looked like my father; meant advancement and money in the bank that I could spend on loud ear-rings and unsensible coats and pointy shoes with loud buckles on them; meant sex with strangers on strange weekends that I could hardly remember now, except for the sense in my euphoric body that I'd abandoned Edgware, not Edgware the place, but the Edgware in my mind with its Sunday lunches and three streets to get to somewhere that wasn't a house. London meant having Elsie and losing her father. London meant Danny. It was the geography of my coming of age. As I drove into Stamford, having unpinned Elsie's fingers from my jacket and kissed her suddenly flushed cheeks and promised on an impulse to collect her from school myself, I suddenly missed London as if it were a lover, a far-off object of desire. Though, actually, the city had betrayed me after Elsie was born, had become a grid of playgrounds and crèches and babysitters and Mothercares. A parallel universe I'd never even noticed until I'd joined it, working in the week, pushing a buggy on Saturday and Sunday, swearing revenge.

This was what I had dreamed of. Time. Me, alone in the house, and no child and no nanny and no Danny and no schedule that ticked away in my mind. There was a miaow and a prickle of claws on my leg. Opening the cat food at arm's length, I filled Anatoly's bowl and shoved it and him out of the back door. A breath of air blew a whiff of the tuna and rabbit in jelly back into my face, provoking a heaving cough and memories of seasickness. How could something like that be good even for a cat? I washed up Elsie's bowl and mug from breakfast, and made myself a cup of instant coffee with water that hadn't properly boiled, so the granules floated to the surface. Outside, rain dripped on to my waterlogged garden; the pink hyacinths that I'd been so excited about yesterday had tipped sideways in the rubbly soil, and their rubbery petals looked grimy. Apart from the sound of rain I could hear nothing, not even the sea. A feeling of dreariness crept over me. Normally, I would have been at work for two, maybe three or, in a crisis, four hours by now; the phone would be ringing, my in-tray would be overflowing, my secretary would bring me a cup of tea and I'd be dismayed by how quickly the morning was going. I turned on the radio: 'Four small children died in a . . .', and turned it off again hastily. I wished that someone had sent me a letter; even junk mail would be better than nothing.

I decided I ought to work. The drawing that Elsie had done for me last week, when I'd complained about forlorn spaces on the sallow, peeling walls of my study, gazed accusingly down at me from where I'd pinned it above my desk. The room was dank and chilly, so I switched on the bar fire; it heated up my left leg and made me feel droopily in need of a morning nap.

The screen of my word processor glowed green. A cursor pulsed at a healthy sixty beats a minute. I clicked the mouse on the hard disk, then on the empty folder called Book. 'Even a journey of a thousand miles must begin with a single step,' somebody irritating had once said. I created a file and labelled it 'Introduction'. I opened the file and wrote 'Introduction' again. The word sat, pitifully small, at the head of a green, blank space. I highlighted it and upped the typesize, then changed the font so that it thickened and slanted. There, that looked better, more impressive anyway.

I tried to remember what I'd written in my proposal for the publisher. My brain felt as shiny and empty as the screen in front of me. Perhaps I should start with the title. What does one call a book about trauma? In my proposal I'd simply called it 'Trauma', but that sounded bald, a kind of scholarly idiot's guide, and I wanted this to be controversial, polemical and exciting, a look at the way trauma as a label is misused, so that real sufferers remain invisible, while disaster junkies jump on the bandwagon. I typed, in large print, above the 'Introduction', 'The

Hidden Wound' and centred it. That sounded like a book about menstruation. With a smooth swipe of the mouse, I erased the letters. 'From Shell Shock to Culture Shock'. No, no, no. 'Trauma Victims and Trauma Addicts'? But that was a small strand of the book, not its overall pattern. 'Soul Searching'. That was a title for a religious pamphlet. 'On Grief's Track'. Yuk. How about 'The Trauma Years'? I'd save that for my memoirs. At least time was passing now. For nearly three quarters of an hour I typed and erased titles, until at the end I was back at the start. 'Introduction.'

I ran myself a bath and filled it with expensive oils and lay in its slippery warmth till my fingers shrivelled, reading a book about end-games in chess and listening to the sound of rain. Then I ate two pieces of toast with mashed sardines on top and the remains of a cheesecake that had been sitting shrink-wrapped in the fridge for days and two chocolate biscuits and a rather pulpy slice of melon.

I went back to the melancholy green on the computer screen and typed firmly: 'Samantha Laschen was born in 1961 and grew up in London. She is a consultant psychiatrist who heads the new Referral Centre for Post-Traumatic Stress Disorder based in Stamford. She lives in the Essex countryside with her five-year-old daughter and her cat, and in her spare time plays chess.' I crossed out the bit about the cat (too fey). And the bit about chess. I erased my age (too young to be authoritative, too old to be prodigious) and the bit about growing up in London and now living in Essex (boring). I erased Elsie – I wasn't going to wear my daughter like an accessory. I looked at what was left; maybe we doctors were too hung up on status. There, I liked it: 'Samantha Laschen is a consultant psychiatrist.' Or what about just 'Samantha Laschen is . . .' Minimalism has always been my style. I lay back in my chair and shut my eyes.

'Don't move,' said a voice, and two warm and callused hands were put over my closed eyes.

'Mmmm,' I said, and tilted back my head. 'Blindfolded by a strange man.'

I felt lips at the pulse of my throat. My body slipped in the chair, and I felt its tensions uncurl.

'Samantha Laschen is . . .' Well, I can't argue with that. But maybe there are better ways for you to spend your days than writing three words, eh?'

'Like what?' I asked, still blind, still limp where I sat with my face in the fold of his rough hands.

He swivelled the chair around and when I opened my eyes his face was a few inches from mine: eyes so brown under their straight dark eyebrows that they were nearly black, hair an unwashed tangle over a battered leather jacket, stubbly cleft chin, smell of oil, wood shavings, soap. We didn't touch each other. He looked at my face and I looked at his hands.

'I didn't hear you arrive. I thought you were building a roof.'

'Built. Installed. Paid for. How long have we got before you have to collect Elsie?'

I looked at my watch.

'About twenty minutes.'

'Then twenty minutes will have to be enough. Come here.'

'Mummy.'

'Yes.'

'Lucy said your hair has died.'

'She didn't mean it's dead, she probably meant that I dye it. Colour it.'

'Her mummy's hair is brown.'

'Yes, well – '

'And Mia's mummy's hair is brown too.'

'Would you like my hair to be brown as well?'

'It's a very bright red, Mummy.'

'Yes, you're right, it is.' Sometimes I still got a shock myself when I met my face in the speckled bathroom mirror on a groggy morning: white face, fine lines beginning to grow and spread around the eyes and a flaming crop of hair on a nobbly neck.

'It looks like' – she stared out of the window, her stolid body leaning out from her safety straps – 'like that red light.'

Then there was quiet, and when I next glanced round she was fast asleep, thumb babyishly in her mouth, head tilted to one side.

I sat on one side of Elsie's narrow bed and read her a book, occasionally pointing to a word which she would falteringly spell out or madly, inaccurately, guess at. Danny sat on the other and twisted small scraps of paper into the shape of an angular flower, a nimble man, a clever dog. Elsie sat between us, straight-backed, eyes bright and cheeks flushed, self-consciously sweet and serious. This was like a proper family. Her glance darted between us, tethering us. My body glowed with the memory of my brief encounter with Danny on my dusty study floor and in anticipation of the evening ahead. As I read, I could feel Danny's gaze on me. The air felt thick between us. And when Elsie's speech slipped, stopped, and her eyelids closed, we went into my bedroom without a word and took off each other's clothes and touched each other, and the only sound was the drip of rain outside or sometimes a breath that was louder than normal, like a gasp of pain. It felt as if we hadn't seen each other for weeks.

Later, I took a pizza out of the freezer and put it in the oven, and while we ate it in front of the fire which Danny had lit, I told him about progress with the trauma unit, and Elsie's first days at school, about trying to start the book and my encounter with the farmer. Danny talked about what friends he'd seen in London and perching on damp crumbling rafters in the bitter cold, and then he laughed and said that as I rose up through my profession, so he fell: from acting, to resting, to carpentry, now to doing odd jobs, building a roof for a cantankerous old woman.

'Don't,' he said, when I started hastily to say something about success being about more than work, 'don't bluster. You don't need to worry so. You like what you do and I like what I do.'

When the fire died away, we went up the creaking stairs once more, looked in at Elsie sleeping in a nest of duvet and soft toys, made our way to the double bed and lay facing each other, sleepy and uncomplicated.

'Maybe we could,' he said.

'Could what?'

'Live together. Even' – his hand rubbed my back, his voice became very light and casual – 'even think of having a child.'

'Maybe,' I muttered sleepily. 'Maybe.'

It was one of our better days.

Five

'Everything all right, sir?'

'No.'

'Let me cheer you up. Fancy something to read?'

Detective Angeloglou tossed a pamphlet on to Rupert Baird's desk. Baird picked it up and grunted at the faded print.

'*Rabbit Punch*? What's this?'

'You're not a subscriber? We've got the full run of issues downstairs. It's the house magazine of ARK.'

'ARK?'

'It stands for the Animal Rights Knights.'

Baird groaned. He gently patted the hair on top of his head which covered but did not conceal the bald scalp underneath.

'Really?'

'Oh, yes. They're the ones who broke into the mink farm over at Ness in '92. They set the mink free.' Angeloglou consulted the file he was carrying. 'They fire-bombed the supermarket in Goldswan Green in '93. Then nothing much till the university explosion last year. They've also been involved in some of the more extreme veal protests, the direct actions against farmers and transport companies.'

'So?'

'Look at this.'

Angeloglou opened the magazine to its central pages, a section under the headline in red ink: 'Butchers shopped.'

'Is this relevant?'

'This is one of the services they provide to readers. They print the names and addresses of people they accuse of torturing animals. Look, here's Professor Ronald Maxwell of the Linnaeus Institute. He researches bird-song. He uses caged birds. Dr Christopher Nicholson has been sewing up the eyelids of kittens. Charles Patton runs the family fur company. And here we have Leo Mackenzie, Chairman of Mackenzie & Carlow.'

Baird seized the magazine.

'What is . . . what was he meant to be guilty of?'

'Experiments on animals, it says here.'

'Bloody hell. Well done, Chris. Have you checked it out?'

'Yes. At its Fulton laboratories, the company are working on a project, partly financed by the Department of Agriculture. It's on stress in animal husbandry, they told me.'

'What does it involve?'

Angeloglou smiled broadly.

'This is the good bit,' he said. 'The research involves giving pigs electric shocks and lacerating them in various ways and testing their responses. Have you ever seen a pig being killed?'

'No.'

'They cut the throat. Blood all over the place. They make black pudding with it.'

'I can't stand black pudding,' said Baird, turning several pages of the magazine over. 'I don't see a date. Do we know when this was published?'

'You don't get *Rabbit Punch* at your local newsagent.

Its publication is best described as intermittent, and its distribution is patchy. We obtained this copy six weeks ago.'

'Was Mackenzie warned about this?'

'He'd been told about it,' said Angeloglou. 'But it was nothing new. From what they say at his head office, he was used to things like this.'

Baird frowned with concentration.

'What we need now are some names. Who was it who headed the animal operation? Mitchell, wasn't it?'

'Yes, but he's arse-deep in the West Midlands at the moment. I've been on the phone to Phil Carrier who was his DI. He's spent the last couple of months wandering around burnt barns and wrecked lorries. He's going to come up with some names.'

'Good,' said Baird. 'Let's move quickly on that. What's the latest with the Mackenzie girl?'

'She's conscious. Not critical.'

'Any chance of a statement?'

Angeloglou shook his head.

'Not at the moment. The doctors say she's in deep shock. Hasn't said anything yet. Anyway, she was hooded, remember. I wouldn't hold my breath for anything there.'

As recently as 1990, Melissa Hollingdale had been a biology teacher in a comprehensive school without even an unpaid parking ticket on her record. Now she was an habituée of police interrogation rooms with a file that scrolled up the screen for page after page. Looking through the one-way mirror, Chris Angeloglou sat and stared at this impassive woman in her mid thirties. Her long thick dark hair was tied up behind, no make-up. Her skin was pale, smooth, clean. She dressed for speed.

A flecked turtleneck, jeans, trainers. Her hands, laid palm down and steady on the table in front of her, were surprisingly dainty and white. She waited with no sign of impatience.

'We'll start with Melissa, then?'

Angeloglou turned. It was Baird.

'Where's Carrier?'

'He's out. There's a report of a bomb sent to a turkey farm.'

'Christ.'

'Inside a Christmas card.'

'Christ. Bit late, isn't it?'

'He'll be over later.'

A constable appeared carrying a tray with three cups of tea. Angeloglou took it. The two detectives nodded at each other and went in.

'Thank you for coming to see us. Cup of tea?'

'I don't drink tea.'

'Cigarette?'

'I don't smoke.'

'Do you have the file, Chris? What are Miss Hollingdale's qualifications for being here?'

'She's a coordinator for the Vivisection and Export Alliance. VEAL.'

'I've never heard of it,' said Hollingdale evenly.

Angeloglou looked down at his file.

'How long have you been out now? Two months, is it? No, three. Malicious damage, assaulting a policeman, affray.'

Hollingdale allowed herself a resigned smile.

'I sat down in front of a lorry at Dovercourt. Now what is all this about?'

'What is your current occupation?'

'I'm having difficulty finding an occupation. I appear to be on various blacklists.'

'Why do you think that is?'

She said nothing.

'Three days ago a businessman called Leo Mackenzie and his wife were murdered in their home in the Castletown suburb of Stamford. Their daughter is critically ill in hospital.'

'Yes?'

'Do you ever read a magazine called *Rabbit Punch*?'

'No.'

'It's an underground magazine produced by a terrorist animal-rights group. The most recent issue published the name and address of Mr Mackenzie. Six weeks later he, his wife and his daughter had their throats cut. What do you have to say about that?'

Hollingdale shrugged.

'What do you feel about activism of this kind?' Baird asked.

'Have you brought me in here for a discussion about animal rights?' Hollingdale asked with a sarcastic smile. 'I'm against any creature having its throat cut. Is that what you want me to say?'

'Would you condemn such acts?'

'I'm not interested in making gestures.'

'Where were you on the night between the seventeenth and the eighteenth of January?'

Hollingdale was silent for a long time.

'I suppose I was in bed, like everybody else.'

'Not everybody. Do you have any witnesses?'

'I can probably find one or two people.'

'I bet you can. By the way, Miss Hollingdale,' added Baird. 'How are your children?'

She started, as if in pain, and her expression hardened.

'Nobody will tell me. Will *you*?'

'Mark Featherstone, or should we call you by your adopted name of Loki?'

Loki was dressed in extravagantly varied fabrics, sewed together into a shapeless tunic over baggy white cotton trousers. His red hair was knotted into dreadlocks which hung down over his back at stiff angles, like giant pipe cleaners. He smelled of patchouli oil and cigarettes.

'Does that rhyme with "hockey" or with "chokey"? I suppose "chokey" would be more appropriate.' Angeloglou consulted his file. 'Breaking and entering. Burglary. Assault. I thought you were against violence?'

Loki said nothing.

'You're a clever man, Loki. Chemical engineering. A Ph.D. Useful training for manufacturing explosives, I suppose.'

'Were they blown up, then, this couple?' said Loki.

'No, though my colleagues will no doubt be asking you about the parcel received at Marshall's Poultry.'

'Did it go off?'

'Fortunately not.'

'Well, then,' said Loki contemptuously.

'Mr and Mrs Mackenzie's throats were cut. How do you feel about that?'

Loki laughed.

'I guess he'll think twice before torturing animals again.'

'You sick bastard, what do you think you'll achieve by murdering people like that?'

'Do you want a lecture about the theory of revolutionary violence?'

'Try us,' said Baird.

'The torture of animals is part of our economy, part of our culture. The problem is no different from that faced by opponents of slavery or the American colonists, any oppressed group. You just have to make the activity uneconomic, unpalatable.'

'Even if that involves murder?'

Loki leaned back in his chair.

'Wars of liberation have their price.'

'You little shit,' said Baird. 'Where were you on the night of the seventeenth of January?'

'Asleep. A broken sleep. Like the Mackenzies.'

'You'd better hope you have a witness.'

Loki smiled and shrugged.

'Who's hoping?'

'Let me read you something, Professor Laroue,' said Baird, holding a sheet of typescript. 'Forgive me if I don't do the style justice:

> *All of us accept limits to our obligation to obey the law. After the Holocaust we may further accept that there are times when we are obliged to violate the law, even to violate the limits of what we would normally consider to be acceptable behaviour. I anticipate that future generations will ask us about our own holocaust, the holocaust of animals, and ask us how we could stand by and do nothing? We in Britain are living with Auschwitz every day. Except this time it's worse because we can't plead ignorance. We have it for breakfast. We wear it. What will we say to them? Perhaps the only people able to hold their heads up will be those who did something, those who fought back.*

'Do you recognize that, Professor?'

Frank Laroue's hair was cut so short that it was almost like a film of gauze draped across his skull. He had very pale-blue eyes, with curiously tiny pupils, so that he looked already flash-bulb blind. He was dressed in an immaculate fawn suit, with a white shirt and canvas shoes. He had a pen in his fingers which he rotated compulsively, sometimes tapping it on the table.

'Yes. It is a part of a speech that I delivered at a public meeting last year. Incidentally, it has never been published. I would be interested to know how you got a copy of it.'

'Oh, we like to get out in the evenings. What did you mean by that passage?'

'What is all this? My views about our responsibilities towards animals are well known. I've agreed to come and answer questions but I don't understand what you want.'

'You've written for *Rabbit Punch*.'

'No, I haven't.' He gave a half-smile of acknowledgement. 'Things I have written or things I have said may have been reproduced there, as in other magazines. That is quite a different matter.'

'So you read it?'

'I've seen it. I have an interest in the field.'

Chris Angeloglou was leaning against the wall. Baird took his jacket off and draped it over the chair on the opposite side of the table from where Laroue was sitting. Then he sat down.

'Your speech is a clear incitement to violence.'

Laroue shook his head.

'I'm a philosopher. I made a comparison.'

'You suggested it was people's duty to take violent action in defence of animals.'

There was a short pause. Then, patiently, 'It's not a

matter of my suggestion. I believe that, objectively, it is people's duty to take action.'

'Is it *your* duty?'

'Yes.' He smiled. 'It follows.'

'*Rabbit Punch* believes the same thing, doesn't it?'

'How do you mean?'

'The magazine publishes the names and addresses of people it accuses of harming animals. The point of this is to encourage violent action against those people?'

'Or their property, perhaps.'

'That wasn't a distinction you made in your lecture.'

'No.'

Baird leaned heavily across the table.

'Do you believe it was wrong to kill Leo Mackenzie and his family?'

Tap, tap, tap.

'Objectively speaking, no, I don't,' he said. 'Could I have some tea or water or something?'

'What about the innocent victims?'

'Innocence is a difficult term to define.'

'Professor Laroue, where were you on the night of the seventeenth of January?'

'I was at home, in bed with my wife.'

Baird turned to Angeloglou.

'Give me the file, will you? Thanks.' He opened it and thumbed through some pages before finding what he wanted. 'Your wife is Chantal Bernard Laroue, is she not?'

'Yes.'

Baird ran his finger down the page.

'Hunt sabotage, hunt sabotage, public order, public order, obstruction, she's even moved on to some assault here.'

'Good for her.'

'But not necessarily good for you, Professor Laroue. Would you like to talk to your solicitor?'

'No, officer.'

'Detective Inspector.'

'Detective Inspector.' A smile spread across Laroue's pale bony face and he raised his eyes to meet Baird's gaze for the first time. 'This is all crap. Speeches and where was I on the night of the whatever. I'm leaving now. If you want to talk to me again, make sure you've got something to talk to me *about*. Will you open the door, please, officer?'

Angeloglou looked at Baird.

'You heard the bastard,' said Baird. 'Open the door for him.'

In the doorway, Laroue turned and faced the two detectives:

'We're going to win, you know.'

Paul Hardy said nothing at all. He sat in his long canvas overcoat, as if removing it would itself be a minor concession. Once or twice he pushed his hand through his curly brown hair. He glanced at Baird and Angeloglou in turn, but mostly he stared into space. He didn't reply to questions or acknowledge he had even heard them.

'Do you know about the Mackenzie murders?'

'Where were you on the night of the seventeenth?'

'You realize that if charges are preferred, your silence may be cited in evidence against you.'

Nothing. After several futile minutes there was a tap at the door. Angeloglou answered it. It was a young WPC.

'Hardy's brief's here,' she said.

'Show him in.'

Sian Spenser, a firm-jawed woman in her early forties, was out of breath and cross.

'I want five minutes alone with my client.'

'He hasn't been accused of anything.'

'Then what the hell is he doing here? Out. Now.'

Baird drew a deep breath and left the room, followed by Angeloglou. When Spenser brought them back into the room, Hardy was seated with his back to the door.

'My client has nothing to say.'

'Two people have been murdered,' Baird said, his voice raised. 'We have evidence to suggest that animal-rights activists were involved. Your client has been convicted of conspiracy to cause criminal damage. He was fucking lucky that he wasn't caught with the explosives. We want to ask him some questions.'

'Gentlemen,' said Spenser. 'I want my client out of this building within five minutes or I'll file a prerogative writ.'

'DC Angeloglou.'

'Sir?'

'Let it be noted for the record that Paul Michael Hardy has refused any cooperation with this inquiry.'

'Have you quite finished?' Spenser asked with a quizzical expression that was almost amused.

'No, but you can take your piece of filth out with you.'

Hardy stood and moved to the door. He paused in front of Angeloglou. A thought seemed to occur to him.

'How's the girl?' he asked, then walked away without waiting for an answer.

An hour later, Baird and Angeloglou were in Bill Day's office for a debriefing. Bill Day was standing at the window looking out into the darkness.

'Anything?' Day asked.

'Nothing concrete, sir,' said Angeloglou cautiously.

'I didn't expect anything,' said Baird. 'I just wanted to get a feel for the people. Get the smell of it.'

'And?'

'I think it's an avenue worth going down.'

'What have we got?'

'Almost nothing. The reference in the magazine, the message written at the scene.'

'*Almost* nothing?' Day asked sarcastically. 'Scene of crime?'

Baird shook his head.

'It's not good. There was this huge reception a couple of days before. Hair and fibres is a total disaster. The girl's room may be better.'

'What about the girl?' Day asked. 'Have we got anywhere with her?'

Baird shook his head.

'What are we going to do with her?'

'She's ready to be discharged.'

'Is this a problem?'

'It's possible, just possible, mind, she may be at some risk.'

'From these animal-shaggers?'

'From whoever.'

'Can they keep her in the hospital for a few more days?'

'This may be for months, not days.'

'What's her mental state?'

'Upset. Traumatic stress, that sort of thing.'

Day grunted.

'Jesus, we got through two world wars without fucking stress counsellors. Look, Rupert, I'm not happy with all this but go ahead and find her somewhere discreet. For

God's sake, make sure it's somewhere the press won't find.'

'Where?'

'I haven't a clue. Ask Philip Kale, he may have some names.'

Baird and Angeloglou turned to leave.

'Oh, Rupert?'

'Yes?'

'Find me some bloody evidence. I'm getting nervous.'

Six

In just a couple of weeks I had managed to construct a life for myself. I had a house and a garden. The house was old with large windows and a solid, four-square shape and stood on what must have been a quayside long ago. Now it looked forlornly across marshland to the sea, half a mile away.

In the hectic few days after buying the house in November I had asked around in the estate agent and in the shop a couple of miles up the road in Lymne and found a child-minder. Linda was small and slight with a pasty complexion and seemed older than her twenty years. She lived in Lymne and though she was lacking in GCSEs, she had the two main qualifications I was interested in: a driving licence and an air of calm. When Elsie first met her she went and sat on her lap without a word, which was enough for me. At the same time I arranged for Linda's best friend, Sally, to come two or maybe three times a week to clean the house.

The nearest primary school, St Gervase's, is in Brask, three miles on the other side of Lymne, and I went and looked through the railings. There was a green playing field, bright murals on the wall, and I didn't see many tears or children left to fend for themselves. So I walked into the office and filled out the form, and Elsie was accepted on the spot.

It had all seemed almost alarmingly easy: a grown-up life to go with my imminent grown-up job. A few weeks into January, when Britain was starting to get going again after Christmas and when Danny had been staying for five days and was still showing no sign at all of going again, filling my house with beer cans and my bed with warmth, I went to Stamford General Hospital to meet the deputy chief executive of the trust who administered it. He was called Geoffrey Marsh, a man of about my own age so immaculately turned out that he looked as if he was just about to present a television news programme. And his office looked big and elegant enough to double as the studio for it. I felt immediately underdressed, which must have been part of the point.

Geoffrey Marsh took me by the hand – 'Call me Geoff, Sam' – and told me that he was immensely enthusiastic about me and about my unit. He was convinced it was going to be a new model for patient management. He took me for a walk up staircases and along corridors to show me the empty wing that I would fill. There was almost nothing to see except how big it was. It was on the ground floor, which I liked. There was a patch of green outside a window. I could do something with that.

'What used to be here?' I asked.

He shook his head as if this were an unimportant detail.

'Let's head back to my office. We've got to arrange some brain-storming sessions, Sam,' he said. He used my name like a mantra.

'About what?'

'About the unit.'

'Have you read my proposal? I thought the staffing and therapeutic protocols I laid out there were clear enough.'

'I read it last night, Sam. A fascinating starting-point,

and I want to assure you that it is firmly my belief that this unit, and you, will put the Stamford General Trust on the map, and my aim is that it must be as good as it can be.'

'I'll need to liaise with social services, of course.'

'Yes,' said Marsh, as if he hadn't heard, or hadn't wanted to hear. 'First I want to get you together with my Human Resources Manager and the management working party for the current programme of expansion.' We were back in his office by now. 'I want to show you the energy-flow structure I have in mind.' He drew a triangle. 'Now at this apex . . .' His phone rang and he answered it with a frown. 'Really?' he said and looked at me. 'It's for you. A Dr Scott.'

'Dr Scott?' I said in disbelief, taking the receiver. 'Thelma, is that you? . . . How on earth did you find me? . . . Yes, of course, if it's important. Do you want to meet in Stamford? . . . All right, whatever you want. It'll be your chance to see the new style I'm living in.' I gave her an address and the elaborate directions I already had off by heart about the third exit on the roundabout and level crossings and duck pond with no ducks in it and said goodbye. Marsh was already on another phone. 'I'm afraid I've got to go. It's urgent.' He nodded at me and gave me a brisk wave in a pantomime of being busy. 'I'll ring you next week,' I said, and he nodded in response, obviously engrossed in something else.

I drove straight home. Danny's van was still in the drive but he wasn't in the house and his leather jacket was no longer hanging on the hook. A few minutes later Thelma spluttered up in her old Morris Traveller. I smiled as I watched her stride across to the path, her head darting around, assessing where I'd ended up. She wore jeans and a long tweed coat. Thelma could look inelegant in anything. I didn't find her comic, though. Nobody whose research had been supervised by Thelma Scott found her comic. I opened the door and gave her a big hug, which required some dexterity as she was getting on for a foot shorter than I was.

'I can see the house,' she said. 'Where are the elms?'

'I can take you round the back and show you the tree stumps. This is the first place the beetles came when they got off the ferry from Holland.'

'I'm amazed,' she said. 'Green fields, silence, a garden. Mud.'

'Nice, isn't it?'

She gave a dubious shrug and walked past me into the kitchen.

'Coffee?' she said.

'Make yourself at home.'

'How's the book going?' she asked.

'Fine.'

'Bad as that? Danny still around?'

'Yes.'

Without asking, she opened the food cupboard and removed a packet of ground coffee and some biscuits. She heaped tablespoon after tablespoon of coffee into a jug. Then she sprinkled some salt on top.

'A pinch of salt,' she said. 'That's my secret for good coffee.'

'What's your secret for why you're here?'

'I've been doing some work for the Home Office. We're looking at the neurological pathology of childhood recall. It's all to do with the capacity of small children to give evidence in criminal trials.' She poured the coffee into two mugs with a great show of concentration. 'One result of becoming a member of the fairly great and good is that you get tickets to things you were never able to get tickets to before.'

'Sounds nice. Are you here to ask me to the opera?'

'Another result is that people ring you with odd requests. Yesterday somebody asked me something about post-traumatic stress disorder, about which I know almost nothing.'

I laughed.

'Happy is the doctor who *knows* that she knows nothing about post-traumatic stress.'

'Not only that, it concerned a problem that has arisen in Stamford. I was struck by the remarkable coincidence that the best person I know in the field has just moved up the road from Stamford, so I came to see you.'

'I'm flattered, Thelma. How can I help you?'

Thelma took a bite from a biscuit and frowned.

'You should keep biscuits in a tin, Sam,' she said. 'Left in an open packet, they go soft. Like this one.' But she finished it anyway.

'Not if you eat the whole packet in one day.'

'We have a nineteen-year-old girl whose parents have been murdered. She was attacked also but survived.'

'Using my famous forensic skills, I think I can guess at the case you're talking about. This is the murder of the pharmaceutical millionaire and his wife.'

'Yes. Did you know him?'

'I think I may have used his shampoo occasionally.'

'So you know the details. Fiona Mackenzie's life is not in any immediate danger. But she is scarcely speaking. She has refused to see anybody she knows. I understand that there are no surviving relatives in Britain, but she won't see any family friends.'

'You mean nobody at all? It's none of my business, but she should be encouraged to restore some sort of connection.'

'She allowed the family's GP to visit her. I think that's all.'

'That's a start.'

'What would you recommend for a case such as hers?'

'Come on, Thelma, I can't believe you've come up here from London for my advice about a patient I've only read about in the papers. What's going on?'

Thelma smiled and refilled her mug.

'There's a problem. The police consider that she is possibly still at risk from the people who murdered her parents and tried to murder her. She needs to be kept reasonably secure, and I wanted some advice about what might be best for somebody who has suffered as she has.'

'Do you want me to see her?'

Thelma shook her head.

'This is all unofficial. I just wanted to know what your first thoughts on the subject might be.'

'Who's treating her? Colin Daun, I suppose.'

'Yes.'

'He's all right. Why not ask *him*?'

'I'm asking you.'

'You know what I'm going to say, Thelma. She should be in a familiar environment with family or friends.'

'There is no family. The possibility of her staying with friends has been considered, but the matter is academic because she has rejected the idea out of hand.'

'Well, I don't think staying in hospital for an extended period will do her much good.'

'It's not practical, anyway.' Thelma drained her coffee. 'This is a lovely house, Sam. Large, isn't it? And quiet.'

'No, Thelma.'

'I wasn't saying . . .'

'No.'

'Just wait a moment,' Thelma said, with a more insistent tone now. 'This is a severely troubled girl. Let me tell you what I know about her. Then say no.' She sat back, marshalling her thoughts. 'Fiona Mackenzie is nineteen years old. She is academically clever, although not brilliant, and apparently she has always been eager to please and to conform. A slightly anxious girl, in other words. I gather she was quite dominated by her father, who had a very forceful personality. Since puberty, she has been somewhat overweight.' I remembered the plump, smiling face of the girl in the news. 'When she was seventeen she had a nervous breakdown and was institutionalized in a godawful private unit up in Scotland for almost six months. In the process she lost almost half her body-weight and plumpness became anorexia that nearly killed her.'

'How long has she been out?'

'She was discharged in the summer, missing the last term of school and her A levels; I think the plan was that she was going to go to a crammer this year and do them. And then she immediately spent a few months going around South America; I think her parents felt it would mark a new beginning. She's only been back a couple of weeks, if that. It seems that the people who committed these murders didn't expect her to be there. It may be the weak link in the crime. Hence the danger she's in and the help she needs. Aren't you intrigued?'

'Sorry, Thelma, the answer is no. For the last eighteen months I haven't seen Elsie except on weekends, and as soon as she fell asleep on Saturday and Sunday I would

47

do paperwork until two in the morning. Mainly I just remember migraines in a fog of fatigue. If you have seriously considered that I could have a traumatized young woman actually staying in my house where I have my little daughter . . . And staying here because she may be in danger. It's not possible.'

Thelma bowed her head in acknowledgement, although I knew her well enough to know she wasn't convinced.

'How *is* little Elsie?'

'Cross, insubordinate. All the usual. Just started a new school.' I was worried by the interested, predatory look that came over Thelma's face when I mentioned Elsie and my home. I had to get on to something else. 'Your research sounds interesting.'

'Mmm,' she said, busily dunking, refusing to be so crudely drawn.

'I've been overseeing some work on trauma in children which might interest you,' I continued, stubbornly, on the same doomed track. 'Obviously, you know that children relive past traumas in repetitive play. A team down in Kent is trying to assess the effect this has on their memory of the event.'

'So it's not your own research?'

'No,' I said with a laugh. 'The sum total of my research on childhood memory is a mnemonic game that Elsie and I play. It's just for fun, but I've always been interested in systems of organizing mental processes and this is one of the oldest. Elsie and I invented the image of a house, and we know in our minds what it looks like and we can remember things by putting them in different places in the house and then retrieving them when we want to remember them.'

Thelma looked dubious.

'Can she manage that?'

'Surprisingly well. When she is in a good mood we can put something on the door, on the doormat, in the kitchen, on the stairs and so on and later she can usually remember them.'

'It sounds hard work for a five-year-old.'

'I wouldn't do it if she didn't like it. She's proud of being able to do it.'

'Or pleased to get your approval,' Thelma said. She stood up, a dumpy and dishevelled creature covered in crumbs. 'And now I must go. If you have any more thoughts about our problem, please phone me.'

'All right.'

'You can post a reminder to yourself on the front door of Elsie's imaginary house.'

I felt I needed to say something.

'You know, when I became a doctor I had an idea about making the world a saner, rational place. I sometimes think that when I began treating victims of trauma, I gave up on the world and just tried to help people deal with it.'

'That's not a small thing,' Thelma said.

I saw her to the door and watched her walk across to the car. I stayed in the doorway for several minutes after she'd gone. It was ridiculous, entirely out of the question. I sat down on the sofa and pondered it.

Seven

'This crackling's a bit soft.' Danny held up a bendy, pale-brown strip that looked as if it had been torn from the sole of a shoe rather than the back of a pig.

'Blame Asda. Or the microwave. I just followed the instructions on the packet.'

'I like it chewy. It's like chewing gum.'

'Thanks, Elsie, and take your feet off the table – just because you've got another INSET day off school doesn't mean you can start copying Danny and slouching around. Pass the apple sauce, Danny. From a tin,' I added.

'Didn't your mother ever teach you to cook?'

'Help yourself to some spinach. Microwaved in the bag.'

I slid two slabs of whitish meat on to my plate.

'Do a bird,' said Elsie.

'Wait,' said Danny.

'Just a small bird.'

'All right.'

Danny ripped a corner of a page of a newspaper and made some surprisingly deft movements with his large chafed fingers and, in a few seconds, perkily standing on the table was a something with two legs and a neck that could plausibly be described as a bird. Elsie gave a shriek of approbation. I was impressed as ever.

'Why is it that men can always do these things?' I asked. 'I could never do origami.'

'This isn't bloody origami. It's just a nervous habit for when I've got nothing better to do.'

That was certainly true. Already, tiny paper creatures were infesting the house like moths. Elsie was collecting them.

'Now I want a puppy,' she said.

'Wait,' said Danny.

'Can we paint after lunch? I've finished anyway. I don't like it. Can I have ice-cream for pudding?'

'Have two more mouthfuls. We're all going for a walk after lunch and . . .'

'I don't want to go for a walk!' Elsie's voice climbed up the scales. 'I'm tired of going for walks. My legs are tired. I've got a cough.' She coughed unconvincingly.

'Not a walk,' said Danny quickly. 'An adventure. We'll find shells and make a . . .' Inspiration failed. 'Shell-box,' he said without much conviction.

'Can I go on your shoulders on the adventure?'

'If you walk the first bit.'

'Thanks, Danny,' I said as Elsie marched out of the room to find a bag for the shells. He shrugged and shovelled a forkful of meat into his mouth. We'd had a good night, and now we were having a reasonable day; no bickerings. He'd said nothing at all about his next job or about having to get back to London – he always spoke about London as if it were an appointment, not a city – nor had I asked him. We were getting on better. We had to talk, but not just yet. I stretched, pushed away my plate; tired, languid and comfortable.

'It'll do me good to get out of the house.'

I never went for the walk because, as I was pulling

Elsie's red elephant boots on to her outstretched feet and she was shouting that I was hurting her, we heard a car draw up outside. I straightened up and peered out of the window. A tall stout man with a ruddy face on which he was already preparing a smile got out of the driver's seat. Out of the passenger seat came Thelma, wearing an extraordinarily unbecoming track suit. I turned to Danny.

'Maybe it would be nice for you and Elsie if you went off on your adventure alone.'

His expression didn't change, and he took hold of her hand and led her, ignoring her single squeal of protest, through the kitchen and out of the back door.

'No.'

'Miss Laschen . . .'

'Dr Laschen.'

'Sorry. Dr Laschen, I do assure you that I understand your reluctance, but this would be a very temporary arrangement. She needs to be in a safe place, anonymous and protected, with someone who understands her position, just for a short time.'

Detective Inspector Baird gave a reassuring smile. He was so big that as he walked into my living room, ducking his head under the door-frame, leaning against the mantelpiece, he made the house seem frail, as if it were built of canvas flats like a stage set.

'I have a daughter and a time-consuming job and . . .'

'Dr Scott tells me your job at Stamford General is months away.'

I shot a venomous glance at Thelma, who was sitting unconcernedly bang in the middle of the sofa, stroking Anatoly with great deliberation and apparently not listening to anything that was being said. She looked up.

'Have you got anything to eat with this cup of tea apart from stale custard creams?' she asked.

'It's not practical,' I said.

Detective Inspector Baird gulped tea. Thelma lifted her glasses away from the bridge of her nose, and I could see the deep red groove they'd made there. She rubbed her eyes. Neither of them said anything.

'I've only just moved here. I wanted a few months off.' My voice, too high with indignation, filled the quiet room. Shut up, I told myself; just keep your mouth closed. Why didn't Danny and Elsie come home? 'This time is important for me. I'm sorry about the girl but . . .'

'Yes,' said Thelma. 'She needs help.' She popped a whole custard cream into her mouth and chomped vigorously.

'I was about to say that I'm sorry about her; however, I don't think that it's . . .' The sentence trailed away and I couldn't remember how I was going to end it. 'How long did you say?'

'I didn't. And you must make your own mind up.'

'Yeah yeah. Detective Inspector Baird, how long?'

'It would not be more than six weeks, probably much less.'

I stayed silent and thought furiously.

'If I were to consider it, how would I know I wasn't putting my daughter at risk? If I decide to have her.'

'It would be discreet,' Baird said. 'Completely. Nobody would know she was here. How would they? It's just a precaution.'

'Thelma?'

She peered up at me, a troll come in from the cold. 'You're in the right area of expertise, you live near by. You were the obvious choice.'

'If she came,' I said feebly, 'when would she arrive?'

His brow wrinkled as if he were recalling the departure time of a commuter train.

'Oh,' he said casually. 'We thought tomorrow morning would be an appropriate time. Say, nine-thirty.'

'Appropriate? Make it eleven-thirty.'

'Good, and that means that her doctor will be able to accompany her,' said Baird. 'So that's all settled.'

Thelma took my hand as she left.

'I'm sorry,' she said, but she wasn't.

'I'll be gone before she arrives.'

'Danny, you don't need to go; I just think it would be a bad idea to be round when . . .'

'Don't talk shit, Sam. When you were deciding about this girl, did I come into the equation?' He stared at me. 'I didn't, did I? You could at least have *talked* to me about it before saying yes, pretended that it mattered what I thought about it. Is this girl's future more important to you than ours?'

I could have said that he was right and I was sorry, except I knew I wasn't going to go back on my agreement to take the girl. I could have pleaded. I could have become angry in response. Instead I tried to reconcile our differences in the old familiar way. I put my arms around him, I pushed back his hair and stroked his stubbly cheek and kissed the corner of his furious mouth and started to undo the button on his shirt. But Danny pushed me away angrily.

'Fuck me and I'll forget, eh?'

He pulled on his shoes and picked up the jacket which he'd slung over a chair.

'Are you going?'

54

'Looks like it, doesn't it?' He paused in the doorway. 'Bye Sam, see you. Maybe.'

Eight

The most tiresome thing about having a guest – or in this case a pseudo-guest – coming to call is the apparent tradition that you are meant to clear up for them. Fiona Mackenzie was due mid morning. This gave me a couple of hours after taking Elsie to school to dither around the house. I had to be tactical about this. Clearing up the house in any meaningful sense was obviously impractical. Establishing order was an even more forlorn hope which needed to be explored in detail with Sally. But Sally was very slow and she had a complicated emotional life and any conversation with her got lost in its labyrinths. For the moment I had time to push a few things out of the way so that doors could be entered, hallways walked along, chairs sat on.

The surface of the kitchen table was almost invisible, but it only took the transfer of Elsie's bowl and cup into the sink, the stowing of her cereal packets into a cupboard, the disposal of a few days' worth of opened envelopes in the bin, and almost half of it was available for use once more. I pushed the window above the kitchen sink slightly up and opened the door to the garden. The house would at least smell a bit cleaner. I wandered up and down looking for anything else that I could tidy up. One of the radiators was leaking rusty liquid on to the floor so I put a cup under it. I looked into the lavatory and thought about cleaning it. I needed bleach or one of those liquids with nozzles designed for squirting under the rim. I made do with flushing it. That was enough for one day.

Looking from a first-floor window, I could see sunlight streaking the lawn and I could hear a bird singing in a twittery sort of way. Things like this were presumably among the benefits of living in this godforsaken bit of countryside. One was supposed to find bird-song beautiful. Was it a skylark? A nightingale? Or did they only sing at night? A robin? A pigeon? Except that I knew that pigeons cooed instead of singing. I was running out of birds. I ought to get a book about bird-song. Or a CD or something.

This was all wrong. I was curious, but most of all I was irritated at having committed myself to an arrangement which was out of my control. I felt bad about Danny; worse than bad – uneasy. I knew I ought to ring and admit I was wrong, but I kept putting it off. I find it hard to be in the wrong. I made myself some instant coffee and compiled a cross list inside my head: it was a distraction for me; a waste of my time; it was an unprofessional way to deal with a person who needed help; it might even be dangerous; it would do no good for Elsie; I didn't like the idea of somebody else in my space; and I didn't like the idea of indistinct, open-ended commitments. I felt exploited and sulky. I retrieved one of the old envelopes from the bin and made a real list.

As eleven-thirty approached, I hovered near the window which looked out at the approach to the house. Another morning entirely wasted. I tried to tell myself that I should be savouring these entirely useless bits of filler time. After years without a spare moment I was wandering around from room to room without even being able to form a coherent impulse. Finally I heard a car pulling up near the front door. I looked out of the window, keeping myself far enough back so that I would be invisible to anybody looking up at the house. It was an entirely anonymous four-door thing, wedge-shaped like a super-market cheddar. There were no blue lights or orange lines. Three of the doors opened at once. Baird and another man in a suit got out of the front seats. From the rear door stepped a man in a long charcoal-grey overcoat. He straightened up with obvious relief, for he was tall. He looked around briefly, and I glimpsed a swing of lank dark-blond hair, a thin and aquiline face. He bent down and looked back inside the car and I thought of the way, only a year ago, I had cursed the straps on Elsie's baby-seat, the awkward angles at which I had had to extract her from the old Fiat. I saw a jeaned leg emerge and then a young woman stepped out. She was blurred by the coarse grain of the old window. I saw jeans, a navy-blue jacket, dark hair, pale skin, nothing else. I heard a knock at the door and walked down the stairs.

Baird stepped into my house with an avuncular, posses-sive air that repelled me. I suspected that all of this wasn't his idea, or at least that *I* wasn't his idea, but that he was going to make a show of seeing it through. He stepped to one side to allow the others to pass. The man in the long coat was leading the girl by the arm, gently.

'This is DC Angeloglou,' Baird said. 'And this is Dr Daley.' The man gave me a curt nod. He was unshaven but looked none the worse for that. He looked around him with narrowed eyes. He seemed suspicious, as well he might. 'And here is Miss Fiona Mackenzie. Finn Mac-kenzie.'

I held my hand out to her, but she wasn't looking at me

and didn't see it. I turned the action into a meaningless fluttery gesture. I invited them through to where there was a sofa and we all sat down awkwardly. I offered them tea. Baird said that Angeloglou would make it. Angeloglou stood up looking irritated. I went with him, leaving silence behind us in the sitting room.

'Is this really a good idea?' I whispered as I rinsed out some mugs.

He shrugged.

'It might do some good,' he said. 'We've got sod all else, but don't tell anyone I said so.'

When we returned, it was to a silent room. Baird had picked up an old magazine from the floor and was looking at it absently. Dr Daley had removed his coat and, wearing a rather startling yellow shirt which might have come from an expensive Italian designer or from an Oxfam shop, was sitting beside Finn on the sofa. I held out two mugs of tea and Daley took them both and placed them on the table. He felt in his trouser pockets as if he'd lost something and didn't know what it was.

'Can I smoke?' His voice was almost unnaturally deep, with a certain languid drawl. I remembered the type from med school. Socially assured in a way I never felt myself to be.

'I'll get an ashtray,' I said. 'Or an equivalent.'

I immediately felt more at home with him than with Baird or Angeloglou. He was well over six foot; the cigarette packet looked slightly too small in his long-fingered hands. He lit a cigarette immediately and was soon tapping the ash into the saucer I gave him. He must have been in his mid forties, but he was hard to assess because he looked tired and distracted. He had dark smudges under his grey eyes and his straight sheet of hair was a bit greasy.

It was a curiously crowded face, with fierce eyebrows, high cheek-bones and a wide, sardonic mouth. Finn looked small and frail and rather bland beside him. The paleness of her face was only accentuated by her thick dark hair and her sombre clothes. She had evidently not eaten for days; she was gaunt, her cheek-bones prominent. She was unnaturally still, except that her eyes flickered, never settling on anything. Her neck was bandaged and the fingers of her right hand constantly strayed to the edge of it, picking at it.

I ought to be saying that my heart went out to this cruelly abused creature, but I felt too compromised and confused for that. This was an absurd setting for meeting a new patient, but then she wasn't my patient, was she? But exactly what was she? What was I meant to be? Her doctor? Older sister? Best friend? A stool-pigeon? Some kind of amateur police forensic psychologist sniffing for clues?

'Are you enjoying life in the country, Dr Laschen?' asked Baird airily.

I ignored him.

'Dr Daley,' I said, 'I think it would be a good idea if you and Finn went upstairs to look at the room where Finn will be staying. It's the room at the back on the left looking over the garden. You can have a look round and tell me if I've forgotten anything.'

Dr Daley looked quizzically at Baird.

'Yes, now,' I said.

He led Finn out of the room and I heard them mounting the stairs slowly. I turned to Baird and Angeloglou.

'Shall we step out into some of this countryside that I'm meant to be enjoying so much? You can take your tea with you.'

Baird shook his head as he saw the state of my kitchen garden.

'I know,' I admitted, kicking a pink plastic object Elsie must have dropped out of the way. 'I had this vision of being self-supporting.'

'Not this year,' said Angeloglou.

'No,' I said. 'It seems as if I've got other things to do. Look, Inspector . . .'

'Call me Rupert.'

I laughed. I couldn't help myself.

'Are you serious? All right. Rupert. Before I start anything, there are some things we need to talk about.'

I extracted the old envelope from the pocket of my jeans.

'Is this official?' he asked.

I shook my head.

'I don't give a fuck whether it's official or not. You got my name as an authority on trauma.'

'An authority on trauma with an isolated house in the country near Stamford.'

'Fine, well, I should start by saying, even if it's only to you two that, in my professional capacity, I don't consider this to be professional.'

'It's convenient.'

'I don't know whose convenience we're talking about, but Finn ought to be in familiar surroundings with people she knows and trusts.'

'The people she knows and trusts are dead. Apart from that, she has absolutely refused to see anybody she knows. Except for Dr Daley, of course.'

'As I'm sure you've been told, Rupert, that is a standard response to what she's been through, and it's not in itself a justification for projecting her into an entirely new environment.'

'And we have some reason to believe that her life could be in danger.'

'All right, we're not arguing about that. I just wanted to give you my objective medical opinion.' I looked down at my envelope. 'Secondly, do you see me as playing some sort of informal part in your investigation, because if you do . . .'

'Not at all, Dr Laschen,' Baird said in a soothing tone that enraged me. 'Quite the contrary. As you know, Miss Mackenzie has said nothing about the murders. But there's no question of you being expected to poke around trying to stir up memories and find out clues. This would do more harm than good. Anyway, I understand that this is not your therapeutic style.'

'That's right.'

'If Miss Mackenzie should wish to make a statement, she is no different from any other citizen. Just contact me and we will be glad to hear what she has to say. We in our turn may occasionally visit her here as part of our inquiries.'

'What makes you think she's under threat?'

Baird did a mock double take.

'Have you seen her throat?'

'Do murderers normally come back if they've failed the first time?'

'This is an unusual case. They wanted to kill the entire family.'

'Rupert, I'm not interested in the details of your investigation. But if you're trusting me to look after Finn, you must trust me with any relevant information.'

'Fair enough. Chris?'

Angeloglou, caught with a mouthful of tea, choked and spluttered.

'Sorry,' he said. 'It's possible that there is an animal rights connection. It's a line of inquiry.'

'Why would they want to kill Finn?'

'To save little pigs from having lotions and potions administered to wounds deliberately fostered in their flesh. She is guilty by family association.'

A sudden thought occurred to me.

'When I was at university I was part of a group of hunt saboteurs. For a bit. I was arrested and cautioned.'

'Yes, we know.'

'Well, how do you know she's safe with *me*?'

'You've taken the Hippocratic oath, haven't you?'

'Doctors don't take the Hippocratic oath any more. That's a myth.'

'Oh,' said Baird, disconcerted. 'Well, please don't kill her, Dr Laschen. The investigation's going slowly enough as it is.'

I looked at my envelope once more.

'I have friends, a child, people coming to the house. What am I supposed to tell them? I've already told Danny – my, uh, boyfriend – who she is.'

'It's best to keep it simple. Complicated stories have a way of going wrong. Couldn't she be some sort of student, staying with you? What about that?'

I was silent for a long time. I couldn't deal with this.

'I'm not interested in all these cloak-and-dagger games. I can't manage it and it's not going to be much help to Finn.'

'That's why we're making it as simple as we possibly can. Dr Laschen, I know this isn't ideal. Other arrangements would probably be worse.'

'All right, I suppose I've already agreed.'

'She could be helping you.'

'I wish.'

'And you don't have to change her name much. Call her Fiona Jones. That should be easy for us all to remember.'

'All right. But listen to me, Rupert, I reserve the right at any time to terminate this arrangement. If you don't agree to that, you can take her away with you now. If, at any time, I feel this charade is bad for me, bad for my daughter or, for God's sake, bad for Finn, then it ends. All right?'

'Of course, Dr Laschen. But you'll be fine. We all have great confidence in you.'

'If that's so, then your confidence is too easily earned.'

When we returned inside, I asked Dr Daley to help me take the mugs back to the kitchen. I wanted to talk to him alone. There was no chance of Finn following us through. There seemed to be no chance of that poor damaged girl doing anything at all.

'Sorry to lure you into the kitchen,' I said. 'We should have had a proper talk before Finn arrived, but it all seems to be beyond my control. Which I don't like.'

Dr Daley smiled with an automatic politeness. I stepped forward and looked at him.

'How are *you*?'

He returned my assessing stare. He had very deep eyes, opaque. I liked that. Then his face relaxed into a smile.

'It's not been a good time,' he said.

'Are you sleeping?' I asked.

'I'm fine,' he said.

'You don't have to impress me. You can save all that for your practice manager. I like vulnerable men.'

He laughed and then was silent for a moment. He lit a cigarette.

'I feel I could have handled this better. And I'm sorry about all this as well,' he said, gesturing with a vague kind of grace, as if at the whole situation in which we found ourselves. 'I've only been obeying orders.'

I didn't say anything. He began talking as if he couldn't tolerate the silence.

'Incidentally, I wanted the chance to tell you that I read your article in the *BMJ*, 'The Invention of a Syndrome', or whatever it was called, the one that caused all the fuss. It was splendid.'

'Thanks. I didn't think doctors like you would read it.'

His colour rose slightly and his eyes narrowed.

'You mean a GP out in the provinces.'

'No, I didn't mean that. I meant a doctor outside the speciality.'

It was an awkward moment, but then Daley smiled again.

'I can remember a bit of it by heart: "dogma, based on unexamined premises and unsupported by demonstration". The stress counsellors must have needed some counselling of their own after reading that.'

'Why do you think I'm out here in the sticks setting up my own unit? Who else would employ me? By the way, I mean "the sticks" in the nicest possible way.'

'That's all right,' said Dr Daley. He rolled up his shirt-sleeves and picked up the mugs. 'You wash, I'll dry.'

'No, *you* wash and then put them in the rack and they can dry on their own. How is Finn?'

'Well, the superficial lacerations . . .'

'I don't mean that. You're her doctor, what do you make of her?'

'Dr Laschen . . .'

'Call me Sam.'

'And call me Michael. If you mean her mood, her degree of shock, then I'm talking beyond my field of competence.'

'That doesn't stop other people. What do you think?'

'I think she is severely traumatized by what happened. Understandably traumatized, I would say.'

'How is her speech?'

'You mean from her injuries? It has been affected. There is some degree of laryngeal paralysis. There may have been minor lesions in the vocal cords.'

'Any stridor or dysphonia?'

Daley paused in his scouring of a mug.

'Is this your field?'

'More like a hobby. It's one up from stamp-collecting. Or one down.'

'Perhaps you should have a word with Dr Daun at Stamford General,' said Daley, returning to his scrubbing. 'Anyway, she's all yours now.'

'No, she isn't,' I replied. 'She's your patient. I insist on that. This is irregular enough as it is. I'm helping out in an informal, I hope, supportive way. But I understand you've been her GP for years, and it's absolutely essential that you should remain in place in her eyes as the doctor. Is that acceptable to you?'

'Sure. I'll do anything at all to help.'

'I hope you'll come to see her regularly then; you're her only link to the world she comes from.'

'There we are, finished,' he said, having washed up not just the mugs but my breakfast things and yesterday's dinner things as well. 'I should say that I felt dubious about this. I mean about this as a plan. But the way it's worked out, I don't think Finn could be in better hands.'

'I hope everybody is going to carry on being this supportive of me when it has all gone wrong.'

'Why should it go wrong?' Daley asked, but he laughed as he said it, his eyebrows slanting into a dark upturned 'V'. 'The only thing I want to say is that I'm worried about Finn being so cut off from her normal surroundings, from people she knows.'

'I feel the same, I promise.'

'You know about these things, but if I could just make a single suggestion, it would be that we should arrange for her to see people. Assuming that's what she wants and the police agree, of course.'

'We'll take it slowly for a bit, shall we?'

'*You're* the doctor,' Daley said. 'Well, I'm a doctor as well, but what I mean is you're *the* doctor.'

'I don't know *what* you mean,' I protested. 'I'm *a* doctor. You're *a* doctor. And we'll just try to make the best of this stupid and tragic situation that we possibly can. Meanwhile, I shall want the details of medication, history and so on, and your number. I don't want to have to go to Baird every time I need some information.'

'It's all in my bag in the car.'

'One more thing. This situation is ridiculously vague, so I want to be firm about one thing. I'm going to tell you and I'm going to tell Baird that I want a strict time-limit for all of this.'

Daley looked taken aback.

'What do you mean?'

'If things work out, there's the danger that we'll become a replacement family for Finn in her new life. That's no good. What's the date now, January the twenty-fifth, isn't it?'

'The twenty-sixth.'

67

'I'm going to be clear with Finn that whatever happens, however things go, this arrangement is until the middle of March – let's call it March the fifteenth – and no more. All right?'

'Fine,' said Daley. 'I'm sure it will be less than that anyway.'

'Good. So, shall we join the ladies?'

'You think it's a joke, Sam. You wait until you get invited for dinner by the neighbours.'

'I'm looking forward to it. I've already got my face-powder ready.'

Nine

I turned to face the girl. I hadn't looked at her properly until now. Her pale oval face, behind the swing of dark-brown hair, was perfectly expressionless. Under her neat thick eyebrows, her brown eyes were unfocused. She was attractive, she could be lovely in different circumstances, but hers was a face from which all character seemed to have been wiped.

'Let me show you round the house,' I said. 'Though that won't take long.'

She stooped to pick up the small suitcase which was beside her, although she looked too weak and listless to carry anything at all.

'Here, let me take that for you. We'll start with your bedroom, though you've seen that already.' She flinched as my hand touched hers on the handle of her case. 'Your hands are cold; I'll put the heating on in a minute. Come this way.'

I led the way up the stairs, Finn following obediently behind. So far, she had not said a word.

'Here. I'm sorry about all the boxes; we can move them into the attic later.' I put her suitcase by the bed, where it stood, forlornly small in the high-ceilinged room. 'It's all a bit bare, I'm afraid.' Finn stood in the middle of the room, not looking. Her arms hung by her sides, pale fingers loose as if they didn't belong to her at all. I gestured vaguely at the wardrobe and small chest of drawers that Danny had found for me in a nearby village. 'You can put your stuff in there.'

I led the way back into the corridor. I saw something small and white and angular on the floor. I crouched and picked it up delicately between two fingers.

'And this, Finn, is a paper bird created by my semi-detached partner, Danny.' Was he still my semi-detached partner, or had he become quite detached? I pushed the thought away for later. 'Look, I can make it flap, sort of. Lovely, don't you think? After living in this house for a few days you will start to find these little creatures among your clothes, in your hair, sticking to you, in your food. They get everywhere. Men, eh?'

I was talking to myself largely.

'That's my room. And this' – she walked two feet behind me and stopped when I stopped – 'is the room of my little girl, Elsie.' The door jammed on a jumble of blonde-maned Barbie dolls, pencil cases and plastic ponies. 'Elsie is short for Elsie.' I looked at Finn and she didn't laugh – well, what I had said wasn't particularly funny – but she gave me a little nod, more like a single convulsive jerk. I saw the plaster around her throat.

Downstairs I showed Finn my study ('out of bounds to everyone'), the living room, the kitchen. I pulled open the fridge door.

'Feel free to take whatever you want. I don't cook but I *do* shop.'

I pointed out tea and coffee and the hole where the washing machine would be and I told her about Linda and Sally and the routines. 'And that's about it, except of course that's the garden' – I pointed out of the window at the soggy undergrowth, the mulched heaps of leaves that

70

hadn't been cleared, the frayed edges of the balding lawn – 'ungardened.'

Finn turned her head, but still I couldn't tell if she saw anything at all. I peered into the fridge again and pulled out a carton of country vegetable soup.

'I'm going to heat us up some soup. Why don't you go and get freshened up in the bathroom, then we can have lunch together.' She stood, stranded in the kitchen. 'Upstairs,' I said encouragingly, pointing, and watched as she turned slowly round and made her way up the broad shallow steps, one at a time and stopping on each step, so slowly, like a very old woman.

Sometimes I see trauma victims who don't speak for weeks on end; sometimes words pour from them like a great muddy flood with no barriers. Quite recently a middle-aged man came to me after being in a train crash that he had been lucky to survive. All his life, he'd been reticent, buttoned up. In the crash he'd emptied his bowels (his phrase, through puckered-up lips) in shock, something that seemed to affect him as deeply as all the deaths he had witnessed. Afterwards, when he was released from hospital, he became incontinent with speech. He told me how he would stand at the bus stop, walk into a shop, stand at his front door, and tell anyone who came near him what had happened to him. He played the scene over and over, yet got no relief from its telling. It was just like scratching an unbearable itch. Finn would speak in her own time; when she spoke I would be there to hear, if it was to me she chose to speak. In the meantime she needed to be given a structure to feel safe in.

I looked at her as she lifted very small puddles of soup in her spoon and carried them carefully to her mouth. What would she say if she could talk?

'Elsie gets back here at six,' I said. 'Some days it might be earlier; often I collect her from school myself. She's excited that you're coming. I will tell her only what we'll tell other people: that you're a student who is staying with us. Fiona Jones.'

Finn got up, the chair scraping noisily against the tiles of the floor in the kitchen that was too quiet, and took her bowl, still half-full of soup, over to the sink. She washed it and balanced it on the draining-board among all the other dishes, and she sat down at the table once more, facing me and not looking at me. She put her hands around the cup of tea I'd made for her and shivered. Then she raised her velvet eyes to mine and stared at me. It was the first time she had done so and I was unaccountably startled. I felt as if I could see into her skull.

'You're safe here, Finn,' I said. 'You don't have to tell me anything unless you want to; you don't have to do anything. But you're safe.'

The second-hand on the kitchen clock, the glowing green digits clicking over on my radio clock, the deep metronome of the grandfather clock's pendulum in the hall, all agreed with me that it was a long, slow afternoon. Time, which had always hurtled through my days, slowed to a painful dawdle.

I ran Finn a hot bath, which I filled with my favourite bath oil. She went into the bathroom, locked the door, and I heard the sound of undressing and of her getting in, but she was out again and dressed in the same clothes as before in under five minutes. I asked her to help me choose curtains for her room, and we knelt by the piles of fabric that I pulled out from under my bed where I'd stored them, and she watched as I held up pleated lengths and said nothing. So I chose her something cheerful in dull red and yellow and navy, though it was much too long for the small square window, and hung it up. I left her in her bedroom so she could unpack, thinking she might like to be alone there for a bit. Before I left the room I saw her looking into her open case at clothes which were all still in their packets. A few minutes later she came downstairs again and stood in the doorway of my study where I was tidying away folders. I took her out into the garden, hoping that the bulbs the previous owner was sure to have planted had poked through the neglected soil, but all we found were a few snowdrops in a cracked flowerpot.

We went back inside and I lit a fire (mostly consisting of firelighters and tightly crumpled balls of newspapers), and she sat a while in my only easy chair, staring into the erratic flames. I sat near her, on the rug, reading through chess problems I'd saved up from the week's papers. Anatoly clattered through the cat flap and into the living room, and he pushed his moist jaw against my hunched knees a few times and then lay between us. Two women and a cat by the fire: it was almost cosy.

Then Finn spoke. Her voice was low, husky.

'I'm bleeding.'

I looked in horror at her neck, but of course she didn't mean that. Her eyebrows were puckered in a kind of vacant puzzlement.

'That's OK.' I stood up. 'I've got plenty of Tampax and towels and stuff in the bathroom. I should have thought to tell you. Come on.'

'I'm bleeding,' she said again, this time almost whispering. I took hold of her thin, chilly hand and pulled her to her feet. She was several inches shorter than me and she looked terribly young. Too young to bleed.

'This,' said Elsie, 'is a shoulder.' She plunged her thin rectangle of toast into the runny yolk and sucked it noisily; it slipped down her chin like yellow glue. 'Do you have shoulders?' She didn't wait for a reply; it was as if Finn's silence had loosened her own guarded tongue. 'We had chicken nuggets today and Alexander Cassell' – she pronounced it *Ale-xxonder* – 'put his in his pocket and they *squished* together.' She gave a squeal of appreciation and sucked her toast again. 'Finished. Do you want to come and see my drawing?' She slithered from her chair. 'This way. My mummy says I draw better than her. Do you think that's true? My favourite colour's pink and Mummy's is black but I hate black except I like Anatoly and he's all black like a panther. What's yours?'

Elsie didn't seem to notice that Finn wasn't replying. She displayed her picture of her house with a front door up to the roof and two crooked windows, she showed her how she could do somersaults, crashing into the legs of the chair, and then she demanded a video and together they sat through the whole of *101 Dalmatians*, Finn in the chair, Elsie on the rug, both staring at the screen full of puppies, Finn vacantly and Elsie avidly, and when I took Elsie up for her bath ('why do I *always* have to have baths?') Finn stayed staring at the blank screen.

Evenings would be the worst, I thought: stretches of time with just the two of us and no structure and Finn just sitting and waiting, but waiting for nothing. I thought of the way she'd looked at me. I rummaged through the freezer: Marks & Spencer steak and kidney pudding, Sainsbury's chicken kiev, a packet of lasagne (serves two), spinach and cheese pie (serves one). I pulled out the lasagne and put it in the microwave to defrost. Perhaps there were some frozen peas. I wondered where Danny was; I wondered who he was with, and if he had sought comfort and pleasure elsewhere, taking his rage to a different bed. Was he with someone else now, as I nursed a mute invalid? Was he laying his roughened hands on someone else's compliant body? For a few moments, at the thought, I could hardly breathe. I suppose he would say that I'd been unfaithful to him, in my fashion. Finn, sitting passively in the next-door room, represented a kind of treachery. I wished he was here now and I was heating up lasagne and peas for him instead; then we could have watched a movie on the telly and gone up to bed together and pressed up against each other in the dark. I wished that I could banish Finn, and my foolish and hasty decision to take her in, and return to the past of two days ago.

'Here we are.' I carried the tray into the living room, but Finn wasn't there. I called upstairs, at first not loudly, then with greater impatience. No answer. Eventually I knocked at her bedroom door, then opened it. She lay, fully clothed, on her bed. Her thumb was in her mouth. I pulled the duvet over her, and as I did so her eyes opened. She glared at me and then turned her head to the wall.

And so ended Finn's first day. Except later that night when I'd gone to bed myself and outside it was quite dark in the way that only the countryside can be dark, I heard a thump from Finn's room. Then another, louder. I pulled on my dressing gown and padded along the chilly corridor. She lay quite asleep, both hands covering her face like someone hiding from an intrusive camera. I went back to my warm bed and heard nothing more except the hoot of an owl, the sigh of the wind, horrible unfiltered country sounds, until morning.

Ten

Finn was a chilly presence in the house. I'd see her out of the corner of my eye: slumped somewhere, shuffling somewhere. In all the debates about safety and status, what hadn't been discussed was what she was actually meant to *do* in my house from hour to hour. In the first couple of days she was with us she woke early; I heard the slap of naked feet on the bare boards of the landing. At breakfast-time I knocked on her bedroom door, asking if I could bring her anything. There was no reply. I saw nothing of her until I returned from driving Elsie to school. She would be sitting on the sofa watching daytime television, game shows, public confessions, news broadcasts, Australian soap operas. She was impassive, almost immobile, except for worrying at the plaster on her neck. Fidget, fidget, fidget. I brought her coffee, black with no sugar, and she took it and cupped her hands around it as if to draw its warmth into herself. That was the closest to human contact for the whole day. I brought her toast but half an hour later it was untouched, the butter congealed.

When I encountered Finn, I would talk to her casually, in the sort of spirit that you might speak to a patient in deep coma, not knowing whether it was for your benefit or theirs. Here's some coffee. Mind your hands. It's a nice day. Budge up. What are you watching? The occasional questions came out by mistake and provoked awkward silences. I was embarrassed and furious with myself for being embarrassed. I was professionally as well as personally discomfited. This was supposed to be my field and I was behaving absurdly, as well as ineffectually. But it was the situation itself that was disastrous, not my behaviour within it. Admitting a severely traumatized woman to my home, establishing her in the context of my own family, such as it was, was contrary to any normal procedure. And I was missing Danny in a way that took me by surprise.

As I drove to Elsie's school in the afternoon of Finn's third mute day, I went over possibilities in my mind. I walked into Elsie's class and found her engaged in a picture almost as large as herself. She was glaring with ferocious concentration and gouging a few final touches into it with a black crayon. I knelt beside her and looked over her shoulder. I could smell her soft skin, feel her cotton-wool hair against my cheek.

'That's a good elephant,' I said.

'It's a horse,' she said firmly.

'It *looks* like an elephant,' I protested. 'It's got a trunk.'

'It *looks* like an elephant,' Elsie said, 'but it's a horse.'

I wasn't going to let this go.

'I look like an ordinary woman. Could *I* be a horse?'

Elsie looked up at me with a new-found interest.

'*Are* you?'

I felt a stab of remorse at what I was allowing to be inflicted on this cross little flaxen-haired goblin. I should be doing something for her. I had to do something. Straight away. I looked around.

'Who have you been playing with, Elsie?'

'Nobody.'

'No, really, who?'

'Mungo.'

'Apart from Mungo.'

'Nobody.'

'Name one person you've been playing with.'

'Penelope.'

I went to the teacher, Miss Karlin, a teacherly dream in a long flowery dress and wire-rimmed spectacles, her hair carelessly tied up, and asked her to point out Penelope, and she told me that there was nobody in the class or, indeed, the school with that name. So could she point out somebody that Elsie had played with or stood next to for more than two minutes? Miss Karlin pointed to a mousy-brown-haired girl called Kirsty. So I loitered at the edge of the class like a private detective and when a woman approached Kirsty and attempted to insert her into a little duffle-coat, I accosted her.

'Hello,' I said ruthlessly, 'I'm very glad that Elsie – that's my little girl over there on the floor – and Kirsty have become such good friends.'

'Have they? I didn't . . .'

'Kirsty must come and play at Elsie's house.'

'Well, maybe . . .'

'What about tomorrow?'

'Well, Kirsty's not really used . . .'

'It'll be fine, Miss Karlin tells me that they're absolutely inseparable. Linda will pick them both up and I'll drop Kirsty back. Could you give me your address? Or would you prefer to collect her?'

That was Elsie's social life sorted out. The rest of the day was unsatisfactory. After we arrived home, I steered Elsie away from Finn's presence as much as was possible. The two of us ate alone together and then I took Elsie up to her room. She had a bath and I sat on the edge of her bed and read books to her.

'Is Fing here?'

'Finn.'

'Fing.'

'Finn.'

'Fing.'

'Fin-n-n-n-n-n.'

'Fing-ng-ng-ng.'

I gave up.

'Yes, she is.'

'Where is she?'

'I think she's asleep,' I lied.

'Why?'

'She's tired.'

'Is she ill?'

'No. She just needs rest.'

This stalled Elsie for long enough for me to get her on to another subject.

On the following morning, I made a dismal attempt at retreating to my room and staring at the computer screen. I double-clicked the chess program. I thought I might as well have a quick one. A king's pawn opening, the program took me into a complicated version of the Sicilian Defence. Without much thought, I established a favourable pawn structure and simplified with a series of exchanges. The program's position was losing but it took a long and intricate series of manoeuvres to queen a pawn. Served the machine right, and a whole hour had gone. Bloody hell. Time for work.

I took a business card out of my pocket and ran it along the interstices of my keyboard. I managed to prod out a surprising amount of dust, fluff and hair that had been trapped underneath, so I began to tackle the problem systematically. I ran the card between the number line of keys and the QWERTY line, between the QWERTY line and the ASDF line, between the ASDF line and the ZXCV line. By the end I had a small grubby pile, about enough to stuff the pillow of a dormouse. I blew it hard and it drifted down behind my desk.

The very idea of getting any work done was absurd. I hate spiders. It is a ridiculous distaste, because I know how interesting they are and all that, but I can't bear them. I felt as if I had glimpsed a spider in the room and it had scuttled away. I knew it was in the room somewhere and I could think of nothing else. Finn was in the house and I felt as if she was rattling around in my brain. I looked at the business card, the corners of which were now grubby and curled. It was the one that Michael Daley had left with me. I dialled the number of his surgery. He wasn't there and I left my name. Less than a minute later he rang back.

'How's she doing?' he asked immediately.

I described Finn's demeanour and expressed my doubts about the whole affair. When I had finished, there was a long silence.

'Are you there?'

'Yes,' Daley started to say something and then stopped. 'I'm not sure what to say. I think you're being put in an impossible position. I'm worried about Finn as well. Let me think about this.'

'To be honest, Michael, I think this is a farce. I don't believe it's doing anybody any good.'

'You're probably right. We must talk.'

'We *are* talking.'

'Sorry, yes. Can I come and see her?'

'When?'

'Straight away.'

'Haven't you got surgery?'

'It's finished and I've got a spare hour.'

'That's fine. Christ, Michael, a doctor who offers to make housecalls. We should have you stuffed.'

Daley arrived barely a quarter of an hour later. He was dressed for work, with a dark suit, a bright tie and a jacket. He'd shaved and brushed his hair, but he had a pleasingly incongruous appearance. His expression was concerned, unsettled even.

'Can I see her?'

'Sure, she's watching TV. Take as much time as you want. Do you want tea or something?'

'Later. Give me a few minutes. I'd like a look at her.'

Daley disappeared into the living room and shut the door. I picked up a newspaper and waited. I could hear the TV through the wall, nothing else. After some time, he emerged, looking as sombre as before. He came through to me in the kitchen.

'I'll have that tea now,' he said. He ran his hand through his hair.

I filled the kettle and plugged it in.

'Well?'

'She didn't speak to me either. I had a quick look at her. Physically, she's fine. As you already know.'

'That's not the issue, is it?'

'No.'

I moved mugs around, found tea-bags, rattled spoons, while waiting for the kettle to boil.

'A watched kettle takes about three minutes to boil,' I said.

Michael didn't reply. Finally, I put two mugs of tea in front of him and sat opposite.

'I can't give you my undivided attention for long,' I said. 'Linda will be back with Elsie and Elsie's new friend, or ersatz friend at least.'

'I've got to go anyway,' said Michael. 'Look, Sam, I'm sorry about you having been landed with all this. It's not working. And it's not your fault. Don't do anything. Give me a day or so. I'll ring Baird and we'll get her off your hands.'

'That's not what I mean,' I said uneasily. 'It's not a question of getting anybody off my hands.'

'No, no, of course not. I'm speaking as Finn's doctor. I don't believe this is appropriate for her. Secondly, and quite separately, it's no good for you either. I'll ring you tomorrow afternoon and let you know what we're going to do.'

He rested his head in the cup of one hand and smiled at me. 'OK?'

'I'm sorry about this, Michael,' I said. 'I hate feeling that I can't do something, but this . . .' I gave a shrug.

'Absolutely,' he said.

The first appearance of Kirsty was not promising. Elsie ran straight past me. Linda came in holding a grim-faced child by the hand.

'Hello, Kirsty,' I said.

'I want my mummy,' she said.

'Do you want an apple?'

'No.'

'I want to go home,' Kirsty said, and she began to cry, really cry, with big tears running over her red cheeks.

I picked her up and carried her through to the living room. Finn wasn't there, thank Christ. Holding Kirsty in my left arm, I pulled a box of toys from behind the sofa and shouted to Linda to bring Elsie down, by force if necessary. There were dolls without clothes, clothes without dolls.

'Would you like to dress the dollies, Kirsty?' I asked.

'No,' said Kirsty.

An equally cross Elsie was dragged into the room.

'Elsie, wouldn't you like to help Kirsty dress the dollies?'

'No.'

The phone rang out in the hall.

'Answer that, Linda. You love the dollies, don't you, Elsie? Why don't you show them to Kirsty?'

'Don't want to.'

'You're supposed to be fucking friends.'

Both of them were crying when Linda came back into the room.

'It's a Thelma for you,' she said.

'Christ, tell her to . . . no, I'd better take it in my office. Don't let anybody leave this room.'

Thelma was ringing to find out how it was going, and I described the situation as quickly as I could. Even so, it was more than twenty minutes before I could get off the line and I left my office expecting screams and blood on the walls and legal action from Kirsty's mother and the intervention of Essex social services and an inquiry culminating in my being struck off. Instead, the first sound I heard was miniature tinkling laughter. Linda must be a miracle worker, I thought to myself, but as I turned the corner I saw Linda standing in the hall by the partially open door.

'What . . .?' I began, but she held a finger to her lips and gestured me forwards with a smile.

I tiptoed towards her and stared through the crack.

There was a thin scream of delight which crumbled into gurgling laughter.

'Where'd it go?'

'*I* don't know.'

Whose voice was that? It couldn't be.

'You do, you do,' two little voices were insisting.

'But I *think* it might be in Kirsty's ear. Shall we look? Yes, there it is.'

There were more tiny shrieks.

'Do it again, Fing. Do it again.'

Elsie and Kirsty were kneeling on the carpet. Very slowly, I peered round the edge of the door. Finn was sitting in front of them holding a little yellow ball from the play-box between the thumb and index finger of her left hand.

'I don't think I can,' she said and rubbed her hands together, transferring the ball from her left to her right hand. 'But maybe we can try.' She held her left hand forward. 'Can you blow?'

Elsie and Kirsty blew with furrowed brows and round cheeks.

'And say the magic word.'

'Abracadabra.'

Finn opened her left fist. The ball was gone, of course. It was a terrible magic trick, but both little girls gasped in amazement and shrieked and laughed. None of them saw us, and I stepped back into the hall.

'Let's not get in the way,' I whispered, and we tiptoed away.

'I'm amazed,' said Kirsty's mother, as she stood in the doorway waiting to leave two hours later. 'I've never seen Kirsty like this in anybody else's house.'

'Oh, well,' I said modestly, 'we tried to make her feel at home.'

'I don't know how you did it,' said Kirsty's mother. 'Come on, Kirsty. Goodbye, Elsie, would you like to come and play with Kirsty some time at our house?'

'I don't want to go,' said Kirsty, tears in her eyes once more. 'I want to stay with Fing.'

'Who's Fing?' asked Kirsty's mother. 'Is that *you*?'

'No,' I admitted. 'She's – Fiona's – someone who's staying with me.'

'I don't want to go,' shrieked Kirsty.

Kirsty's mother picked her up and carried her out. I shut the door behind her. The screams receded into the night. There was the slam of a car door and they ceased. I knelt and held Elsie close.

'Did you like that?' I asked softly in her ear.

She nodded. She had a glow about her.

'Good,' I said. 'Run upstairs and take your clothes off. I'll come up in a minute and put you in the bath.'

'Can Fing come? Can she read me a story?'

'We'll see. Now go on.'

I watched the back of her strong little body making its way up the stairs. I turned and walked back into the sitting room. The television was on. Finn was sitting watching. I sat next to her, and she showed no sign of having noticed me. I looked at the screen and tried to work out what the programme was. Suddenly I felt her hand on mine. I turned and she was looking at me.

'I've been a drag,' she said.

'That's all right,' I said.

'Elsie gave me a present.'

I couldn't help laughing.

'And what might that be?'

'Look,' Finn said and held her fist out. She slowly unfolded the fingers and there, neatly perched on her palm, was one of Danny's paper birds.

That night I rang Danny. I rang at ten, at eleven, then at twelve, when he answered in a thick voice, as if I'd woken him.

'I've missed you,' I said.

He grunted.

'I've been thinking about you all the time,' I continued. 'And you were right. I'm sorry.'

'Ah, Sammy, I've been missing you too,' he said. 'Can't seem to get you out of my head.'

'When will you come?'

'I'm rebuilding a kitchen for a couple who seem to think that sleep's a luxury and weekends don't exist. Give me a week.'

'Can I bear to wait for a week?' I asked.

'But then we need to talk, Sam.'

'I know.'

'I love you, you difficult woman.'

I didn't reply, and he said sombrely, 'Is it such a hard word for you to say?'

Eleven

We stood side by side in front of the long mirror in my bedroom, looking like two witches in a coven. I had dressed in a black knee-length skirt, black coarse-silk shirt and black waistcoat, and then, taken aback by how *red* my hair looked topping such dark attire, I'd even pulled on a black cloche hat. Finn was wearing her black polo-necked sweater, and I'd lent her a shapeless charcoal-coloured shift to go over the top of it. It came down to her calves, but actually she looked rather touching and graceful standing in its inky folds. Her glossy head came barely to my shoulder; under its fringe her face was pale and her lips looked slightly swollen. Suddenly, never taking her eyes from her reflection, she did a small and disconcerting jiggle; one bony hip jutted out from the enveloping shift. If it had been in different circumstances I might have giggled and offered some ironic or self-mocking remark. As it was, I remained silent. What, after all, was there to say?

Out of the picture except for one plump knee sat Elsie, off school with a cold which seemed to consist of a theatrical sniffle every twenty minutes. If I turned round – which I didn't yet want to do for I felt that some subtle drama was going on for Finn in front of this mirror – I would have seen her sitting, legs tucked up under her bottom, draping herself in the cheap round beads which she was scooping from a lidded box. As it was, I heard her muttering to herself: '*That* looks nice, I'm so proud of you. A little princess.'

Outside, it was raining. The countryside gets wetter when it rains than cities. It's to do with the increased surface area from all those leaves and blades of grass. Much of it still seemed to be hanging in the air as well, as if the marshland and mud were so sodden already that it was incapable of absorbing any more moisture. This was my bit of England, undecided whether it was in the sea or on land. A loud revving and a splutter of pebbles signalled the arrival of a car.

'Danny,' I said. Elsie slithered off my unmade bed, pulling a mess of duvet behind her, loops of coloured glass bouncing round her neck, a crown of pink plastic falling out of her unruly hair as she made for the stairs.

'Are you sure about this?' I asked Finn, again. She nodded.

'And you're sure you want me there too? I won't be able to sit anywhere near you, you know.'

'Yes. Sure.'

I wasn't sure. I know that funerals help us to realize that loved ones are dead and not returning; I know that we can say goodbye at a funeral and start to mourn. I've been to funerals – well, one funeral in particular – when this has been true, the start of the melting of the great ice-block of grief. The familiar words do touch you, and the faces around you, all wearing the same look of battened-down grief, make you part of a community, and the music and the sobs inside your chest and the sight of that long box and the knowledge of what's inside it well up into a kind of sorrow that's the beginning of a thaw.

But at this funeral there would be police and journalists and photographers and busybodies peering eagerly at her. Finn would have to see all the people that she'd hidden from since the day she lost her parents. We'd be escorted there by plain-clothes policemen, and she'd be flanked by them throughout the ceremony, bodyguards for a girl still at risk. People talk too easily about facing up to loss, coming to terms with it. Finn seemed to me more in need of protection than self-knowledge. Avoidance is a common and ill-advised coping strategy for people suffering from post-traumatic-stress depression; Finn was certainly avoiding. But safe, soothing routines may be the best way for them to start the healing process.

'It's your choice,' I said. 'If you want to leave, just tell me. All right?'

'I just need to . . .'

She didn't finish her sentence.

'Let's go and meet Danny then.'

She looked at me imploringly.

'He's not going to bite you. At least, not in a horrible way.'

I took Finn by the hand and pulled her out of the room. Later, Danny laughed about his first sight of Finn, she and I descending the stairs in melodramatic black, but then he looked up at us, hair over his shoulders, unsmiling. Finn didn't smile either, but nor did she hesitate. She let go of my hand, and the two of us – me clip-clopping behind in my leather buckled shoes and she softly padding in front in her pumps – approached him. She stopped in front of him, looking tiny against his bulk, and lifted her eyes to his. Still no smile from either of them.

'I'm Finn,' she said in a murmury little voice from behind her silky curtain of hair.

Danny nodded. He held out his hand and instead of shaking it, she laid her thin fingers against his palm, like a small child deciding to trust someone. Only then did Danny look past Finn at me.

'Hi, Sammy,' he said nonchalantly, as if he'd been away for an hour, not nearly two weeks. 'Do you know what you look like?'

'I'm sure you'll tell me.'

'Later I will.'

Elsie came in from the kitchen.

'There's a man called Mike.'

'It's time for us to be off, Finn.'

Danny bent his head down and kissed me on my lips. I put the flat of my hand against his cheek and he leaned into it briefly, and we smiled at each other. I smelled his skin. Then Finn and I went into the rain. Daley got out of his car. He was dressed in a crinkled navy-blue suit with wide lapels. He looked more like a slightly hungover jazz musician than a mourner. Finn stopped suddenly, one foot in the car.

'No.'

I laid my hand on her back.

'Finn?'

Daley stepped forward.

'Come on, Finn,' he urged. 'It'll be . . .'

I interrupted him.

'You don't have to do this,' I said.

'You go,' Finn said suddenly. 'You and Michael go for me.'

'Finn, you ought to go, don't you think, Sam?' Daley said. 'You should see people.'

'Please, Sam. Please will you go for me?'

Daley looked at me.

90

'Sam, don't you think it would be good for her to go? She can't go on not seeing people like this.'

A look of panic came into her eyes. I was getting wet and wanted to move from the muddy gravel and pouring rain. We couldn't force her.

'She should make up her own mind,' I said.

I beckoned to the figures in the doorway, who ran out to hear the change of plans. The last glimpse I had of Finn was of her being led into the house, a small damp figure resting limply against Danny, while Elsie skipped behind them and the rain rained on.

During the service I was silent and still, Daley was silent and fidgeting endlessly. He ran his fingers through his silky hair, rubbed his face as if he could wipe away the dark shadows under his eyes that made him look so dissolute, shifted his weight from foot to foot. Finally, I put a calming hand on his arm.

'You need a holiday,' I whispered. An elderly woman sitting on the other side of me, a pork-pie hat jammed on her head, warbled. 'Bread of Hea-a-a-aven,' she sang, in a passionate vibrato. I mouthed the words and looked around. I was trying to get a feel of the world of Finn and her family. For me, Finn so far was pitifully isolated. This funeral felt unreal. I had no connection at all to the dead couple, except through their daughter. I hardly knew what they looked like, except from the photograph I had seen in all the papers – a blurred picture taken at a charity ball, him burly and her skinny, both smiling politely at a face out of the frame, while the fact of their terrible death cast them into history. 'Fe-e-e-d me ti-ill I-I want no more.'

Sometimes I wonder if people can smell suburbia on me, like a dog is supposed to be able to sniff out fear. I think I can smell wealth and respectability a mile off, and I smelled it here. Modest black skirts and neat black gloves, grey gaberdine suits with a dash of glamour at the neck, sheer black tights, low shoes (my buckles gleamed loudly in the dull air of the Victorian church), small ear-rings on a hundred lobes, make-up which you couldn't detect but knew was there on the faces of all the middle-aged women, the low-key, well-bred grief, a discreet tear here and there, modest and expensive bouquets of early spring flowers laid on the two coffins that sat so baldly on the catafalque. I had had to arrange a funeral once and I had gone through the catalogues and learned the vocabulary. I glanced from face to face. In one pew ahead of me sat seven teenage girls; from the angle at which I sat their sweet profiles overlapped each other like angels on a gilt Christmas card. I noticed that they were all holding hands or nudging each other, and they tilted their heads occasionally to catch whispers from one side or the other. Finn's schoolfriends, I decided, and made up my mind to try to bump into them later. Across from me a plump woman in shiny black with a large hat was sobbing into her copious handkerchief. I knew at once that she was the cleaner, the one who'd found the bodies. She was the only person I saw that day who displayed raw, noisy, undignified grief. What would happen to her?

We knelt in silence to remember the dear departed, to the cracking of a dozen ageing knees. I wondered what all these people were remembering – what conversation, what row, what little incident bobbed above the implacable surface of death to remind them? Or were they remembering that they'd left the oven on, or planning what to wear to the concert that evening or wondering if any dandruff was falling on to their dark-fabricked shoulders?

Which ones had been close to Finn – the old friends of the family who'd known her all through her childish years, had seen her suffer and seen her grow into a lovely young woman, the ugly duckling into the graceful swan? Which were the vague acquaintances who'd turned up because the couple had been slaughtered and there were police and journalists at the door of the church?

'Our Father,' intoned the vicar.

'Who art in heaven,' we followed obediently. 'Hallowed be thy name . . .' And the cleaner, whatever her name was, sobbed on.

Ferrer, that was it. She hung behind as people started to make their way up the aisle, and I forced myself against the flow towards her. She was scarcely visible, bent over between two pews. I got closer and saw she was picking things up from the floor and putting them into her bag. She started to put on her coat and knocked her bag all over again.

'Let me help you,' I said and bent down and felt under the bench for keys and a purse and coins and folded pieces of paper that had fallen out of it. 'Are you coming next door?' I saw her face close up, the skin pale, the eyes swollen with crying. 'Next door?'

There was a prod in my back and I turned to see the detective, Baird. He nodded at me with a smile, then remembered himself and looked sombre.

'You've met Mrs Ferrer,' he said.

'Has anybody done anything for this woman?' I asked. Baird shrugged.

'I don't know, I think she's going back to Spain in a few days.'

'How are you?' I asked her. She didn't respond.

'It's all right,' Baird said, in the loud slow voice English people use when speaking to foreigners. 'This is Dr Laschen. She is a doctor.' Mrs Ferrer looked anxious and distracted. 'Um . . . doctoray, medico.'

Mrs Ferrer ignored me and began talking quickly and incoherently to Baird. She had things for the 'little girl'. Where was she? She was going home and wanted to get things to Miss Mackenzie. Say goodbye to her. She must say goodbye, couldn't go before she had seen her. She started crying again, hopelessly. I noticed that her hands were trembling. In my professional judgement, she was a total mess. Baird looked nervously across at me.

'Well, Mrs Ferrer, if you pass anything on to me, then in due course . . .' He looked over at me and nodded me away. 'Don't worry, doctor, I'll take her across.'

'You look like a bridge player. Help us out here.'

Two women – one woman with coarse brown hair and a strong nose, the other smaller with perfect white hair under a tiny black hat – beckoned me into their conversation. When I was about thirteen, my mother had forced me into the school bridge club as part of my upwardly mobile social education. I'd lasted about two weeks, enough to learn the point counts of the court cards and not much more.

'If I open two no trumps, what does that mean to you, eh?'

'Trumps,' I said gravely. 'Are they the black cards or the red ones?'

Their faces fell and I backed away, teacup in hand, an apologetic smile on my lips. Over the other side of the hall I saw Michael deep in conversation with a balding man. I wondered who'd arranged all of this – booked the hall, made the sandwiches, hired the tea urn. My attention was snagged suddenly.

'I was hoping to see Fiona, poor girl. Has anyone spoken to her?'

I stood still and sipped my empty cup.

'No,' came the answer. 'I don't think so. I heard she'd been taken abroad to recover. I think they have some relatives in Canada or somewhere.'

'I heard she was still in hospital, or a nursing home. She nearly died, you know. Poor darling. Such a gentle, trusting girl. How will she ever get over this?'

'Monica says' – the voice behind me sank to a stage whisper so that I could hear it more clearly than ever – 'that she was, you know, raped.'

'No, how terrible.'

I moved away, grateful that Finn had been spared this. The mourning process could wait. Baird had been standing dutifully with Mrs Ferrer in a corner, and I saw them making their way towards the door. I caught Mrs Ferrer's eye and she came across to me, seized my hand and mumbled what seemed to be thanks. I tried to say to her that if there was anything I could do I would do it, and that I would find out her address from Baird and come to see her. She nodded at me but I wasn't sure if she had taken it in and she released my hand and turned away.

'How's the cleaner?' a voice said behind me. Michael Daley.

'Aren't you her doctor?'

'She's registered with me. I took her on as a favour to the Mackenzies.' Daley turned and followed her progress out of the room with a frown, before turning back to me. 'Does she know who you are?'

'Baird introduced us; I don't think she understands the connection between me and Finn,' I said.

'What did she want?'

'Help, I should say, and urgent help at that. And she wants to give Finn some of her things. And to see her, before she goes back to Spain.'

Daley sipped reflectively at his sherry.

'Sounds good to me,' he said. 'I suppose it would be good for Finn to see someone she knows.'

'I don't know if it's safe, but on the other hand she might be an unthreatening kind of presence,' I said.

'It's fine,' he said.

There was a pause. He gave a half-smile. 'There are one or two people I should make a pretence of talking to. I'll pick you up on the way out.'

Standing in a huddle in the corner of the room were the girls I'd noticed in the church. I made my way over to them and when I caught the eye of one, I moved into their circle.

'You must be friends of Finn's?'

A tall girl with dark shoulder-length hair and freckles over the bridge of her pert nose held out her hand, looked suspiciously at me, and then back at her friends. Who was I?

'Just from school,' she said. 'I'm Jenny.'

I'd wanted to find out about Finn from people who knew her, but now I couldn't think what to say.

'I knew her father. Professionally.'

They all nodded at me, incurious. They were waiting for me to move on.

'What's she like, Finn?' I asked.

'Like?' This from a blonde girl with cropped hair and

a sharp nose. 'She's nice.' She looked around for confirmation. The girls nodded.

'*Was* nice,' another girl said. 'I went to visit her at the
hospital. They wouldn't let me anywhere near her. Seems
pretty stupid.'

'I suppose . . .'

'Are you ready to go?'

I turned with a start to see Michael's face. He hooked
an arm under my elbow and nodded at the girls. They
smiled back at him in a way they hadn't smiled at me.

The car park of the little parish church at Monkeness was
right by the sea wall, and we sat there for a few minutes.
I nibbled at a walnut cake that I'd scooped up from a tray
on the way out, and Michael lit a cigarette. It took several
matches, and finally he had to crouch down in the shelter
of the wall.

'Did Finn get on with her parents?'

He gave a shrug.

'Were they close? Did they argue? Help me out here,
Michael, I'm living with this girl.'

He took a deep drag from his cigarette and gave a
gesture of helplessness.

'I think they were close enough.'

'Michael, there must have been problems. She was
hospitalized because of depression and anorexia. You
were her doctor.'

'Yes, I was,' he said, looking away from me over at the
indistinct sea. 'She was a teenager, it's a messy time for
most of us, so . . .' He gave a shrug and didn't finish his
sentence.

'Was it difficult for you being a friend of her parents?'

Dalcy turned to face me with his tired dark eyes.

97

'It's been very difficult for me being a friend of Leo and Liz. Did the police tell you what they did to them?'

'A bit. I'm sorry.'

We got into the car and drove off. The countryside seemed grey, scrubby, indistinct. I knew it was my own mood. I had been to a funeral and felt no grief. I had just been uselessly thinking. I looked out of the window. Reed city.

'I'm not right for Finn,' I said. 'And I wasn't particularly proud of myself today.'

Michael looked round.

'Why and why?'

'I think Finn was telling me something in wanting me to go to the funeral of her parents and all I did was snoop around and try to find out about what she was like.'

Michael seemed surprised.

'Why did you do that?' he asked.

'I can't see a patient in a vacuum. I want a context.'

'What did you learn?'

'Nothing, except what I already knew: that our knowledge even of our close friends and relations is strangely vague. "Nice." I learned that Finn is nice.'

He put his hand on my arm, took it away to change gear, put it back on my arm.

'You should have told me. If you want, I'll introduce you to some people who knew the family well.'

'That would be good, Michael.'

He turned and gave me a mischievous smile.

'I'll be your ticket into rural society, Sam.'

'They won't have me, Michael. I'm lower middle class.'

He laughed.

'I'm sure they'll make an exception in your case.'

Twelve

'She thinks I'm a layabout. Why should I be polite to her?'

'You are a layabout. Just don't be completely rude. Or go for a long walk and don't be here at all.'

Danny put his hands around my waist as I stood at the sink, and bit my shoulder.

'I'm hungry and I like to be here.'

'I'm washing the dishes,' I said crossly. Danny was getting on my nerves today, just as he'd got on my nerves yesterday. Although, after we had returned from the funeral and talked at length to Finn about it, and Michael Daley had stayed for a drink – Danny glowering at him as if he and I had spent the day in a double bed together, not at a funeral, and Michael oddly nervy with Danny – and Elsie had been put to bed, we'd had a passionate reunion, the next two days had not gone well. He'd hung around in his normal kind of way, getting up late, eating huge breakfasts while Sally cleaned around him, going to bed in the small hours of the morning and leaning into me with beery breath, and this had irritated me. He'd not put himself out for Finn, although he hadn't actually been rude, and this had irritated me too. He'd left his dishes unwashed in the sink, his clothes unwashed in the corner of my room, he'd almost picked my fridge clean without replacing anything, and then I was irritated by my own prissiness. Didn't I want Danny to be Danny? 'Can't you lay the table or something?' I complained.

'Lay the table? Let her get her own fork out of the drawer. She's not going to be here for at least fifteen minutes. Why don't we just go upstairs?' Now his hands were under my shirt.

I pushed his roving hands away with my soapy ones.

'Elsie and Finn are next door.'

'Half-way through the puzzle.'

'She's quite nice to have around, isn't she?'

Danny let me go and sat down heavily at the kitchen table. 'Is she?' he said.

'What's wrong with that?'

'Oh Christ,' he ran his hand through his hair. 'I don't want to talk about your patient.'

I took five forks from the plastic basket by the sink and clattered them on to the table in front of him.

'Quiche is in the fridge. Warm it up. Ice-cream in the freezer. I think you're jealous of her.'

'And why would I be jealous?' Now Danny's arms were folded across his chest and he was glaring at me.

'Because I like her and Elsie likes her and you don't feel quite so much like the king of the castle when you deign to visit us in the country – that's why.'

'And do you know what I think, Sam? I think you've stopped separating work from home. You're in trouble here. And have a think about this while you're at it: first of all I have to compete with a dead man for your love, and then with an invalid child. How can I ever win?'

There was a loud knock on the front door. For once I was glad Roberta had arrived early.

I am sometimes unkind to Roberta because I am scared

of the mixed and contradicting emotions I have always had for her. I don't want to know if she is unhappy. When we were girls, Roberta was designated the pretty one and I was the clever one. She never had a chance. She wore the pink dresses and had the row of dolls along the shelf in her bedroom; I wore trousers (even though, to my disgust, they had heel straps and no pockets) and read books by torchlight under my covers. She painted her manicured nails with pearly varnish (I bit mine), wore pretty blouses and plucked her eyebrows. When her breasts started to develop she and mum made a special trip to Stacey's department store to buy pretty little bras with matching knickers. When she got her periods, a sense of glamour and mystery surrounded the sanitary towels and blood stains. She was an insecure little girl, who went into womanhood bravely and fearfully, as if it were her terrible vocation.

When I was working seventy-two-hour weekend shifts as a junior doctor at the Sussex by the river, she was a mother and living in Chigwell, and while I became thin and haggard and middle-aged, she became rounder, wearier, middle-aged. Her husband called her Bobsie and once told me that my sister made the best scones in Essex. But then, what did she think when she looked across at me? Did she see a successful doctor or a scraggy unmarried mother with a vulgar on–off boyfriend and vulgar red hair, who couldn't even cook quiche when her sister came to lunch?

'And how are you enjoying staying with Sam, Fiona?'

'It's nice.'

Finn had hardly touched her food. Once an anorexic always an anorexic they say, like alcoholics and smokers. She had sat with an anxious half-smile on her face as

Danny had slouched and made flirtatious remarks and I had scowled and Bobbie had made bright remarks about how we could all see more of each other.

'Do you like country life or do you prefer the town?' Bobbie, in her social anxiety, sounded as if she were talking to a six-year-old.

'I'm not sure . . .'

'Auntie.' Elsie had insisted on sitting so close to Roberta she was practically in her lap. Her sharp little elbows jabbed my sister every time she spooned more chocolate-chip ice-cream into her smeared and eager mouth.

'Yes, Elsie.'

'Guess what I'm going to be when I grow up?'

This was the kind of conversation Bobbie could deal with. She turned away from the three adult faces ranged opposite her.

'Let's see. A doctor like mummy?'

'Nowayhosay!'

'Um, a nurse?'

'No.'

'A ballerina?'

'No. Give up? A *mummy*, like you.'

'Are you, dear, that's lovely.'

Danny smirked and spooned more ice-cream on to his plate, slurped it loudly into his mouth. I glared across at him.

'You're her role model, Roberta,' he said.

Bobbie smiled uncertainly. We're bullying her, I thought.

'Let me clear the dishes,' she said, stacking plates with a clatter.

'I'll put the kettle on,' I said, 'and then maybe we can all go for a walk.'

'Not me,' said Danny. 'I'm going to stay and lie about, I think. That's what I *really* like doing, eh, Sammy?'

Finn followed Roberta and me into the kitchen, carrying a couple of glasses as her excuse. She turned to my sister, who was furiously scrubbing clean dishes.

'Where did you get your jumper?' she asked. 'It's pretty; it suits you.'

I stopped in the middle of the room, kettle in hand. Bobbie smiled with delighted embarrassment.

'A little shop near us, actually. I thought maybe it made me look too fat.'

'Not at all,' said Finn.

I felt a wash of emotions – astonishment at Finn's aplomb, shame at my own neglect of Bobbie, a rush of swamping tenderness for my sister, who could be made so happy by such a small remark. But then I heard Bobbie asking Finn what exactly she was studying. There was a ring at the front door, a murmur of voices, and Danny appeared in the kitchen doorway.

'A man called Baird,' he said.

'I'll see him in the kitchen. Can you take the others through into the living room?'

'I feel like a fucking butler,' Danny said, looking across at Roberta. 'I mean a damned butler.'

Baird came into the kitchen and began fidgeting with a mug on the table.

'Do you want me to put some coffee into that for you?'

'No, thanks. Your extractor fan wants fixing. It gets rid of kitchen odours. I could have a look at it if you want. Take it apart.'

I sat down opposite him.

'What's up?'

'I was just passing.'

'Nobody just passes Elm House.'

'Dr Daley says that Miss Mackenzie's shown some signs of improvement.'

'Some.'

'Has she said anything about the crime?'

'Rupert, has anything happened?'

'Everything's fine,' he said formally. 'I just wanted to see how you were.'

'We're fine too.'

He stood up as if he was about to go.

'I just wanted to ask,' he said, as if it was an afterthought, 'that you keep a lookout for anything unusual.'

'Naturally.'

'Not that there'll be anything, but if you notice anything unusual, or if Miss Mackenzie says anything, dial 999 and ask for Stamford Central 2243. That's the quickest way of reaching me any time, day or night.'

'But of course I won't be using that number, Rupert, because you explained to me how perfectly safe this situation was and that I had nothing to worry about.'

'Absolutely. And that's still the case, although we had hoped for a conviction by now. Is this the only exterior door apart from the one at the front?' He grasped the handle and tried it. It didn't seem very firm.

'Should I have bars put on?'

'Of course not.'

'Rupert, wouldn't it help if you told me who we were supposed to be looking out for?'

'You're not supposed to be looking out for anybody.'

'Do you have a suspect or a description or an Identikit picture?'

'We're pursuing various possibilities.'

'Rupert, nothing's going to happen here. Nobody cares about Finn, and nobody knows she's here.'

'That's the spirit.'

'For God's sake, Rupert, there was that lorry-park fire on Monday. How many veal transporters were destroyed? Forty?'

'Thirty-four lorries suffered varying degrees of damage.'

'So shouldn't you be out harassing animal liberationists rather than worrying me?'

'I believe that some of my colleagues are following a line of inquiry there as well. As a matter of fact . . .' The sentence died away.

'Have you got a suspect? Why are you really here?'

'Looking in. I'll go now. We'll keep in touch.'

'Do you want to see Finn?'

'Better not. I don't want to make her nervous.'

We walked to his car together. A thought occurred to me.

'Have you heard from Mrs Ferrer?'

'No.'

'She wanted to see Finn, bring her some stuff, and I thought it might be helpful to Finn to meet her.'

'That's probably not such a good idea at the moment.'

'I thought I might go and see her. I'm worried that nobody has given her any kind of help. Also I'd like to talk to her about the family, about Finn. I wondered if you could give me her address.'

Barid paused and looked back at my house, apparently deep in thought. He rubbed his eyes.

'I'll think about it.'

We shook hands and for just a fraction of a second he delayed letting go. I thought he was about to say something, but he stayed silent, just nodding a goodbye. As I turned round to return to the house I saw Finn's pale face at her window. I wasn't going to be put off so easily. And anything that delayed joining Danny and Roberta for a few minutes was additionally attractive. I picked up the phone and called Michael Daley.

Thirteen

'How are you coping?' Daley asked.

'What with?'

He laughed.

'I don't know where to begin. With Finn. With a child. Moving to the country. With a big new job.'

'I'm coping. That's what I do.'

Michael was driving me on the Stamford ring road towards the Castletown area of Stamford where Mrs Ferrer lived. Michael had been resistant at first but I told him that after meeting Mrs Ferrer, I felt a certain responsibility for her. I was worried about her mood. Also, if she wanted to see Finn, then that might be good for both of them, and I was determined to encourage it. Certainly, the cleaner had seemed pretty determined to track down Finn and say goodbye. At any rate, I wanted to talk to her. No, I didn't want to talk to her on the phone. After my experience at the funeral, I thought it would take a good deal of patience, not to mention sign language, to establish meaningful contact with her.

'Just give me her address and I'll go there in the morning.'

'I think she's at work in the morning. If you can wait until the afternoon, I'll come with you. After all, I am supposed to be her doctor. It could count as a home visit.'

As we drove, Michael pointed out remains of Roman

fortifications, the traces of a siege in the civil war, an ancient mount, but then we left the interesting local sites behind and drove among school playing-fields, allotments, roundabouts, superstores, petrol stations, about which there was nothing to say.

'How are *you* coping?'

'Fine,' said Daley, a little sharply. 'Why do you ask?'

'Politeness.'

'You don't need to be polite with me.'

'You haven't seen me not being polite.'

'I could deal with it.'

Michael never took his eyes off the road and I couldn't see the expression in his eyes.

'Do you resent me being here?' I asked.

'In my car?'

'Here, on the scene. When you are Finn's doctor.'

'I've already told you that I don't.'

'It would be natural.'

We were back in a residential area of terraced houses.

'If we turned left here, we'd get to the Mackenzies' old house. But we just turn right here into the less salubrious part of Castletown. We're alike I think, you and me.'

I smirked at his apparent flirtatiousness.

'How so?'

'We like challenges. We take things on.'

'What do you take on?'

'When I was a child, I used to be scared of heights. There was a sort of tower near where I went to prep school, a monument built by an eccentric old duke. There were a hundred and seventy steps, and when you were at the top it felt as if you were falling. I made myself climb it every week of term.'

'Did it cure you of your fear of heights?'

'No. Then it would have become boring. My work's just a job. Except for people like Mrs Ferrer, of course. But my real life's largely outside it. I make myself do things. Gliding. Riding. Have you ever been sailing?'

'No, I hate water.'

'You can't live here and not sail. You must come in my boat.'

'Well . . .'

'This car's another example. Do you know anything about cars?'

'We don't seem alike to me. I never do things I'm afraid of.'

'It must be somewhere here.'

'Here? Can we park?'

'Trust me. I'm a doctor. I have a sticker in my window. I'm paying a call.'

'Does she live in Woolworths?'

We were in a busy shopping street. Mrs Ferrer lived in one of those rooms that you don't notice, a doorway between shops leading up to a first floor that you wouldn't suspect is there. A door from the street led up some grey-carpeted stairs to a landing from which there were two doors. One had the nameplate of a dentist on the door, the other had nothing.

'This must be it,' said Daley. 'Handy for the shops, at any rate.'

There was no bell or knocker. He rapped at the door with his knuckles. We waited in awkward silence. There was nothing. He knocked again. Nothing.

'Maybe she's at work,' I suggested.

Daley turned the handle of the door. It opened.

'I don't think we should go in,' I said.

'The radio's on.'

'She probably forgot to switch it off when she went out.'

'Maybe she can't hear us. Let's go up and see.'

There were more steps. No carpet this time. As I reached the top my face was hit by a breath of stifling hot air. Michael grimaced at me.

'Is there something wrong with the electrics?' I asked.

'A reminder of Spain, I suppose.'

'Mrs Ferrer!' I called. 'Hello? Where's the radio?'

Michael pointed ahead of me into the tiny, squalid kitchen.

'I'll find the heater,' he said.

I walked into the kitchen, in which the music was echoing tinnily. I found the radio by the sink, pushed at buttons ineffectually and then pulled the plug out from the wall. There was a shout which I thought at first was a delayed throb from the radio, but then I realized it was my name: 'Sam! Sam!' I ran through to the other room and found a complicated and strange scene. Looking back on it even a few minutes later, I wasn't able to recall how I had put it together in my mind. I could see a woman lying on the bed with all her clothes on, a grey skirt, a brightly coloured nylon sweater. No head. Yes, there was a head but it was obscured by something, and Michael was picking frantically at it, tearing it. It was plastic, a bag, like the bags you put fruit in at the supermarket. Michael was pushing his fingers into her mouth and then firmly pushing down on the woman's chest and doing things with her arms. I looked around for a phone. There. I dialled.

'Ambulance, please. What? Where are we? Michael, where are we?'

'Quinnan Street.'

'Quinnan Street. By Woolworths. Above Woolworths, I think. And police as well.' What was his name? Rupert. Rupert. 'Tell Inspector Baird at Stamford CID.'

I put down the receiver and looked round. Michael was sitting still now, obscuring most of Mrs Ferrer's body, though I could see her open eyes, disordered grey hair. He stood up and walked past me. I heard a tap running in the kitchen. I walked over and sat by the body. I touched her hair and tried to arrange it slightly, except that I couldn't remember which way it was supposed to go. Who was left to know?

'I'm sorry,' I said aloud to myself, to her. 'I'm so, so sorry.'

The ambulance arrived within five minutes, a man and a woman in green overalls ran in at high speed, then slowed down and stopped after a brief examination of the body. They looked around as if they had woken from a dream and had noticed us for the first time. As we were introducing ourselves, two young police constables came up the stairs. I asked about Baird, and one of them spoke into a radio. I whispered to Daley, feeling guilty and conspiratorial.

'How did she die?' I knew the answer.

His faced looked dazed.

'Suffocated.'

I had an ache in my stomach that seemed to be rising in my oesophagus and becoming a throbbing headache. I was unable to think clearly except for a feeling that I wanted to leave but probably had to stay. I felt strangely grateful a few minutes later at the sight of Baird, who entered the room, apparently filling it, with a distracted-looking, rumpled man who was introduced to me as Dr

Kale, the Home Office pathologist. With a nod Baird walked past me and stood over the body for a moment in silence. Then he turned to me.

'What were you doing here?' he asked in a subdued tone.

'I was concerned about her. I met her once and she seemed to be crying out for help. But I was too late, it seems,' I said.

'You mustn't reproach yourself. This wasn't just a cry for help. She really meant to die . . . Has the body been moved?'

'No. Michael tried to revive her.'

'Was death recent?'

'I've no idea. It's hard to tell in this heat.'

Baird shook his head.

'Awful,' he said.

'Yes,' I said.

'You don't need to stay. Either of you.'

'I suppose we'd better tell Finn.'

'I'd like to, if that's all right.' It was Michael. 'I'm her doctor, after all.'

'Yes, you are.'

So we made our way to Elm House in a cumbersome fashion. Michael drove me back to his surgery, where I had left my car. Then the two of us drove in an absurd convoy out of Stamford, and all the way I thought of a woman coming on a murder scene, the blood and the suffering, and finding it all too much to bear and having nobody to help her and that I'd already known this and had been too late.

We came on Finn in the kitchen tracing letters with Elsie. Without a word I took Finn and Elsie by the hand

and walked outside where Michael was waiting. I held Elsie tight in my arms and prattled to her about her day at school, at the same time watching as Michael and Finn walked down in the direction of the sea. I saw their silhouettes, and behind them the reeds were tipped golden with the low sun, although it was barely four o'clock. They talked and talked and sometimes leaned one on the other. Finally they walked back towards us and I put Elsie down and, still without talking, Finn fell into my arms and grasped me close to her so that I felt her breath on my neck. I felt Elsie pulling at me from the side, and we all laughed and walked inside out of the wind.

Fourteen

'Am I your patient?'

I felt like a mother being asked where babies come from, having already considered the different answers I could give when the question was posed. I felt torn for a moment between the desire to reassure and the responsibility to be clear.

'No. You're Dr Daley's patient, if you're anybody's. But you shouldn't think of yourself as a patient.'

'I'm not talking about me, I'm talking about you.'

'What do you mean?'

'I don't know what I'm doing in your house. Am I in hiding? On the run? Am I a lodger? A friend? A sick person?'

We were sitting in a sort of pseudo-bistro establishment near the old harbour in Goldswan Green, half an hour up the coast and almost empty on this cold Monday in February. I was eating a bowl of pasta and Finn was pushing her fork into a side salad served as a main course. She stabbed a leaf of some kind of bitter lettuce that I found inedible and rotated it.

'You're a bit of all of them, I suppose,' I said. 'Except for the sick person.'

'I *feel* sick. I feel sick all the time.'

'Yes.'

'You're the expert, Sam,' Finn said, pushing the salad around her plate. 'What *should* I be feeling?'

'Finn, in my professional capacity, I usually make a point of not telling people what they should do or feel. But in this case I'm going to make an exception.'

Finn's expression hardened in alarm.

'What do you mean?'

'Speaking as an authority in the field of post-traumatic stress disorder, I would strongly advise you to stop playing with your salad and scraping the fork on the plate, because it's getting on my nerves.'

Finn looked down with a start and then relaxed into a half-smile.

'On the other hand,' I continued, 'you could move some of it from your plate into your mouth.'

Finn shrugged and pushed the whole large leaf into her mouth and crunched at it. There was a sardonic sense of triumph.

'There we are,' I said. 'That wasn't so difficult.'

'I'm hungry,' Finn said, as if she were examining the behaviour of an exotic creature.

'Excellent.'

'Perhaps I could order some of the pasta you've got.'

'Take mine.'

I pushed the dish across and she dipped into it, almost excited by the novelty of what she was attempting. For several minutes neither of us spoke. It was enough for me to see her eat.

'Maybe I've had too much, all at once,' Finn said, when the two plates were clean.

'It wasn't all that much. What I forgot to eat, mostly. Do you want some coffee?'

'Yes. White.'

'Good, Finn. Some more protein and calcium. We can start building you up.'

She started to laugh, then stopped herself.

'Why did she do it?'

'Who? Mrs Ferrer?' I shrugged, then took a chance. 'She wanted to come out to see you, you know. She was going back to Spain, but she wanted to see you first.' I remembered her frantic desire to visit the 'little girl' – then I remembered her lying dead on the bed in her cheerful jumper.

Finn's face darkened. She seemed to be looking through me at something far away.

'I wish, I think I wish, that she had. I'd liked to have seen her. It was the horror of what she'd seen, I suppose.'

'It must have been something,' I said absently.

'You sound suspicious.'

'I didn't mean to.'

'Do you think I was stupid? With the bonfire?'

On that shambolic Saturday afternoon, Danny had left shortly after Rupert and Bobbie – he'd picked up his holdall and shoulder-bag, ignored Michael and Finn, and given me a curt nod. When I'd tried to detain him ('I know this isn't ideal, but let's talk about it later') he'd said wearily that he'd been waiting for three days to talk to me, and I'd just been spiky and hostile, and didn't I know by now that my 'later' never arrived and anyway he had things to do in London? To which I hissed, babyishly, that he was behaving just like a baby. Then, he'd left. This was becoming a habit. Neither Finn nor Michael said anything about it, and Elsie scarcely seemed to notice that he was no longer with us. As for me, Mrs Ferrer's death, my concentration on Finn, had pushed him to the edge of my mind.

Then, on the following Sunday morning, Michael

Daley had suddenly turned up. I was in the garden piling planks, canes, old branches on to a bonfire when his Audi pulled into the drive. He didn't come over but removed a dozen or so stuffed Waitrose bags from the back. Was he buying food for us now? No such luck. He had brought some of Finn's clothes which the police had released from the house.

'Where am I supposed to put all of this?' I asked as we ferried bags up the path into the hallway.

'I thought it might be a step back into normality,' Daley said.

'I wondered how long Finn could keep padding around in my rolled-up jeans.'

'Sorry I can't stay,' said Daley. 'Give her my regards.'

'Regards,' I said. 'I never know what they are.'

'You can think of something.'

'Are you all right?'

'What do you mean?'

'You've lost another patient.'

'Is that a joke?' he asked and said nothing more. He left without seeing Finn. I called her down.

'Look what the doctor brought you,' I said.

She was visibly startled. She pulled a maroon crushed-velvet blouse from one of the bags and held it up.

'I've got some work to do outside,' I said. 'I'm burning almost everything that's movable in the garden. I'll leave you to go through it, if you want.'

She nodded but said nothing. I left her, and when I looked back, before closing the front door, I saw her kneeling on my hall floor holding the velvet to her cheek, as if she were a tiny lost child.

Gardening would always be a mystery to me, but I loved making fires. There had been rain and it was a tricky business but that only increased the ultimate satisfaction. I had screwed newspaper into balls at various points on the windward side of my pile of rubbish. I lit them and they crackled, glowed and went out. I looked in the shed and found an almost empty box of firelighters and a washing-up-liquid bottle that didn't smell of washing-up liquid any more. I wrapped up the entire box in newspapers and pushed it deep into the recesses of the rubbish pile. I sprayed all that was left of the petrolly liquid over it. I had created a small incendiary device and wasn't sure whether it would ignite my pile of rubbish or simply blow it up. I lit a match and tossed it at the heap. There was a low thud, as if a punch-bag had been dropped on to a concrete floor. I saw a yellow glow, heard crackling, then flames escaped from the pile, and I was pushed back by a soft invisible pillow of heat against my cheeks and forehead.

I felt the usual thrill at the transition from the stage when the fire couldn't be started to the stage when it couldn't be stopped. I began to feed the flames with scraps from all over the garden. There were old grey wooden lattices, a pile of ancient planks by the back wall of the house, all of them soon cracking in the core of heat, sending sparks flying high. I felt a presence at my side. It was Finn, the reflection of the flames dancing in her eyes.

'Good fire, eh?' I said. 'I should have been a pyro-maniac. I *am* a pyromaniac. I can't imagine robbing a bank or killing somebody, but I can understand the pleasure of setting fire to something big and watching it burn down. But this will have to do.'

Finn leaned close to me, placing a hand on my shoulder. I could feel the brush of her lips as she whispered into my ear. She finished and moved back, but she was still close. I could see the golden down on her cheeks.

'Are you sure?' I asked.

She nodded.

'Wouldn't you like to drop it into an Oxfam shop or something?'

She shook her head.

'I don't want anybody else to wear it.'

'Whatever you think is right.'

So she went back into the house and a minute later she emerged with an armful of skirts, dresses and shirts. She came past me and heaved them on to the pyre. The bright fabrics ballooned, bubbled and burst. She made trip after trip. There were some beautiful things among them, the things she must have bought after she'd lost weight, and Finn must have detected a wistful expression on my face, because she broke off from one of her journeys to push a trilby hat on my head and wind a damson cashmere scarf around my neck. The hat fitted me perfectly.

'Rent,' she said with a smile.

She kept nothing for herself at all. When it was all over we contemplated the fire together, watching the fragments of braid and ribbon being consumed, and I felt a little sick, like a champion eater who has been out-gourmandized.

'So what do we do now?' Finn asked finally.

'I think that tomorrow I'll take you shopping.'

'I'm sorry, Sam,' Finn said, swallowing the last of her coffee. 'Oh, it's bitter. Nice. I know it was melodramatic, burning them all like that. It felt like something that I had to do.'

'You don't have to explain it to me.'

'Yes, I do. This is hard for me to put into words, but what I feel is something like this. In a way I feel contaminated by those people who tried to . . . you know.

My life has been ripped apart and completely changed by them. Do you see what I mean? You like to feel that your life has been directed in a good way. But I felt, feel, that my life has been put in a certain direction by people who hated us. I had to cut all that away and be reborn. Remake myself. Do you see what I mean?'

'I understand completely,' I said with deliberate bland acceptance. 'But you're used to doing that, aren't you?'

'How do you mean?'

'You suffered from anorexia, it was life-threatening. But you moved on. You know how to recover, and that's a wonderful thing.' I paused for a moment, wondering how far I could take this. 'You know, it's funny. The first sight I had of you was in some old photo of you, plump, jolly-looking. And here you are, a different person, secure, alive.'

I looked at Finn. Her hand was trembling so much she had to put her knife down.

'I hated that girl. Fat Fiona Mackenzie. I feel no connection to her. I made myself a new life, or thought I had. But now it's hard for me to accept the good things. Meeting you and Elsie and all of this. I sometimes think that I've met you and Elsie because of, you know, *them*. I'm not sure if I should be talking about this. Should I be talking about this?'

I kept feeling different things and I was rather afraid that I was saying different things at different times. If I was discussing her case with a colleague we could have considered the different therapeutic options and the varying, much-disputed rates of success for each one. With one or two of my most trusted friends, I might have remarked that in the treatment of post-traumatic stress disorder we were still stuck in medieval times, in the age of superstition, of humours and agues and bleedings. Finn was looking to me for the sort of authority people expect from doctors. And I knew so much about the subject that I was less certain about it than somebody who knew less than I did might have been. Most of what people thought they knew about trauma and its treatment was wrong. The truth seems to be that talking about the experience makes some people better, some people worse and leaves other people about the same. That isn't what people like to hear from doctors.

I took a deep breath and aimed for as much of the truth as we could both manage.

'I don't know, Finn. I wish I could give you an easy answer and make you feel better, but I can't. I want you to feel that you can tell me anything. On the other hand, I'm not the police. I'm not after you for evidence. And I can't say this too often: I'm not your doctor. There isn't some schedule of treatment involved here. But if I can be disloyal to my great and noble profession for a moment, that may not be entirely a bad thing.' I reached across the table and took Finn by the hand. 'I sometimes think that doctors find it particularly difficult to accept suffering. You had a most terrible, unspeakable thing happen to you. All I can say is that the pain will diminish over time. It will probably be better when the bastards who did it are caught. On the other hand, if you have specific physical symptoms, you must mention them to me or to Dr Daley and he'll deal with them. All right?'

'Sort of.'

'Good enough.'

'Sam?'

'Yes?'

'I'm in the way, aren't I?'

'Everything in my life has always been in the way of everything else. But I've decided that you are one of the nice things and that's all that matters.'

'Don't feel you have to be nice, Sam. I'm stopping you writing your book, for a start.'

'I was doing a good enough job of not writing it before you arrived.'

'What's it about?'

'Oh, you know, trauma, what I do, all that stuff.'

'No, really, what's it about?'

I narrowed my eyes in mock disbelief. I summoned the waitress and ordered two more coffees.

'All right, Finn, you asked for it. The basis for the book is the status of post-traumatic stress as an illness. There is always a question of whether a pathology, I mean, a particular illness, actually exists before it has been identified and given a Latin name. Bobbie, of all people, once asked me a good question. She asked if Stone Age men suffered from traumatic stress after fighting a dinosaur. First I explained to her that there were no dinosaurs during the Stone Age, but her question stayed with me. We know that Neanderthals suffered bone fractures, but after terrible events did they have bad dreams, did they have triggered responses, did they show avoidance?'

'Well, did they?'

'God knows. What I'm planning to do is to give a brief history of the condition, in which it was largely described by false analogies with recognizable physical traumas, and then I'll analyse the amazing inconsistencies of diagnosis and treatment in the subject in Britain at the moment.'

'Are you going to study *me*?'

'No. And now let's spend some money.'

★

We spent a delirious couple of hours drifting up and down the paved pedestrianized concourse in Goldswan Green's shopping district. I tried on an absurd little pillbox hat with a veil, which would have gone perfectly with a black dress, black stockings and plain black shoes, none of which I possessed. But I bought a navy-blue velvet waistcoat and thought about some ear-rings until I realized that the point of the expedition was to kit out Finn rather than me and turned my attention to her. We found a large basics store and equipped her from the inside out: socks, knickers, bras, tee-shirts, two pairs of jeans – one black, one blue. My own tendency would have been to rush around and grab almost at random, and I was impressed by Finn's gravity and exactitude. There was nothing frivolous or light-hearted about her choices. She selected clothes with the precision of a person setting off to climb a mountain, in which every surplus ounce would be a liability.

As we drifted around the shop I noticed that another woman was eyeing us. I wondered if it was because we were buying so much and then forgot about her until I heard a voice behind me.

'It's Sam, isn't it?'

I turned with a sinking feeling of non-recognition. The woman was familiar, but I could see that I wasn't going to be able to place her quickly enough.

'Hello . . .'

'It's Lucy, Lucy Myers.'

'Hello . . .'

'From Bart's.'

Now I knew who she was. Christian Society. Glasses, which she no longer wore. Went into paediatrics.

'Lucy, how are you? Sorry, I didn't recognize you at once, it must be your glasses. Lack of.'

'And I wasn't really sure it was you, Sam, because of your hair. It looks really . . . really . . .' Lucy looked for the right word. 'Brave,' she said desperately. 'I mean, interesting. But I know all about you. You've come to Stamford General.'

'That's right. Is that where you're based?'

'Yes, for years. I grew up there.'

'Oh.'

There was a pause. Lucy looked expectantly at Finn.

'Oh,' I said. 'This is Fiona. Jones. We're working together.'

They nodded at each other. I didn't want to prolong this.

'Look, Sam, it's great to see you. When you're in the hospital we must, you know . . .'

'Yes.'

'Well, I must get on with my shopping.'

'Yes.'

Lucy turned away.

'You weren't very nice to her,' Finn whispered to me as we inspected some cardigans.

'She wasn't a friend, we were just in the same year. The last thing I want is to get thrown together as soul mates out here in the middle of nowhere.'

Finn giggled.

'And I only like seeing people by appointment,' I added. 'Here.' I brandished a grey cardigan at her. 'I order you to buy this.'

'Buy it for yourself.'

'If you say so.'

I lay in bed with my eyes open in the dark. The day after tomorrow was Valentine's Day. Would Danny come with a red rose and a sarcastic smile, a cross word and a kind look? Would he ever come again, or had I lost him, carelessly, without really meaning to, just because I hadn't been looking his way? I'd write to him tomorrow, I promised myself, I'd make things all right again, and on this resolution I fell asleep.

Fifteen

On Wednesday, when I had shuffled down the cold stairs wrapped in Danny's dressing gown, which he'd forgotten to take in his hurry to be gone, a letter lay on the doormat. But it was too early for the postman to have been and the 'SAM' that was written in blue Biro on the envelope showed this was Elsie's handiwork, not Danny's. After I'd turned up the thermostat and put on the kettle, I slipped a finger under its sealed flap. She had stuck a pink tissue-paper heart on to white card. Inside the card was written, in tilted letters that belonged to Elsie but which had clearly been spelt out by Finn, 'Happy Valentine's Day. We love you.'

The 'we' had bothered me, although it touched me too. In a moment of weakness, I had let Elsie stay at home with another of her not very serious colds, and we'd sat, the three of us, at the kitchen table, eating Rice Krispies and toast. Nothing had come from Danny – no card, no phone call, no sign that he was thinking of me. I wished that I had never sent him yesterday's rather raw letter. Well, who cared about Valentine's Day, anyway? I did.

We'd drifted around in the morning, pottering. For a while, Finn looked through the bundle of letters that Angeloglou had brought over the previous day – letters that friends had written to her and left with the police for delivery. They made quite a thick parcel, which she propped rather secretively against her knees. I watched her very carefully to see if she became agitated, but she seemed strangely unaffected. It was almost as if she had no interest in them. After a bit, she pushed them all together again, and took them up to her room. She never mentioned them to me and I never saw her looking at them again.

Finn had become fascinated with the subject of trauma, with herself, perhaps, and I told her about its beginnings, about railway spine and shell-shock, how the First World War doctors thought it was caused by the impact of the artillery. I was amused by Finn's interest and just a little concerned whether such an absorption in her own condition was entirely healthy. We were planning to head out for a walk as soon as the rain eased. But the rain didn't ease off. It grew heavier and more dense, and the windows were now almost opaque, as if we were living behind a waterfall.

'It's like being on an ark,' I said, and of course Elsie asked what an ark was. Where should I begin?

'It's a story,' I said. 'A long long time ago, God – he had made the world, in the story, but he thought it had all gone wrong, that everyone was behaving badly. So he decided to make it rain and rain and rain to cover the whole world and kill everybody . . .'

I stopped and looked anxiously over at Finn, who was stretched out on the sofa. Even the word seemed insensitive. How had she taken it? Finn wasn't looking at me. She was looking across at Elsie. She rolled off on to the ground and scrambled over to where Elsie was seated by her box of toys.

'But he didn't kill everybody,' Finn said. 'There was a man called Noah and there was Mrs Noah and their children, and God loved them. So God told Noah to build a huge boat and to put all the animals on the boat, so that they could be saved. So he built the boat and put every animal he could find inside. Like dogs and cats.'

'And lions,' said Elsie. 'And pandas. And sharks.'

'Not sharks,' said Finn. 'The sharks were all right. They could look after themselves in the water. But the others, the family and the animals, they all stayed in the ark. And it rained and rained and the whole world was covered with water and they stayed safe and dry.'

'Did it have a top?'

'It had a roof. It was like a house on a boat. And at the end, when the water had gone away, God promised that he would never do it again, and do you know what he did to show his promise?'

'No,' said Elsie, her mouth gaping open.

'Look, I'll show you. Where are your felt-tips?' Finn reached into Elsie's playbox and took out some pens and a pad of paper. 'See if you can guess what I'm drawing.' She drew a crimson curve. Then she drew a yellow line along its top edge. Then blue.

'I know,' said Elsie. 'It's a rainbow.'

'That's right. That's what God put in the sky as a promise that it would never happen again.'

'Can we see a rainbow? Now?'

'Maybe later. If the sun comes out.'

Which it didn't. We had a good old-fashioned rural ploughman's lunch as invented by some flash git who lived in a city. Good fresh bread, bought half-baked from the supermarket. I unpeeled the polythene from a wedge of cheese. Some tomatoes from a packet. A jar of relish. Sunflower spread. Finn and I shared a large bottle of

Belgian beer. Elsie chattered, but Finn and I didn't say much. Beer and cheese and the rain on the roof. It felt enough for me.

I got some logs from the shelter at the side of the house and made a fire in the grate in the living room. When the flames were shimmering, I got the chessboard and pieces and set them out on the rug. As I played through an old Karpov–Kasparov world-championship game, Finn and Elsie were on the other side of the chimney-breast. Elsie was drawing with fierce concentration while Finn told what sounded like a story in a conspiratorial, low voice. Sometimes Elsie whispered something back.

I looked down at the board and lost myself in Karpov's strategic spiders' webs, turning the tiniest of advantages into an irresistible attack, and Kasparov's heady plunges into awesome complication, confident that he would be able to emerge ahead. I was playing around with variations, so the games took a very long time to get through. After some time, I don't know how long, I heard a clink of china and a warm familiar smell beside me. Finn was kneeling beside me with a tray. She had made tea and toast and a couple of hot-cross buns for Elsie.

'How will I ever manage to go back to an office?' I said.

'I don't know how you can lose yourself like that in a game,' Finn said. 'Are you just playing through something that someone else has already played?'

'That's right. It's like watching thought in action.'

Finn crinkled her nose.

'Doesn't sound like much fun to me.'

'I'm not sure that *fun* is exactly the right word. Who said that life should be fun? Do you know the moves?'

'What do you mean?'

'That a bishop moves diagonally, that a king moves one square and all that.'

'Yes, I know that much.'

'Then look at this.'

I quickly returned the pieces to their starting positions and began to play through a game I knew by heart.

'Who wins?' Finn asked.

'Black. He was thirteen years old.'

'Friend of yours?'

I laughed.

'No. It was Bobby Fischer.'

'Never heard of him.'

'He became world champion. Anyway, his opponent was overconfident and neglected his development.'

I played White's seventeenth move.

'Look at the board,' I said. 'What can you see?'

Finn pondered the position for more than a minute with that grave concentration of hers that so impressed me.

'It looks as if White is in a better position.'

'Very good. Why?'

'Both Black's queen and his horse . . .'

'His knight.'

'His knight . . . are being attacked. He can't save them both. So how did Black win?'

I reached forward and moved the bishop across the board. I looked with amusement at Finn's puzzled expression.

'That doesn't do anything, does it?'

'Yes, it does. I love this position.'

'Why?'

'White can do lots of different things. He can take the queen or the knight. He can swap off the bishop. He can do nothing and try to batten down the hatches. Whichever he chooses, he loses in a completely different way. Go on, try something.'

Finn looked for a moment and then took Black's bishop. In just four moves there was a beautiful smothered mate by the knight.

'That's wonderful', said Finn. 'How could he work out all that in his head?'

'I don't know. It hurts me just to think about it.'

'It's not my sort of game, though,' Finn said. 'The pieces are all out in the open. Poker is my game. All that bluff and deception.'

'Don't let Danny hear that or he'll keep you up all night at it. Anyway, that's the whole beauty of the game. Chess, I mean. Two people sit across the board from each other. All the pieces are in full view and they manipulate each other, bluff, lure, fool each other. There's no hiding-place. Hang on a second.' I reached for a book that was beside the board and flicked to the epigraph. 'Listen to this: "On the chessboard lies and hypocrisy do not survive long. The creative combination lays bare the presumption of a lie; the merciless fact, culminating in a checkmate, contradicts the hypocrite."'

Finn gave an almost flirtatious little moue.

'Sounds a bit scary to me. I don't want to be laid bare.'

'I know,' I said. 'We need our little self-deceptions and strategies. In real life, I mean, whatever real life is. Chess is a different world, where all that gets stripped away. In the match I just showed you, a little boy lured a grown-up master chess player into destroying himself in the open.' I saw that I was losing her attention. 'We must have a game some time. But not today.'

'Definitely not,' said Finn firmly. 'I don't want to be at

131

your mercy. At least not any more than I am already. More tea?'

'*I* want to play chest.'

It was Elsie, her drawing finished or abandoned.

'Chess,' I said. 'All right. What is this piece called?'

'Don't know.'

'How can you remember all those moves?' Finn asked.

'Because I'm interested in them.'

'My memory is totally useless.'

'I doubt that. Let me show you something. Choose seven or eight objects from the room and tell us what they are.'

After Finn had done that, we sent her out of the room for a couple of minutes, then called her back. She squatted back down on the floor with Elsie and me.

'All right, Elsie, what were they?'

Elsie closed her eyes and wrinkled her forehead and her little round nose.

'It was a chess piece . . . and a cup . . . and a lamp . . . and a picture of a sheep and a pink felt-tip and a yellow felt-tip . . . and Fing's shoes and Mummy's watch.'

'Brilliant,' I said.

'That's pretty good for a five-year-old, isn't it?' Finn said. 'How did she do that?'

'She practises,' I said. 'Centuries ago, remembering things was an art that people used to learn. The way you do it is to have a building in your mind, and you put things in different places in the building, and when you want to remember them, you go into the building – in your mind's eye – and retrieve the objects.'

'What do you have, Elsie?' Finn asked.

'I've got my special house,' Elsie said.

'So where was the chess piece?'

'On the front door.'

'And where was the cup?'

'On the doormat.'

'How did anybody ever think of doing that?' Finn asked.

'There's an old story about that,' I said. 'A sort of myth. In Ancient Greece a poet was reciting at a banquet. Before the end of the feast, the poet was called away, and a few minutes later the banqueting hall collapsed and everybody was killed. The corpses were so badly damaged that the next of kin couldn't recognize them and claim them for burial. But the poet was able to remember where everybody had been sitting, and because of that he could identify all the bodies. The poet remembered all the guests because he had seen them in a particular location, and he realized that this could be a means of remembering anything.'

Finn's face was pensive now.

'Memory and death,' she said. 'I wouldn't dare to wander in the house of my own mind. I'd be frightened of what I might find there.'

'*I* wouldn't,' Elsie said proudly. '*My* house is safe.'

I stayed up till late. No Danny.

Sixteen

The next evening I went to what Michael Daley had called a social occasion when he invited me to accompany him. 'You wanted me to launch you into local society,' he said, so I had to be a sport and say yes.

I pulled garments from their hangers and tossed them on to the bed. There was a long maroon woollen dress with a high waist that I liked, but it seemed too sombre. I rejected a couple of black miniskirts, the delicate blue dress with the soft neckline and three-quarter-length sleeves that I never threw away and never wore, the loose silk black trousers that had started to resemble pyjamas, and finally put on a black voile top and calf-length satin skirt. I pulled out my favourite black shoes with no heel (I tower over most men anyway) and a clunky silver buckle, and hung ear-rings on my lobes in a jangle of hot colour. Then I examined myself in the mirror; I didn't look very respectable. I put on no make-up, except for a slash of red on my lips to match my hair. I pulled Finn's trilby from the top of the wardrobe and jammed it on my head. I wished it was Danny taking me to this party; without him, I was dressed up and stepping on to the set of the wrong play. Where was Danny now? I had swallowed my pride and tried to telephone him, but there had been no reply, not even his voice on the answering machine telling me he wasn't there but would ring me back as soon as he could.

Elsie was already asleep in a nest of duvet. I knelt beside her and breathed in her clean fragrance: her breath smelled of hay and her hair of clover. My hat touched her on the shoulder and she grimaced in her sleep and curled up on her side, muttering something which I couldn't catch. Her paintings were stuck all around her room, more every day. Rainbows; and people with arms and legs coming out of their bulbous heads, eyes askew; animals with five legs; daubs of violent colour. Finn had labelled each picture neatly with Elsie's name and the date she had drawn it. Sometimes there was a title: one, a scribble of purple with eyes and hands adrift in the chaos of colour, was called 'Mummy at work'. It occurred to me that if I died now Elsie would have no real memory of me. She'd miss Finn when the time came for her to go, but she'd get over it quickly.

Linda and Finn turned from the sofa as I came into the living room. They were eating microwaved popcorn and drinking Coke in front of the TV. Finn had resolutely opposed all my suggestions that she contact her old friends, but an unlikely friendship had grown up between these two, comradely and consoling.

'I'm off. What are you watching?'

'Linda brought round a video of *Dances With Wolves*. You look nice.' Finn smiled sweetly and poured a handful of popcorn into her mouth. She seemed completely comfortable; she'd kicked off her shoes and her legs were tucked up under her, a floppy cardigan was wrapped around her; she'd plaited her hair and looked pre-pubescent. I tried to imagine her as fat and found that I couldn't.

Kevin Costner was dancing around naked, his white buttocks shining cutely.

'Such an irritating actor,' I said waspishly. Linda turned to me, shocked.

'He's gorgeous.'

Outside, a car horn sounded. I picked up my coat.

'That'll be Michael. I won't be gone long, Linda. Help yourself to anything you want. Finn, see you in the morning.'

And I was gone, into the cold night air, into the warm interior of Michael's car, meeting his appreciative gaze, sinking into my coat, leaning back in the seat. I love being driven, probably because I almost never am. Michael drove with deliberation, and his big car slipped smoothly along narrow lanes. He was wearing a navy-blue coat over a dark suit and looked rather expensive and less louche than usual. Sensing my eyes upon him he turned, met my gaze, smiled.

'What are you thinking, Sam?'

I spoke before my brain intercepted me.

'I was wondering why you've never married, had children.'

He frowned.

'You sound like my mother. My life is the way I want it to be. Here we are' – we were in Castletown with its stone lions on gate pillars and lawns – 'we'll be there in a couple of minutes.'

I sat up a bit straighter in the seat, pushed back a wisp of hair that had escaped the hat.

'How many people are going to be there?'

'About thirty. It'll be a buffet supper. Laura's one of the more bearable consultants at your hospital. Her husband Gordon works in London, in the City. They're very rich. There'll be a couple of other doctors.' Michael smiled with a touch of mockery. 'A cross-section of provincial society.'

He turned off the road and pulled to a halt at the beginning of the drive. The house ahead was dismayingly large. Was I dressed right?

'It's the sort of house I imagine Finn's parents living in,' I said.

'It's just a couple of streets away,' Michael said and looked serious for a moment. He got out of the car and came round to my door, which he held open for me. Not something Danny would do. 'Laura and Gordon were close friends of Leo and Liz. There'll be other friends there as well, I suppose.'

'Remember I don't know her though, Michael.'

'You don't know Finn,' said Michael with a conspiratorial smile. 'I'll try to remember that.'

He took me by my elbow and steered me up a driveway lined with rhododendrons. A Mercedes was parked outside the Georgian house, whose porch was lit by a lamp. Behind the thin curtains I could see the shapes of groups of guests, hear the chink of glasses, the hum of voices and the laughter of people at ease with each other. I should have worn the delicate blue dress, after all, and lined my lips with pink. Michael ostentatiously sniffed the air.

'Can't you smell it?' he asked.

'What?'

'Money. It's in the air. Everywhere. And all we can do is smell it.' For a moment he sounded bitter. 'Do you ever have the feeling that people like Laura and Gordon are on the inside and we're outside with our noses pressed against the glass?'

'If you ring the bell perhaps they'll let us inside as well.'

'You've spoiled my image,' he said.

He thumped the heavy brass knocker and almost immediately a handsome woman with iron-grey curls and a taffeta skirt down to the ground opened the door; the hallway behind her was wide and its walls were lined with paintings.

'Michael!' She kissed his cheek three times, French fashion. 'And you must be Dr Laschen. I'm Laura.'

'Samantha,' I said. Her handshake was firm. 'Thank you so much for inviting me.'

'We're so looking forward to having you at the hospital. Not long now, is it?'

But she didn't wait for a reply. I probably wasn't supposed to talk shop. And I couldn't mention Finn. That didn't leave much I was interested in. The room was full of people standing in exclusive knots, in their hands glasses full of amber-coloured wine. The men were all in dark suits; men only take risks with their ties. Most of the women wore long dresses, and dainty jewellery flashed from their ears and fingers. Michael seemed surprisingly at home here. He broke through a closed circle of four people and said affably:

'Hello, Bill' – a large man in, God, one of those things wrapped round the waist, shook him by the hand heartily – 'Karen, Penny, Judith, isn't it? May I introduce a new neighbour of ours? This is Samantha Laschen – Samantha's a doctor. She's setting up a new centre of her own at Stamford General.'

There was a murmur of subdued interest. 'Something to do with trauma. People getting upset after accidents, that sort of thing, isn't it?'

I grunted something meaningless. Running down the

trauma industry was *my* job. I wasn't so keen on it being done by an oafish amateur. There was a polite chorus of greeting, then a little pause. But these people were social pros. Within half an hour I'd talked about gardening to Bill, country versus town to a rotund man with a gravelly voice and permanently raised eyebrows whose name I never discovered. A high-bunned woman called Bridget told me about the latest activities of the animal rights terrorists. Dogs seized from a research facility, sabotage at the university, vandalism of farm vehicles.

'I don't eat veal myself,' she confessed. 'I read an article once about how the calves are so weak that they can't even stand up, poor things. I always found the meat rather tasteless anyway. But these other things are something different. The point is that these are city people who don't understand rural traditions.'

'You mean like forcing beagles to smoke cigarettes?'

I looked round at the speaker to my right. A saturnine young man with close-cropped hair and extraordinarily pale eyes nodded at me and drifted away towards a tray of drinks.

'Don't mind him,' said Bridget. 'He just does it to annoy.'

I was passed expertly from group to group, while women in black skirts and white shirts poured wine into my glass, or handed me tiny canapés with a firm curled shrimp or a shred of dill-topped smoked salmon in the middle, until I found myself once more standing next to Laura.

'Samantha, this is my husband Gordon. Gordon. Samantha Laschen. You remember, Michael's friend. And this is Cleo.' Cleo was taller than me, and broad. She was dressed in pillar-box red, and her hair, which once must have been blonde but had now turned a rusty grey, hung loosely about the pouches of her ageing, intelligent face.

'We were just talking about Leo and Liz.'

I composed my face into an expression of blank interest and wondered if there was any mayonnaise on my chin. I stroked it as if I were thinking. Nothing. Or perhaps I'd only smeared it.

'You must remember. Leo and Liz Mackenzie, who were murdered in their own house last month.'

'I read about it,' I said.

'And their daughter, of course, Fiona, lovely girl. She survived, of course, she was in Stamford General for a while. She was terribly wounded and distressed, I heard. Terrible thing.'

'Awful,' I said.

'They were friends of ours, neighbours almost. We used to play bridge with them every first Thursday of the month. Leo had the best memory for cards I ever saw.'

'Such a waste,' said Gordon, nodding vigorously and pulling his features into the settled grimace of sorrow. They had evidently performed this double act of shocked remembrance before.

'What happened to Fiona?' This was from Cleo, who had managed to get hold of a plate and now scooped up a handful of asparagus wrapped in bacon from a tray as the waitress passed.

'Nobody knows where she is at the moment. She's disappeared.'

'Michael would know, of course.' Gordon turned to me. 'He's her GP. But he's the soul of discretion.'

'What was Fiona like?' I blessed Cleo for asking the questions that I felt unable to, at the same time noting how they talked about the girl as if she had died.

'Lovely. She had her weight problems, of course, poor thing. Donald,' Laura caught the arm of a cadaverous man passing and pulled him into our circle. 'Cleo was just asking what Fiona was like. She used to spend time with your daughter, didn't she?'

'Fiona?' He frowned. A piece of asparagus slid from its bracelet of bacon as I lifted it to my mouth and landed between my feet.

'You know, Fiona Mackenzie, whose parents both . . .'

'Oh, Finn.' He reflected for a moment. 'Rather a nice girl, not loud like some of them are, or forward. Sophie hasn't seen her since she went away, of course, though I think she sent a letter to the police station to forward.'

I tried to prod something specific out of him.

'Difficult age, though, isn't it?' I said. 'Boyfriends. Parties, all that.' I lobbed the remark into the conversation, then shut my mouth firmly, as if it hadn't come from me.

'Boyfriends? Oh, I don't think she had anything like that. No, as I say she was very pleasant and polite; a bit under the thumb of Leo, I always used to think. Nice girl, as I said.'

That was that. We began to eat supper at half-past nine. Game pie and rocket salad, little crescents of choux pastry filled with fish, chicken satay on skewers, lots of different cheeses, looking grand on a large wooden platter, tangerines heaped in a bowl. I sipped and ate and nodded and smiled, and all the time I kept thinking that Finn must have been in this house – and how could she have come from this kind of high-ceilinged world and yet have fitted so easily into mine? I sat on a yellow-covered chair, my plate propped on my knees, and for a moment was overcome with the familiar agony of not belonging, not here, not to the semi I grew up wanting to escape from, and now (I felt a wave of panic run through me) not to my own house, where a young girl with soft hair was looking over my daughter, singing lullabies that only mothers should sing to their children. If I had been alone I might even have wrapped my arms around myself and rocked, in the age-old gesture of distress which my patients often use. I wanted Elsie, and I wanted Danny, and they were all that I wanted. 'Fuck you, Danny, I'm not going to sit around moping,' I muttered under my breath.

'*Clockwork Orange?*'

'What?' I frowned and looked round, startled out of my reverie. It was the man with the close-cropped head.

'Your outfit. You've come as a character from *Clockwork Orange.*'

'Never seen it.'

'It was a compliment. You look like one of the characters who break into the houses of blindly respectable people and shake them up a bit.'

I surveyed the room.

'You think this lot need shaking up?'

He laughed.

'Call me a wet liberal, but after an evening like this, I start to think that the Khmer Rouge had the right idea. Raze all the cities. Kill everybody wearing spectacles. Drive the rest out into the fields and turn them into manual labourers.'

'You wear spectacles yourself.'

'Not all the time.'

I looked at the man and he looked at me. After thirty seconds' acquaintance I would say that he was the most attractive man I had met since I had left London. He raised his glass in an ironic toast, displaying a wedding ring. Oh, well.

'You're a friend of Dr Michael Daley.'

'We're not exactly friends.'

'The hunting doctor.'

'What?'

'You've heard of the flying doctor. And the radio doctor. And the singing nun. Michael Daley is the hunting doctor.'

'What do you mean?'

'What I say. He rides horses which ride after wild animals and sometimes catch them, and tears them apart. And the triumphant hunters then daub entrails on to each others' faces. Another of those country traditions you were being lectured about.'

'I didn't know Michael did that. I can't imagine him hunting somehow.'

'I'm Frank, by the way.'

'I'm . . .'

'I know who you are. You're Dr Samantha Laschen. I've read some of your very interesting articles about the construction of illness. And I know that you're setting up the new trauma unit at Stamford General. The Stamford Trust's potential new cash cow.'

'That isn't precisely its point,' I said with as much asperity as I could express with a straight face. Frank's ambiguously probing and humorous manner both attracted and unsettled me.

'Well now, Sam, we must meet for a drink some time in a real place, and we can discuss subjects such as how the function and purpose of something like your trauma unit can be different from what it first appears.'

'Sounds a bit abstract to me.'

'How is the unit going?'

'I'm starting in the summer.'

'So what are you doing now?'

'A book and things.'

'Things?'

Frank took not a glass but an entire bottle of white wine from a passing tray and filled our two glasses. I looked ruminatively at his wedding ring once more, a feeling of recklessness that was just another way of being unhappy rising in me. He looked at me with narrowed, thoughtful eyes.

'You're a paradox, you know. You're here at the house of Laura and Gordon Sims, but you're not, thank goodness, a member of their circle of bridge players and tuft-hunters. You arrive at the party with Michael Daley but you claim not to be a friend. It's all quite mysterious. Why would an expert in traumatic stress . . .?'

'Hello, professor.'

Frank turned.

'Why, it's the hunting doctor. I've been telling Dr Laschen about your hobbies.'

'Have you told her about your own hobbies?'

'I have no hobbies.'

I turned to Michael and was surprised to see his jaw set in anger. He looked at me.

'I should explain to you, Sam, that Frank Laroue is one of the theorists behind all the barn-burning and veal-protesting and laboratory break-ins.'

Frank gave an ironic bow of the head.

'You flatter me, doctor, but I don't think that activists need instruction from a humble academic like me. You are far more effective on the other side.'

'What do you mean?'

Frank winked at me.

'You shouldn't be so modest about your recreational

144

activities, Dr Daley. Let me blow his trumpet for him. He is the adviser to an informal secret committee composed of academics and policemen and other stalwart citizens, which monitors the actions and publications of people like me, who are concerned with ecological issues, ensuring that we can be harassed occasionally, *pour décourager les autres*. Is that about right?'

Michael didn't reply. 'I'm afraid we have to go now, Sam.'

Michael had taken my arm, which in itself tempted me to resist and stay, but I yielded to the pressure.

'See you,' said Frank in a low voice as I passed him.

'Was that true, what Frank said about you?' I asked when we were back in the car. Michael started the car and we drove away.

'Yes, I ride to hounds. Yes, I advise a committee which monitors the activities of these terrorists.' There was a long silence as we left Stamford. 'Is this a problem?' he said, finally.

'I don't know,' I said. 'Something about it leaves a bad taste. You should have told me.'

'I know I should,' he said. 'I'm sorry.'

'It's all so childish,' I said. 'People spying on each other.'

Michael veered sharply, braked and came to a halt. He turned the key and the car shivered and fell silent. I could hear the sea, softly, down below. He turned to me. I could only see his silhouette, not his expression.

'It isn't childish,' he said. 'Do you remember Chris Woodeson, the behavioural science researcher?'

'Yes, I know about that.'

'We all know that behavioural scientists put rats in mazes, don't we? So somebody sent him a parcel bomb which blew his face off, blinded him. He has three children, you know.'

'Yes, I know.'

'Frank Laroue can be charming sometimes, the ladies love him, but he plays with ideas and sometimes other people put them into practice and he doesn't take responsibility.'

'Yes, but . . .'

'I'm sorry, I should have told you this earlier. Baird told me not to tell you, but I'm going to tell you anyway. There's a magazine published by animal activists, it's illegal and underground and all that, and it prints the addresses of people who are claimed to be torturers of animals, as an obvious invitation to people to take action against them. In December, an edition of the magazine appeared with the home address of Leo Mackenzie, pharmaceutical millionaire.'

'For God's sake, Michael, why wasn't I told about that? Baird just mentioned animal activists vaguely, as a possibility; he never told me about a direct connection.'

'It wasn't my decision.'

I couldn't see his expression. Was he remorseful? Defiant?

'Knowing this, and the police knowing this, I can't believe you thought it was a good idea to stick Finn in the middle of nowhere with me and Elsie.'

'We wouldn't have considered it if we didn't think it was safe.'

'That's easy for *you* to say, Michael.'

'Perhaps I should say that I was first told about this edition of the magazine by Philip Carrier, one of the detectives running the animal rights investigation. It wasn't the publication of Leo's address that he rang me about.'

'No? What was it then? *My* address, presumably. That's all I need.'

'No, they printed *my* name and address.'

'Yours?' I felt a flush of embarrassment. 'God, I'm so sorry.'

'That's all right.'

'What are you doing about it?'

Michael started the car and we moved off once more.

'I double-lock the door at night, that's about all. Don't worry, I'm strong.'

'All that riding to hounds.'

'I do other things as well. I must show you my boat. We should go out on it for a day. Get away from all of this.'

I mumbled something.

'What are you doing on Saturday?'

I mumbled something else.

'I'll pick you up after breakfast.'

That night I couldn't sleep. I put on my dressing gown – Danny's, full of his smell in its towelly folds – and sat by my window and listened to the sea. I think that I cried. If Danny had come into the room then I would have laid him on the bed without a word. And I would have undressed him slowly and kissed him tenderly and covered his nakedness with my body, pulling apart my gown and sinking on to him, drawing him into me, watching his face all the while. I would have asked him to take us away, live with us, to marry me, to give me a child.

At dawn I fell asleep.

Seventeen

'A cash cow?'

Geoff Marsh looked amused, almost flattered by the suggestion.

'That's what the man said to me.'

'You shouldn't believe everything that strange men say to you at parties. Who was it?'

'A man called Frank Laroue, an academic.' Geoff Marsh's face broke into a knowing smile. 'A friend of yours?'

'I know Laroue. He probably believes that the whole of western medicine is a capitalist plot to keep the workers unhealthy, but in this case he has a point. Post-traumatic stress is a growth area, no doubt about it.'

It was the Monday after the party, and Geoff and I were in the middle of a working breakfast of coffee and croissants. I had mischievously quoted Laroue at Geoff and was surprised to find it taken seriously.

'There can't be much money in trauma,' I said.

Marsh shook his head vigorously and swallowed a mouthful of pastry.

'You'd be surprised. You saw the judgment last week in favour of the trauma suffered by the Northwick firemen. What were the damages and the costs? Five million and change?'

'Good for the firemen.'

'Good for *us*. I suspect we will now be finding insurance companies insisting on a pre-emptive policy of stress counselling to safeguard them against future litigation. And we are in a position to be ahead of the market in supplying that counselling.'

'I thought the purpose of this unit was to fill a therapeutic need, not to protect the investment of insurance companies.'

'The two go together, Sam. You should be proud of this potential. After all, the unit is your baby.'

'I sometimes feel that my baby isn't turning out the way I had planned.'

Geoff drained his coffee-cup and his face assumed a sententious expression.

'Well, you know, you have to allow your children to go their own way.'

'Thank you, Dr Spock,' I said sourly. 'The baby hasn't even been born yet.'

Geoff got up and wiped his lips with a napkin.

'Sam, I want to show you something. Come over here.'

He led me to one window of his large, high, corner office. He pointed down to a corner of the hospital grounds where a few men in orange helmets were standing disconsolately outside a Portakabin.

'We're expanding,' he said. 'Stamford is expanding. We're in the right place. Close to London, close to Europe, green-field sites. I have a dream, Sam. Imagine this hospital trust realizing its full potential and being floated on the Stock Exchange. We could be the Microsoft of primary healthcare.'

I followed his gaze, aghast.

'I suppose now you're going to ask me to turn the stones into bread. Unfortunately I can't stay the full forty days here in the wilderness because I've got to get back to making so-called progress on my book.'

Geoff looked confused.

'What are you talking about, Sam?'

'Nothing much, Geoff. I'll see you next week, back in the real world.'

'This *is* the real world, Sam.'

As I drove on the now-familiar route out of Stamford I reflected gloomily that he was probably right, and then I considered the rest of my world – Elsie, Danny, Finn, my book – and felt even worse. Elsie was at school, Danny was God knows where, and when I arrived home Finn was sitting on a sofa holding a magazine but not reading it. I looked with a pang towards my office, then took a deep breath and walked over to her.

'Walk?' I suggested.

We set off in silence, turning left and walking parallel with the sea for a mile or so and then turning off sharply to the left again. We were walking along the edge of a ploughed field by a ditch so wide as to be almost a canal. All we could see ahead of us were flimsy lines of trees ranged as straight as the posts of a fence – defences against the wind, I supposed.

I was thinking hard. It was the nineteenth of February. Finn had been with us for four weeks. There were two, maybe three, weeks to go before I called a halt. But for Elsie, a temporary expediency had become her life. She loved coming downstairs each morning to find us both (Finn in my old dressing gown, me in clothes that were not office ones) sitting at the kitchen table drinking coffee, chatting. She loved me to drive her to school each morning and stand at the classroom door with the other parents and kiss her quickly on her cold cheek when the bell rang and say, 'I'll collect you this afternoon.' And each day, when the bell sounded again at three-forty, she would run out with her coat and her pack folder and usually a piece of stiff paper with colourful daubs on it, and I could see that she was very happy to be like the other children. I was even careful to wear my least exotic clothes when I collected her. I tried to chat to the other mothers about head-lice lotion and the next school jumble sale. For a bit I, too, wanted us to blend in with the scenery. At teatime Finn would make Elsie toast and honey; it became a kind of ritual. At bedtime she'd pad silently into Elsie's room to say good-night while I read her books. I realized one day that she had made us feel like a real family, rather than a mother and daughter, in a way that Danny had never done. And I knew, too, that that was because I'd never allowed Danny to.

But for Finn as well as for me it was a false, fairy-tale existence. Soon she would have to return to a world of friends and solicitors, A levels, obligations and parties and competition, sex, university, chance, pain.

We arrived at a small, austere church, little more than a box, with a single window in its grey walls and a notice outside announcing that it dated from the eighth century. It had been used as a barn, a cowshed and, according to local tradition, a storehouse for smuggled casks of wine. And please do not throw litter. I asked Finn directly if she had thought about what she was going to do. She shrugged, kicked a stone out of her path, dug her hands further into her pockets.

'You can't stay here, you know that. My job starts in a couple of months. And anyway, your life isn't here.'

She muttered something.

'What?' I looked across at her, her face was set against the wind, sullen.

'I said,' she responded angrily, 'that my life isn't anywhere.'

'Look, Finn . . .'

'I don't want to talk about it, OK? You're not my *mother*.'

'Talking of which,' I said as matter-of-factly as possible, jarred by the tone of her voice, '*my* mother is arriving tomorrow for lunch.'

Finn looked up. Her face lost its mutiny.

'What's she like? Is she anything like you?'

'I don't think so.' I stopped myself and smiled. 'Maybe more than I like to believe. She's more like Bobbie, perhaps. Very respectable. She hates me not being married. I think she's embarrassed in front of her friends.'

'Does she want you to marry Danny?'

'God, no.'

'Is Danny coming again soon?'

I shrugged, and we set off again, continuing the huge, slow circle that would take us home.

'Sam? Who was Elsie's father?'

'A nice man,' I replied curtly. Then I relented and shocked myself by saying something to Finn which I had said to almost nobody else. 'He died a few months before Elsie was born. He killed himself.'

Finn said nothing. That was the only right response. I saw an opportunity.

'You never talk about your past, Finn. I understand that. But tell me something. Tell me about something that was important to you, a person, an experience, anything.'

Finn tramped on and gave no sign that she had heard me. I worried that I might have repelled her. After a hundred yards she spoke, still walking, still looking straight ahead.

'Did you hear how I spent last year?'

'Someone told me you were going round South America.'

'Yes. It all seems vague and far away now, so much so that I can hardly tell one country from another. It was a strange time for me, a kind of convalescence and a rebirth. But I do remember one time. I was in Peru and went to the Machu Picchu site which used to be something important in the Inca empire. If you're there at the time of the full moon, you can pay seven dollars for what's called a *boleto nocturno*, and you can visit the site at night. I went and looked at the Intihuatana – that's the only stone calendar that wasn't destroyed by the Spaniards – and I stood there in the moonlight, and I thought about light and about the way empires decay and die like people. The Inca empire is gone. The Spanish empire is gone. And as I stood there I thought about how all that survived were those ruins, the bits and pieces, and that beautiful light.'

I had never heard Finn talk like this before and I was deeply affected.

'Finn, that's beautiful,' I said. 'What made you want to tell me that now?'

'You asked me,' she said, and I felt the smallest chill of dismissal, unless it was just the chill of the wind blowing in off the North Sea.

As we came in sight of the house again, Finn said, 'What are you going to cook for her?'

'Them. Dad's coming too. Oh, I don't know, I'll go to the supermarket and buy something ready-made.'

'Can I do the lunch for you?'

'Cook it?'

'Yes. I'd like to. And could we invite Dr Daley as well?'

I was surprised to realize that there was a small bit of me that resented Finn's continuing attachment to Michael Daley. It was understandable. He was a contact with normality, he was good-looking, he was the family doctor. Yet, perversely, my vanity wanted her to depend on me, even as I was hardening my resolve that she should leave within a couple of weeks.

'I'll ring him.'

'And Danny?'

'Maybe not Danny this time.'

For a brief moment, I saw Danny's night-face, tender and stubbly and quite without his habitual daytime irony – the face I hoped that he turned only towards me – and felt a panicky lurch of desire. I didn't even know where he was. I didn't know if he was in London or away. What on earth was I doing in this muddy wasteland anyway, helping a fucked-up girl and losing my lover?

My uneasy feeling hung over me all day like bad weather and wouldn't disperse even when I drove to fetch Elsie from school. She was sullen also and I tried to cheer her up by telling her how Finn and I had visited a church that in the olden days was a secret pirate store where they used to keep the treasure they had smuggled ashore from their pirate ships.

'What treasure?' she asked.

'Gold crowns and pearl necklaces and silver ear-rings,' I said. 'And they buried them and drew a map and then the pirates signed it using their own blood.'

We returned home, Elsie determined to draw her own treasure map. Finn and I sat with mugs of coffee in the kitchen while Elsie crouched over the table, her forehead wrinkled, a little tip of tongue projecting from a corner of her mouth, using almost every colour from her box of Magic Markers. The phone rang and Linda answered it.

'It's for you,' she shouted from upstairs.

'Who is it?'

'I don't know,' she said.

I huffed and picked up the phone in the living room.

'Is that Dr Laschen?'

'Yes, who is this?'

'Frank Laroue. I enjoyed meeting you on Saturday and I hoped we could meet again.'

'That would be nice,' I said calmly, while my mind flapped in panic. 'What would you like to do?'

'Would you like to invite me round for tea at your new house? I always like seeing people's houses.'

'And your wife?'

'My wife's away.'

'I'm afraid my house isn't really in a fit state for anybody to visit at the moment. What about a drink in town?'

We agreed a date and place, and I rang off before I had a chance to change my mind. I wondered if I should tell Michael Daley but quickly dismissed the idea. I was going to go on his boat. That was enough. I owed myself some fun, and fuck Danny.

'We're like three pirates, aren't we, Elsie?' said Finn, as I returned to the kitchen. 'Mummy and me and you.'

'Yeah,' said Elsie.

'Is it finished?'

'Yeah.'

I laughed.

'So shall we all sign the treasure map, you and me and Finn?'

Elsie's eyes lit up.

'Yea-a-ah,' she said enthusiastically.

'So let's find the red Magic Marker.'

'No,' said Elsie. 'Blood. Sign it in blood.'

'Elsie!' I said sharply, glancing fearfully over at Finn. She got up and left the room. 'Elsie, you mustn't talk like that.'

Finn came back into the kitchen and sat next to me.

'Look,' she said. She was holding a needle between her thumb and first finger. She smiled. 'It's all right, Sam. I'm better. Not perfect, but better. Look, Elsie, it's easy.' She jabbed the needle into the end of her left thumb, then leaned forward and squeezed a crimson drop on to Elsie's map. With the eye of the needle she arranged the drop into a fair approximation of an 'F'. 'Now for you, Sam.'

'No, I hate needles.'

'You're a doctor.'

'That's why I became one, so that I can put needles into other people.'

'Hand.' Finn said firmly. 'It's all right. I've got a new one for you.' I reluctantly held out my left hand and flinched as she jabbed the needle into the tip of the thumb. She squeezed it on to the paper.

'I suppose I'll have to write Samantha,' I grumbled.

'"S" will do,' laughed Finn.

I formed my blood into an 'S'.

'Now, what about Elsie,' said Finn.

'I'll use Mummy's blood,' she said with finality.

Finn squeezed another drop from my thumb and Elsie smeared it into something that looked like a raspberry that had been trodden on. I contemplated my thumb.

'It hurts,' I said.

'Let me see,' said Finn. She took my hand and looked at the thumb. There was a dot of red, and she leaned

156

forward and dabbed it off with her tongue, looking up at me with her big dark eyes.

'There,' she said. 'We're blood sisters.'

Eighteen

'Sam, Sam, wake up.'

A whisper close to my ear pulled me up through a tumble of dreams to focus on a white face, a whimper of terror. I sat up and looked at the pale-green numbers of my clock-radio.

'Finn, it's three in the morning.'

'I heard something outside. There's someone outside.'

I frowned in disbelief, but then I heard it too. Something creaked. I was up now, wide awake in the pitch-black chill. I took Finn by the hand and raced down the corridor into Elsie's room. I picked her up, duvet, teddy and all, and carried her back into my bedroom with her thumb still in her mouth and one arm still out-flung. I laid her on my bed where she muttered, rolled more securely into a ball of duvet and bear and slept on. I picked up the phone. Nine nine nine.

'Hello, what service?'

I couldn't remember the number Baird had given me. I almost howled in frustration.

'I'm at Elm House near Lymne. There's an intruder. We need the police. Please tell Detective Inspector Baird at Stamford CID. My name is Samantha Laschen.' Oh God, she wanted it spelled out. Why couldn't I be called Smith or Brown? She was finally finished, and I replaced the receiver. I thought of the autopsy reports on the

Mackenzies and suddenly I felt as if there were insects crawling over my flesh. Finn was holding me tight. What was the best thing to do? My mind teemed with possibilities. Barricade the door to the bedroom? Go downstairs on my own and perhaps delay any intruder long enough for the police to arrive? Suddenly it was only Elsie that I cared about. She hadn't asked for this, none of this was her responsibility. Would she be safer if I could somehow separate her from Finn?

'Finn, come with me,' I hissed.

I had a vague plan of getting a weapon from somewhere but then – too soon, surely, to have responded to my call – there was the sound of car engines, scraping gravel, and flashing lights. I looked out of the window. There were police cars, dark shapes moving around. I saw a dog. I went to Finn and held her close, murmuring into her hair.

'It's OK now, Finn. You're safe. The police are here. You did well, honey, you did very well. You can relax now.'

There were knocks at the door. I looked out of the window. There was a group of uniformed officers on the path and a second group further away. Another car was pulling up. I ran down the stairs, pulling a robe around me, and opened the door.

'Is everybody all right?' the officer in front asked.

'Yes.'

'Where is Fiona Mackenzie.'

'Upstairs, with my daughter.'

'May we come in?'

'Sure.'

The man turned around.

'Secure the first floor,' he said.

Two officers, one of them female, brushed past me and ran upstairs, their feet clattering on the wood.

'What's going on?'

'Bear with us a moment,' the first officer said. Another policeman ran up and whispered in his ear. 'We've apprehended a man. He says he knows you. Can you come and make an identification?'

'Yes.'

'Do you want to get dressed?'

'That's all right.'

'Come this way, then. He's sitting in the car over there.'

My heart beat almost painfully as I approached the silhouetted figures in the car and then I just had to laugh. It was a dishevelled Danny, firmly pinioned between two officers.

'That's all right,' I said. 'He's a friend. A close friend.'

The officers let him go with some reluctance. I saw that one of them was holding a handkerchief against his nose.

'Very well, sir,' said the other. 'I should avoid lurking in gardens in the middle of the night, in future.'

Danny didn't answer. He glowered at them and at me and walked towards the house. I caught up with him at the front door.

'What were you up to?'

'My fucking van broke down in the village, so I walked. Somebody grabbed me so I hit back.'

'I'm glad you came, oh, my God, I'm glad,' I said and slid my arms around his waist. 'And I'm sorry.' A giggle rose in my chest like a sob.

There was another scrape of gravel in the drive behind me. I turned and saw an unmarked car scraping to a halt. The door opened and a burly figure emerged. Baird. He stumbled forward towards us. He stopped and scrutinized Danny blearily.

'What a bloody shower,' he said and walked past into the hall. 'I need some bloody coffee.'

'Your men were on the scene with improbable speed,' I said.

Baird was sitting at the table with his head in his hands. Danny was standing in the far corner with a glass of whisky, occasionally topped up from the bottle which he was holding in his other hand.

'They were in the vicinity,' Baird said.

'Why?'

'I understand that you've encountered Frank Laroue.'

'Did Daley tell you?'

'We believe him to be a dangerous man, Sam. And now he has contacted you.'

I was confused for a moment.

'What did . . .? Are you tapping my phone?'

'It was an obvious precaution,' Baird said.

'Fuck,' said Danny, and walked out.

'How much does he know?' Baird asked.

'How much do *I* know? Why wasn't I told any of this? Is Laroue a suspect?'

Baird frowned and looked at his watch.

'Bloody hell,' he said. 'I think it is likely that the Mackenzie murders are linked to the wave of terrorism in the region of Essex around Stamford. We thought it possible that there might be a move against Fiona Mackenzie here. Please offer your friend my apologies.' He got up to go. 'For your information, tomorrow . . .' He paused and smiled wanly. '*Today*, there will be an operation led by a colleague of mine named Carrier, involving arrests across the county. Among them will be Frank Laroue, who will be charged with various offences of conspiracy and incitement to violence.'

'Oh dear,' I said. 'So I suppose the drink I was going to have with him will have to be postponed.'

'That was not especially prudent,' Baird said. 'Anyway, I'm convinced that you are now perfectly safe.'

'What if it *wasn't* the animal terrorists who killed the Mackenzies?'

'In that case the murderers were probably burglars.'

'What did they steal?'

'It went wrong, they were disturbed. Whatever the case, you're safe now.'

'No, I'm not. I've got my parents coming for dinner later today.'

At ten later that morning there was a timid knock on the door. A thin young man, boy, really, whose hair was scraped back into a pony-tail, was standing there with a bag and a nervously adoring smile. It faded when he saw me.

'Miss Fiona wanted some vegetables,' he said and pushed the bag into my hands.

'Real farm produce, whatever next?' asked Danny. 'Real home-cooking, perhaps?'

Finn and Elsie came out of the kitchen. They both had their sleeves rolled up, and Elsie had wrapped a dish towel around her waist like an apron.

'Why don't you two go out for a walk before your mother arrives?' asked Finn.

Was this the girl who only a few weeks ago had been unable to piece two words together? She was wearing her new, dark-blue jeans and a white cotton shirt; her dark hair was brushed back into a pony-tail and tied with a velvet bow. Her face was tanned from our windswept walks and flushed from the heat of the stove. She looked clean and young and soft, with her supple limbs and her strong slim shoulders; I knew if I stood closer to her I would be able to smell soap and talcum power on her. She made me feel old and weathered. Coming forward, she took the bag from me, peering into its interior.

'Potatoes,' she said. 'And spinach. Just what we wanted, eh, Elsie?'

'Who was that boy?' I asked.

'Oh, that was Roy, Judith's son,' she replied airily. She knew far more local people than I did. She giggled. 'I think he fancies me,' and then she flushed from the roots of her hair down to her throat, on which the scar was already fading.

Danny looked after her as she went.

'She's looking well.'

'You and that boy with the pony-tail,' I said.

Danny didn't laugh.

Outside the sky was a bright pale-blue, and although it had snowed a few days ago – spitty, mean little flakes that scattered along the ridges of the red-soiled fields – the air was gentle. I had turned all the heating off and opened the windows. In the garden, among the weeds and undergrowth, daffodils glowed and tulips stood in a row of tightly unopened buds.

'Shall we have a walk then?' asked Danny. 'When are your parents descending?'

'We've a good couple of hours. Let's go through Stone-on-Sea' – though the sea had long since been pushed back by the sea walls, leaving the village surrounded by desolate marshland and strange, land-locked jetties – 'and to the coast that way.'

It was so mild we didn't even need jackets. Through the kitchen window I could see Finn bending over something, a furrow of concentration on her brows. Elsie was out of sight. Danny pulled me closer to him, and for a long time we walked in silence, strides matched. Then he spoke.

'Sam, there's something I need to talk to you about.'

'What's that?' His tone was unusually serious, and an unaccountable fear invaded me.

'It's to do with Finn, of course, and you, and Elsie too. Oh hell, I don't know, come here.'

And he stopped and pulled me against him and buried his face in my neck.

'What is it, Danny? Talk to me, we should have talked a long time ago, please tell me.'

'No, wait,' he murmured. 'Bodies talk better.'

I pushed my hands under his sweater and shirt and felt his warm, strong back naked under my fingers. With his face still nuzzling me, stubble grazing my cheek, he undid the belt on my jeans like a blind man and slid one hand inside my trousers, cupping my buttocks. My breath came in shallow gasps.

'Not here, Danny.'

'Why? There's no one to see.'

Around us the marshes spread out in every direction, punctuated by stunted trees and rusting boats stranded when the sea was tamed by the walls. Danny undid my bra with one expert hand. I pulled back his head by his long, not-quite-clean hair and saw his face was screwed up in a kind of concentrated disquiet.

'Don't be anxious, my love,' I said, and undid his

trousers and let him tug down mine, and he pushed into me despairingly while my jeans and knickers puddled round my pinioned ankles. So we stood tangled together in a great empty space under a tepid sun, and I thought how undignified I must look and hoped no farmer would decide to walk this way and wondered what my mother would say.

'This,' Danny was speaking with his mouth full and I could see my mother looking across the table at him with a pucker-mouthed distaste, 'is great, Finn.'

Finn had served us roast leg of lamb spiked with garlic and rosemary, jacket potatoes with sour cream as well as butter, coarsely chopped spinach, and she'd even remembered to buy mint sauce from the supermarket yesterday. My father – dressed in his version of casual, which meant a tweed jacket, trousers of an indeterminate greyish colour, the first button undone on his well-ironed shirt and a parting like a new pink road running though his thinning grey hair – had produced two bottles of wine. My mother ate her food neatly, dabbing her lips after each mouthful, taking cautious sips of wine every so often. Finn ate almost nothing, but she sat at the table with bright eyes and a nervous smile hovering on her lips. On one side of her sat Danny, who was on his best behaviour but rather subdued, I thought. On the other sat Michael Daley, determinedly animated, diligently charming to everyone. He had arrived in a flurry of yellow roses (for me), anemones (for Finn, who'd clutched them to her like a shy bride), wine, firm handshakes. He listened to my mother attentively when she spoke about the terrible morning they'd had, asked my father respectfully about the route they'd taken to come here, lifted Elsie, wriggling, on to his shoulders, bent consolingly towards Finn every time he spoke to her, his dark-blond hair flopping over his eyes as he did so. He wasn't suave; he just seemed attractively eager to please. He turned on his chair like a weather-vane, swinging at every remark. He handed out vegetables, jumped up to help Finn in the kitchen. He was full of a strange nervous energy. Suddenly I wondered, appalled, if he was falling in love with Finn, and then I wondered if he was falling in love with me. And if he was, what did I feel about that?

I looked at the two men on either side of the girl: one so dark, surly and gorgeous; the other fairer, more enigmatic. And I could see which of them my mother liked with every grim mouthful that she diligently chewed. There was a strange tension between the men; they were in competition, but I couldn't work out over what, exactly. Danny incessantly made paper shapes, twisting scraps of his paper napkin into flowers and boats.

Over baked apples (stuffed, by Elsie, with raisins and honey, though Elsie by now had retired to her bedroom, saying she was going to make a picture) my mother said, in her ever-so-interested voice, 'And how's work, Samantha?'

I mumbled something about being at a waiting stage, and the conversation would have petered away (indeed, I saw Michael sitting up a bit straighter, waiting to leap gallantly into the silence he knew was coming), when my dad coughed formally and laid down his napkin. We all turned to him.

'When I was a prisoner in Japan,' he began, and my heart sank. I'd had this conversation before. 'I saw lots of men die. They died like flies.' He paused; we waited with the automatic respect of people who must bow their heads before a tragedy. 'I saw more than any of you will ever see and more I'm sure than any of your precious patients see.'

I looked at Finn, but her head was bent and she was chasing a raisin around her plate with a fork.

'I came back home and I just got on with things. I remember everything.' He laid his hand over the tweed at his breast. 'But I put it to one side. All this talking about trauma and stress and victims, it does no good, you know, it's just opening up old wounds. Best to let things lie. I don't doubt your motives, Samantha. But you young people think that you have a right to happiness. You have to endure. Trauma!' He guffawed. 'That's just modern rubbish.' He picked up his wine glass and took a mouthful of its contents, his eyes glaring over the rim. My mother looked anxious.

'Well . . .' began Michael in an understanding tone.

'Dad . . .' I started in a wail that I recognized belonged to my childhood.

But Finn's voice cut through, soft and clear.

'As far as I understand it, Mr Laschen, trauma is an over-used word. People use it when they often just mean grief or shock or bereavement. Real trauma is something different. People don't just get over it. They need help.' Her eyes flicked to mine for a moment, and I gave her a little smile. The room felt oddly quiet. 'Some people who are traumatized find life is literally unbearable. They're not weak cowards or fools; they've been injured and they need to be healed. Doctors heal the body's wounds, but sometimes you can't see the wounds. They are there, though. Just because you suffered and didn't complain, do you think other people should suffer as well?' No one spoke. 'I think Sam helps people a lot. She saves people.

It's not about happiness, you see, it's about being able to live.'

Michael leaned across and took the fork, which she was still pushing around her plate. He put his arm around her, and she leaned into him gratefully.

'Finn and I are going to make everybody coffee,' he said, and led her from the room.

My mother noisily clattered our pudding plates together.

'Teenage girls are always very intense,' she said understandingly.

I looked over at my father.

'You know what the problem is?' he said.

'No,' I said.

'Your door's sticking. I'll bet it's the hinges. I'll look it over later. Have you got any carbon paper?'

'Carbon paper? Why would I have that?'

'For spreading down the lintel, find where it's rubbing. There's nothing like carbon paper for that.'

Nineteen

Once, when I was about ten, we went on our summer holiday to Filey Bay up on the east coast. I've never been back, and all I remember about the place is sand-dunes and a fierce and dirty wind – how it swept along the sea front in the evenings, rattling the cans that had been left lying on the pavements, sending crisp packets into the air like small tatty kites. And I remember, as well, that my father took me out in a pedal-boat. My legs would hardly reach the pedals, and I had to sit forward on the seat while he sat back, his legs – skinny and shiny white in his unaccustomed shorts – skittered away. I looked down into the water and suddenly could no longer see the bottom, just a depthless grey-brown. As if it happened yesterday, I can feel the panic that flooded through me, leaking into all the compartments of my mind. I screamed and I screamed, clutching my bewildered father's arm, so that my mother, waiting on the shore, thought something terrible had happened, though our little red boat still bobbed safely a few yards out. I don't feel safe with water, and although I know how to swim I try to avoid doing so. When I take Elsie to the swimming pool I tend to stand knee-deep and watch her splash about. The sea, for me, is not a place to have fun; it's not a giant leisure centre but a terrifying expanse that sucks up boats and bodies and radioactive waste and shit. Sometimes, especially in the evening when the layered grey of the sea blurs with the darkening grey of the sky, I stand and look out at the shining water and imagine the other, underwater world that lies hidden beneath it and it makes me feel dizzy.

So what did I think I was doing going sailing with Michael Daley? When he'd phoned me up to arrange it I'd replied, in my enthusiastic voice, that I would love to go out in his boat. I like people to think that I'm brave, dauntless. I haven't screamed with fear since I was a little girl.

'What shall I bring?' I asked.

'Nothing. I've got a wet suit that should fit you and a life-jacket, of course. Remember to wear gloves.'

'Wet suit?'

'You know, the kind of rubber suit divers wear – you'll look good in one. If we capsized you'd freeze without it at this time of year.'

'Capsize?'

'Has this phone got an echo or is it just you?'

'I can't possibly fit into this.'

I was looking at something that resembled a series of black and lime-green inner tubes.

'You have to take your clothes off first.' We were in my living room. Danny had gone to Stamford to buy some paint, Finn had gone to the corner shop for milk and bread and Elsie was at school. Michael was already wearing his wet suit, under a yellow waterproof. He looked slim and long, but faintly absurd, like an astronaut without his spaceship, like a fish out of water.

'Oh.'

'Put a swimsuit on underneath.'

'Right. I think that I'll do this in my bedroom. Help yourself to coffee.'

Upstairs I stripped down, put on my swimming costume and started to push my legs into the thick black rubber. God, it was tight. It closed elastically around my thighs and I tugged it up over my hips. My skin felt as if it were suffocating. The worst bit was getting my arms into the sleeves; I felt as if my body was going to buckle under the pull of the rubber. The zip did up behind but I couldn't reach it – indeed, I could hardly lift my arms higher than horizontal.

'Are you all right?' called Michael.

'Yes.'

'Do you want any help?'

'Yes.'

He came into the room and I saw us both in the mirror, long-legged moon-walkers.

'I was right, it does suit you,' he said and I pulled my stomach in self-consciously as he did up the zip, its cold metal and his warm fingers running up my knobbled spine. His breath blew against my hair.

'Put your boots on' – he handed me a pair of neat rubber shoes – 'and then we can go.'

The wind blew in icy gusts up the pebbly beach, where Michael's boat was pulled up in a line with other dinghies. His boat-house was apparently where he kept his wind-surfers and spare tack; his dinghy lived outside in all weathers. A strange humming sound, a bit like forests on a fierce winter night, came from the denuded boats: all those cord-things ('Shrouds,' said Michael) which held the masts up were rattling. The small waves were white-tipped. I could see squalls rippling across the slatey water. Michael tipped his head back.

'Mmm. Good sailing weather.'

I didn't like the sound of that. Out in the estuary I could see the single small shape of a white-sailed dinghy, tipping alarmingly so that it seemed to stand up out of the water. There was no one else around at all. The horizon disappeared into a misty greyness. It was the kind of day when it never became completely light; a dank gauze lay across the water.

Michael pulled the thick green tarpaulin off his boat (a Wayfarer called *Belladonna*, he told me, because of her black spinnaker; I didn't ask what a spinnaker was). He leaned into the bottom of the boat and pulled out a life-jacket.

'Put this on. I'll just get her rigged.'

He shook a large rust-coloured sail out of a nylon bag and started to push long flat sticks into pockets in its fabric.

'Battens,' he explained. 'The sails would flap all over the place without them.'

Then he unhooked a wire from the base of the mast and cleated it into the top of the sail; the bottom he threaded through the boom – I knew the name for that – and fastened firmly.

'That's the mainsail,' he said. 'We won't actually haul it up until we push her into the water.'

The next sail he buckled to another wire which he unclipped from the mast. He attached its outer edge to the forestay with lots of small hooks and left the sail puddled on the deck. Then he pulled a long rope through a hole at the base of its triangle and trained the ends along either side of the boat, pushing each through the handles, and tying a knot shaped like a figure of eight to stop it escaping. Finally, he produced a small black flag, tied it to a string secured to the mast and pulled it up until it wavered and then jerked into place on the mast's tip.

'Right, let's pull her into the water.'

I was struck by his air of authority. His hands were strong and meticulous, his concentration was all on the job. It struck me that he must be a good doctor, and I wondered how many of his patients fell in love with him. Together we pulled the *Belladonna*, still on the trailer, down to the water's edge, where Michael pushed her into the choppy waves while I held the rope.

'Don't worry about getting wet,' he called as he clambered into the boat and started putting the rudder in and hauling up the slapping expanses of sail. 'You'll actually feel warmer once there's a bit of water between your suit and your skin.'

'Right,' I said in a quavering voice and waded into the sea, painter in my blue hands, which stung where they hadn't turned numb, for I'd forgotten my gloves. 'When?' I yelled.

'What?'

'When will I feel warmer? Ice is coursing around my body, Dr Daley.'

He laughed, his even white teeth gleaming, the sails rolling wildly around him. Suddenly, as first the front sail and then the back one were pulled up the mast, the boat stopped jerking around and strained purposefully; it was no longer like holding a twitching kite; more like holding a dog who is eager to be off.

'Push her nose out a bit,' Michael called. 'That's the way, and then jump in. *Jump*, I said, not fall.'

I landed in the bottom of the boat, flapping like a fish, and hit my knee. The boat keeled immediately and water slopped over the side. My face was about six inches above sea-level.

'Come over to my side,' instructed Michael, who did not seem unduly alarmed. 'Now, sit on the side here, beside me, and put your toes under that strap there, it's called the toe strap. That way if you lean out you won't fall in.'

He was holding the tiller in one hand, and with the other he leaned forward to push down the centreboard and gathered in the rope attached to the small sail and pulled it taut. The sails stiffened and I could feel the boat lose its sluggish sideways drift and pick up speed. Indeed, it picked up far too much speed for my liking.

'Right, Sam, while we're on this tack and the wind's quite gentle . . .'

'Gentle!' I squawked.

'It won't really pick up until we're around the point and out into more open waters.'

'Oh.'

'All you've got to remember is that we are using the wind to take us where we want to go. Sometimes it will be coming from the side, and that's called reaching; some-times it will be right behind us, that's called running. And sometimes we will be almost going into it . . .'

'And that's called falling over, I suppose,' I croaked.

He grinned at me.

'Your only job is to hold this jibsheet' – he tossed the rope attached to the small sail into my lap – 'and control it. The more we go into the wind, the tighter you pull the sail in. When we are running, you let that sail right out. When I shout "Go about", all you have to do is let out the sail, and then pull it in on the other side. I'll look after everything else. Right?'

'Right.'

'There are some spare gloves in the bow.'

I edged forward to get them, but the boat suddenly keeled further over.

'Lean back; no, Sam, lean *back* so we keep the boat upright. Sam, *back*.'

I leaned and I felt as if I were suspended over the water, held only by brittle toes. My hands crabbed in the cold, my curved back ached, my neck lolled so that if I rolled my eyes I could see the water underneath me, alarmingly far down. The centreboard was lifting out of the water; if I looked forward, I could see water on the other side slopping into the boat. I shut my eyes.

'We're going about, Sam. When I say "Lee-oh", you pull your rope free and let it flap. Then you move swiftly across to the other side as she swings around. Got it?'

'No. If I move, the boat's going to fall over.'

'Capsize.'

'You fucking call it capsize; I call it fall over.'

'Don't worry, Sam, we're not going to capsize; it's not so windy.' I didn't like the patronizing patience in his voice.

'OK, let's go!' I shouted and tugged the rope out of its cleat. The sail flapped wildly, the boat bucked, the noise was deafening. I lunged into the middle of the boat and tripped over the centreboard. Michael pushed the tiller across and calmly stepped over to the other side, pushing my head down as he did so. The boom whipped past just above me; Michael pulled in his sheet, then mine. The noise subsided, the flapping ceased, the boat lay flat and trim on the grey water. I moved over to join him. If my hands hadn't been stiff with cold they would have been shaking.

175

'Next time, why don't you wait until I say Lee-oh?' he said mildly.

'Sorry.'

'You'll soon get the hang of it. This is all right, isn't it?' The boat was quite level now and scudding along with its sails bellied and taut. 'Just sit back and enjoy it. Look, there's a heron. I often see it when I'm sailing. Over there' – he pointed to a distant outcrop of rocks in the dark water – 'is Needle Point. That's where two currents meet. Very tricky area; especially at spring tide.'

'We're not going there now, are we?' I asked nervously.

'I think,' he replied gravely, trimming his sail, 'that we'll save that for another day.'

For a few minutes, as long as the *Belladonna* kept on that course and all I had to do was sit still and watch the water coursing by and Michael's steady profile, fair hair slicked away from his high, calm forehead, I did almost enjoy myself. The waves slapped underneath us in a steady rhythm, a finger of sun pointed through the leaden sky. Another dinghy passed behind us and the two sailors raised their gloved hands in a comradely fashion, and I managed to wave back, a cheery smile fixed to my face. Once we even had something approaching a conversation.

'You hate to be in someone else's hands, don't you?'

'I don't actually trust that many people's hands,' I replied.

'I hope you trust mine.'

Was he flirting? Because this wasn't very good timing.

'I'm trying to.'

'You must be a difficult woman to live with, Dr Laschen. Does Danny find you difficult?'

I didn't reply; a damp wind stung my cheeks and the grey sea galloped past.

'Though he seems quite able to look after himself, protect himself. A worldly kind of chap, I should imagine.'

If my mind hadn't been so fixed upon the far-off shoreline and the dip and thrust of the boat, the word 'chap' would have struck a false note. As it was, I just nodded and fiddled with the soggy knot on my rope which lay idly in my lap.

But then Michael pulled the tiller towards him until the wind was right behind us, pulled up the centreboard with one smooth movement, let out his sail until it opened like a luscious, over-blooming flower and told me to pull my sail across so that it filled with wind on the other side.

'A spot of running now, I think,' he said. 'Move across; our weight should be evenly distributed.'

The bow of the dinghy lifted, and we creamed through the waves.

'Be alert, Sam. If the wind shifts we'll have to jibe.'

'Jibe? No, don't explain. Just tell me how to stop it happening.'

Michael was concentrating, now glancing up at the flag to check the direction of the wind, now adjusting his sails ever so slightly. The boat queasily rolled; we lifted and fell with a yawing motion that did strange things to my innards. My tongue was starting to feel gravelly and too large for my mouth.

'Um, Michael.'

'Mmm.'

'Can you stop this boat moving around for a bit? I feel a bit . . .'

'The wind's shifting, we're going to jibe. Let your sails flap.'

It could only have taken a second. For a brief moment

we seemed to stop dead in the water while the sails hung limp. Then I watched in horror as the boom swung from its outstretched position and flung with a great sideways swipe towards us. The boat heeled over sharply. My stomach lurched and I stood up, thinking only that I had to get to the edge of the boat before I threw up.

'Duck, Sam,' said Michael.

The boom cracked me just above the ear with such ringing force that for a moment the world went black. I careered across the boat, tipping it wildly, and the boom swung back again. This time it missed me (I was already down and almost out) but smacked into Michael's head as he rose to rescue me. We ended up sitting in the dinghy's watery bottom like two large black beetles, the boom banging above us, both sails loose and wild. It felt much safer when I couldn't see what was happening.

'Sit still,' he commanded.

'But . . .'

He put up one hand and very gently, very carefully, hooked a dislodged ear-ring safely back into my ear lobe.

'Who else would wear such absurd dangly ear-rings out sailing? Are you all right?'

Actually, I was all of a sudden and quite without reason feeling perfectly calm. The queasiness in my stomach was subsiding; the bang of my frightened heart was diminishing; only the side of my head felt swollen and sore. The boat still bucked in the gusts, but with the sails adrift the wind could get no purchase. Michael was such a solid presence near me, so sure of himself. I could see the faint graze of his stubble, the emphatic bow in his upper lip, his large pupils in his grey eyes.

'I wouldn't put you in danger, Sam,' he said softly, staring at me.

I managed a grin.

'On our next date, Michael, perhaps I could take you to see a film.'

Twenty

Michael and I were silent in the car on the way back to the house. I felt I'd disappointed him, and I hate so much to disappoint anybody that it makes me bad-tempered, and I was afraid I would snap at him and I didn't want to say anything I would regret, so it was better to say nothing at all. He put on a tape of some classical-sounding music and I pretended to be absorbed in it. Dusk was turning into night and as we wound through the lanes that followed the line of the coast I caught tantalizing glimpses of glowing interiors of the houses we passed. The darkness concealed the oddness of the landscape and made it seem almost reassuring, the way countryside is meant to be. By the time we arrived, I felt that the volcano in my chest had become dormant once more. I took a deep breath.

'I don't think I'm a natural sailor.'

'You did very well.'

'Yeah, I know. And Nelson was sick every time he went to sea. But it was really nice of you to take me out.' Michael stayed silent with a half-smile on his face, and I babbled to fill the gap. 'Let's try it again some time. I'm sure I'll be better.'

Bloody hell. What had I committed myself to? But Michael seemed satisfied enough.

'I'd like that very much,' he said.

'You'll soon have me tacking and jibing and booming like nobody's business.'

He laughed, and we both got out of the car and walked towards the house, Michael holding my arm. It was dark now and through the window I could make out signs of movement inside. I stepped forward and looked. The fire was blazing. Danny was sitting in the armchair to one side. He had his back to me and I could see little more than the back of his head and the bottle of beer that he was balancing on the arm of the chair with his right hand. But I knew what his expression would be. He would be dreamily staring into the fire. Elsie was in her pyjamas, her hair washed and combed flat, her face red and blotchy with excitement and with the reflection of the flames. She was piling up her wooden bricks. I could hear nothing but I could see her lips moving in a constant chatter directed at Finn who was lying beside her, also with her back to me, so I couldn't see if she was talking back. Probably she was just lying there with her eyes half closed. I suspected that Elsie responded to Finn's sense of repose as well as her youth. They were two girls together in a sense that I would never be able to be. It was a lovely scene, so much so that I felt an ache of exclusion, or was it guilt at being absent?

I felt a hand on my shoulder. Michael.

'What a beautiful family group,' I said, with more than a hint of dryness.

Michael took some time to reply. He just looked, with fascination, at the fireside scene. His jaw clenched with obvious satisfaction.

'It's you, you know,' he said.

'What do you mean?'

'When I was first talking with the police and we asked

around, everybody said how wonderful you were. And you have been. I can't believe what you've done with Finn.'

I gave a frown and pushed Michael back in a half-jocular fashion.

'I don't need your flattery, Dr Daley. Besides, I've supplied no treatment of any kind. Anything Finn has done, she's done for herself.'

'You underestimate yourself.'

'I've never underestimated myself in my life.'

'You're wrong, you know. As a GP I often think of what the job was like a hundred years ago when there were no antibiotics, no insulin, just morphine, digitalis, one or two other things. A doctor had almost nothing in his bag that could change the course of an illness. What he was was a healer. He would sit by a patient and by his presence would help him, maybe just holding his hand.' Michael's face was just inches away from mine now, he was speaking in barely more than a whisper. 'You're a bloody-minded woman. You're arrogant. You're accomplished. You can be harsh with the rest of us. But you've got it, you know, that healing human quality.'

I didn't say anything. Michael raised his hand and with just a finger lightly touched my hair. Was he going to kiss me, out here, with Danny just a few feet away? What would I do? In what must have been less than a second I imagined myself having an affair with Michael, us naked together, and then all the conflicts and anguish and betrayals. I took his hand in a friendly, sisterly fashion.

'Thank you for the compliment, Michael, however misconceived. Come in and have a drink. Grog, or whatever you sailor types like.'

182

He smiled and shook his head.

'I must get back, and out of these things. Good night, clever woman.'

I went into the house feeling that glow that you can only experience when you have been flattered grossly. As I pushed the door of the living room open, three heads, three expressions, turned towards me. Danny, with a hint of an ironic smile. Was he rebuking me for something? Elsie's whole face glimmered as if the fire were inside her. Finn rotated slightly, like a cat that had appropriated my hearthrug and been partially stirred from a long sleep. I felt a quiver of disquiet deep inside me.

'Look, Mummy, look,' said Elsie, as if I had been there all the time.

'It's incredible. What is it?'

'A secret. Guess.'

'A house.'

'No.'

'A boat.'

'No.'

'A zoo.'

'It's not a zoo. It's a secret.'

'So how has your day been?'

'I went out with Dan and Fing.'

I looked expectantly at the grown-ups.

'We built a sand-castle,' said Finn. 'With stones. And tins.'

'Thanks, Finn,' I said. And I went and sat on the armchair and kissed Danny on top of his cross head. 'And thank you.'

'I'm going into town tomorrow,' Danny said.

'Work?'

'No.'

It was an awkward, unsatisfactory moment, with Finn and Elsie just beside us.

'Is everything all right?' I murmured.

'Why shouldn't it be?' Danny replied in that normal tone that I found so difficult to read.

'No reason,' I said.

There was a slightly unpleasant silence, during which I saw Finn and Elsie exchanging smiling glances.

'What's up?' I asked.

'Ask Elsie what's hanging on the door,' Finn said.

'What's hanging on the door of your safe house, Elsie?'

In her excitement, Elsie looked like a party balloon that had been blown up almost too far and if it were released would shoot around the room out of control.

'There's a spade hanging on the door,' she said.

'And ask Elsie what's on the doormat.'

'What's on the doormat, Elsie?'

'A sand-castle,' Elsie said with a shriek.

'A sand-castle on the *doormat*? That's a funny thing.'

'And ask Elsie what's in Mummy's bed.'

'What's in Mummy's bed?'

'A big hug.' And Elsie ran forward and threw her arms around me. The feeble pressure on my shoulders almost made me cry. I mouthed a thank-you to Finn over Elsie's shoulder.

Elsie wanted Finn to put her to bed but I wasn't going to be cheated out of that and I insisted and then *she* insisted and I carried Elsie's wriggling body up the stairs, promising that Finn would come and kiss her good-night *and* tell her a story. After I'd peeled off the wet suit and pulled on some jeans and a T-shirt, I brushed her teeth and then rather grumpily read her a book of tongue-twisters.

'Can I see Fing now?'

'Kiss me good-night first.'

With a sigh she pushed her lips forward and then I was dispatched downstairs to fetch Finn. She slipped past me to keep her appointment with my delinquent daughter. Danny was still sitting in the chair, but I saw he had a fresh bottle of beer. I noticed three empty bottles next to the foot of the chair.

'Let me have a sip,' I said, and he handed me the bottle. 'What's up?'

'It's time I was in London again, that's all.'

'All right.'

There was another silence and, again, it wasn't a comfortable one. I sat on the floor at his feet and leaned back against him, feeling his knees against my shoulder-blades. I sipped at the bottle and then passed it back to him.

'What do you think of Finn?' I asked.

'What do you mean?'

'How does she seem to you?'

'I'm not a doctor, doctor.'

'You're a human being.'

'Thanks, Sam.'

'You spent the day with her, Danny. Tell me what you think?'

'Interesting girl.'

'Interesting *damaged* girl,' I said.

'You're the doctor.'

'Do you find her attractive?'

Danny frowned.

'What the fuck are you talking about?'

'When Michael dropped me off, we looked in at the house. I saw Finn stretched out on the floor in front of the fire. I thought that, if I were a man, I might find her very attractive. A lovely seductive creature.'

'Well, you're not a man.'

There was a silence. I listened for Finn's tread on the stairs. Then I heard a distant giggle from Elsie. Finn would be a few minutes yet.

'Danny, have you got a problem with this?'

'With what?'

'With Finn, this set-up, you know.'

I felt Danny's hand on my hair. Suddenly he grasped it and pulled my head back. I felt his lips against mine, I tasted his tongue. His left hand ran up my stomach. I felt an ache for him. He stopped and sat back. He gave a sardonic smile.

'You know I'd never tell you how to run your life, Sam. But . . .'

'Shhh,' I said.

There were steps outside and Finn drifted in and sat near us on the mat in front of the fire.

'Elsie's almost asleep. I've made a couple of salads,' she said. 'Some garlic bread. I didn't think you'd want much. I hope that's all right.'

'You didn't have any other culinary plans, did you, Sam?' Danny asked sarcastically.

Finn giggled.

'Sounds good to me,' I said.

Danny drank a couple more bottles of beer. I drank wine. Finn drank water. The salads were crispy and colourful. You could almost mistake them for the ones you get in plastic beakers at M&S. I talked a bit about the day's sailing. Finn asked a couple of questions. Danny said almost nothing at all. Afterwards, we took mugs of coffee back to the living room where the fire had burned down to its embers. Danny had yet another bottle of beer. I put some small pieces of firewood on the embers and blew and blew until there were flames once more. The wind was rattling the window frames and blowing drops of rain against the glass.

'It's the sort of night when it feels wonderful to be in front of a fire,' I said.

'Stop that crap, Sam,' said Danny.

'What do you mean?'

'You're talking like a fucking advertisement for something.'

He walked over to the window.

'This isn't you, Sam. What are you doing here? There's just trees out there and mud and marsh and rain and then the sea. Real people can't live here, only dressed-up oafs who go hunting.'

'Stop it, Danny,' I said, with a glance across at a shocked Finn.

'Why? What do you think about it, Finn? Do you like living out here.'

Finn looked panic-stricken.

'I don't know,' she mumbled. 'I've just got some clearing up to do. In the kitchen.'

She hurried from the room and I turned to Danny in a rage.

'You fucking buffoon,' I hissed. 'What are you playing at?'

He shrugged.

'The countryside pisses me off. This whole thing pisses me off.'

'How could you talk like that in front of Finn? How *could* you? What's going on? Do you resent Finn, or Michael? Are you jealous?'

Danny raised the bottle and drained it.

'I'm off to bed,' he said and left the room.

I leafed through a magazine for a few minutes until Finn joined me.

'I apologize,' I said. 'Danny can be strange.'

'That's all right,' Finn said. 'I like Danny. I like the way he can just say anything. I like his difficulty. I've always gone for that sort of grim man.'

'I haven't.'

Finn smiled and sat next to me on the rug in front of the fire. She pressed close. I could smell her soft, warm skin.

'Do you have a boyfriend?' I asked.

'Do you know what I hate about all of this, what's happened to me?'

'What?'

'There's an idea that suffering has made me this delicate, saintly creature and everybody gets worried if they say the wrong thing when I'm in earshot. No, I didn't "have a boyfriend". When I was fat no one was interested in me, of course, and I guess I wasn't interested either. Or I was terrified. Maybe that's what being fat was partly about for me. After I lost all that weight but wasn't like a bicycle frame either, I felt completely different, and then I had sex with boys sometimes. Especially in South America; it was part of the adventure. Well – ' she gave a harsh, unlikely chuckle – 'Mummy always said I was too young to get tied down. Does it shock you?'

Well, yes.

'No, of course not. I'm afraid that I, and all of this,' I gestured at our surroundings, 'must seem a bit staid to you.'

'Oh, no, Sam.' Finn turned to face me. She stroked my

cheek and kissed it, very softly. I wanted to draw back, but forced myself not to. 'I don't think you're staid.' She sat back. 'I used to be – for God's sake, I *am* – someone who acts on impulse. When Danny was talking about the countryside I sort of agreed with him. But at the same time, for me it's not boring. I have this idea in my head that won't go away. There are people out there in the dark who put tape round my face and cut my throat and they would do it again if they had the chance.'

'Don't, Finn.'

'But it's more than that, Sam. I have this image playing over and over in my head. I don't know whether it's a dream. I imagine this house in the middle of the night. Torchlight outside, a window sliding up. A creaking on the stairs. I wake up with masking tape over my mouth, a blade at my throat. Then they move to your room. Then to Elsie's . . .'

'Finn, stop that,' I was almost shouting. 'You mustn't say that. You have no right to say that.'

I felt a sour taste in the back of my throat. I wanted to be sick.

'Whose feelings are you protecting?' Finn asked. 'Mine or yours?'

'Mine, for once.'

'So you know how it feels.'

I felt cross.

'I knew how it felt already, Finn. I knew. It was wrong of you to say that about Elsie. Don't bring my daughter into this.'

'I'm desperate for them to be caught, Sam.'

There was something eerily theatrical about all of this.

'We all want that.'

'I want to help. I've been thinking and thinking, trying

to remember something, anything that could help the police. A smell maybe, a voice. I don't know.'

My mind was clouded by it all, by the wine, the warmth of the fire, the lateness of the hour. I tried to make myself think clearly. Was she trying to tell me something?

'Finn, is there something you're holding back, something you haven't told the police?'

'I don't think so. At least . . .'

'Was there anything else that happened to you during the assault? Have you told the police everything?'

'Why should there be anything? I wish there was. Maybe there's something I'm not facing up to. Perhaps I'm being cowardly. Sam, I want to help. Can you do anything for me?'

She put her arms around me and held me, so close that I could feel her heart beating. She was hugging me desperately. This was creepy, all wrong, as if I were being seduced by somebody who knew I couldn't reject them. I put my arms around her like a mother comforting a child, but at the same time I was watching myself putting my arms around her, wondering what I was doing. I was dubious about my role as Finn's doctor, dubious about my role as Finn's friend, and now she was expecting me to become some sort of psychological detective, some sort of soul mate.

'Sam, Sam,' she moaned. 'I feel so lonely and helpless.' If this was a crisis, I wished I felt a bit more in control of it, less manipulated.

'Stop this and calm down. Stop!' I pushed her away. Her eyes were puffy and wet, she was panting. 'Listen to me. We're here to support you. You are protected. No harm will come to you. All right? Secondly, it is entirely possible that there could be a degree of memory loss associated with emotional and physical trauma and it is remediable. But now, late at night, when we're tired and overwrought, is not the time to talk about it. Things can be done, but I doubt whether I would be the right person to do them. For a variety of reasons. Above all, there are kinds of therapeutic help that you can't get from me and you can't get in this environment. We have to think about that. I regard you . . . That's too clinical. You are a dear friend. But we have to think about things. But not now. Not even tomorrow. Now go to bed.'

'Yes, Sam,' she said in a frail, chastened voice.

'Now,' I said.

She nodded and took a final sip of her coffee and left the room without a further word being exchanged. When she was gone I gave a great sigh. What had I brought into my house? And now Elsie adored Finn more than anybody else in the world. What was I doing to everybody?

I went upstairs. I let my clothes fall and got between the sheets in my dark bedroom and felt the warmth of Danny's body. I ran my hands over him, under, over, between. I needed him badly. He turned and clutched me fiercely. He kissed me hard, his teeth nipping at my lips. I felt his hands rough on my body. I bit into his shoulder to stop myself from screaming with a pleasure that was almost fear. He pinned my arms above my head with one large hand and felt me with the other, felt me as if he were learning me all over again. 'Don't move,' he said as I wriggled in his grasp. 'Lie quite still now.' And as he thrust into me I felt he was fucking me with all the suppressed passion, anger even, of the evening. He didn't speak my name, but he looked at me steadily and I shut my eyes to escape from his. Afterwards I felt battered, wounded. Danny's breathing became slow and regular and I thought he was asleep. When he spoke it was in the drowsy, slurred tone of a man half asleep, who can scarcely order his thoughts.

'Have you been looking at Finn?' he murmured. 'Really looking at her. Like the great doctor you are.' I began to answer but he continued speaking as if I wasn't there and he was just thinking aloud. 'Or is it all Sam and Elsie and the house and the countryside and a new best friend?' The bed creaked as he turned, and I felt his breath on my cheek. 'Have you looked at her, Sam? What's your sort of word? Objectively. Scientifically.'

'Are you obsessed with her, Danny?' A horrible thought came into my mind. 'Is that it? Were you fantasizing about Finn?'

I was breathless, my heart racing, I could feel its beat in my ears.

'You just don't get it, do you?'

I felt him turn away from me.

'Night, Danny.'

'Night, Sam.'

When I woke the next morning, Danny had gone.

Twenty-One

'Am I allowed in here?'

'So long as you don't try to do anything,' Finn replied.

'Don't worry.'

My kitchen was like a mad scientist's laboratory, steam and heat and mysterious clatters and hums. Everything was being used. On the hob a pan sizzled and the lid of a saucepan was shivering as vapour puffed over the rim. A bowl of water contained what looked like soggy leaves. The chicken breasts were in the oven. Finn was chopping something very quickly on a board, rat-a-tat-tat, like a snare-drum roll.

'What I don't understand,' I said, 'is the way you're doing all the different bits at the same time. When I try to cook, I have to do one thing after another and even then I get it wrong.'

A couple of old friends were coming round for supper. Normally I would have got a take-away in or popped various pre-cooked dishes into the microwave, but Finn said to leave it all to her, that she would do something simple. After dropping Elsie at school, we had driven twenty miles through villages, past antique emporia and the paddocks of riding schools, along the coast to a super-market which was comfortingly identical to the one I used to go to on the way home from work when I lived in

London. I bought some frozen stuff and bin-bags and washing-up liquid and Finn headed for the real food: chicken breasts not wrapped in Cellophane, mushrooms and rice in expensive small boxes, rosemary, garlic, olive oil, vegetables, red and white wine. As the trolley filled, I tried to talk her out of it.

'Sarah and Clyde are just like me. They've lived on take-away vindaloos all their professional lives. Their tastebuds have been burned away. They won't know the difference.'

'Enjoy yourself while you're alive,' Finn replied. 'Because you're a long time dead.' It was with difficulty that I did not gasp.

'That's why I've never bothered about what food I eat.'

'Shame on you, Sam. You're a doctor.'

Finn was becoming alarmingly imperious and I was becoming strangely passive, like a guest in my own house. It occurred to me, before I hastily pushed the thought away, that in the last few weeks, as she had recovered and bloomed again, so my grip on my own life had weakened. Elsie seemed half in love with Finn, Danny was gone again, my trauma unit had become someone else's capitalist dream, my book stayed unwritten.

During the early evening my kitchen looked like a casualty department. I did some work and played a bit with Elsie and put her to bed, and when I came back a couple of hours later, without much appearing to have been done it had subsided into something tidier: an intensive-care unit, maybe. There was beeping and bubbling, but only the occasional moment of activity, a stir here and a sniff there.

Sarah and Clyde arrived, just after seven, panting and virtuous in their fluorescent cycling gear. They had taken the train to Stamford and biked out. They headed up for

194

a bath and came back down in jeans, loose shirts. This was the authentically miraculous bit. Even if supper had consisted of nothing more than pizza in cardboard boxes brought to the house by motorbike and six-packs of beer, I still would have been rushing round in a panic. But this evening there was an air of serenity. A couple of bottles of wine stood open on the table next to the olives and some little things of salami and cheese that Finn had put together, and the table was laid and there was a general smell of nice food hanging around the place, but without any sense that anybody was actually doing anything. Finn wasn't red-faced and dashing off to the kitchen every two seconds to deal with some crisis. She was there, pouring out wine, and not being ostentatious. She had put on a pair of pale slacks and a smockish black top and tied her hair back. Fuck, I was impressed with her.

Maybe I'd become friendly with Sarah and Clyde not just because we'd trained together but because they were tall and rangy like me. Sarah's flowing hair was grey now and she had wrinkles round her eyes. Clyde still had the chiselled, long-boned Clark Kent looks of the rower he had been at university, but he'd got thinner, so his prominent Adam's apple seemed even larger. We were all big and looked at each other from the same level. Clyde and Sarah were GPs together at a practice in Tower Hamlets. When they had a free weekend, they would put their bikes on to a train, head out from London and cover a couple of hundred miles by Sunday evening, hopping between the houses of friends. I was the first pit-stop on this weekend's route.

'And tomorrow we're staying with Helen – you know, Farlowe.'

'Where does she live?'

'Blakeney. North Norfolk.'

'Jesus, you'll have earned your dinner tomorrow night.'

'That's the whole point.'

We took our drinks outside and wandered in the grounds, as I sarcastically called the neglected garden. Sarah identified birds by their songs and Clyde told me the names of the plants in the garden, some of the nicest examples of which, it emerged, I had weeded in a fit of enthusiasm and tossed on to my compost heap. Finn called us in and we had little bowls of succulent rice with reconstituted mushrooms, followed by chicken cooked in olive oil and garlic and rosemary, with new potatoes and spring greens.

'Unlike me,' I explained to Finn across the table, 'Sarah and Clyde have stayed in London and are doing a real job.'

'You shouldn't do yourself down, Sam,' she said, with feeling.

Sarah laughed.

'Don't worry, Fiona,' she said. 'Sam is not generally famous for her English modesty and reserve.'

'Anyway, it's not modesty,' I said. 'The point is to be self-deprecating so that other people then step in and say how wonderful you are. It's a way of inviting praise.'

Finn shook her head with a wistful smile.

'I don't believe that,' she said. 'I don't believe that most people are independent enough to look at what someone does and make up their mind about it for themselves. It's too much trouble. People take you at your own valuation. If you say you're good, most people will believe you. If you're modest, they'll agree with you.'

Finn's fervent statement was followed by a cavernous silence which was broken by Clyde.

'And what do *you* do? And we don't expect you to be modest about it.'

'I'm writing a thesis,' Finn said.

'What about?'

'It's to do with the history of science.'

'In what way?'

'You don't want to hear all about my work.'

'Yes, we do.' Sarah insisted warmly. 'Remember, we're all licensed to boast about ourselves now.'

Finn glanced across the table at me. I tried to think of some way to stop this disaster but everything that came into my mind seemed as if it would make matters worse. There was a long pause as Finn leaned over for the wine, filled her glass and then took a sip.

'You really want to hear about this?' she asked.

'We're on the edge of our seats,' said Clyde.

'Well, you asked for it. I'm writing a thesis on the taxonomy of mental disorders, using post-traumatic stress disorder as the principal subject.'

'What does that mean when it's at home?'

Finn gave me the most imperceptible of winks across the table before she replied.

'Basically, the question that fascinated me is the extent to which a particular pathology exists before it has been named. Has it been discovered, identified or invented? There have always been broken legs and tumours. But did Neanderthals suffer from post-traumatic stress disorder after they had been in battle with their flint knives and axes?'

'There was shell-shock after the First World War, wasn't there?' Clyde said.

'Yes, but do you know where the term came from?'

'No.'

'They thought the explosions of the shells were causing physical damage to the nerves around the spine. The reason for this is that the condition was first given medical status after survivors of a Victorian rail crash presented symptoms of shock but no physical injuries. They assumed it was caused by the physical impact and called it "railway spine". When similar symptoms were observed in the trenches, they assumed it was caused by shockwaves from the shells. They needed to believe it was a version of the sort of thing they called injury. Maybe the soldiers were just displaying a natural response to the madness of fighting in the trenches. But then people with the power to do so call some of these forms of behaviour symptoms and call them a disorder and treat it in a medical environment.'

'Do you think it's an invention?'

'That's what Sam is investigating.'

'How did you two get together?'

'Someone in my department knew about Sam's research. I've got a background in statistics and Sam had a spare room and it seemed a good idea for me to stay here for a while. I'm very lucky. I suspect that Sam's work is going to redefine the subject and put it on a proper systematic basis for the first time. I'm just lucky to be tagging along with her for a bit.'

Sarah looked across at me.

'Fiona makes it sound fascinating. How's the research going?' There was a silence. 'Sam?'

'What?'

'How's the research going?'

'Sorry, I was miles away. Fine, it's going fine.'

'And she can cook as well.'

'Yes,' I said, feebly.

★

I absolutely wouldn't let Finn do the washing-up. I sent her through to the living room with Clyde while I washed and Sarah dried.

'How's your book going?'

'Not,' I replied.

'Oh dear – well, when you've written it, would you like me to have a look?'

'That'd be great, except you might have to wait a long time.'

'And how's Danny?'

'I don't know really,' I said, and to my horror I felt tears prick at my eyelids.

'Are you two OK?'

I shrugged, not wanting to trust my voice.

Sarah glanced across at me, then meticulously polished off a spoon and put it in the drawer. 'Fiona's a real find,' she said.

'Yes,' I said a bit gloomily.

'She idolizes you, you know.'

'Oh, I don't think so.'

'Of course she does. I was looking at her during the meal. She looks at you constantly. She was echoing your expressions, your posture. After everything she said, she almost seemed to check with you, just for a fraction of a second, as if she needed to be reassured about your reaction.'

'That sounds almost creepy.'

'I didn't mean it that way.'

'Anyway, it's common, isn't it, with . . . er, teachers and pupils. It's like patients becoming attached to their doctors. And it's only for a short while.'

Sarah raised an eyebrow.

'Really? I thought she was helping with your project.'

'She is for the moment. but this isn't a permanent arrangement.'

'I'm amazed you can manage without her.'

Sarah and Clyde were leaving almost at first light, so after coffee and some shoptalk, they went up to bed. Finn was lying on the floor with a book.

'That was extraordinary.'

'What?'

'I almost had a heart attack when Clyde starting asking you about your research.'

Finn put down the book and sat up, her knees pulled close to her chest.

'I felt awful for you,' she said. 'I just tried to think of anything I could to be convincing. I hope it was all right.'

'All right? You made me want to read your thesis. I can't believe how much you've taken in. You're an amazing girl, Finn. Woman.'

'It's not me, it's you, Sam. I'm just interested in you and your work. When Clyde asked me about what I was doing, I completely panicked for a second. Then, do you know what I did? I imagined myself as you and tried to say what you would say.'

I laughed.

'I wish I was as good at being me as you are,' I said.

I turned to go but Finn continued talking.

'I want all this to go on, you know.'

'How do you mean?'

'I love it. Don't smile. I really do. I love you and I love being with Elsie and looking after her. I think Danny's wonderful. And Michael . . . he saved my life, really. I'd be nothing without him. I don't know what I could ever

200

do to pay him back for what he's done for me.' She looked up at me, almost pleading. 'I want it to go on and on.'

It was a moment I had been waiting for and now I was relieved it had come. I knelt beside her.

'Finn, it can't. You have a life of your own. You have to go back into it, and soon. Look at yourself, you can do anything. You can do it.'

Finn's eyes filled with tears.

'I feel safe here, in this house,' she said. 'I'm frightened of outside.'

Twenty-Two

The first time I met Danny was at a party, although as a rule I never meet anyone at a party except for people whom I already know. It was at that mellow, sozzled stage of the evening when most of the guests have gone and the hosts are carrying glasses into the kitchen or emptying overflowing ashtrays, and the remaining guests are entirely comfortable, and the music is sweet and slow. The pressure to perform has dropped away, and you no longer have to be bright or have to smile, and you know the evening is at an end and suddenly you want it to go on a little longer. And Danny crossed the room, his eyes on me. I remember hoping that he wasn't stupid, as if someone so handsome couldn't be intelligent too, as if life is divided up fairly like that. Before he addressed a single word to me, I knew we'd have an affair. He told me his name and asked me mine; told me he was an unsuccessful actor and a quite successful carpenter, and I said I was a doctor. Then he said quite simply he'd like to see me again and I replied that I'd like that too. And then when I got back to my flat, and after I'd paid the babysitter and kicked off my shoes and looked in on a sleeping Elsie, I'd listened to the messages on my answering machine, and there was his voice, asking me to dinner the next day. He must have rung me as soon as I'd left the party.

The point is, Danny doesn't play games. He comes and

he goes, and sometimes I don't hear from him for days or even know where he is. But he's always been straightforward with me; we quarrel and then we make up, we shout and then we apologize. He's not devious. He wouldn't keep away in order to teach me a lesson. He wouldn't fail to telephone just to keep me waiting for him, just to make me suffer.

For days, I waited for Danny to call me, I checked my machine whenever I came in. I checked that Elsie hadn't knocked the receiver off its hook. When the telephone rang I'd feel as nervous as a teenager, would wait for its second or third ring before picking it up, but it was never Danny. At night I'd stay up long after Finn went to bed, because I thought he'd walk in through the door, quite casual, as if he'd never been away. I'd wake up in the dark and think he was there, my body alert with hope. I slept like a feather, fluttering into consciousness at any noise – a car on the distant road, wind in the trees, the unnerving hoot of an owl in the dark. There was never any reply when I called his flat, and he never left his own machine on. After nearly a week I called his best friend, Ronan, and asked him as casually as I could if he'd seen Danny recently.

'Had another row, Sam?' he'd said, cheerfully. Then, 'No, I haven't seen Dan. I thought he was with you.'

I thanked him and was about to put the phone down when Ronan added, 'While we're talking about Dan, though, I've been worried by him lately. Is he OK?'

'Why? What do you mean?'

'It's just that he's been a bit, well, gloomy. Brooding. Know what I mean?'

'Mummy?'

'Yes, my love.'

'When's Danny coming again?'

'I'm not sure, Elsie. He's busy. Why, do you miss him?'

'He promised to take me to a puppet show, and I want to show him how I can do cartwheels now.'

'When he comes, he'll be so proud of your cartwheels. Come here and give me a hug, a bear-hug.'

'Ow, you're hurting me, Mummy. You shouldn't hold on so tight. I'm only little.'

'Sam.'

'Mmmmm.'

'Is Danny coming again soon?'

'I don't know. For God's sake, Finn, don't you go on about Danny as well. He'll come when he bloody feels like it, I suppose.'

'Are you OK?'

'Yes, of course. Oh fuck, I'm going for a walk.'

'Do you want me to . . .'

'Alone.'

'Sam, your father and I wondered if you and Elsie and Danny would like to come over for the day next Sunday. We thought, well, that it was time we made the effort to get to know your young man better.'

'Mum, we'd love to, that's really nice of you, I appreciate it – but can I get back to you about it? Now's not a good time.'

'Oh' – a familiar huffy tone of injured pride that gave me an unfamiliar, unwelcome rush of homesickness – 'all right then, dear.'

Not a good time.

*

I went around the supermarket like a fury, my head hurting after a long depressing morning spent interviewing secretaries in the hospital. Frozen peas. Bubble bath with a cartoon character I don't recognize on the bottle. Fish fingers. Pasta in three colours. Tea-bags. Digestive biscuits and jammy dodgers. Fuck Danny, fuck him fuck him fuck him. Garlic bread. Sunflower spread. Sliced brown bread. Peanut butter. I wanted him back, I wanted him, and what should I do oh what should I do? Wings of chicken, oriental-style. Crisp green apples, all the way from the Cape, but that was OK nowadays. Three cartons of soup, lentil and spinach and curried parsnip, suitable for the microwave. Vanilla ice-cream. Pecan pie, heat from frozen. Belgian beer. I should never have moved to the country and I should never have taken in Finn. Cheddar cheese, mozzarella cheese. Cat food in rabbit and chicken and salmon flavours and the fat face of a purring mog on the tin. Crisps. Nuts. Television dinner: serves one.

The door was locked when I arrived home. I let myself in and called upstairs for Finn, but there was nobody there. So I unloaded all the shopping, pushed food into the already crowded freezer, filled up the kettle, turned on the radio, turned it off again. Then I took a deep breath and went in to my study to check the answering machine. Its little green eye wasn't blinking: no one had rung me at all.

But there was an envelope on my desk and it had my name on it. And – I put my hand on the wood of the desktop for a moment – the handwriting was Danny's. He'd been here, come in while I was out and left a note so he wouldn't have to say it to me. I picked up the envelope and turned it over, held it for a moment. There were two sheets of paper. The top one was his. The paper was grubby and smeared. There were few words, obviously written in haste, without care, but they were unmistakably his.

> Sam
> Goodbye. I'm sorry. I
> Danny

That was it. His apparent attempt at self-justification had fizzled, and he hadn't bothered even to complete it. My breath rose and fell in my chest. The desk was grainy under my hand. I put Danny's letter carefully down. My hands were trembling. Then I looked at the sheet of paper beneath, a forest of blue loops and underlinings.

> *Darling Sam* – how very intimate she'd become, all of a sudden. Perhaps she felt almost sisterly towards me now, having run off with my lover – *It's a madness, I know. We couldn't live without each other.* – How touching, I thought, love like the magazines say that it can be; love as a landslide, a destiny, a madness. – *I'm sorry to hurt you, so sorry. Love, Finn.*

I folded Danny's pitiful scrawl and Finn's letter back in the envelope and put it where it had been. Danny and Finn, Danny and Finn. I took the photograph of Danny, back to the camera and head turned towards it, caught unawares, and put it neatly in the drawer of my desk. I ran into Finn's room. The bed was made, a towel neatly folded on the bed. I clattered down the stairs. One of Finn's jackets, the navy-blue one, was missing. Was it some crazy joke that I wasn't getting the point of? No. They had gone. I said it aloud as if it was the only way I could take in what had happened: 'They've run away. Finn.' I made myself say it. 'Danny.' I looked at my watch. In two hours Elsie would be back. The memory of her little body wrapped around Finn's slim one, of her pale grave face tilted up towards Finn's smiling one, her cartwheel practised nightly in preparation for Danny's return, momentarily stopped me dead. Bile rose in my throat. I went to the kitchen sink, splashed cold water over my face and drank two glasses more. Then I returned to my study and picked up the phone and pressed the button three times.

'Stamford Central 2243.' There was a pause. 'Chief Inspector Frank Baird, please. Well, get him then.'

Baird arrived in less than half an hour, Angeloglou with him. They both looked agitated, solemn. They could hardly meet my eye. My fidgety mind suddenly fixed on the contrast between them. Baird large, his suit tight under the arms, red hair across a large head. Angeloglou was neater, his tie pulled all the way up against his collar, a full head of dark curls. How did he brush it? They seemed newly wary of me. I was transformed from a professional person to a jilted woman. And although they didn't say it, they both clearly thought Danny was little short of criminal, running off with Finn. There wasn't much I could say to them, the story was simple enough. Any fool could understand it. Angeloglou wrote some things down in a notebook, they read the letters that the two of them had left behind, and together we went to Finn's bedroom and stared into the wardrobe. One shirt was left hanging among the clatter of empty hangers; no underwear; no shoes; nothing. The room had been left quite tidy, one twist of tissue in the waste-paper basket and the duvet folded back. I was quite tart with Baird. I'm afraid, but I think that he understood. Just before he left he stood in the doorway, twisting the plain wedding ring on his thick finger, flushed with embarrassment.

'Miss Laschen . . .'

'Doctor Laschen.'

'Doctor Laschen, I'm . . .'

'Don't say anything,' I said. 'But thanks, anyway.'

I still had thirty minutes left until Elsie came. I tidied the kitchen, wiped clean the table and opened the window, because outside it had turned into a balmy spring day. I picked four orange tulips from my garden and put them in the living room. I ran into Elsie's room and made her bed, turned down the sheet on it and put her balding teddy on the pillow. Then I rummaged in the kitchen cupboards for her supper. Sonic the Hedgehog spaghetti shapes; she loved those. And I'd bought that ice-cream at the supermarket. I brushed my teeth in the bathroom and stared at the staring face that looked back at me out of the mirror. I smiled at myself and myself obediently smiled back.

Elsie ate her Sonic shapes, and her ice-cream, and had Pocahontas bubbles in her bath. Then we played a rather forlorn game of charades and I read her three books. Then she said, 'Where's Fing?'

What had I agreed with myself to say?

'She's not here at the moment.' No, that wasn't it. 'Finn's gone away, my darling. She was only ever going to stay here for a bit. She has her own life to lead.'

'But she didn't say goodbye.'

'She told me to say goodbye for her,' I lied. 'She sent a kiss.' I kissed Elsie's baffled brow and the shiny softness of her hair. 'And a hug.' I hugged Elsie, feeling her stubborn shoulders beneath my nervous hands.

'But where's she gone?'

'Well, actually' – a terrible brightness in my voice – 'she's gone to stay with Danny for a bit. So that's nice, isn't it?'

'But Danny's *ours*.'

'Ah, my love, we're each other's anyway.'

'Mummy, that's too *tight*.'

After Elsie had gone to sleep, I had a long bath. As I lay in the hot water I thought of Danny and Finn. I imagined them. Her smooth young body engulfed by his strong one; the arrow of dark hair on his chest; her tender breasts. I imagined their legs, hers so pale and his so hairy and muscled, tangled on my bed; Danny's emphatic feet, the second toe much longer than the big one, hooked under her acquiescent calf. Had he looked at her with the same gravity with which he used to look at me? Of course he had. They loved each other, didn't they, that's what Finn had said? They must have said it to each other too. How could I have not seen? Even now I didn't see it properly: when I looked back over the weeks it was as if a darkness had suddenly dropped over the string of days. Had they fucked in this house, muffling their sighs? They must have, in this house, in the place I had made for them by my trust. By my blindness. We must have sat together all three, and all the time I thought I was the centre and all the time I was on the outside, while they looked at each other, sent electric pulses rippling across the spaces between them, touched feet under the table, sent messages between the lines. Had he groaned when he came into her, that tearing sound of grief? In my mind I saw them, him rearing up above her, sweat on his straining back, her smiling into his frowning, effortful face. I washed vigorously, massaged shampoo into my scalp and, although I felt tired, I felt terribly awake. When I looked in the mirror afterwards, my ghastly red hair plastered down on my scalp, I fingered the slight bags under my eyes, ran a hand down the dry skin of my face. I looked like an ageing crow.

Then I dressed in an old track suit and made a fire, rolling newspapers into tight balls, chucking empty envelopes and loo rolls and cereal packets among the logs until it was blazing with a quick heat that would soon die away. There was a knock at the door.

'Sam.'

Michael Daley stood on the doorstep with his arms held open: theatrical, tragic, ridiculous. What did he expect me to do? Walk into them? He looked the way I felt. Pale and shocked.

'Well, Michael, what a surprise. I wonder what brings you here?' I said sardonically.

'Sam, don't go cold on me. I've just spent an hour with that policeman, Baird. I'm so sorry, I can't believe it, but I'm so sorry. And I feel responsible. I want to know if there's anything, anything at all, that I can do. I'm on my way to London, but I had to stop in and see you.'

To my horror, I felt tears stinging my eyes. If I started crying I'd not stop. Oh God, I didn't want Michael Daley to see me crying. I had to concentrate.

'What's in London?'

'Nothing important. I'm flying to Belfast for a conference. Fund-holding. A nightmare. I'm sorry . . .' His voice died away. I half-turned towards the house and then felt his hands on my shoulders, holding me steady. He smelled of cigarettes and wine. His pupils were dilated.

'You don't need to be brave with me, Sam,' he said.

'Oh yes I do,' I snapped, shaking him off.

But he cupped my chin in one hand and traced a tear with the other. We stared at each other for a long moment. What did he want from me?

'Good-night, Michael,' I said and closed the door.

Twenty-Three

I don't get dumped. I dump. I don't get humiliated. That's
for other people. When I was growing up it was always
me who sat down with the boy and looked him in the eye
– or when I couldn't be bothered, rang him up – and told
him that it was time we stopped seeing each other and all
that. It was for my boyfriends, my ex-boyfriends, to go
red and feel hurt and rejected. And I've never had
insomnia. Even in the worst times, or at least until I moved
to the country, I slept undisturbed. But in the middle of
the night after it, after Danny and Finn had gone, I found
myself awake, my skin prickling, my mind humming, like
an electric motor that had been left on and was running
uselessly, burning itself out. I felt a familiar pressure
against my right arm. Not Danny. Elsie, heaving gently,
fast asleep. She must have climbed up into the bed without
waking me. I kissed her hair and her nose. With a loose
flap of duvet I wiped her forehead where a hot tear had
fallen. I looked around at the window. The curtains were
dark. I couldn't see my watch. I couldn't see the dial of
the clock-radio and if I moved I would wake Elsie and she
wouldn't go back to sleep.

I would like to have taken a scalpel and made a thousand
incisions into Danny's body, slowly, one by one. I couldn't
believe he had done this to me. I wanted to track him
down wherever he was and just ask him did he realize

what he had done to Elsie, who depended on him so much? Did he realize what he had done to me? I wanted him back, I desperately wanted him back. I wanted to find him to explain that if he returned we could make things all right. We would work things out. I could move back to London, we could get married, anything, just so that we could go back to the way things had been.

And Finn. I would like to take her pretty little face and punch it over and over again. No. Stamp on it. Mash it. I had let her into my house, into the most intimate recesses of my life, revealed secrets I had never let anyone else see, trusted her with Elsie. I had been closer to her than I had been to my own sister, and she had huffed and puffed and blown my house down. Then I remembered the details of Dr Kale's autopsy on her parents and the bandage across Finn's neck when I had first seen her, fearful and silent on my sofa. She had been porcelain that I thought might topple and shatter. I had watched her turn soft and human again, and this was what she had done. Or was this just another symptom? Was this a cry for help from a sad, lonely girl? And wasn't Danny absconding nothing more than the characteristic behaviour of a weak man? Isn't it just what men do when flattered by the attention of a beautiful young girl? Tears were running down the sides of my face. Even my ears were wet.

After an hour of heaving sobs I descended into cool stillness. I could look at my responses with objectivity, or so I thought. I felt the pain in layers. The core of it was the betrayal of trust by Finn, the abandonment of me and Elsie by Danny. I felt scalded by this, as if nothing else could ever matter, but the sensation grew numb and I thought of other things. There was the sense of professional failure. I had said over and over again that Finn was not my patient, I had resisted the whole stupid arrangement. But even with all that taken into account, it was a total disaster. A traumatized victim of a murderous assault had been in my care and the episode had ended not in cure but in horrible farce. She had run off with my lover. I prided myself as a person who hunted alone and didn't care what other people thought of me, but I couldn't help caring now. The faces of professional rivals and foes came into my mind. I thought of Chris Madison up at Newcastle and Paul Mastronarde at the London, finding it funny and telling people that of course it was awful but to be honest it served me right, always so arrogant. I thought of Thelma, whose idea this had been. I thought of Baird, who had seemed dubious enough about me from the first and all the rugby-club gang at the police station. They must all be having a good laugh.

Then – oh, God – I thought of my parents and of Bobbie. I don't know which seemed worse: the mingled shock, shame and disapproval which would be the first response of the family or the sympathy that would follow in its wake, the outstretched arms offered to Samantha, the prodigal daughter. There was just the hint of a moment where I felt that I would rather go back to sleep and never wake up again than face the ghastliness of what the daylight held for me. It was going to be so horrible and so boring and I didn't have the strength.

Low blood sugar, of course. The subdued metabolic function characteristic of the early morning, dispersed by activity and nourishment. The curtains were grey now and Elsie was stirring on my arm. Her eyes opened and she sat up as if she were on a spring. My arm had gone to sleep. I rubbed it fiercely and life trickled back into it. Fuck the world. I would survive this and I wouldn't bother what anybody thought. Nobody was going to catch me showing weakness. I took Elsie under her armpits, threw her upwards and released her. She fell on the blanket with a shriek of terrified pleasure.

'Do it again, Mummy. Do it again.'

The following day I made an adventure of our girls' breakfast. Bacon and eggs and toast and jam and a grapefruit, and Elsie ate her half and deliriously purloined segments of mine. I had coffee. At half-past eight I drove Elsie to school.

'What's that tree like?'

'A man with green hair and a green beard. What's *that* tree like?'

'I said tree already.'

'No, *I* said, *I* said.'

'All right, Elsie. It looks . . . In this wind it looks like a green cloud.'

'No, it doesn't.'

'Does.'

'Doesn't.'

'Does.'

'Doesn't.'

The game finished in a crescendo of laughing contradiction.

On the drive back, the clouds had come into focus, the buildings were standing out more clearly against the sky. I had a sense of resolve. I would look after Elsie and I would work. All the rest was waste. I made myself more coffee and went into my study. On the computer I disposed of everything I had written so far. It was dross, the useless product of half-hearted activity. I looked through a file to remind myself of some figures and then I closed it and began to write. It was all in my head anyway. I could check the references later. I wrote for almost two hours without looking away from the screen. The sentences ran off my fingers, and I knew they were good. Like God creating the world. Just before eleven I heard the front door open. Sally. Time to refill my coffee mug anyway. As the kettle boiled, I gave her a brief, sanitized account of what had happened. My voice was level, my hands didn't tremble, I didn't blush. She didn't care much and I didn't care what she thought about it. Sam Laschen was in control once more. Sally began to clean and I returned to my study. At lunch-time I had a five-minute break. There was half a carton of pre-cooked lasagne in the fridge. I ate it cold. The era of proper food was past. After another hour I had finished a chapter. I clicked a couple of times with the mouse. Four and a half thousand words. At this rate the book would be finished in a couple of weeks. I reached into my filing cabinet and pulled out two folders of processed data. I worked my way through them very quickly, again to remind myself. It took only a few minutes before they were back in the cabinet. I opened a new file: Chapter Two. Definitions of Recovery.

A movement caught my eye. It was outside. A car. Baird and Angeloglou got out. For a moment a part of me assumed that this must be a sort of memory or a hallucination. This had happened yesterday. Was I replaying a horrible dream I had in my mind? It couldn't be happening again. There was a knock at the door. It was just some routine matter, a form that needed signing or something.

When I opened the door, they were looking at each other shiftily.

'Yes?' I said.

'We thought you might have heard something,' said Baird.

'Danny hasn't rung, and if he bloody does . . .'

The two officers looked at each other again. What was up?

'That's not what we meant. Inside?' said Baird in a dismal attempt at a casual tone. There were none of the usual smiles and winks. Baird looked like a man imitating professional police behaviour. Beads of sweat shone on his brow although it was cold and damp.

'What's this about?'

'Please, Sam.'

I led them through and they sat side by side on my sofa like Tweedledee and Tweedledum. Baird was stroking the hairy back of his left hand with the fingers of his right. A man about to make a speech. Angeloglou was still, not catching my eye. His cheek-bones were accentuated by the tightness with which he held his face, his jaw.

'Please sit down, Sam,' Baird said. 'I've got some bad news for you.' He was still fingering his hand. The hairs were a startling red even more so than those on his head. I couldn't take my eyes off them. 'Yesterday evening we were called to a burnt-out car just outside Bayle Street, twenty miles or so along the coast. We quickly established that it was the Renault van registered to Daniel Rees.'

'Christ,' I said, 'Did he crash . . .?'

'There were two badly burned human bodies in the car. Dead bodies. The effects of the fire were extremely severe and there are some identification tests still to be carried out. But I should prepare yourself for the near-certainty that these are the bodies of Mr Rees and Miss Mackenzie.'

I tried to hold on to the moment, grasp the shock and confusion as if it were a precious state of mind. It could never get worse than this.

'Did you hear what I said, Dr Laschen?'

Baird spoke softly, as if to a small child seated on his lap. I nodded. Not too hard. Nothing hysterical or over-eager.

'Did you hear what I said, Dr Laschen?'

'Yes, of course. Well, thank you, Mr Baird, for coming to tell me. I won't take up any more of your time.'

Chris Angeloglou leaned forward.

'Is there anything you would like to ask us? Anything you want to say?'

'I'm sorry,' I said, looking at my watch. 'The problem is that it's almost time for me to go and get . . . er . . . my child.'

'Can't Linda do that?'

'Can she? I can't . . .'

As Baird spoke I had been entirely clear about what was happening. While listening to the information I had also been observing with a professional interest the manner in which he conveyed painful news. And I had considered my own response with total clarity. I felt tears running down my face and realized I was crying with sobs that shook my whole body. I cried and cried until I felt myself almost gagging with all the grief and pain. I felt a hand on my shoulder and then a mug of tea was pressed against my lips and I felt surprised because not enough time seemed to have passed for tea to be made and brewed and poured out. I gulped and sipped some tea and burned my mouth. I tried to speak and couldn't. I took some deep breaths and tried again.

'Crashed?' I asked.

Baird shook his head.

'What?' It was hardly more than a croak.

'A note was found by the car.'

'What does that mean?'

'It was addressed to you.'

'To me?' I said inertly.

'The note is written by Miss Mackenzie. She writes that after the realization of what they have done, done to you, above all, they feel there is nothing to live for and they have elected to die together.'

'They committed suicide?' I asked stupidly.

'That is our working assumption.'

'That's ridiculous.' The two were silent. 'Don't you hear what I'm saying? It's ridiculous and impossible. Danny would never, never, have killed himself. Under any circumstances. He . . . How did they?'

I looked at Baird. He had been clutching a pair of gloves in one hand and now he was twisting them, hard, as if he were trying to wring water out of them.

'Is this something you need . . .?'

'Yes.'

'The car was set alight using a rag inserted into the petrol tank. It appears that they then shot themselves, each with a single shot to the head. A handgun was retrieved at the scene.'

'A gun?' I said. 'Where did they get a gun from?'

Rupert swallowed painfully and shifted his position.

'The gun was registered to Leopold Mackenzie,' he murmured in a low voice.

It took me a moment to realize what I was hearing, and when I did realize I felt dizzy with rage.

'Are you suggesting that Finn had gained possession of her father's gun?' Baird shrugged shamefacedly. 'And

that she had it in this house? Didn't you know that Mackenzie had a gun and that it was missing?'

'No,' said Baird. 'This is difficult for us and I know it
must be difficult for you.'

'Don't patronize me, Rupert, with all your prepared
psychological jargon.'

'I didn't mean that, Sam,' Baird said softly. 'I meant
that it must be difficult for *you*.'

I started.

'What do you mean?'

'I mean this happening again, for a second time.'

I sank back in my chair, miserable and defeated.

'You bastards. You have done your research, haven't
you?'

Twenty-Four

'I can count to a hundred.'

'No! Go on then.'

'One, two, skip a few, ninety-nine, a hundred.'

I chuckled appreciatively, hands on the wheel, eyes on the road, dark glasses covering my bloodshot gaze.

'And listen. Knock knock.'

'Who's there?'

'Isobel.'

'Isobel who?'

'Isobel necessary on a bicycle? And listen, listen. How does Batman's mummy call him in for supper?'

'I don't know. How does Batman's mummy call him in for supper?'

'Dinner-dinner-dinner-dinner, dinner-dinner-dinner-dinner. Batman!'

'Who told you that one?'

'Joshua who loves me and kisses me on the slide when Miss isn't looking and we're going to get married when we're growed. And how many ears does Davy Crockett have?'

'I don't know, how many ears does Davy Crockett have?'

'Three. A left ear, a right ear and a wild ear. I don't understand that joke.'

'Well, it's a wild *front* ear. Who told it to you?'

'Danny. Danny sang it one day, and then he laughed a lot.'

'Look,' I said brightly. 'Here's Kirsty's house.'

Kirsty came to the door, white socks pulled firmly up to her plump knees, smocked blue dress with a crisp white collar, red coat trailing behind, shiny hair-slide in her shiny brown hair.

'Isn't Fing coming with us?' she asked when she saw me and Elsie. Behind her, Mrs Langley was mouthing widely: 'I-haven't-told-her-yet.'

'Fing's . . .' began Elsie importantly.

'Not-today-Kirsty-but-we're-going-to-have-a-love-ly-time-and-where-are-your-swimming-things-and-jump-in-the-car-and-don't-you-look-smart-and-up-you-go,' I rattled out, as if I could push the question away if I spoke fast enough and long enough, replace it by thoughts of chloriney water and crisps afterwards, and an afternoon spent in the hot dark of the old cinema, where balding velvety seats flipped back and popcorn rolled along the floor, where cartoon characters could be bashed and squashed and dropped in boiling oil and still come back to life.

Mrs Langley leaned in through my window, looking avidly sympathetic, and placed a smooth hand over my callused one, which was clenching the steering-wheel. She files her nails, I thought.

'If there's anything I . . .'

'Thank you. I'll bring Kirsty back this afternoon.' I grabbed away my hand and turned the key in the ignition. 'Are you both belted in, girls?'

'Yes,' they chorused, sitting neatly side by side, two pairs of feet dangling in their patent-leather shoes, two eager faces.

'OK, let's go.'

Kirsty and Elsie floated decorously in their rubber rings and armbands, so buoyed up their torsos hardly got wet. Their white legs scampered in the water, their faces were pink with the sense of their own courage.

'Look at me,' said Kirsty. She slapped her nose and chin into the water for a nanosecond and came up triumphant with one lock of hair dripping. 'I can go underwater. I bet you can't do that.'

Elsie looked at me for a moment, my anxious little landlubber. I thought she would cry. Then she ducked her head down into the pool, struggling clumsily amid her bright orange floats.

'I did it,' she said. 'I did it, Mummy, did you see?'

I wanted to pick her up and hold her.

'My two little fish, aren't you?' I said. 'Shall I be a shark?'

Under the water, I was weightless and half blind; my eyes squinted through the thick green water and the luminous legs swirled like seaweed; my hands held out for flickering ankles. The tiles were reassuringly only a few inches away from my submerged body. I heard the girls squeal and giggle as I floundered beneath them. I'm not a fish, not me. I only like solid ground.

In the changing room a teenage girl nudged her friend as I tugged vests over wet heads, forced stubborn feet into recalcitrant shoes and buckled stiff straps. She pointed at me with her eyes.

Chicken nuggets and chips and bright pink ice-lollies for lunch. Popcorn, savoury and sweet mixed, and fizzy orange in a huge cardboard cup with two stripy straws poking from the top. The girls watched a cartoon and I let the screen slip into a blur as I looked beyond it and they both held my hands, one sitting on either side of me. Their fingers were sticky, their heads were tilted towards my shoulders. The air all around us felt second-hand, overused. I tried to match my breath to theirs, but couldn't. It came in ragged unsymmetrical tearings out of lungs that hurt. I put my dark glasses on as soon as we came out into the foyer.

'Mummy.'

'Yes, my love.' Kirsty was safely returned to her mother and we were driving through a milky mist towards home.

'You know in the video,' except Elsie pronounced it 'vidjo', a surviving trace of baby-talk, the last frail brown leaf left hanging on the tree, 'of *The Lion, the Witch and the Wardrobe*?'

'Yes.'

'When he's killed by the wicked witch and he lies with the mouses?'

'Yes.'

'And then he comes back to life, he *does*. Well . . .'

'No. Danny and Finn won't come back like that. We'll miss them and we'll remember them, and we'll talk about them to each other, you must talk to me whenever you want to, and they won't be dead here.' I put one hand against my thundering heart. 'But we won't see them again.'

'But where are they? Are they in heaven now?'

Charred lumps of flesh, hilariously grinning skulls with burnt-out eyes, features pouring in a ghastly river down their ruined faces, melted limbs, on a metal tray in a fridge a few miles from where we were driving.

'I don't know, my sweetheart. But they are peaceful now.'

'Mummy?'

'Yes.'

'Was I brave to put my head in the water?'

'You were *very* brave; I was proud.'

'Brave as a lion?'

'Braver.'

As we drove towards the house, it looked as if a party was going on, looming out of the fog. A flock of white lights; a herd of cars. We pulled to a halt and I softly touched the tip of Elsie's nose with my forefinger.

'Beep,' I said. 'We're going to run through these rude men with their cameras and their tape recorders. Put your head on my shoulder and let's see if I can get to the door before you count to a hundred.'

'One, two, skip a few . . .'

'Your father and I think you ought to come and stay with us for a few days. Until all the fuss has died down.'

'Mum, that's . . .' I paused, searching for what I ought to say. 'Kind of you, but I'm all right. We have to stay here.'

My parents had arrived just after us. They marched into the house like two guards, left–right, chins up, eyes ahead. I was grateful for their resilience. I knew how much they must be hating all of this. They brought a fruit cake in a large maroon tin, a bunch of flowers wrapped in Cellophane and some Smarties and a colouring book for Elsie, who hates colouring books but loves Smarties. She took them off to the kitchen to eat meticulously, colour by colour, leaving the orange ones till last. My father made a fire. He stacked twigs in a neat pyre over half a fire-lighter and then arranged four logs on top. My mother made tea with a bustling air and thumped a hunk of fruit cake in front of me.

'At least let us stay here then.'

'I'll be fine.'

'You can't do everything by yourself.'

Something in the tone of my mother's voice made me look at her. Beneath her glasses, her eyes swam; her lips were tautened against emotion. When had I last seen her cry? I leaned forward in my seat and touched her knee, under her thick wool skirt, awkwardly. When had I last touched her, apart from those stiff pecks on the cheek?

'Let it be, Joan. Can't you see Samantha's upset?'

'No! No, I *can't* see she's upset. That's my point, Bill. She should be upset; she should be – be – prostrated. Her friend, I always did think she was sly that one and I told you so that day we met her, and her boyfriend run off together and kill themselves in a car and it's all over the newspapers. And everything.' She gestured vaguely at the window, at the world beyond. 'And Samantha sits there as cool as anything, when all I want, all I want, is to *help*.' She paused, and perhaps I would have leaned forward and hugged her then, but I saw her give a twitch and she said the final thing, the thing she must have promised herself not to say: 'It's not as if it's the first time this has happened to Samantha.'

'Joan . . .'

'That's all right, Dad,' I said and I meant it. The pain of that being said to me by my mother was so intense that it almost became an astringent twisted pleasure.

'Elsie shouldn't be here at all,' my mother said. 'She should come away with us.'

She half-rose, as if she were going to make off with my daughter at once.

'No,' I said. 'Elsie is with me.' As if on cue, Elsie appeared in the living room, crunching on her last Smarties. I pulled her on to my lap and put my chin on her head.

There was a knock at the door.

'Who is it?' I called.

'Me. Michael.'

I let him in, closing the door quickly behind him. He took off his coat and I saw he was wearing old jeans and a faded blue cotton shirt, but otherwise he looked relaxed, steady.

'I've brought smoked salmon and brown bread and a bottle of Sancerre, I thought we might . . . oh, hello, Mrs Laschen, Mr Laschen.'

'They're just going, Michael,' I said.

'But Samantha, we've only just . . .'

My father nodded insistently at my mother and took her arm. I helped them on with their coats in silence and steered them to the door. My mother looked back at Michael and me. I don't know which disquieted me more, her puzzlement or her approval.

Elsie was waiting for me in my bed that night. As I slipped under the cover, she shifted, wrapped a tentacle arm around my neck, butted her face into my shoulder, sighed. Then, with the miraculous ease that children have, she closed her eyes again and sank into sleep. I lay awake for a long time. Outside it was moonless and dark. Everyone had gone home; I could hear nothing but the wind in the trees, once or twice the faint shriek of a bird out at sea. If I put my hand to Elsie's chest I could feel her heartbeat.

Her breath blew warmly against my neck. Every so often she would murmur something indistinguishable.

Michael hadn't stayed long that evening. He had opened the wine and poured me a glass, which I'd knocked back without tasting, as if it were schnapps. He had spread the butter he'd brought with him on to slices of the bread and covered them with smoked salmon, which reminded me horribly of raw human flesh, so I nibbled a bit of the crust and left it at that. We didn't talk much. He mentioned a couple of details from the Belfast conference he thought might interest me. I said nothing but stared at the dying embers of the fire my father had made. Anatoly wrapped his black length around our legs and purred loudly.

'It seems unreal, impossible, doesn't it?' he said. 'I've known Finn for years,' he said. 'Years.'

I said nothing. I felt unable even to nod.

'Well.' He stood up and pulled on his coat. 'I'm going to go, Sam. Will you be able to sleep? I could give you something.'

I waved him away. When he had gone, I went upstairs. I held Elsie against me and stared, wide-eyed, dry-eyed, at the silent dark.

Twenty-Five

'It's a bad business, these suicides.'

'I'm coping.'

'Bad for us, I mean.'

'No, I don't know what you mean.'

Geoff Marsh fingered the knot of his tie as if attempting to establish by touch alone whether it was in the centre of his neck. This meeting had been arranged a fortnight earlier to discuss some possible new sources of funding that had arisen. These we had disposed of over a cup of coffee. I had stood up to go, but he had gestured me back into my chair and started to look worried.

'This couldn't have come at a worse time,' he said.

I bit back a retort and said nothing.

'You should have told us, Sam.'

'What should I have told you, Geoff?'

Geoff reached for a pad and looked at some jottings in a display of bureaucratic efficiency.

'You were technically in our employment, Sam,' he said after a pause. He gave that shrug of helplessness that I had come to know well. It was an acknowledgement of the implacability of the political and economic climate which cruelly constrained him. He continued, 'The last thing I want to do is make anything of that, of course, but you should have told us that you were doing sensitive work that would impact on our project.'

I was going to have to work with this man for a long time, so it was difficult for me to think of what I could decently say. I took a deep breath.

'I thought I was being a good citizen. The police asked me for help. They insisted on secrecy. I didn't even tell my own family.'

Geoff placed his two hands delicately on the edge of his grossly oversized desk. I felt like a schoolgirl in the headmaster's office.

'It's going to be in the papers,' he said, with a frown.

'It's already in the bloody papers,' I said. 'My front lawn is like Greenham Common.'

'Yes, yes, but so far there has been no mention of, well . . .' Geoff gestured around him vaguely. 'Us, all this, the unit.'

'Why should they mention that?'

Geoff stood up and walked over to the window and stared out. I tried to think of a way of bringing this tiresome meeting to an end. After a couple of minutes' silence, I couldn't bear it any longer.

'Geoff, if there's nothing more, I've got things to do.'

Geoff turned suddenly as if he had forgotten I was in the room.

'Sam, do you mind if I am entirely frank?'

'Go ahead,' I said drily. 'Don't spare my feelings.'

He joined his hands in a pose of statuesque gravity.

'The whole subject of post-traumatic stress disorder is still controversial. You've told me that enough times. We're creating a new centre for it here and at the same time I don't want to tell you how many wards I've been closing over the past couple of months. And the Linden Report – you know, into that photogenic six-year-old girl who died in Birmingham after we'd turned her away –

that's coming out in a couple of weeks. And I'm just waiting for some bright medical correspondent to put all that together with your thing . . .'

'What do you mean, *my* thing?'

Geoff's face had become pinker and harder.

'Since I'm looking into the abyss,' he said, 'maybe I'll tell you. We chose you to superintend the largest project of my reign . . . my tenure, whatever you like to call it. Sir Reginald Lennox on my committee says that post-traumatic stress disorder is an excuse for weaklings and nancy boys, to use his expression. But we've brought in the famous Dr Samantha Laschen to fight our corner. And about a month before taking up her post, she has shown the world what she can do by treating a traumatized woman in her own home. An irresponsible journalist might point out that the result of Dr Laschen's personal brand of treatment was that the patient fell in love with Dr Laschen's own boyfriend, they absconded and then both committed suicide.' Geoff paused. 'Any such summary would, of course, be most unfair. But if such an argument were to be made, it would in truth be difficult to argue that the treatment of Fiona Mackenzie was one of your great successes.'

'I wasn't treating Fiona Mackenzie. She wasn't my patient. The point was to provide her with a safe and secure – and temporary – refuge. And as a matter of fact I was against the idea myself.'

I was whining and making excuses and I despised myself for it. Geoff looked unimpressed.

'It's a subtle distinction,' he said, dubiously.

'What is all this, Geoff? If you've got anything to say, just say it.'

'I'm trying to save you, Sam, and save the unit.'

'*Save* me? What are you talking about?'

'Sam, I'm not expressing a personal view, I'm just putting forward a few pertinent facts. If this trust becomes embroiled in a public scandal in the media, things will be awkward for everybody.'

'I don't want to be belligerent about this, but are you making some sort of threat? Do you want me to resign?'

'No, absolutely not, not at present. This is your project, Sam, and you're going to see it through, supported by us.'

'And?'

'Perhaps we should consider a strategy of containment.'

'Such as?'

'That was what I had hoped we could discuss, but it occurred to me that one possibility might be a judicious interview with the right journalist, a sort of pre-emptive strike.'

'No, absolutely not.'

'Sam, think about it, don't just say no.'

'No.'

'Think about it.'

'No. And I've got to go now, Geoff. I've got doctors to talk to. Lest we forget that the point of this project is to provide a medical service.'

Geoff walked with me across his vast office to the door.

'I envy you, Sam.'

'That's hard to believe.'

'People come to you with their symptoms and you help them and that's it. I argue with doctors and then I argue with politicians and then I argue with bureaucrats and then I argue with doctors again.'

I turned back to the office and looked at the Mexican tapestry, the sofa, the desk that was about the size of Ayers

Rock, the panoramic view across fens and marshes or whatever it was that lay between Stamford and the sea.

'There are some compensations,' I said.

We shook hands.

'I need to be able to look my board in the face without too much embarrassment. Please don't do anything to embarrass me. And if you do, tell me first.'

When I arrived home, it took me fifteen minutes to play through the messages on my answering machine. I lost count of the different newspapers whose representatives left their numbers and of the different euphemisms they employed, the offers of deals, sympathy, consultation fees. Buried among them were messages from my mother, baffled by the tirade of beeps caused by the preceding messages, and Michael Daley, and Linda, who was going to be late today, and from Rupert Baird, who asked if we could have a word about Finn's effects.

Her effects. The idea irritated me and then made me feel so sad. What was to be done with her few things? Presumably they now had no significance as part of an investigation. They weren't evidence of anything except two wasted lives and a landscape of emotional damage. Our possessions were supposed to drift down from one generation to the next, but I couldn't even think of anyone to give Finn's pitiful few things to. I wondered what would happen to her untouched inheritance.

Even so, if there was nothing to do, at least I would do it straight away. I took a cardboard box from the kitchen and ran up the stairs to the room from which I had deliberately excluded myself, Finn's room. Even now there was a feeling of transgression as I pushed the door open and stepped inside. It was pathetically bare, as if it had been unoccupied for months. For the first time I realized that Finn had accumulated none of the burrs and barnacles that stick to most of us as we pass through life. Apart from some paperbacks piled on a shelf, there was not a single personal object in view, not even a pencil. The bed was carefully made, the rug straight, the surfaces were all bare. There was a musty smell and I hastily pushed the window open. There was nothing in the wardrobe but a rattle of metal clothes hangers. I looked at the books: some thrillers, *Bleak House*, *The Woman in White*, poetry by Anne Sexton, a battered guide to South America. I took that and tossed it out of the door on to the landing. I felt like escaping to South America. Escaping anywhere. The rest of the books I put in the box, and as I did so a white envelope fell from the pages of one of them on to the floor.

I picked it up and was about to put it in the box too when I saw what was written on it and stopped. In large childish capital letters it said: MY WILL. Finn, so scared, so preoccupied with death, had written a will.

I had a sudden tremulous conviction that she had impulsively left everything to me and that this would be a further public disaster. I slowly turned the envelope over. It wasn't sealed. The flap had simply been tucked inside without being stuck down, the way one does with greetings cards. I knew that what I was doing was wrong, possibly illegal, but I opened it and unfolded the paper inside. It was a blue form, headed 'Make Your Own Will' at the top, and it had been filled out very simply. Under the box marked 'Will of' there was written: Fiona Mackenzie, 3 Wilkinson Crescent, Stamford, Essex. In the box marked 'I appoint as my executor' there was written: Michael Daley, 14 Alice Road, Cumberton, Essex. In the box marked 'I leave everything I own to' there was written: Michael Daley, 14 Alice Road, Cumberton, Essex. It was signed and dated Monday 4 March 1996. She ticked that she wished to be cremated.

At the bottom were two boxes marked 'Signed by the person making this will in our presence, in whose presence we then signed'. In these, in different hands, were written: Linda Parris, 22 Lam Road, Lymne. Sally Cole, 3b Primrose Villas, Lymne.

Finn had gone completely mad. Finn had gone mad and then my fucking child-minder and my fucking cleaner had joined in a mad conspiracy under my own roof. My head was spinning and I had to sit on the bed for a moment. And what conspiracy, anyway? A conspiracy to leave your wealth in a mad way after your death? Old ladies left millions to their cats; why shouldn't Finn leave everything to Michael Daley? But as I thought of his ineffectual role in all of this as Finn's doctor, as Mrs Ferrer's doctor, I became angry. Who knew about this will? The idea of the wealth of the Mackenzie family being handed over to Michael Daley suddenly seemed unbearable. Why shouldn't I destroy the will, so that some sort of justice could be done? Anyway, if the person who was the executor also got all the money, it could hardly be legal, so it might as well be destroyed anyway. As I pondered this I saw there was another slip of paper in the envelope. It was hardly larger than a business card. On it was Finn's unmistakable handwriting: 'There is another copy of this will in the possession of the executor, Michael Daley. Signed, Fiona Mackenzie.' I gave a shiver and felt as if Finn had come into the room and caught me rummaging through her things. I blushed until I felt my cheeks sting.

I carefully replaced both pieces of paper in the envelope and placed it into the cardboard box. Then I spoke aloud, even though I was alone.

'What a bloody mess.'

Twenty-Six

I don't believe in God, I don't think that I ever have, although I have a dim and suspiciously hackneyed memory of kneeling by my bed like Christopher Robin and rattling off Our-Father-who-art-in-heaven-hallowed-be-thy-name. And I do recall being terrified when very young of that prayer that goes: 'If I should die before I wake I pray the Lord my soul to take.' I would lie in my knee-length nightie with the frills round the wrists and the shell-white buttons closed up to the demure neckline, blinking worriedly in the darkness, Bobbie's breath rising and falling from the bed across the room, and try to keep off the great wall of sleep. And I have always hated the idea of the capricious deity who answers some people's calls for help and not others'.

But when I woke in the grey light of the March morning, on the narrow hem of a bed almost entirely occupied by an out-flung Elsie, I found myself to my shame muttering, 'Please God, dear God, let it not be true.' Morning, though, is harsh. Not as bad as night, of course, when time is like a great river spilling over its banks, losing all onrushing momentum, lying in shallow stagnant pools. My patients often talk to me about night terrors. And they talk too about the terror of waking up from dreams into an undeceived day.

I lay for a few minutes until the first panic had subsided

and my breathing grew steady. Elsie shifted abruptly beside me, yanked the duvet cover off me and wrapped herself in it like some hibernating creature. Only the top of her head showed. I stroked it, and it too disappeared. Outside I could hear the sounds of the day: a dog barking, cock crowing, cars changing gear at the sharp corner. The journalists had gone from my door, the newspapers were no longer full of the story, the phone did not ring every few minutes with solicitous or curious inquiry. This was my life.

So I jumped out of bed and, quietly so as not to wake Elsie, got dressed in a short woollen dress, some ribbed tights and a pair of ankle boots, methodically threading the laces into little eyelets and noticing while I did so that my hands were no longer shaking. I looped dangly earrings into my lobes and brushed my hair. I wasn't going anywhere, but I knew if I shuffled round in leggings that had lost their stretch I'd add to my despondency. Thelma had once said to me that feelings often follow behaviour, rather than the other way round: behave with courage and you give yourself courage; behave with generosity and you start to lose your mean-spirited envy. So now I was going to face the world as if it didn't make me sick with panic, and maybe my nausea would begin to fade.

I fed Anatoly, drank a scalding cup of coffee and made a shopping list before Elsie woke and staggered into the kitchen. She had a bowl of Honey Nut Loops, which I finished for her, and then a bowl of muesli, picking out the raisins with her spoon and handing the soggy beige remainder to me.

'I want a stick insect in a jar,' she said.

'All right.' I could cope with cleaning out a stick insect's home.

She looked at me in surprise. Maybe she'd started too low, a grave negotiating mistake.

'I want a hamster.'

'I'll think about it.'

'I *want* a hamster.'

'The trouble with pets,' I said, 'is that they need cleaning out and feeding, and after the first few days you'll get bored, and guess who'll do it. And pets die.' I regretted the words as soon as I spoke them, but Elsie didn't blink.

'I want *two* hamsters, so if one dies, I'll still have the other.'

'Elsie . . .'

'Or one dog.'

Letters abruptly slapped through the letter-box and on to the tiled floor.

'I'll get them.'

Elsie slid from the table and retrieved a pile of envelopes, more than usual. The brown for bills I put to one side. The slim white ones, with my name formally typed and the stamp franked in the corner, I peered at suspiciously and put to the other side. They were almost certainly from newspapers or TV programmes. The handwritten ones I opened and quickly glanced at: 'Darling Sam, if there's anything we can do . . .'; 'I was so surprised when I read . . .'; 'Dear Sam, I know we've lost touch recently, but when I heard about . . .'

And there was one envelope I didn't know what to do with. It was addressed to Daniel Rees in neat blue-Biro capitals. I supposed I'd better send it on to his parents. I held up the envelope to the light, stared at it as if it held the key to a mystery. The gummed seal of the envelope was detached in one corner. I slid my finger under the flap and opened it a bit further. Then all the way.

239

Dear Mr Rees,

Thank you for your inquiries this morning concerning weekend breaks in Italy. This is to confirm that you have booked two nights, half board, in Rome, for the weekend of May 18/19. We will send you your flight details and tickets shortly. Can you confirm the names of the passengers are Mr D. Rees and Dr S. Laschen?
Yours sincerely,
Miss Sarah Kelly
Globe Travel

I folded the letter up and slid it back into its envelope. Rome with Danny. Hand in hand in T-shirts and in love. Under the starched sheets in a hotel bedroom, with a fan stirring the baked air. Pasta and red wine and huge and antique ruins. Cool churches and fountains. I'd never been to Rome.

'Who's the letter from, Mummy?'

'Oh, nobody.'

Why had he changed his mind so abruptly? What had I done, or not done, that he could forgo Rome with me for death in a burnt-out car with a fucked-up girl? I pulled out the letter again. 'Thank you for your inquiries this morning . . .' It was dated 8 March 1996. That was the day that it happened, the day he went off with Finn. Pain gathered, ready to spring, above my eyes.

'Will we be late for school again, Mummy?'

'What? No! No of course we won't be late for school, we'll be *early*. Come on.'

'I just signed where she told me to.'

'But *Sally*, how could you not look? It was her will, and she was a distressed young girl.'

'Sorry.' Sally went on scrubbing the oven. That was it.

'I wanted to speak to you about it, Linda, before Elsie comes back.'

'She said it was nothing.' Linda's eyes filled with tears. 'A formality.'

'Didn't you read it?'

She just shrugged and shook her head. Why hadn't they been nosy like me?

Michael's house was not large, but it was lovely in a cool and modish kind of way. The downstairs floor was entirely open-plan and the French windows in the uncluttered kitchen opened out on to a paved courtyard in which stood a small conical fountain. I looked around: well-stocked bookshelves, vivid rugs on austere floors, tortured black-and-white drawings writhing on serene white walls, pot plants that looked green and fleshy, full wine racks, photographs of boats and cliffs and not a single person in them. How could a GP afford such style? Well, at least he was living up to the status he would soon acquire. We sat at a long refectory table and drank real coffee out of mugs with delicate handles.

'You were lucky to catch me. I'm on call,' he said. Then he reached over and took my hand in both of his. I noticed his nails were long and clean.

'Are you all right, Sam?'

As if I were a patient. I pulled away.

'Does that mean you aren't?' he asked. 'Look, this is a horrible business, horrible for you, horrible for me too. We should try and help each other through it.'

'I've read Finn's will.'

He raised an eyebrow.

'Did she show it to you?' I shook my head and he sighed. 'So is that what this is about?'

'Michael, do you *know* what's in her will? You've got a copy.'

He sighed.

'I know I'm the executor, whatever that means. She asked me.'

'Do you mean you've got no idea?'

He looked at his watch.

'Has she left everything to you?' he asked with a smile.

'No. She's left everything to you.'

The expression on his face froze. He stood up and walked to the French window with his back to me.

'Well?' I demanded.

He looked round.

'To me?' He ran his fingers through his hair. 'Why should she do that?'

'But it's not on, right?'

Michael's face took on a quizzical expression.

'I don't know what to say. It's all so . . .'

'So unethical,' I said. 'Dubious.'

'What?' Michael looked up as if he had only just heard. 'Why would she do that? What was she up to?'

'Are you going to accept it?'

'What? It's all so sudden.'

There was a sudden beeping sound and he put his hand in his jacket pocket.

'Sorry, I've got to rush,' he said. 'I'm stunned, Sam.' Then he smiled. 'Saturday.' I looked puzzled. 'Sailing, remember? Might be good for us. Get things in perspective. And we should have a proper talk.'

I'd forgotten about that arrangement: sailing was all I needed.

'It'll do me good,' I said hollowly.

I held Elsie like a precious jewel; I was scared that I would break her with the might of my love. I felt so strong, so alive, so euphoric with grief and rage. My blood was coursing around my body, my heart was beating loudly; I felt clean and supple and untired.

'Did Danny,' I asked carefully, casually, 'ever say anything to you about Finn?'

She shrugged.

'What about Finn?' I stroked Elsie's silky hair and wondered what secrets were locked inside her neat skull. 'Did she say anything about Danny?'

'Nope.' She shifted in my lap. 'Danny used to *ask* me about Finn.'

'Oh.'

Elsie looked at me with curious wide eyes.

'And Danny said that you're the best mummy in the world.'

'Did he?'

'*Are* you?

After Elsie was asleep. I prowled around the house, pulling curtains aside, forcing myself under beds, reaching into corners. At the end of it I had on the kitchen table in front of me a battered menagerie of six tiny paper animals, three little birds, two sort of dogs, something baffling. I looked at them and they looked back at me.

Twenty-Seven

She had his dark eyes and the heavy eyebrows that almost joined in the middle of the forehead. The hair itself was lighter in colour and finer, and her skin was different in texture and heavily freckled already, though it was only just spring. Danny's skin was pale, but always clear. He always went a lovely smooth caramel-brown. I could remember the smell of it, and the slight dampness, when he had been in the sun.

I had never met any of Danny's family. He told me they lived in the West Country, his father owned a construction company, he had a brother and a sister, and that was all. I was typing away at the book – it was going really fast now, it would be finished in a matter of weeks – when the phone rang. I left the answering machine to deal with it.

'Hello, Dr Laschen. This is . . . um . . . my name's Isobel Hyde, we've never met, but I'm Danny's sister and . . .'

I gave a shiver and felt repulsed. What on earth could she want with me? I picked up the phone.

'Hello, this is Sam Laschen, I was hiding behind the answering machine.'

There were some awkward halting exchanges as she thought that I thought she just wanted to grab any of Danny's possessions that had been left with me and I didn't know what she wanted. I said there was nothing valuable but of course she could have it all and she said that wasn't what she meant and she was down in London for a few days and wondered if she could pop out in the train to see me. I don't know why, irrational instinct maybe, but I didn't want her to come to the house. I had had enough of people seeing where I lived in any case, and I didn't know what ghoulish motives might impel a woman to see the setting where her dead brother had been with a woman that he abandoned and all that. In fact I didn't know what the hell was going on, so I said I would meet her off the train at Stamford on the following morning and we could go to a pub.

'How will we recognize each other?' she asked.

'Maybe I'll recognize you, but I'm tall and I've got very short red hair. Nobody who's actually free to walk the streets looks remotely like me in this entire county.'

I almost cried when she got off the train, and I couldn't speak. I just shook her hand and led her off to a café opposite the station. We sat and played with our coffee-cups.

'Where are you from?'

'We're living in Bristol at the moment.'

'Which part?'

'Do you know Bristol?'

'Not really,' I confessed.

'Then there's not much point in going into detail, is there?'

I could see that Danny's easygoing charm was a family trait.

'I didn't bring any of Danny's things,' I said. 'There were a couple of shirts, some knickers, a toothbrush, a razor, that sort of thing. He never seemed to have much. I could send them if you like.'

'No.'

There was a silence which I had to break.

'It's interesting for me to meet you, Isobel. Eerie, too. You look so like him. But Danny never talked about his family. Maybe he didn't think that I'm the sort of person you take home to Mum. He left in a horrible way. And I'm not sure what the point of all this is, although of course I am deeply sorry for all of you.'

Once more there was a silence, and I began to feel a little alarmed. What was I going to do with this woman, staring at me with Danny's gaze?

'I'm not really sure myself,' she said finally. 'It may seem stupid, but I wanted to meet you, to look at you. I'd wanted to for ages and I thought that now we might never meet at all.'

'That's understandable, in the circumstances. I mean, that we might never meet.'

'The family is in a terrible state.'

'I'm not surprised.'

I hadn't allowed myself to think about Danny's parents. Isobel had been looking down into her coffee but now she raised her large heavy-lidded dark eyes and looked at me. I felt a ripple of lust flow through me and I clenched my teeth so that it hurt.

'Are you coming to the funeral?'

'No.'

'We thought not.'

A horrible thought occurred to me.

'You weren't, by any chance, coming to ask me not to come?'

'No, of course not. You mustn't think that.'

Isobel seemed to be trying to gather courage for some great leap.

'Isobel,' I said, 'is there something you want to tell me, because if not . . .'

'Yes, there is,' she interrupted. 'I'm not good at putting things but what I wanted to say is that you know that Danny had loads of affairs, loads and loads of women before you.'

'Well, thank you, Isobel, for coming all the way here by train to tell me that.'

'I don't mean that. That's the way he was, you know that, and women always fell for him. But what I wanted to say is that you were different. You were different for him.'

Suddenly I felt I was in danger of losing emotional control over myself.

'That's what I thought, Isobel. But that's not how it turned out, is it? I ended up like the others, dumped and forgotten about.'

'Yes, I know about that and I don't know what to say except that I couldn't believe it. I just couldn't believe it. I don't believe it.'

I pushed my coffee cup to one side. I wanted to draw the encounter to a close.

'No, but you see it did happen, whatever your instinct tells you. It was a kind impulse to come and say that to me, and yet it does no good at all. What am I expected to do with what you say? To be honest, I'm just trying to put it all behind me and move on.'

Isobel looked dismayed.

'Oh, well, I wanted to give you something, but maybe you won't want it.'

She rummaged in her bag and produced a sheaf of photocopies. I could instantly see the bold handwriting was Danny's.

'What's this?'

'Danny used to write to me, about two letters a year. This is a copy of the last one he wrote to me. I knew that the break-up must have been terrible for you. And then the deaths. I suppose it must have been a public humiliation as well.'

'Yes.'

'I wasn't being tactless, was I? I just thought this letter might be a sort of comfort.'

I expressed a hollow gratitude but I wasn't really sure how to respond, although I did take the letter, gingerly, as if it might hurt me. She just got on the train and I gave a small wave at a woman I knew I would never see again. I was half-tempted to throw away the photocopied letter unread.

An hour later I was in the CID section of Stamford Central police station. A WPC brought me tea and sat me at Chris Angeloglou's desk. I looked at his jacket, draped over the back of his chair, at the photograph of a woman and lumpy child, played with his pens, and then Angeloglou himself appeared. He put his hand on my shoulder in a carefully rehearsed spontaneous gesture of reassurance.

'Sam, are you all right?'

'Yes.'

'I'm afraid Rupert's busy.'

'How's the investigation going?'

'All right. Last week's raids went quite well. We've got some interesting stuff.'

'About the murders?'

'Not exactly.'

I sighed.

'So charges are not imminent. Look at this letter. It was written by Danny to his sister just a couple of weeks before he died.'

Chris took it and pulled a face.

'Don't worry, you only need to read the last couple of pages.'

He leaned on the edge of his desk and scanned them.

'Well?' he said, when he was finished.

'Is that the letter of somebody about to run off with another woman?'

Chris shrugged.

'You've read it,' I said. 'Never met anyone like her before, I don't want anyone else any more, I want to marry her and spend the rest of my life with her, I love her child, my only worry is whether she'll have me.'

'Yes,' said Chris uneasily.

'And there's this.'

I handed him the letter of confirmation from the travel company. He scrutinized it with a half-smile.

'Do you arrange to run away with somebody when you've planned something like that?'

Chris smiled, not unkindly.

'I don't know. Maybe you do. Was Danny the impulsive type?'

'Well, sort of . . .'

'The kind of man who might just get up and leave . . .'

'Yes, but he wouldn't have done this,' I said lamely.

'Is there anything else,' Angeloglou asked gently.

'No, except . . .' I felt desperate. 'Except for the whole thing. Have you thought about it?'

'What?'

'This young girl writes a will . . .'

'How do you know about the will, Sam? All right, don't tell me, I don't want to know.'

'She writes a will and the next moment she's dead. Isn't that peculiar?'

Angeloglou thought silently for a time.

'Had Finn ever talked about dying?'

'Yes, of course.'

'Had she ever talked about suicide?'

I paused for a moment and swallowed hard.

'Yes.'

'So,' said Chris. 'And, anyway, what were you suggesting?'

'Have you even considered that they could have been murdered?'

'For God's sake, Sam, who by?'

'Who stands to gain a fantastic amount from Finn's death?'

'Is this a serious accusation?'

'It's a serious nomination.'

Chris laughed.

'All right,' he said. 'I give in. Can I keep these pieces of paper?' I nodded. 'Out of compassion for everybody, including you, I'm going to make this little inquiry as discreet as possible. But I'll ring you tomorrow. And now, doctor, go home and take a pill or have a drink or watch TV or all three at once.'

But it wasn't the following day. At seven o'clock at the end of the same day, Chris Angeloglou rang me.

'I've made some inquiries about your suspect.'

'Yes?'

'Let's get this clear, Sam. The still-burning car was found shortly before six p.m. on the ninth.'

'Yes.'

'On the eighth, Dr Michael Daley flew to Belfast to attend a conference for fund-holding general practitioners. He spoke at the conference on the ninth and flew back to London in the late evening. Enough?'

'Yes. Actually, I knew that. I'm sorry, Chris. Silly me and all that.'

'That's completely all right. Sam?'

'Yes?'

'We all feel bad that we let you in for this. We'll do anything we can to help.'

'Thank you, Chris.'

'You're the expert on trauma, Sam, but I think the truth is that we need to improve our investigation and you need to improve your grieving.'

'Sounds good to me, Chris.'

Twenty-Eight

Six years ago my lover, the father of my unborn child, had killed himself. Of course, everyone had told me I mustn't, not for one minute, blame myself. I said it to myself, in my doctor's tone of voice. He was a depressive. He had tried it before. You thought you could save him but we can only save ourselves. And so on.

One week ago my lover – the only other man I'd ever really loved – had killed himself. People's admonitions that I should not blame myself were beginning to sound a bit frantic. Danny's funeral was the next day but I was not going to attend. He'd died in another woman's arms, hadn't he? He'd run away from me entirely. At the thought of Danny and Finn together, I felt hot, loose; almost excited and almost despairing. For a moment I was quite sick with jealousy and hopeless lust.

'I'm off out now, Sally,' I said a few minutes later. 'I won't be back before you leave so I've left the money on the mantelpiece. Thanks for making everything look so much better.'

'Not going to work?' Sally looked at my faded blue jeans, ripped at one knee, my beaten-up leather jacket.

'I'm going sailing.'

She pulled a face. Of disapproval?

'Nice,' she said.

Finn's two doctors, one her supposed protector, the other the sole beneficiary of her will, didn't have much to say to each other on the short drive to the sea. Michael seemed preoccupied and I looked out of the window without seeing anything. When the car pulled to a halt he turned to me.

'You forgot to put your wet suit on,' he said.

It was in a carrier bag between my feet.

'You forgot to tell me to put it on.'

We continued in silence. I looked for the sea. The day was too grey. The car turned off on to a narrow road between high hedges. I looked inquiringly.

'I've moved the boat near to the boat-house.'

It felt like driving in a tunnel and it was a relief when we came out into the open. I saw some boats. When the car stopped I heard them rattling in the wind. There were a few wooden shacks, with peeling paint. One of them was abandoned and open to the sky. There was nobody around at all.

'You can change in the car,' Michael said briskly.

'I want a changing room,' I said in a sulky tone and got out of the car. 'Which one's yours?'

'I don't really want to go to the trouble of opening it up. The car would be better if it's all right with you.'

'It isn't.'

Michael extracted himself awkwardly from the car. He was already in his rubbers, big and slick and black.

'All right,' he said with an ill grace. 'Over here.'

He led me to a seasoned wooden building with double doors facing the sea and handed me his bunch of keys.

'The door might be a bit stiff,' he said. 'It hasn't been used since last spring. There's a life-jacket hanging on a hook.' He padded off the coarse yellow grass and along the pebbly beach to the boat. 'Stay near the front or you'll probably tread on something sharp or pull something down on you.'

I looked along the shoreline. Nobody, and no wonder: the sky was all shades of slate and the water was whipped up by vicious squalls. White spray flew off the waves. I could hardly see the point from where I stood and the wind on my face felt icy. I scraped the key into the lock and with difficulty turned it, pushing one of the doors narrowly open. Inside, there was a jumble of objects: yellow and orange life-jackets hanging from a large hook on the wall to my left, two fishing rods standing propped against the opposite wall, several large nylon bags which, when prodded by my curious foot, turned out to contain sails. At the back of the shed lay a windsurfer. There were buckets, bailers, boxes with nails and hooks and small implements I didn't recognize, a few empty beer bottles, an old green tarpaulin, some pots of paints, sandpaper, a tool box, a crowbar, a broom. A thick smell of oil, salt, sweetness, rot, decay. There was probably a dead rat in here.

I laid the wet suit on a rough wooden bench and started to pull off my clothes, shivering in the icy, stagnant air. Then I tugged on the unwelcoming rubber. It closed relentlessly around my limbs. God, what was I doing here?

I'd dropped the little rubber shoes on my way to the bench so I gingerly hobbled across the shed to pick them up, trying to avoid stepping on wood chips and grit with my bare feet, and then tottered back. Sitting on the bench once more I rubbed the soles of my feet to remove the debris that had stuck to them. Something – it felt like a straw stalk – had caught between two toes. I prised them apart and removed it. A pink bit of paper twisted into the shape of something with four legs and a sort of head and a funny little tail. I rotated it in my fingers, a little cousin to the six creatures standing on my kitchen table.

Could Michael have brought it along? Could it have stuck to his clothes? 'It hasn't been used since last spring.' Last spring Danny and I had been squabbling in London. Danny had been here. I was in a fever. I knew that I needed to think clearly but the objects in the room were shifting in shape, making me dizzy. My stomach shifted. I felt each hair on my skin prickling against the inside of my outer, rubber, skin. There was a light of clarity on the edge of my mind and I had to calculate my way towards it, but everything I had been sure of was now twisted out of shape. Danny had been here.

'Remember your life jacket, Sam.'

I turned to the door where Michael was standing, silhouetted against the grey. I closed my fist around the little paper creature. He came towards me.

'Let me help you with that,' he said. He pulled the zip up behind me, so hard that it made me gasp. I was aware of his large physical presence. 'And now the boots.' He knelt in front of me. I sat down and he took both my feet in turn and gently eased them into the boots. He looked up with a smile. 'The slipper fits, Cinderella,' he said. Danny had been here. He took a yellow life-jacket from the hook and slipped it over my shoulders. 'And, finally, your gloves.' I looked down at my closed fist. I took the gloves in my left hand.

'I'll put them on in a minute.'

'Fine,' he said. 'We're ready.'

With an arm gently on my back, he escorted me down to the boat and we climbed on board. He looked at me, and with the wind blowing in our faces I couldn't make out his expression.

'Now, let's have a bit of fun.'

I'd been here before, the wet rope callusing my palm as I pulled it taut, the boat rising steeply in the wind, sails cracking in the gusts, iron-grey water slopping over the sides, the weird cries of seabirds as we scudded our lonely way out to open sea, the curt commands of 'lee-oh' as I cast myself desperately from side to side, the silent minutes of leaning back against the boat's violent heeling. Danny had been in the boat-house. I tried to think of an innocent explanation. Could Danny have gone there on a walk with Michael? The door hadn't been opened since last spring. Michael had said so. The little paper creature was still clasped in my frozen fist.

We tacked swiftly away from the shore and the spray stung my face so that if I was crying he wouldn't know. And I didn't know. Images passed through my mind: Finn when she arrived at my house, so white and mute; Danny staring at her across the table – and the expression that I could vividly recall wasn't one of desire, then, but of discontent; Danny with Elsie, lifting her on to his lap, leaning down to her so that his black hair tangled with her blonde wisps. I tried to cling to wisps of thought. Danny had been there. Danny hadn't run away with Finn. Danny hadn't committed suicide.

'You're silent, Sam. Are you getting the hang of it?'

'Maybe.'

At that moment a gust caught us, and the boat lifted up so it was almost vertical. I leaned my whole weight out.

'There we are, we're almost round the point.' Michael sounded completely calm. 'Then we needn't go so close to the wind. Ready about . . .'

And we swung, with a neat whip of the boom and a smack of the sails, into open sea, with the wind steady from the side. I looked back, and I couldn't see the shore we'd started from. It was lost in mist and grey glare.

'That was pretty good.'

'Thanks.'

'Are you beginning to feel better, Sam?'

I attempted a shrug and a neutral mumble.

'What was that?'

'I don't feel sick,' I said. He looked at me closely. He turned away. He was holding the tiller and mainsheet with one hand now and fiddling with something in his other. I looked around. Then he was close beside.

'What did you find, Sam?'

There was a metallic cold sensation in the pit of my stomach.

'Nothing,' I said.

Very quickly, before I could move, he seized my right wrist and opened the fingers. He was strong. He took the small paper animal from me.

'I suppose,' he said. 'It might have stuck to your clothes.'

'Yes,' I said.

'Or it might have got stuck on *my* clothes.'

'Yes,' I said.

He gave a spooky little giggle and shook his head.

'Sadly not,' he said. 'Pull your jib in tighter, Sam, we're going to beat a bit.'

The wind was getting stronger again; it bit into my left cheek. Michael pulled on the tiller so that the boat swung away from the wind and let the mainsail billow. We had safely rounded the point and were now heading back to the coastline, towards the sharp needles of rocks that he'd pointed out last time. I turned and looked at him from close up. His strange face looked its best in the wind and the spray. The fog in my mind was slowly dispersing. Finn had been murdered. Danny had been murdered, and I was going to be murdered. I had to speak.

'You killed Finn.'

Michael looked at me with a half-smile playing across his features but said nothing. His pupils were dilated: there was excitement coursing under that composed surface. What had he once told me about liking a challenge?

'A spot of running now, let your jib out, Sam.'

I obediently spooled the rope out and the small sail filled with wind. The boat sat back, lifted its bows; water surged beneath us.

'And did Danny stumble on it? Is that it? So you killed Danny, staged the suicide? And that note, that awful note.'

Michael gave a modest shrug.

'Unfortunately a degree of coercion was required to produce that. But you're failing to appreciate the whole picture, Sam.'

'And then . . .' I didn't care about anything, I didn't care about my own life, I just had to know. 'You and Finn killed her parents together, I suppose.' The *Belladonna* was taking us towards the treacherous cross-currents: I saw the way he was measuring distance with his calculating sailor's gaze. I looked down towards the water. Death by drowning.

'Something like that,' he replied casually, and smiled again as if a joke had occurred to him. His teeth and his grey eyes shone, his hair whipped back in the wind and spray: he looked eager, rather beautiful, appalling.

And then I thought of Elsie. I remembered how her

body felt against mine; I could almost feel her strong little arms around my neck. I remembered how she'd looked that morning when I'd dropped her off at school, in her purple tights and her spotty dress and her solid legs and her freckles. The shine on her hair. Her concentration, pink tip of tongue sticking out when she painted. I wasn't going to die out here and leave my daughter an orphan. I idled with the rope between my fingers.

'Why kill Finn then?'

He laughed then; really threw back his head and guffawed as if I'd made a brilliant joke.

'For the money, of course. But you're still not seeing the whole, beautiful picture.'

Then the boat tilted violently, as if the wind had suddenly changed direction. The sails flapped and the boom lurched. Without Michael saying anything, I tightened the jib as he pulled in his mainsail, and the boat raced towards the violent eddy. I could see it now: the shiny patch of sucked-in water. The outcrop of rocks was getting closer, their crags and splinters coming into focus. The wind was suddenly up and I could only shout.

'Needle Point?' I asked.

He nodded.

'You're going to kill me.'

But I spoke too quietly for him to have heard and he was immersed in the business of sailing. I looked at the bottom of the boat. A bailer. A long metal pole. A spare sail stowed at the bows. A coil of rope. A pair of oars. The boat was like a bucking horse now, thwacking its nose over and over into the trough of the sea. Suddenly it stopped, halted in its tracks, and I could feel no wind at all, although all around me I could see the wild sea. The sails wilted. We were in the eye of the storm. I looked across at Michael, who was looking at me. He shook his head, as if in disappointment.

'It's so irritating and unnecessary,' he said. 'Like the bloody cleaner.'

'Like Mrs Ferrer? You . . .?'

Michael turned away. He was looking from side to side, trying to assess where the wind would come from. He said nothing, and we sat side by side – me and the man who was going to kill me – in the becalmed moment. For an instant Michael seemed almost embarrassed by the awkward hiatus. Then it hit us full from behind and the boat jolted. Its sails smacked loudly, like a gun going off, and it lifted its bow so high out of the water that I was flung to its bottom. For one moment I thought it would do a backward somersault on to us. I looked up, my legs thrashing, and saw Michael's face looking down at me. It loomed out of the weather, handsome and polite.

'Sorry, Sam,' he said, leaning towards me as if he were bowing. He had the pole in his hand.

I rose, bailer in my hand, and hurled myself at the boom. It swung towards Michael but he ducked. I threw the bailer at his head and kicked wildly at him. He grunted and let go of the tiller and mainsheet and pole. Water was pouring in now and the boom was crashing from side to side. Michael dived at my waist and brought me down to the bottom of the boat once again. His face was a few inches from mine; a trickle of blood oozed down his forehead. There was a trace of stubble beneath the sweat and spray. I brought my knee up under the cage of his straining body and kneed him sharply in the groin, then, as he spasmodically jerked, I bit at the nearest lump of flesh. His nose. He shouted and punched at my jaw, my neck, into my breasts, into the bouncy rubber of my stomach. One finger pierced my eye so that for a moment the world was a red ball of pain. I could feel his breath and I could feel the blows rain down on my body, my jaw, my ribs.

Michael heaved himself into position, knees on my outstretched arms, and put his hands around my neck. I spat at him, my blood on his bloody, grimacing face. This was it. I was to be throttled and tossed overboard like a bit of live bait. He started to squeeze, slowly and with concentration. Behind his head I saw the giant shape of Needle Point bearing down on us, blotting out the sky. I bucked under Michael's body. I needed to live. I needed to live so badly. I thought that if I could say Elsie's name out loud I would live. I opened my mouth and felt my tongue slide forward, my eyes roll back. If I could say Elsie's name I would still live, though my world had gone black.

There was a jolt from beneath the hull, a screeching sound of wood on rock. Michael was thrown off me. Black waves; black rocks all around. I knelt up, grasped the pole, and as Michael stood on the breaking boat I thrust it into his body with all the force I could manage and saw him tip. It wasn't enough. I looked around, desperately, hungrily. The tiller. I pulled it sharply towards me. The wild boom jibed and viciously struck him; his body crashed into the sea.

'Elsie,' I said. 'Elsie, I'm coming home.' Then the boat broke against the rocks and the water closed around me.

Twenty-Nine

First I was dimly aware of movement. I knew I'd been gone, lost somewhere timeless, dark. My eyelids fluttered. I saw a face. I yielded with relief to the blackness once more. On later attempts – I didn't know how much later – the light became easier to take and the shapes that sometimes moved around my bed became clearer, but I still couldn't make sense of them. I started to put imaginary faces on the shapes. Danny, Finn, my father, Michael. It was all too much effort.

One day, the light seemed greyer and more bearable. I heard a footstep and felt a nudge against the bed. I opened my eyes and everything was clear. I was back and Geoff Marsh was standing over me with a quizzical gaze.

'Fuck,' I said.

'Yes,' he said, looking uneasily at the door. 'Your mother went down to the cafeteria. I said I'd stay for a few minutes. I just walked down from the office for a moment. Maybe I should get a doctor. How are you, Sam?'

I murmured something.

'Eh?'

'All right.'

Geoff pulled a chair over and sat beside me. He smiled suddenly. Almost laughed. I wrinkled my face in puzzlement. Even that small movement made me flinch in pain.

'I was thinking of our last meeting,' he said. 'Do you remember it?'

I gave a slow, painful shrug.

'You agreed that you were going to keep a low profile. Avoid publicity.'

It seemed too much of an effort to speak.

'At least the media aren't interested in post-traumatic stress any more,' Geoff continued jovially. 'Boating accidents, miraculous escapes. I think the unit is safely out of the spotlight.'

I gathered all my resources and grabbed Geoff's sleeve.

'Michael.'

'What?'

'Daley. Where?' I forced myself. 'Where is Michael Daley?'

Suddenly Geoff looked scared and shifty. I tightened my grip on his sleeve.

'Is he here? Must tell me.'

'They haven't told you? You haven't been conscious really.'

'What?'

'I think you should talk to a doctor.'

'*What?*'

I was shouting now.

'All right, Sam,' Geoff hissed. 'For God's sake, don't make a scene. I'll tell you. Daley is dead. He was drowned. They only found his body yesterday. It was amazing that anybody could survive that. I don't know how you got to the shore. And then it was hours before you were found. With the shock and the exposure, you're lucky to be alive.' He tried to remove his sleeve from my grasp. 'Could you let me go now?'

'Baird. Get me Baird.'

'Who's Baird?'

'Detective. Stamford CID.'

'I think I should get a doctor first. And your mother's been here for days.'

I was almost at the limit of strength. Trying to shout, I could only manage a croaking whisper.

'Baird. Now.'

I was woken by a murmured conversation. I opened my eyes. Rupert Baird was talking to a middle-aged man in a pinstriped suit. When he noticed I was awake, the man came and sat on the side of the bed. He gave me an almost mischievous smile.

'Hello, I'm Frank Greenberg. I'd been looking forward to meeting you on your arrival. I didn't quite expect it to happen like this though.'

I almost laughed and as I did so realized I was feeling stronger, more supple.

'Sorry to be dramatic,' I said.

'Is this how you generally arrive at your new posts?'

'I didn't know I *had* arrived.'

'Oh yes, in fact your PTSD unit will be just along the corridor. We can wheel you along there for a look in a day or two if you keep improving.'

'I'm feeling better, I think.'

'Good. You may be surprised to learn that you were in a very serious condition indeed when you were brought in.'

'What symptoms?'

'BP crashing. Obvious signs of peripheral vasoconstriction. It was a cocktail of exposure and shock symptoms. You were extremely fortunate. As you can see, you were on the verge of acute circulatory failure.'

'How was I found?'

'A man was walking on the shore with his dog and his mobile phone.'

Baird stepped forward.

'Can I have a word?' he asked.

Dr Greenberg turned to me.

'All right?'

'Yes.'

'No more than five minutes.'

I nodded. Dr Greenberg held out his hand.

'Good to meet you, Dr Laschen,' he said. 'I'll see you again tomorrow morning.'

Baird approached and awkwardly looked for a perch. The moulded plastic chair was in the far corner. He considered whether to sit on the bed in the spot that Dr Greenberg had vacated.

'Take a seat,' I said and he sat uncomfortably on the very edge. He looked utterly miserable.

'I'm glad you're all right, Sam. This is a blighted case, isn't it?' He put his right hand on mine, awkwardly. 'At some point there may be one or two routine questions but there's no need now . . .'

'It was Michael.'

'What do you mean?'

'I was in the boat-house and on the floor I found one of those little paper animals Danny used to make.'

Baird gave a resigned sigh and tried to look sympathetic.

'Yes, well, in itself, that doesn't prove . . .'

'Michael told me, Rupert. He tried to kill me on the boat. That's how we went overboard. He and Finn killed Finn's parents. And he killed Mrs Ferrer. And then Michael killed Finn. He killed Danny.'

Baird responded with a mock double take and his eyes wrinkled into a smile.

'You don't believe me.'

'Of course I believe you, Sam. Now, a cynical copper might say that you have been through a terrible experience, you suffered from concussion and shock and you . . . er . . .'

'Might have imagined it all?'

'I'm an overly cautious man, Sam. I have to imagine what certain sticklers for evidence might say to me as they demoted me to walking the beat again. If you have anything concrete to offer us, Sam, we will be most interested in investigating it.'

I'd been sitting up, but now I sank back exhausted on to my pillow.

'I don't care what you do, Rupert. *I* know, and that's enough for me. Why don't you have a look at Michael's boat-house? I think that's where he kept Danny's body. Where he made him write that suicide note. Shot him.'

Baird was silent for a long time. I couldn't see his face.

'All right,' he said. 'We'll have a look. I think my five minutes must be up and there is one more senior figure who requires to see you straight away.'

'Oh, for God's sake, if it's Geoff Marsh or some other bloody manager, tell them to fuck off.'

Baird smiled.

'I'm sorry, Sam. I'm afraid this is somebody who is too senior for me to give orders to.'

'What is it? A royal visit or something?'

'Close.' Baird walked to the door and spoke to someone outside who I couldn't see. 'She can come in now.'

I looked, expectantly, and a familiar freckled face appeared about a yard below where I was expecting one.

Shoes clicked across the floor and Elsie jumped on to the bed and on top of me. I hugged her so close and tight that I could count the vertebrae in her spine. I was afraid of hurting her with the urgency of my grasp.

'Oh, Elsie,' I said. 'You can be my nurse now.'

She wriggled free of me.

'I am *not* your nurse,' she replied firmly.

'My doctor, then.'

'I am *not* your doctor. Can we go out and play?'

'Not just yet, my love.'

She looked at me with narrowed, suspicious eyes.

'You're not ill,' she announced, almost in challenge.

'No, I'm not. I'm a bit tired, but in a couple of days we can run around and play.'

'I saw a camel.'

'Where?'

'And a *big* camel.'

In the doorway I saw my mother hovering with ostentatious discretion. I waved her over and we hugged like we hadn't hugged for years, and then she started whispering about Elsie with such a show of secrecy that Elsie immediately began asking about it. I started to cry and couldn't conceal it and my mother led Elsie out of the room and I was alone again. I'd suddenly thought of Danny. Not the Danny from the past but the Danny I would never know anything about. I pictured him being held at gunpoint and made to write his note to me and I made myself imagine what he must have felt. He must have died thinking he had betrayed me and that I would never know. Ever since I was a teenager, I have been able to make myself giddy with the thought of my death, the disappearance into oblivion. The idea of Danny's death was more terrible and I felt it not just in my mind but on my skin and and at the back of my eyes and humming in my ears, and it made me cold and implacable.

My mother had moved into the house to look after Elsie. Her sympathy was operatic.

'I suppose the house will hold unhappy memories for you,' she said. 'Can you bear to go back to it?'

I didn't want to be told what to feel.

'The house has Elsie. It has no bad memories for me.'

Within a couple of days I felt strong enough to leave hospital and two days after that I was able to ease my mother on to a train at Stamford and myself out of her debt. Everything was all right, except that I heard nothing from Baird and I knew that there was something I wasn't dwelling on because if I did, I didn't know where it could stop. A full week after I had spoken to Baird, Chris Angeloglou rang and asked me if I could come in to the station. I asked what for and he said they wanted a statement but also that I might learn something to my advantage. Could I come that afternoon?

I was led into an interview room with Chris and Rupert. They were being very nice to me and smiling. They sat me down, brought me tea and biscuits, switched on their double tape recorder and asked me about the events of the day of Michael's death. With all their questions and my replies, additions and insertions, it took me almost an hour and a half, but by the end they seemed well satisfied.

'Excellent,' said Rupert, as he finally switched off the machine.

'So you believe me?'

'Of course we do. Hang on a moment. Phil Kale was supposed to be here at three-thirty. I'll go and see if he's around.'

Rupert got up and left the room. Chris yawned and rubbed his eyes.

'You look the way *I'm* supposed to look,' I said.

'It's all your fault,' said Chris with a grin. 'We've been hard at it since your tip-off. You're going to enjoy this.'

'Good. I need some enjoyment.'

Baird came back in leading the distracted, dishevelled man I remembered from the day we found Mrs Ferrer dead. Now his wire-framed spectacles had a sticking-plaster on one of the hinges and he wore a corduroy jacket of the sort that I had last seen on several of my teachers in the late seventies. Under his arm was a thick stack of files. Chris pulled a chair over and the man sat down.

'This is Dr Philip Kale, Home Office pathologist. Phil, this is our heroine, Dr Sam Laschen.'

We shook hands, which resulted in many files being scattered on the floor.

'DI Baird tells me you've just made a statement about Dr Daley's admission.'

'Yes.'

'Good. I can only stay a minute. They've just pulled a lollipop lady out of the canal. I can just tell you that what you told the police seems to be confirmed by the full range of forensic evidence. God, where should I start?'

'Did you check Michael's boat-house?' I asked.

'Yes,' Kale said. 'There were copious traces of blood in the boat-house. We've done a series of serological tests. We also found fibres and hairs and did a Neutron Activation Analysis on the hair samples. We've cross-referenced them with hair samples from Mr Rees and some found at the Mackenzie house. We're still waiting for some results of DNA tests but I know what they're going to tell us. For undetermined periods and at undetermined times, the bodies of Daniel Rees and Fiona Mackenzie were kept in Michael Daley's boat-house. This is confirmed by my post-mortem findings on the burnt bodies. There was an absence of hyperaemia, no positive protein reaction, and a host of other signs showing that they were dead when the car was set on fire.'

'So Finn's, I mean Fiona's, dead body was in the boat-house as well?'

'Traces of hair and fibre associated with Fiona Mackenzie were found attached to a canvas sheet in a rear corner of the boat-house. The assumption, the near certainty, is that it was used for wrapping her body. And now I must go to the canal.'

'What about Mrs Ferrer?'

Kale shook his head.

'I think you must have misunderstood. I've been over my report. There's nothing I could find.'

'Why would he have done it?' Baird asked.

'I don't know,' I said numbly.

Kale held out his hand.

'Well done, Dr Laschen.'

'Well done?'

'This is *your* triumph.'

'It's not my triumph.'

We shook hands and Kale left the room. Angeloglou and Baird were grinning like schoolboys with a dirty secret.

'What have you got to look so happy about?' I asked.

'We're holding a press conference tomorrow morning,' said Baird. 'We shall be revealing our findings and announcing that the cases involving the murders of Leopold and Elizabeth Mackenzie, Fiona Mackenzie and Daniel Rees are now closed. There are no further inquiries pending. We shall also give you full credit for your own contribution and your heroic actions *vis-à-vis* Michael Daley. You may even be recommended for some form of civilian award. That should square you with the hospital. Everybody will be happy.'

'Let's not overstate it.'

'I don't want to be insensitive to what you've been through,' said Rupert. 'But in the circumstances this must be the best possible conclusion.'

'I'm sorry,' I said. 'I need to think all this through. Do you know how the murders of the parents were committed?'

'You really need to talk to Kale about that. It looks as if Daley and the girl tied up and killed the parents in the middle of the night. Fiona allowed herself to be tied up by Daley. When the cleaner arrived, Daley used a scalpel and made what was basically a shallow incision in her neck and then escaped down the back stairs that lead into the garden. We'd always thought that there was relatively little blood because she had gone into shock with a massive drop in blood pressure. In fact, it was because the wound had been inflicted only a few minutes before. Is everything all right? You don't look happy.'

'I keep going over it in my head, trying to disentangle it.' I said. 'It was all a fake. Finn helped to cut the throats of her own parents and then allowed her own throat to be cut. Is there anything in her past that was consistent with that?'

Chris looked puzzled.

'You mean, had she killed anyone before?'

'No, I don't mean that. Was there evidence of serious conflict with her parents? Or medical instability?'

'There was £18,000,000. I'm afraid there are a lot of people out there who would cut their parents' throats for a lot less than that. And we've ascertained from his bank that Dr Daley was living well beyond his means. He was seriously in debt.'

'What about the stuff on the wall? The animal rights connection?'

'Daley knew about that because he was involved with monitoring animal rights terrorists. It gave him the perfect opportunity to shift suspicion. It's all perfectly simple.'

I forced myself to think, the way I used to do mental arithmetic at school, when I would wrinkle my nose and my forehead and think so hard that it hurt.

'No, it isn't,' I said. 'It may be true but it's not perfectly simple. Why did Finn make a will in favour of Michael Daley? That was convenient for him, wasn't it?'

'Maybe they were going to get married.'

'Oh, for God's sake, Rupert. And there's one other thing.'

'What's that?'

'You may remember that I raised the suspicion about Michael Daley before and you demonstrated to me that he couldn't have any connection with the burning of the car. As far as I understand it, you have no evidence putting him at the murder scene of the Mackenzies and you told me that he was in Belfast when the car was burned.'

The two men looked at each other sheepishly. Or were they winking at each other? Rupert opened his hands in an appeasing gesture.

'Sam, Sam, you were right, we were wrong. What do you want us to do, get down on our knees? I admit, there are one or two loose ends, and we are going to do our best to tie them up, but in real life things are hardly ever neat. We know what was done and we know who did it. We probably will never know exactly how.'

'Would you get a conviction if Michael Daley had got to the shore?'

Baird held up a finger in sanctimonious admonishment.

'Enough, Sam. This is going to be good for all of us. We've got a result. You're going to be a famous heroine like Boudicca and . . . er . . . like . . .' He looked helplessly at Angeloglou.

'Edith Cavell,' volunteered Angeloglou brightly.

'She was executed.'

'Florence Nightingale, then. What's important is that this is over and that we can all get back to our lives. In a few months we'll meet for a drink and laugh about all of this.'

'The George Cross,' I said.

'What?'

'I've always rather fancied the George Cross as a medal.'

'You weren't *that* brave. If you had drowned, you could have got the George Cross.'

I got up to leave.

'If I'd drowned, you wouldn't have known what a wonderful heroine I was. See you on TV, Rupert.'

Thirty

I was doing lots of things at the same time. I was *feeling* lots of things at the same time. For once in my life, it felt good to be absorbed in all that boring stuff that is only noticed when it isn't being done – keeping the house organized, getting things washed, paying some attention to what Elsie was wearing, standing over Sally to make sure she did something more than just wash the kitchen floor and straighten the piles of paper on the kitchen table and take out the rubbish. Once a week Elsie went out and was bullied by Kirsty and once a week Kirsty came to us and was bullied by Elsie. I found a second friend for her, Susie, a thin, anaemic-looking child with ribbons in her blonde hair and a scream like a road drill. For the afternoons when Elsie was alone I bought a big colourful book, and each late afternoon we sat and counted the bananas in each bunch and grouped animals according to legs and wings, or size, or whether they lived in water or on land. Despite all the biology, it was meant to teach her maths.

I got through chapter after chapter of my book, like a burrowing mole. My routine barely altered. Take Elsie to school. Write. Eat sandwich made with what was to hand and didn't have anything growing on it that wasn't easily removable. Go for brisk walk down to the sea to catch the tide at its highest. Look at it and think complicated things. Go back home. Write.

Thoughts rotated in my mind as I went over and over them, constructing more or less plausible structures out of the flotsam and jetsam that I could gather. There were simple bits and complicated bits. The motive for the murders was Finn's inheritance of a great deal of money and perhaps also some sense of grievance. The crime was conceived and committed by Michael Daley with a child who had always been pampered and had, so far as reports showed, never shown any signs of the smallest adolescent rebellion. But of course we psychologists always have a simple response to that. Evidence of rebellion? QED. No evidence at all of rebellion? Worse still, it must have been bottled up, unexpressed, until it all came out at once. QED likewise.

The act itself was simple enough. The murder was presumably being planned anyway when Michael, through his work on the committee monitoring animal terrorism, learned of the threat against Leo Mackenzie. It would be an obvious opportunity. The only requirement was to commit the murders in such a way that it might seem like the work of particularly crazed animal rights activists, hence the trussing up and throat-cutting and wall-daubing. I felt that I had known Leo and Liz Mackenzie only through a couple of blurred photographs in the newspapers and – I felt with a heave in my chest – from a few bland things Finn had said about them. But they didn't seem real to me. What did seem real, a huge stain in the lattices of my logical thought, was the image of Danny with a gun barrel against his temple. Did he cry and plead, or was he brave and silent? What had I been doing at the moment when he knew there was no hope, that he wouldn't be able to bargain himself out of being killed? Feeling angry or sorry for myself, probably.

And he'd killed Finn, his accomplice, too. I thought of the garrulous letter she had written to me, and I just could not understand how she could have produced such a gush of words with a gun to her head. Yet how little I knew her, after all. I kept worrying at all the little memories of Finn in my house, as if I were probing a broken tooth with my tongue. Each touch would provoke waves of pain and nausea, yet I couldn't resist it. Finn sitting numbly on my sofa. Finn in her room. My own brilliant coaxing of her back into life with the use of my own little daughter. Finn destroying her clothes. Conversations in the garden. Sitting drinking wine and giggling together. Telling Finn about chess. Letting Finn look after me. It was a form of self-torture. Confiding in Michael Daley. Michael Daley complimenting me on how well I had handled Finn. Oh God oh God oh God oh God. I was the gull in an extended confidence trick that had begun in blood in a Stamford suburb, continued as a charade enacted in my house and finished in a fire on a lonely stretch of Essex coastline.

Then there was Mrs Ferrer. What was *that* about? Had Michael really said that he had killed her, or had I misunderstood at a moment when I feared for my own life? I tried to go over anything that Mrs Ferrer might have found out. Perhaps as a cleaner she had come across a piece of damning evidence in the house and mentioned it to a man she trusted – her doctor. But what could it have been?

Suddenly, on one rainy spring afternoon, as I stood in grey rain watching the sailing boats in sunshine a mile away, in the middle of the estuary, I asked myself the question that I tried to cure my own patients of asking: 'Why me?' I thought of how I had become part of the murderous deception, and how effectively I had played that part, me with my unmatched expertise, my acuteness of perception, my skill in diagnosis.

'But she wasn't my patient,' I muttered to myself, as if I would be embarrassed for my whining to be overheard by a gull or by the reeds. How I wished that the plan could have been carried out without me or that somebody else could have been chosen, somebody else's life ruined, someone else's lover killed.

'Why me? Why me?' And then I found myself cutting the question short. 'Why? Why?'

I put it to myself as a chess match. If you are a clear bishop ahead, you don't throw yourself into a speculative sacrifice. You simplify. Michael Daley and Finn Mackenzie's motive was disgusting but it was simple. So why was their crime so complicated? I went over the event in my head yet again. I couldn't understand why Finn had to be there for the crime, with all the added risk of Michael Daley being caught. She could have been somewhere else, with a perfect alibi, and there would have been no need for the cutting of her throat and the long, detailed, hazardous charade that ensnared me and Elsie and poor Danny and poor, sad Mrs Ferrer, if indeed she had been ensnared. And then why should Finn change her will so suddenly, leaving everything to the man who would murder her? Did she commit suicide after all? Did Michael kill her because he suddenly decided that half was not enough? Neither version seemed to make sense. I tried to construct a scenario in which Michael killed the parents and forced Finn into complicity by threatening her with murder, but none of it quite worked in my head.

I did no more work that afternoon. I just walked into the wind and rain until I saw by my watch that I had to run to be home to meet Elsie. I was out of breath when I ran along the drive, a sour pain in my chest, and I saw the car was already back. I ran inside and picked up my little bundle and held her close against me, burying my face in her hair. She pushed herself back and reached for some incomprehensible picture she had drawn at school. We got out the paints and covered the kitchen table with newspaper and did more pictures. We did three puzzles. We played charades and hide-and-seek all over the house. Elsie had her bath and we read two whole books. Occasionally I would stop and point to a short word – 'cow', 'ball', 'sun' – and ask Elsie what it was, and she would look at the picture above the text for clues. If it was totally obvious – 'The cow jumped over the . . . What comes next, Elsie?' – she would make an elaborate pretence of spelling out the word – 'Mer . . . oo . . . oo . . . ner . . . moon!' – that in its elaborate mendacity impressed me more than if she had simply been able to read.

After her bath I held her plump, strong, naked body and rubbed my face in her sweet-smelling hair ('Are you looking for nits?' she asked) and I suddenly realized two things. I had spent almost three hours without brooding on horror and deceit and humiliation. And Elsie wasn't asking after Finn or even Danny. In my darker moments I sometimes felt as if there were slime on the walls left by the people who had been inside them, but Elsie had moved on. I held her close and felt that she at least was unpolluted by the evil. I croaked a couple of songs to her and left her.

Though it was barely after eight o'clock, I made myself a mug of some instant coffee or other that was nominally reserved for Linda's use, topped it up with lots of milk and went up to bed. Elsie had survived this horror the way it seems that children are designed to do and I had a sudden impulse to take her away from all of this, go somewhere safe, away from fear and danger. I had never escaped. As a teenager I had kept my head down and worked and worked. I had worked even harder as a medical student and then harder still once I had qualified. There had never been a light at the end of the tunnel. Just the next examination or prize or scholarship or job that nobody thought I could get. Food and fun and sex and the other things that life is meant to consist of had been something to grab bite-sized pieces of along the way.

A thought occurred to me and I gave a bitter smirk. I'd forgotten. Finn had got away from it all, backpacked her way around South America, or whatever the hell it was she'd done. She'd even polluted the idea of safety and purity. I remembered the one item of Finn's that I had held back. I sprinted across the chilly room, grabbed the chunky paperback and sprinted back to bed, pulling the covers over me. I looked at the book properly for the first time. *Practically Latin America: The Smart Guide*. I grunted. *The best guides in the world – five million copies sold*. I grunted again. Getting away from it all, indeed. Nevertheless I began to have a fantasy of taking a year or two years off and heading around South America, just me and Elsie. There were some practical obstacles: my unit was about to open, I had no money, I couldn't speak a word of Spanish. But children are good at languages. Elsie would soon pick it up and she could be my interpreter.

Peru, everybody said that was beautiful. I flicked through the book until I came to a paragraph in the Peruvian section headed 'Problems':

The urban centres of Peru should be treated with caution.

Robbery of tourists is endemic – pockets are picked; bags snatched; the razoring of packs or pockets is a local speciality. Confidence tricksters and police corruption are rife.

I grunted once more. Elsie and I could handle that. Where was it that Finn had gone? Mitch something. I looked in the index. Machu Picchu. That was it. I turned to the entry: 'The most famous and sublime archaeological site in South America.' I could take a year's sabbatical and we could travel round and Elsie would have the advantage of being fluent in Spanish. My eye drifted down the page until it was stopped by some familiar words:

If you are lucky enough to be in the area for the full moon, visit the Machu Picchu site at night. (US $7 for a boleto nocturno.*) Look at the Intihuatana – the only stone calendar that wasn't destroyed by the Spaniards – and contemplate the effects of light and the fates of empires. The Inca empire is gone. The Spanish empire is gone. All that remains are the ruins, the fragments. And the light.*

There it was, Finn's great transcendent experience, pinched from a crappy little travel guide. I remembered Finn's shining eyes, the tremble in her voice as she had described it to me. It felt like my final failure. There had been a little vain bit of me still left in a corner of my psyche which hoped that I had got somewhere with Finn. Despite the wickedness and the deception, she had liked me a bit, just as she had won Elsie's love. Now I knew that even there, where it wouldn't have mattered, she hadn't taken the trouble to toss me something real. It was all fake, all of it.

Thirty-One

'Have you thought of seeing someone about what's happened? I mean, you know . . .'

Sarah was sitting at my kitchen table, making sandwiches. She'd brought cream cheese, ham, tomatoes, avocados – real food – and was now layering them between thick slices of white bread. She was one of the few people I could stand to have around me. She was straightforward and talked about emotions objectively, as if she were a mathematician puzzling over a problem. Now the sun was streaming in through the windows, and we had the afternoon to ourselves before Elsie came home from school and Sarah returned to London.

'You mean,' I took a swig of beer, 'go and see a trauma counsellor?'

'I mean,' Sarah said calmly, 'that it must be hard to get over what's happened.'

I stared at the crooked metal eye of the beer can.

'The trouble is,' I said at last, 'there are so many bits to it. Anger. Guilt. Bafflement. Grief.'

'Mmm, of course. Do you miss him a lot?'

I often dreamed about Danny. Usually, the dreams were happy ones, not of losing him, but of finding him again. In one, I was standing by a bus stop and I saw him walking towards me; he held out his arms and I slid into their empty circle like coming home. It was so physical – his heartbeat against mine, the warm hollow of his neck – that when I woke I turned in the huge bed to hold him. In another I was talking to someone who didn't know about his death, and crying, and suddenly the stranger's face became Danny's and he smiled at me. I woke and tears were streaming down my face.

Every morning, I lost him all over again. My flesh ached for him, not so much with desire as with loneliness. My homesick body recalled him: the way he would cup the back of my head with a hand, the rasp of his roughened fingers on my nipples, his body folded against my folds in bed. Sometimes I would pick Elsie up and hug her until she cried out and struggled to get away. My love for her felt, suddenly, too big and too needy.

Too often I would take out the letter he had written to his sister. I wouldn't read it but would stare at the bold black script and let phrases come into focus. I only had a few photographs of him; he'd always been the one behind the camera, the way most men are. There was one of both of us in shorts and T-shirts; I was looking at the camera and he was looking at me. I couldn't remember who'd taken the picture. There was another of him lying on his back and holding Elsie up on his lifted legs. His face was out of focus in the sunlight, a bleached-out blur where his eyes should be, but Elsie's mouth was agape in panicky delight. Mostly, he was turned away from the camera lens, hidden. I wanted a photo of him that would stare directly at me, like a film star's glossy publicity, for I was terribly scared of forgetting what he looked like. Only in my dreams did I see his face properly.

'Yes', I answered Sarah, picking up a sandwich that

disgorged tomato as I lifted it to my mouth, 'yes, I miss him.' I chewed a bit, then added, 'I don't know how to restore him to his proper size in my memory. If you see what I mean.'

'What about her?'

'Finn, you mean? God, that's complicated. First of all I almost got to love her; she was part of the family, you see. Then, I hated her; I felt almost sick with hatred and humiliation. And then she died and it's as if that's stopped all my emotions in their tracks. I don't know what I feel about her. At sea.' I shivered at the figure of speech, remembering again the dark waters. I saw Michael Daley standing on the breaking boat and, in slow motion, I saw again the metal pole hitting him, the boom striking him, his long body buckling.

'The police keep saying how pleased they are that it's all cleared up, and never mind the loose ends, they can deal with those bit by bit, but I feel bothered. That's too little a word. I can't get it right in my head. There are things, I mean, I don't see how it was possible that . . .' I stopped abruptly. 'Let's have a game of chess. I haven't played for ages.'

I put the chess-board on the table and slid open the lid of the dark wooden box, picking out two smooth-headed pawns. I held out my fists and Sarah tapped my left hand.

'White,' I said, and we arranged the pieces on their squares. They stood there stalwartly in their ranks, the wood gleaming in the shafts of sunlight; a bird chirped outside, not the lonely cry of a seabird that sent shivers down my spine, but the homely mundane chirrup of an English garden bird sitting in a small tree whose leaves were just about to unfurl.

*

Later, after Sarah had left for London and I'd collected Elsie and settled her with Linda, I made a trip to the supermarket. I had been only a few days previously and the shelves and fridge at home were groaning with convenience food. But it calmed me to wheel my trolley up and down familiar alleys, picking out the solid comforting objects which were always in their proper place. I liked to compare the prices of reduced-sugar baked beans, washing powder, peanut butter.

I was hovering over a freezer full of puddings – should it be another pecan pie, or a lemon meringue? – when I heard a voice behind me.

'Sam?'

I took both puddings and turned.

'Why, hello, er . . .' I'd forgotten her name again, just as I had done the last time we'd met. The memory of Finn's shopping expedition surfaced briefly and painfully. That was the day I'd believed she'd started opening up to me. Now I knew it had been just part of the charade.

'Lucy,' she prompted me. 'Lucy Myers.'

'Of course. Sorry, I was miles away.' I balanced the puddings on the overflowing trolley. 'How are you?'

'No, how are *you*? she responded eagerly. 'You've been having such an awful time. I've been reading all about it, well, we all have. We admire what you did so much. So brave. It's all anyone's talking about at the hospital.'

'Great,' I said.

'Yes.' She pulled her trolley in from the centre of the aisle, so that it blocked my path. I was trapped beside the freezer by our trolleys' brimming cages, with Lucy as my beaming keeper. In her trolley I saw dog food, mineral water, leeks, deodorant, kitchen roll and bin-bags. I suddenly felt a bit sick and furtively discarded my lemon meringue pie. 'I mean, I can't believe you're so famous now. People must *recognize* you on the streets and things.'

'Sometimes.' I returned the pecan pie too.

'You nearly drowned. How awful.'

'It was,' I agreed. I must remember cat food for Anatoly.

'And do you know the *really* amazing thing?'

'No.'

She opened up the trolleys and stepped inside, putting her face close to mine. I could see the circles of her contact lenses.

'I knew her.'

'Who?'

She nodded emphatically at me, triumphant to have her own special slice of this delicious drama.

'I knew Fiona Mackenzie. Now isn't that weird, to know you and to know her too?'

'But . . .'

'It's true. My mother and her mother were friends. I even babysat for her when she was little.' Lucy giggled as if it were the most thrilling news in the world, that she had babysat for someone who'd later slaughtered her parents and then been burned up in a car. 'I hadn't seen her for a few years, maybe three years. She came to my sister's wedding with her parents. She . . .'

'Hang on, Lucy.' I spoke slowly as if she didn't understand English very well. 'You met her.'

'That's what I've just been saying, Sam.'

'No, I mean you met her with me. The last time you saw me, in Goldswan Green, I had a young woman with me, remember?'

'Well, of course.'

'Finn. Fiona Mackenzie.'

285

'That was Fiona? She was so slim, but I heard something about her problem.'

I nodded. 'Anorexia,' I said.

She looked at me, her round face creasing, and then a fat man, with his paunch hanging over his belt and sweat spreading under his armpits, heaved his trolley into our parked group.

'Mind where you're standing,' he barked.

'Mind where you're walking,' I snapped back, then looked at Lucy again. I wasn't about to let this woman get away; here at last was somebody who had actually known Finn Mackenzie. 'Tell me about her.'

'Describe her? Oh dear, well, she was,' she held her hands apart as if she were grasping a beach ball, 'rather round, you could say, but nice. Yes' – Lucy looked at me as if she'd given me some kind of key – 'very nice.'

I raised my eyebrows. 'Nice?'

'Yes. Quite quiet, I think, she didn't push herself forward. Perhaps she was a bit shy.'

'So she was nice and quiet?'

'Yes.' Lucy looked as if she were about to burst into tears. How did this woman ever get through the ward rounds? 'It's so long ago.'

'What did she look like then? How did she dress?'

'Well, I couldn't say really. Nothing outrageous, you know. She always looked quite pretty, I think, although she was very plump, of course. She wore her hair long and loose. Look, Sam, it's been lovely seeing you but . . .'

'Sorry, Lucy, your shopping awaits you. See you soon.'

'That'd be lovely.' The eager note of friendship came back into her voice now that we were parting. 'Hey, wait, Sam, what about your trolley?'

'I changed my mind,' I called as I strode empty-handed

down the aisle towards the exit. 'I didn't need anything after all.'

The house was absolutely quiet. Upstairs Elsie lay asleep, clean in her ironed pyjamas. I sat on the sofa, Anatoly on my lap, with only a single lamp to illuminate the room. I remembered one evening here with Danny, a few days after I'd moved and was still surrounded by packing cases and bare boards. He'd rented a video and bought us an Indian take-away which he'd spread out on newspaper in front of us. We sat cross-legged on the floor and watched the film, and I'd laughed so much that I started to weep. Danny had hugged me to him, pushing away the silver-foil containers with their slop of dark-red meats and sinister vegetables, and told me he loved me, and I'd gone on laughing, weeping. And never said it back. Never said I loved him. Not then, not later. So now I sat in his gown, with the cat and the darkness, and I said it to him. Over and over again I said it to him, as though somewhere there in the darkness and quiet he was listening, as though if I said it enough I could bring him back. And then I picked up a cushion and pressed my face into it and cried, heaving my heart out into a plump square of flowered corduroy.

And after that, I thought about Finn. She'd stayed in this house for nearly two months and she had hardly left a trace. She'd burned all her old clothes and taken her few new ones. She'd left no bits and pieces of her life. I looked around the dim room where I sat: its surfaces were cluttered with stuff I'd accumulated even in the last couple of months. The wobbly clay pot Elsie had made for me at school, the papier-mâché peach Sarah had presented me with today, a glass bowl I'd picked up in Goldswan Green because I loved its pure cobalt-blue, the ebony cat, yesterday's list of tasks, a wooden candlestick, a dying bunch of anemones, a box of Lil-lets, a pile of magazines, another pile of books, a pewter mug holding pens. But her room had always looked like a hotel room, and she'd entered it and left it without disturbing its anonymity at all.

What did I know about this girl who'd lived under the same roof as me for two months, shared my meals and charmed my daughter? Not much at all, although I realized as I thought that she had extracted a good deal of information from me. I'd even told her about Elsie's father. What had Lucy called her? And those schoolfriends of hers that I'd met at her parents' funeral? 'Sweet', was it; 'sweet' and 'nice'. And those family friends – they called her 'lovely' in that patronizing way that means 'no trouble'. She seemed memorable to me, with her youthful, soft-skinned radiance. Death usually fixes people, pinning them on to their finished life. But death seemed to be dissolving Finn, dispersing her like a cloud.

Thirty-Two

The days and the nights started to become normal, lacking in obvious incident so that one slid into the other. It would be an overstatement to describe the result as blissful, but it was just about bearable, and that would do for the moment. Things happened, of course. After a month more of grim concentration, the book was finished. My printer coughed out a satisfyingly large pile of paper, which I sent off to Sarah for a quick read and some encouragement. There were developments with Elsie. I started to suspect that if a word in one of her reading books was very short indeed, like 'cat' or 'son', then, given time, and when she was in a good mood, she might be able to work it out without the help of the picture above the text. And she made a third friend: Vanda, whose real name was Miranda. I invited her – or rather Elsie invited her and I confirmed the invitation – to stay the night.

And my unit was about to start, it really was. Two doctors and an SHO were appointed and on their way. I spent many hours in offices talking about details of pay and national insurance, I attended meetings about internal market practice at Stamford, and I went with Geoff Marsh on a round trip of insurance companies discussing the protection we offered against liability over rubber chicken and mineral water. Just one week of Dr Laschen's famous snakebite medicine and you are guaranteed free from all lawsuits. I sounded so marketable, I only wished I could own a piece of myself.

I thought of Danny, but not every bit of the time. He wasn't in every room of my house any longer. Occasionally I would open a door, a cupboard, and there he would be in some silly detail or object or memory but that was all. Sometimes I would wake in the night and cry, which was fine, but the obsessive, pointless speculating about the rest of our lives together, the bitterness at having him snatched away from me by a wicked lunatic, I didn't dwell on that so much any more.

The press attention was slackening off. The articles about the fallibility of the trauma industry had metamorphosed into columnists' analysis of the nature of female courage. My heroism had replaced my failure but I was no more interested in the second than in the first. There were invitations to be photographed in my garden, to discuss my childhood, my influences, to respond to questionnaires, to go on the radio and play my favourite records. I was offered the opportunity of talking to a radio psychiatrist about what it was like to have my lover murdered and then almost to be murdered myself. As, for the time being at least, the most famous expert in Britain on recovery from mental trauma, I decided that such exposure would not be helpful so, to the lightly suppressed exasperation of Geoff Marsh, I turned everything down.

There was one day, though, that didn't merge into all the others. It was the day when Miranda was coming to spend the night with Elsie and I had promised them a midnight feast. Over breakfast, Elsie had ordered biscuits, lollies, miniature salami sausages in silver paper, fromage frais, chocolate fingers, and as I wiped her mouth, brushed her hair and teeth, I calculated how I could go to the supermarket between meetings. We were in a desperate rush out of the door and I noticed it had started to pour with rain in iron-coloured streaks. I threw off my jacket and pulled on a raincoat and put a cap on my head.

'Put your raincoat on, Elsie,' I said.

She looked at me and started giggling.

'I haven't got time to play,' I said. 'Get your coat on.'

'You look funny, Mummy,' she said, in between gurgles.

With a sigh of exasperation I turned to the mirror. I started to laugh as well. I couldn't help it. I *did* look funny.

'You're like Hardy Hardy,' Elsie said.

She meant Laurel and Hardy. She had remembered a scene in one of her videos where they had got their hats mixed up. The cap was too small for me and perched precariously on the top of my head. What the bloody hell was it? I pulled the thing off my head and examined it. It was one of Finn's. I tossed it aside and grabbed my old trilby and we ran for the car.

'That was a funny hat, Mummy.'

'Yes, it was . . . er . . .' Well, why not? 'It was Finn's.'

'That was Fing's too,' she said, pointing at the trilby which nestled neatly on my head.

I stopped short and looked at it.

'Yes,' I said. 'That's right. It was. It . . .'

'Mumme-e-e-e. It's wet.'

'Sorry.'

I ran around the car and let her into the passenger seat and fastened her in, then ran back to the other side and sat beside her. I was very wet.

'You smell like a dog, Mummy.'

We had played musical statues, musical bumps and a

complicated game whose rules I never quite understood but which made Elsie and Miranda echo with laughter. They had their secret midnight feast at a quarter past eight and then I came in in the form of a ghost with a toothbrush to tell them a story. I looked for a book but Elsie said, 'No, out of your head, Mummy,' knowing that I only knew one story, so they sat back while I tried to remember the principal events of 'Little Red Riding Hood'. Did the grandmother die? Well, she wouldn't in my version. I tiptoed through all the details until I reached the climax.

'Come in, Little Red Riding Hood,' I said in a croaky voice.

'Hello, Granny,' I said in a little-girl voice. 'But what big ears you've got, Granny.'

'All the better to hear you with, my dear,' I said in my croaky voice. There were giggles from the bed.

'And what big eyes you've got, Granny,' I said in my little-girl voice.

'All the better to *see* you with,' I said in a croak that made me cough. More giggles.

'And what a big *mouth* you've got, Granny,' I piped. I left a long pause this time and looked at their expectant wide eyes.

'All the better to-o-o-o *eat you up*.' And I leaped on to the bed and enfolded the little girls in my arms and snapped at them with my lips. They shrieked and laughed and wriggled under me. After we composed ourselves, I spoke again in what was left of my normal voice.

'So who was it in the bed, Miranda?'

'Granny,' said Miranda, laughing.

'No, Miranda, it wasn't Granny. Who was in the bed, Elsie?'

'Granny,' said Elsie and they both howled with laughter, rolling and jumping on the bed.

'If something has eyes like a wolf, and it has ears like a wolf, and it has a mouth like a wolf, then what is it?'

'A gra-a-anny,' shouted Elsie and they both howled once more.

'You two are like naughty little wolf-cubs,' I said, 'and it's time you were asleep.' I hugged and kissed them and went downstairs where the lamp was swinging on its flex from their continued bouncing on Elsie's bed. There was a bottle of some old white wine in the fridge and I poured myself half a glass. I needed to think for a moment. There was something buzzing around in the recesses of my skull and I wanted to grab it. If it knew I was chasing it, it would escape. I would have to sneak up on it. I began muttering to myself.

'If something has eyes like a wolf, and it has ears like a wolf, and it has a mouth like a wolf, then it's a wolf.' I sipped at my wine. 'But if it doesn't have eyes like a wolf, and it doesn't have ears like a wolf, and it doesn't have a mouth like a wolf, and it doesn't howl at the moon, then what?'

I found a piece of paper and a pen and began to write things down. I compiled a list and then began to underscore and circle and join things with lines. I let the pen fall. I thought of Geoff Marsh and his medium-term strategy, I thought of Elsie and my new peaceful life, I thought of the absence of press attention and finally and inevitably I thought of Danny.

In a pocket of my purse with some ticket stubs and credit-card slips and my identity card for the hospital and bits of fluff and stupid things I should have thrown away was a slip of paper with Chris Angeloglou's home number on it. The last time we had met he had given it to me, saying if at any time I wanted to talk about things, I should feel free to give him a call. I suspect the plan was for him to apply his own brand of intrusive remedial therapy and I had responded with the driest of smiles. Oh God. The police were totally sick of me. Everybody – the family, the hospital, everybody – just wanted these terrible events to go away. If I let it go, there would be no problem. It would interfere with my work, unbalance me emotionally and stir up old memories for Elsie which could only harm her. And if I actually phoned Chris Angeloglou now, on top of everything else, he would probably imagine that I was asking him out on a date. But when I was sixteen I had sworn a very stupid oath to myself. At the end of your life, it is the things you *didn't* do, not the things you *did* do, that you regret. So, faced with a choice of action or inaction, I promised myself that I would always act. The results had been frequently disastrous and I didn't feel optimistic. I picked up the phone and dialled.

'Hello, is Chris Angeloglou there? Oh, Chris, hi. I was ringing . . . I wondered if we could meet for a drink. There's something I wanted to talk to you about . . . No, I can't do the evening. What about lunch-time? Fine . . . Is that the one in the square? . . . Fine, see you there.'

I replaced the receiver.

'Stupid, stupid, stupid,' I said to myself, consolingly.

Thirty-Three

A resource manager in a suit with strange lapels was trying to explain to me the philosophical difference between hospital beds as an accounting concept and hospital beds as physical objects that people can lie in, and by the time I half-understood it I realized I was running late. I tried to ring Chris Angeloglou but he was out. I conducted another meeting on the phone and another while walking along a hospital corridor. I cut even that short and ran to my car. I stopped to pick up a prescription for Elsie (as if there were any medicine which could cure lack of sleep in association with chronic naughtiness) and drove around the central Stamford car park, getting stuck for long periods behind people manoeuvring into tiny spaces when there were huge sections visibly free ahead.

By the time I puffed into the Queen Anne I was almost half an hour late. I immediately saw Chris seated in the far corner. As I drew closer, I saw he had made a complicated construction out of matches. I sat down heavily with a cascade of apologies and, naturally, it fell over. I insisted on getting drinks, and without waiting for any instructions I went to the bar and hysterically ordered two large gin and tonics, every flavour of crisps they had and a packet of pork scratchings.

'I don't drink,' said Chris.

'I don't really, either, but I thought just this once . . .'

'I mean I really don't drink.'

'What are you, a Muslim or something?'

'An alcoholic.'

'Really?'

'Yes, really.'

'Right. Can I get you a mineral water?'

'This is my third.'

'I'm extremely sorry, Chris. I know how busy you are. I got held up and tried to ring you but you were out. And now I'm babbling.'

Neither of us spoke for a moment and I tried to gauge how angry Chris was and whether this would do any good. He took a sip of his drink and attempted to give me a sympathetic smile.

'You're looking better, Sam,' he said.

'Better than what?'

'We were worried about you. A bit guilty as well.'

'There was nothing really to worry about. My ducking didn't even give me a cold.'

He lit a cigarette.

'Do you mind?' I shook my head. 'I wasn't thinking of that,' he continued.

'What were you thinking about?'

'It was difficult for you, in different ways. We felt sorry for you.'

'It was worse for other people.'

'You mean the murder victims?' Angeloglou laughed as if it required an effort. 'Yeah. Well, it's all in the past now. This new job must be good for you. We're looking for that Kendall girl. You probably saw it on TV.'

I shook my head.

'I don't watch TV.'

'You should. There are some good things on. American programmes mainly . . .'

Angeloglou tailed off and his eyes narrowed. He smiled inquiringly at me. This was the pause being left for me to explain why I had arranged this meeting.

'Chris, what's your version of what happened?'

The interest in his face slackened slightly, as if the dial had been turned down. He had a handsome face, dark, with prominent cheek-bones, a strong jaw-line, over which he sometimes ran his fingers as if he were surprised by its firmness. He was too neat for me. Too well groomed. He had been waiting for me to say that I had been wanting to get to know him better but had held back while the case was going on. But now, how about dinner some time and let's see what may happen? After all, I was a professional woman and one of those feminists and had funny hair, all of which probably meant I was sexually adventurous. Instead I was still being neurotic about the case.

'Sam, Sam, Sam,' he said, as if soothing a child who had woken in the night. 'You don't have to do this, you know.'

'I don't have to do anything, Chris, that's not the point.'

'You had a terrible, terrible time. You were traumatized . . .'

'Don't tell me about trauma.'

'And then you became a big heroine and we gave you lots of credit and were – still are of course – grateful to you. But it's over. I know that you're the expert and I shouldn't be telling you this but you've got to let this go.'

'Answer my question, Chris. Tell me what happened.'

He took a drag on his cigarette that was almost brutal.

'I'm not interested in talking about this case any more, Sam. Everybody involved is dead. It didn't go particularly well for anybody.' I gave a sarcastic snort. 'But we got away with it. I don't want to think about it.'

I sipped deeply from one of the gin and tonics. Then I took a deep breath and said, more or less honestly, 'Listen to me for five minutes and then if you're not interested, I won't mention it ever again.'

'That's the most promising suggestion you've made so far.'

I tried to put my thoughts in some sort of order.

'You believe that Finn and Michael killed the Mackenzies, and then Michael cut Finn's throat, even though it would have been easy for Finn to have been somewhere else with an alibi.'

Chris lit another cigarette.

'For God's sake, Sam, we've been through all this. I don't have to justify these murderers' behaviour to you. Maybe it needed two of them to do the murders. They're sick, fucking psychos, who knows what they enjoy? Perhaps they got a sado-masochistic kick out of a fake murder.'

'There's the murder of Mrs Ferrer.'

'Mrs Ferrer died from pulling a plastic bag over her head. It was a clear suicide.'

'Perhaps. But that still leaves the murder of Danny and Finn. You were the ones who proved to me that Michael couldn't have done it.'

'I can't believe I'm sitting here listening to this. Just concentrate for a moment, Sam. You made a statement to us saying that Michael Daley confessed to the murders. The forensic evidence from the boat-house clearly confirmed your statement. It is not reasonable to doubt that Daley and Fiona Mackenzie killed the Mackenzies and then that Daley, with or without Fiona Mackenzie, killed

Danny Rees, and then Daley killed Fiona Mackenzie, disposing of any link with the crime. If he had managed the fake boating accident with you, then he would probably have got away with it.'

'Can you think of any possible reason why Finn should have suddenly written a will leaving everything to Michael Daley?'

Chris was looking at me now with an expression close to contempt.

'I don't really give a fuck. Patients sometimes fall in love with their doctors, don't they?' He paused before resuming with cruel deliberation. 'Women have been known to behave irrationally in times of great stress. Perhaps she was suffering from trauma, maybe her period was about to start. I'm afraid that this is the way that cases end up. If you've got the right people and not too many loose ends, then that's good enough. Is this what you wanted to see me for?'

'I thought you might be interested in hearing about a couple of funny things that happened to me in the last couple of days.'

'Are you feeling all right, Sam?'

'A couple of months ago I was out doing some shopping for clothes with Finn and I bumped into a woman I'd known at medical school.'

'That's fascinating. I think your five minutes are up . . .'

'Wait. I met her again on Tuesday.'

'Give her my regards if you happen to see her again,' said Chris, raising himself from his seat.

'Sit down,' I said sharply.

Chris frowned, and I saw he was wondering whether to ignore me and walk out, but he gave a sigh and sat back down.

'She had read about me in the papers. She told me it was a funny coincidence because she was a family friend of the Mackenzies. Yet when we had met before, she hadn't recognized Finn.'

Chris's face was impassive, still waiting for the punchline.

'Is that supposed to mean anything?' he asked.

'Yes. Don't you think it's strange?'

He laughed harshly.

'Had Fiona lost a lot of weight, Sam?'

'Yes.'

'Did she avoid meeting people face to face?'

'Yes.'

'So maybe your friend didn't get a proper look, maybe she didn't have her glasses on.'

'And then, when I was reading through Finn's guide to South America, I accidentally came across a passage, and it was the same – I mean exactly the same – as something she had said to me about her trip there. As if she'd learned it by heart.'

Now he was cracking his knuckles, a look of boredom and, almost, of contempt on his face. He didn't bother to say anything.

'And a funny thing happened to me yesterday. I was dashing out of the house and I grabbed a hat at random and it was laughably too small. It just bobbled on top of my head. It made Elsie laugh.'

'I suppose you had to be there to appreciate the full humour of the situation.'

'You see this trilby?' I picked my hat off the table and put it on my head. 'Fits nicely, doesn't it? It was Finn's.'

'Shrank in the wash, did it? Well, I'm certainly glad that you shared that with me, Sam.'

'You put your hats in the washing-machine, do you Chris? That explains one or two things. Did you do science at school?'

'This is crucial to the inquiry as well, I assume. Yes, I did science at school, but I bet I wasn't as good at it as you were.'

'I bet you weren't. Look, I know that reality is complicated, people act illogically, evidence is ambiguous. But . . .' I drained my gin and tonic and slammed the glass so hard on the table that people looked around and Chris shifted uneasily.

'I hope you're not planning to drive home.'

'But,' I repeated. 'This is not just messy. It's impossible. Until the discoveries in Michael's boat-house, it was *possible* that Finn and Danny ran away and then committed suicide. It may have been unlikely and uncharacteristic and deeply upsetting for me personally but it was *possible*. It may be likely and characteristic that Michael killed Finn and Danny and staged their suicide but it is totally impossible.' I paused. Chris didn't respond. 'Well, isn't it?'

He tapped his cigarette.

'In the way that you've described it, maybe. But Michael is dead. Finn is dead. We don't know what happened.'

I don't know if it was the gin and tonic on an empty stomach or my anger but I felt as if the hum of the saloon bar had entered my head like tinnitus. Suddenly I felt in a rage.

'For Chrissake, just pretend for a moment that you aren't a policeman, just pretend for a moment to be an intelligent ordinary person who cares about what actually happened. I mean, don't worry about it, there are no other policemen eavesdropping. You don't have to seem big in front of the boys.'

'You arrogant...' With an obvious effort, Chris stopped himself. 'All right, Sam. I'm listening. I'd really like to know. If we're so stupid, tell us what we've missed. But before you start, I would like to add that you are in danger of becoming a serious embarrassment. To your employers, to us, to yourself, to your daughter. Is this what you want? To become famous as a crazy obsessed woman on the loose? But tell me, I'm listening.'

For a moment I seriously considered picking up the ashtray from the table and braining him with it. Then I cooled down and thought only of throwing the remains of the second gin and tonic over him. I counted to a large number.

'I thought I was doing you a favour,' I said.

'So do me a favour.'

I felt as if I were going to burst.

'I'm not going to do you a favour but maybe I can help you to think for yourself.'

'I've got to go.'

'One more minute. The burnt-out car was found on March the ninth. What was the original theory? They had killed themselves by setting fire to the car with a rag stuffed into the petrol tank, nozzle, whatever?

'Yes.'

'But since traces of both Finn and Danny's bodies were found in the boat-house, it is clear that they were dead when the car was set on fire, yes?'

'Yes.'

'And Michael couldn't have done it. Right?'

'Sam, as I told you, there are some loose ends, some inconsistencies. But try to understand this.' He was speaking very slowly now, as if English was my second language. 'We know as a matter of certainty that Michael Daley killed Danny Rees and Fiona Mackenzie. OK? We haven't yet ascertained exactly how. OK? He was a clever man. But we will find out, and when we do we will inform you. OK?' His face was positively twitching with the effort to remain calm.

I spoke very slowly in response. 'Michael was in Belfast at the time. Yes?'

'Yes.'

'So what is the only other possibility?'

'There are various other possibilities.'

'Such as?'

Chris shrugged.

'Lots. Some form of incendiary device, for example.'

'Was any evidence of such a device found?'

'No.'

'The car would need to have stood there with the dead bodies for two whole days. That's not possible either. And what would have been the point of doing it anyway? Why go to all that trouble to start a fire?'

'He was a psychopathic killer.'

'Humour me for a moment, Chris, and stop talking like a fool. I'm not going to hold you to anything you say, I'm not going to embarrass you again, but just tell me how the car must have been set on fire.'

Chris mumbled something.

'Sorry, I didn't hear what you said.'

He lit another cigarette, blowing out the match with absurd deliberation and placing it in the ashtray before replying.

'It is possible,' he said, 'that Daley had some sort of collaborator.'

'No, Chris, you're wrong. It is impossible that he *didn't* have a collaborator.'

Chris looked at his watch and stood up.

'I've got to go.'

'I'll see you out,' I said.

He was gloomily silent as we walked back towards the police station. Only when we reached the steps at the main entrance did he turn and face me.

'So you think,' he said quietly, 'that we ought to reopen the investigation and try and identify this mysterious assistant?'

'No,' I said.

'Why not?'

'Because I know who it was.'

'Who?'

'It was Finn,' I said, enjoying his gasp of disbelief. 'In a way.'

'What do you mean, "in a way"? What the fuck are you talking about?'

'You find out,' I said. 'That's your job.'

He shook his head.

'You . . .' he said. 'You're . . .'

He seemed completely at a loss. I held out my hand.

'Sorry about being late. I'll be in touch.'

He took it as if he thought it might give him an electric shock.

'You . . . Are you doing anything tonight?'

'Yes,' I said, and left him there on the steps.

Thirty-Four

I could hear steps coming towards the door, see a shadow through the frosted glass, so I stood up straighter in the intimidating porch and put a polite and hopeful expression on my face. I suddenly realized how shabby I was looking. The door was opened a few inches and a woman's face peered round it. I could see she was still in her dressing gown and had applied only half of her make-up. One eye was lined and mascara'd and ready for the day; the vulnerable other one wasn't.

'Laura?' I said through the gap. 'I'm so sorry if this is a bad time. I was wondering if I could have a few minutes with you.' On her face, the expression of irritated politeness towards a stranger who's called at the wrong time was giving way to surprised and, I thought, slightly appalled recognition. 'I'm Sam Laschen,' I added. The door opened wider, on to the wide hall with its polished wooden floor, the restrained sense of money and taste and a daily cleaner.

'My dear, of course, you came to a party, didn't you, with . . .' Alarm and interest pursued each other across her features.

'With Michael Daley. Yes. I'm sorry just to turn up like this. I need to find out something and I was wondering if you could help. I can come back later if that's more convenient.' She looked at me with narrowed eyes. Was

I the gossip item of the year or a dangerous madwoman? The gossip item prevailed.

'No, that is, I don't have to get to the hospital till later today, I was just saying to Gordon yesterday . . . Do come through.' I followed her solid chenilled shape into the room where a few months ago I'd eaten asparagus spears and drunk white wine. 'I'll just go and get some clothes on. Would you like some coffee? Or tea?'

'Coffee.'

'I won't be more than five minutes,' she said, and as she went up the stairs I could hear her calling urgently, 'Gordon. *Gordon!*'

While she was out of the room, I pulled out the mobile phone which the hospital had supplied me with and which I still felt self-conscious using, and dialled.

'Hello, yes, could you give me Philip Kale? No, I'll hold.'

I gave my name and after a few seconds he came on to the line.

'Dr Laschen?' He was obviously puzzled and, as before, in a hurry.

'Yes, well, it's just that I was wondering if you could tell me Finn's — Fiona Mackenzie's — blood type. From your autopsy report.'

'Her blood type? Yes, of course. I'll call you back.'

The prospect of a mobile phone bleeping in my pocket was too much.

'No. I'm all over the place today,' I said. 'I'll call you. In about an hour, say? Thanks so much.'

I could hear the sound of coffee being ground from the kitchen, china clinking. I dialled a second number.

'Hello, is that the hospital? Yes, can you put me through

306

to Margaret Lessing in the personnel office. Maggie? Hello, this is Sam.'

'Sam!' Her voice tinkled down the line. 'Hi, what are you up to?'

'This and that. Can you do something for me? I wanted to have a quick look at Fiona Mackenzie's file from when she was in hospital after the attack. Could you get hold of it for me?'

There was a moment of hesitation.

'I don't see why not.'

'Thanks, Maggie. Shall I pop round later today?'

'Give me a call first.'

'Fine. Speak to you soon.'

Laura felt better, I could tell. Her face was less tentative under her glossy grey curls. She'd put on a greeny-grey knee-length suit, the other eye and a lipsticked smile. She placed a tray down on the table between us – an upright pot, two china cups with little silver spoons on their saucers, a dainty jug half-filled with milk, and lumps of sugar in both pale brown and dense white. I thought of the milk bottle and jam jar standing on my kitchen table, the boxes still unpacked on the uncarpeted floor of my study. I'd never have this kind of style. Thank God.

'How are you? We've all been so admiring.' Laura poured me a deft cup of steaming coffee, and I added a slop of milk.

'Fine, thanks.' I took a sip. 'I wanted to talk to someone who knew Finn.'

Laura looked flattered. She laid a strong, well-manicured hand on my denimed knees.

'What you've been through is terrible; I mean, even for

people like us, right on the sidelines, it's been shocking, and . . .'

'Tell me about Finn.'

She took a sip of coffee and sat back, visibly at a loss. She had wanted *me* to do the talking.

'I didn't know her that well. She was a very kind, gentle girl, who may have suffered at school, as girls do, because she was overweight.' Laura raised her eyebrows at me. 'And she became seriously ill and she went away from us, from everybody who knew her. It was terrible for Leo and Liz. But she got better. Liz told me that Finn was happier than she had ever been. Completely transformed, they said. I think that they saw her trip to South America as a new beginning, a sign that she had grown up.'

This was no good. I didn't want Laura's amateur diagnoses. I wanted information, facts I could make something of for myself.

'You don't have any photographs of her, do you? All the ones in her house were destroyed.'

'I don't think so. It was her parents we saw, really. Hang on a minute.' She left the room, reappeared with a fat square red book and started rapidly turning over colour photos in their transparent pages, tutting and shaking her head. Unknown faces flicked past, unremarkable houses, hills and beaches and formal groups of people. 'Here is a garden party we went to with Liz and Leo. Fiona may have been there. I can't see her.'

The Mackenzie parents, whose out-of-focus faces had been on the front of every newspaper a few months ago, were standing on a smooth lawn, smiling for the camera. She was skinny under a wide-brimmed straw hat; he looked hot and uncomfortable in his suit and tie. On the left of the photo, sliding out of the shot, was a bare arm, a slither of a floral dress and a wave of dark hair.

I put my finger on the arm, as if I could press its flesh. 'That'll be Finn.'

I sat on a bench by the side of a square. A mother was pushing her child on the single swing that stood on the patch of green.

'Dr Kale, please,' I said into my telephone.

His voice came quickly down the line.

'Hello, Dr Laschen. Yes, I've got it here, in front of me. Let's see. Here it is: Fiona Mackenzie's blood type was O, along with about half of the population of Western Europe and the United States. Is that all you wanted?'

At the hospital, Maggie sounded harassed.

'Sorry, Sam, you'll have to give me a bit more time to get the file. These bloody computers, somebody must have logged in wrong and snarled the system up. Would her casualty admission file be any good?'

'Yes.'

'Ring me back.'

'Donald Helman? Hello, I hope this isn't a bad time to ring. My name's Sam Laschen and we met at a party of Laura and Gor . . . Yes, that's right. Laura gave me your number. You said your daughter used to be a friend of Finn's and I was wondering if I could speak to her about it. Oh, when will she back? Well, in that case, there was a friend of Finn's from school who I met, her first name is Jenny, I think. You don't happen to remember her last name? Glaister. Thank you very much for your help.'

Jenny Glaister was home from university for the Easter

holidays. Her parents' large house was about twenty miles from Stamford, standing in its own grounds, and she came on to the gravelled sweep of driveway as I arrived. It was a grey and rather chilly day, but she wore a tiny, brightly coloured silk skirt and a thin shirt. I remembered her articulate self-confidence from the funeral. She was puzzled, but she was interested in me. Everyone was interested enough in the woman they'd read about in the newspapers to let me into their houses for a few minutes. She made us a pot of tea, then sat down facing me, oval face in ringless hands.

'To be honest,' she said, 'Finn wasn't *really* one of our group. I mean, she was and she wasn't.' She bit her lower lip and then added, 'She was self-conscious at school. A bit awkward. One of the difficult things when she . . . you know, became ill and went away, was that some of us felt a bit guilty about her. We thought we might not have included her enough. I mean, maybe she got anorexic because she wanted to be one of us, you know. I saw her briefly when she came back from South America and I hardly recognized her, none of us did: she was so slim and tanned and she had all these fabulous new clothes and she seemed so much more self-confident, less anxious for our approval. We were all a bit in awe of her, as if she were suddenly a stranger. She was quite different from the plump Finn who'd just tagged along.'

I tried to push her for something specific. She made an obvious effort.

'A few weeks ago I would have said that she was intelligent, nice. That kind of thing. And loyal,' she added. 'I would have said Finn was loyal: you could trust her and depend on her. She'd always do her homework, and arrive places on time, and be, well, reliable. Eager. You spent all that time with her at the end. Does she make sense to you?'

'Do you have any photographs?'

We rummaged through a case of photographs that mainly consisted of Jenny looking lovely on horseback, in the sea, with her family, playing her cello, receiving her school prize, going gracefully downhill on skis. No Finn.

'You could try the school,' she suggested. 'There must be a school photo of her and term's not finished there yet. The school secretary, Ruth Plomer, will help. She's a darling.'

Now why hadn't I thought of that?

So I drove to Grey Hall, which wasn't grey but red and magnificent and set back across lovely green lawns from the road. On playing fields I could see a hoard of girls in grey shorts and white Aertex shirts wielding lacrosse sticks while a tall woman barked at them. Inside, the smell of French polish and green vegetables and linseed oil and femaleness met me. Behind closed doors I could hear lessons in progress. This wasn't how I remembered Elmore Hill comprehensive. A woman in overalls directed me down a corridor to the secretary's office.

Ruth Plomer sat, beady-eyed and beaky-nosed as a bird, amid a nest of files and wire baskets and piles of forms. She listened attentively to my request, then nodded.

'To be honest, Dr Laschen, the press has come round here asking for photographs, comments, interviews, and our policy has been to refuse everyone.' She paused and I remained silent. She yielded slightly. 'You just want to *see* a photograph? You don't want to take it away? You don't want to talk to anybody?'

'That's right. I need to see what she looked like before she lived with me.'

She looked puzzled, apparently arguing with herself and finally losing.

'I don't suppose there can be any harm. There are no individual portraits but there is always the group photograph. When was her final year?'

'I think she formally left in the summer of 95, but she was ill for almost all of the academic year. Maybe I could look at the previous year.'

'Wait here; I'll see what I can do.'

She left the room and I heard footsteps retreating and returning. Miss Plomer had a scrolled tube in her hand and unrolled it on her overcrowded desk. I leaned forward, scanning the rows of girls' faces for sight of Finn. She put on her spectacles.

'This is the 1994 line-up. There is a list of the girls' names here. Let's see, yes, she's in the third row back. There she is.' A well-trimmed fingernail touched a figure on the left-hand side of the photo. Dark hair, a slight blur on her features: she must have turned aside as the lens shuttered, just as she'd done with me. I picked up the scroll and held it to the light, staring intently, but it seemed to recede from my gaze. I wouldn't have known it was Finn. I wouldn't have known it was anybody.

'Maggie. Hi, it's Sam again. Have you found it yet?'

'No, there's a hold-up with the casualty file. Somebody must have taken it out and I'm trying to track down who it was. Get back to me.' She was harassed and irritated and eager to get off the line.

Everything was gone. Now what?

Where was it, oh, where was it? I flung open the trunk. Elsie's paintings, dozens and dozens of them, lay there in piles. Some were glued together by their paint. Some still had masking tape on their corners, where they'd been stuck to the walls. Three-legged monsters in green and red, yellow daisies with their straight stalks and two looped leaves, violent purple daubs, faces with wonky eyes, indeterminate animals, lots of seascapes, wavy blue lines traversing the thick white paper. Rainbows with the colours running into each other; the moon and stars bleeding yellow into rough black nights. I lifted each picture, looked at it, turned it over. Surely it would be here. Traces of Finn's presence in the house could be seen: occasional titles, neatly written in with their dates, an adult representation of a dog alongside a child's one, several times whole hasty pictures of horses and trees and sailing boats obviously done by Finn. But I couldn't find what I needed. I'd come to a dead end.

I went into Elsie's room and pulled open drawers. Dolls with pink limbs and gaudy dresses stared at me, knitted animals, little boxes with nothing in them, beads in satisfying primary colours, satiny ribbons, whole armies of those tiny plastic things which are always put into party bags. In her drawing pad there were several paintings, but not the one I wanted. Under the bed was one slipper and three separate socks and Anatoly, asleep. I climbed on to a chair and pulled down from the top of the wardrobe an untidy pile of used paper folded up. On the top, in pencil, was Elsie's name written over and over, in large wonky letters. Underneath was the treasure map. I'd found it.

I jumped off the chair and spread the paper out on the floor tenderly, looking at the daubs of colour and the rusty red letters. An 'S' and an 'E'. And there, an 'F': signed in her blood.

I lifted the paper up very carefully, as if it were like a dream that fades when you try and grasp it. In my study downstairs was a stack of large brown envelopes and I slid the map and its signature of blood inside one and sealed it up. Then I picked up the car keys and ran outside. I had it now.

'You again.'

I had taken a seat but Chris remained standing, hands on hips, looking down at me.

'I've found her. It.'

'What?'

I took the envelope, still sealed, and put it on his desk. 'In here,' I said, speaking very slowly, as if he were demented, or as if I were, 'in here is a picture.'

'A picture. How nice.'

'A picture,' I continued, 'drawn by Elsie.'

'Look, Sam,' Chris bent towards me and I noticed that his face had become rather red, 'I wish you well, honestly I do, but go home, see your daughter, leave me alone.'

'This is a relic from a children's game. Finn and I signed our initials, each in our own blood.' He opened his mouth and I thought he was going to roar at me, but no sound came out. 'Give it to Kale. Have it tested.'

He sat down heavily. 'You're mad. You've gone completely insane.'

'And I want a receipt for this. I don't want it disappearing.'

Angeloglou gave me a fixed stare for a long time.

'You mean you want a record kept of your behaviour? Right,' he shouted and began rummaging feverishly on

314

his desk. He didn't find what he was looking for and he stormed across the room returning with a form. He banged it down on the table and picked up a pen with deliberation.

'Name?' he barked.

Thirty-Five

'I'll have' – I ran a finger down the handwritten menu – 'smoked mackerel and salad. What about you two?'

'Chicken nuggets and chips,' Elsie said firmly. 'And fizzy orange drink. Then chocolate ice-cream for pudding.'

'OK,' I said easily. Elsie looked taken aback. 'Sarah?'

'Ploughman's, thanks.'

'What about drinks? Do you want a shandy or something?'

'Lovely.'

I gave the orders to a barmaid who appeared to be ten months pregnant, took our ticket and our drinks, and we went outside into the gorgeous spring day and sat down, coats still buttoned up, at an unstable wooden table.

'Can I play on the swings?' asked Elsie, and charged off without waiting for a reply. Sarah and I watched her struggle on to the seat of a swing and rock it violently to and fro, as if that would give her momentum.

'She seems well,' commented Sarah.

'I know.' A little boy in a stripy jersey climbed on to the swing next to Elsie's and the two of them stared suspiciously at each other. 'Funny, isn't it?'

'Kids are resilient.'

We sipped our shandy with the sun on the napes of our necks, and didn't speak for a bit.

'Come on, Sarah, don't keep me on tenterhooks. What did you think of the book, then? Plain speaking, mind. Aren't you saying anything because it's so bad?'

'You must know it's good, Sam.' She put an arm around my shoulders and I almost burst into tears; it had been a long time since anyone except Elsie had hugged me. 'Congratulations. I really mean it.' She grinned. 'And wildly controversial of course. I'm amazed you could write something like that in such a short time, and with all that happened. Maybe that's why. It's very good.'

'But?'

'There are a few tiny little things that I wrote in the margin.'

'I mean *really* but.'

'There's no really but. There's a question.'

'Ask away.'

'Not even a question, just a comment.' She paused, picked up her glass and ran a thumb around its rim. 'It feels like a summing-up of a career, not just the beginning of one.'

'I've got a habit of burning my bridges.'

Sarah laughed.

'Yes, but this time you're burning your bridges in *front* of you. All those attacks on hospital managers and jaded consultants, and the stuff about designer trauma.'

The little boy was pushing Elsie on her swing now. Every time she went swooping up, sturdy legs pointing to the sky and head thrown exaggeratedly back, my heart banged anxiously.

Our lunch arrived. My mackerel lay among a few shreds of tired lettuce, looking orange and enormous. Elsie's meal was entirely beige. 'You made the best choice,' I said to Sarah, and called to Elsie, who came running.

*

After lunch, after Elsie had eaten every last chip and scooped up every last drop of ice-cream, we went for a short walk, to the old church I had visited once before, and talked about South America and Elsie's father.

'Do you love it here?' asked Sarah as we walked beneath the enormous sky, beside the sea that was blue and friendly today, the ground spongy under our feet, birds curling overhead.

I looked around. Near here, Danny had made love to me while I kept an anxious eye out for tractors. Near here, Finn had walked her thin body back into health and had made me confide in her. Out there, I had nearly died.

I shivered. We seemed to be making no progress; however far we walked the landscape remained unchanged. We could walk all day and the horizon would just roll away from us.

I had always thought that when people were described as being purple with rage it was a metaphor or hyperbole, but Geoff Marsh really was purple. The arterial pulsation in the neck was clearly visible and I asked him if he was all right, but he waved me into the chair in front of his desk and then sat across from me. When he spoke it was with a forced calmness.

'How is it going?'

'You mean the unit?'

'Yes.'

'The painters are just applying the final coat. And those carpets. Our reception area is looking very corporate.'

'You make that sound a bad thing.'

'I suppose I'm primarily interested in it as a therapeutic setting.'

'That's as may be. But the existence of the unit and its

role in our internal economy depend on its success as a generator of funds and *that* depends on the input of health schemes and insurance companies who believe that a programme of trauma treatment for certain categories of their customers will provide them with legal protection. Battered toddlers and firemen who're frightened of fires aren't going to pay for your precious therapeutic environment.'

I counted to ten and then I counted to ten again. When I spoke it was also with an exaggerated calm.

'Geoff, if I didn't know and love you as I do, I might think you were trying to insult me. Did you summon me here to give you a lecture about first principles in post-traumatic stress disorder?'

Geoff stood up and walked round his desk and sat on the corner in a posture that had probably been taught to him on a management training course.

'I've just given Margaret Lessing an official warning. She's lucky I didn't terminate her.'

'What do you mean, "terminate her"? What are you talking about?'

'This trust has a strict policy on personal privacy which Margaret Lessing violated. I understand that she did so on your instructions.'

'What is this personal privacy stuff? You'd sell copies of our records to Colonel Gaddafi if he offered money for them. What are you playing at?'

'Dr Laschen, as you yourself insisted to me, Fiona Mackenzie was not your patient. It was quite improper of you to ask for her file.'

'I am a doctor in this hospital and I have a right to ask for any file I want.'

'If you read your contract and our own contract of

operation, Dr Laschen, you will see that your so-called rights are based on strictly defined terms of employment.'

'I'm a doctor, Geoff, and I will do what I think is right as a doctor. And incidentally, as a matter of curiosity, when did you start monitoring routine applications for medical files?' I saw a hint of indecision in Geoff's expression and I realized the truth. 'This has nothing to do with ethics, you've been spying on me, haven't you?'

'Was this file on a dead girl required as part of a course of treatment?'

I took a deep breath.

'No.'

'Was it in your capacity as a doctor?'

'Yes,' I said. 'Indirectly.'

'Indirectly,' Geoff repeated, sarcastically. 'Can it be, is it conceivably possible, that despite my warnings, you are, on your own initiative, conducting some sort of private investigation into this case? A case, I should add, that has been closed.'

'That's right.'

'And?'

'What's this "and"? I don't have to answer to you.'

'Yes, you do have to answer to me. I can't believe this. More by luck than anything, we seem to have escaped bad publicity, and this tragic case has been closed. When I heard that you were still meddling in it, my first thought was that you had suffered a breakdown. To be frank, Dr Laschen, I'm not sure whether you require medical treatment or disciplinary action.'

I almost leaped from my chair, and stared at him, so close that I could feel his breath on my face.

'What did you say, Geoff?'

'You heard me.'

320

I reached forward and clenched the knot of his tie, firmly so that my fist pressed up against his throat. He squealed something.

'You pompous bastard,' I said, and let him go. I stepped back and thought for a second. There was no doubt in my mind, and I felt an immediate sense of release. 'You're trying to goad me to resign.' Geoff said nothing and looked at the floor. 'I will, anyway.' He looked sharply, almost eagerly. This was what he had planned for, but I didn't care. 'Professional differences. That's the phrase, isn't it?'

Geoff's eyes darted warily. Was I trapping him in some way?

'I'll issue a statement to that effect,' he said.

'You've probably got it in your drawer already.'

I turned to go, then remembered something.

'Could you do me a favour?'

He looked surprised. He might have anticipated tears or a punch in the face, but not this.

'What?'

'Withdraw the warning against Maggie Lessing. I can look after myself, it'll hurt her.'

'I'll consider it.'

'It's served its purpose, after all.'

'Don't be bitter, Sam. If you had been me, I don't think you would have been able to deal with you any better than I did.'

'I'll leave straight away.'

'That's probably best.'

'Has Fiona Mackenzie's file turned up yet?'

Geoff frowned.

'Apparently it's lost,' he said. 'We'll find it.'

I shook my head.

'I don't think so. I think it will stay lost.' I thought of

321

something and smiled. 'But it doesn't matter. I've got a drawing by my five-year-old daughter instead.'

As I shut the door, the last I saw was Geoff standing there with his mouth gaping open like a landed fish.

Thirty-Six

The estate agent looked about fourteen years old.

'Lovely,' he said. 'Just lovely.'

Those were his first words as he stepped across the threshold.

'Very saleable. Very saleable.'

I showed him around upstairs and it was all lovely and saleable in the extreme.

'I haven't really tackled the garden,' I said.

He shook his head.

'A challenge for the adventurous gardener,' he said.

'That sounds a bit off-putting.'

'Joke,' he said. 'Estate-agent speak.'

'As you can see, we're only a short walk from the sea.'

'Good point,' he said. 'Very attractive. Buyers like that. Sea views.'

'Well, not exactly.'

'Joke. Estate-agent speak again.'

'Right. I don't know what else I should tell you. There's a loft and a shed. But you handled the sale last year, so you probably have the details on file.'

'Yes, we do. But I wanted to come for a look. Sniff the air, get a feel for the property.'

'You were going to give me a valuation.'

'Yes, Dr Laschen. Do you remember what you paid for the property?'

'Ninety-five.' His eyebrows rose. 'I was in a hurry.'

'That's an interesting figure,' he said.

'You mean it was too high. I wish you had mentioned that a year ago when you showed me round.'

'The east Essex market is soft at the moment. Very soft.'

'Is that a problem?'

'An opportunity,' he said and held out his hand. 'Good to meet you, Dr Laschen. I'll ring you this afternoon with the valuation. We need to price this aggressively. I'm sure that we'll have some people to take round by next week.'

'I won't be here. My daughter and I are going back to London on Saturday.'

'Just so long as we have a set of keys and a phone number. In a hurry to get away? What's the matter? Don't you like the countryside?'

'Too much crime.'

He gave an uncertain laugh.

'Joke, right?'

'Yes. Joke.'

That week consisted of nothing but things that needed doing. I sat down with Elsie and asked her if she would like to go back to London and see her old friends.

'No,' she said cheerfully.

I left it at that. The rest was just a process of working my way down a list: telling Linda and Sally, who seemed inured to any more shocks, and paying them in lieu of notice; making arrangements with utility companies; getting boxes out of the attic and putting things into them that, it seemed, I had only just removed from them.

I spent too much time on the phone. When I wasn't trying to track down somebody at the council I was being phoned once more by journalists and doctors. I said no to all the journalists and maybe to most of the doctors. I gradually thinned down the maybes into probablys and by the end of the week I had a temporary-contract consultant post in the Department of Psychology at St Clementine's in Shoreditch. I had phone calls from Thelma asking me what the hell was going on and Sarah telling me that I'd done the right thing and that a friend of hers had gone to America for a year and did I want to borrow his flat in Stoke Newington which was just a couple of streets from the park. I did. The only problem was that it was near Arsenal's football ground and was overrun on alternate Saturdays and occasional weekends and did I mind? I didn't.

In the gaps I kept phoning Chris Angeloglou. They were waiting for the laboratory results. Chris was out and yes, so was DI Baird. They couldn't be reached. They were in a meeting. They were in court. They'd gone home. On Friday morning, the day before I was to move out, I rang Stamford police station once more and was put through to an assistant. Unfortunately DC Angeloglou and DI Baird were unavailable. That was all right, I said, I just wanted to leave a message. Did she have a piece of paper? Good. I wanted to warn Angeloglou and Baird that I was about to offer an interview to a national newspaper in which I would give the full story of the Mackenzie murder case as I saw it, together with my indictment of the police role in failing to reopen the case. Thank you.

I replaced the receiver and began to count. One, two, three . . . On twenty-seven, the phone rang.

'Sam?'

'Rupert, how are you?'

'What do you want?'

'I want to know what you're doing.'

'Do you think it's constructive to make wild threats?'

'Yes, and I'll tell you what I really want. I want a meeting at Stamford police station.' There was a long pause. 'Rupert, are you there?'

'Of course. We'd be happy to see you. I was about to ring you anyway.'

'Apart from you and Chris, I want Philip Kale there.'

'All right.'

'And whoever was in charge of the case.'

'*I* was.'

'I want to talk to the organ-grinder, not his monkey.'

'I'm not sure that the organ-grinder is available.'

'He'd better be.'

'Anything else?'

'Ask Kale to bring his autopsy reports on the Mackenzie couple.'

'I'll see what I can do, Sam, and ring you back.'

'Don't bother. I'll be with you at twelve.'

'That's too little time.'

'You've had lots of time, Rupert.'

As soon as I identified myself at the front desk, a young WPC hustled me through the building and into an empty interview room. When she returned with coffee, Angeloglou and Baird were with her. They nodded at me and sat down. It felt as if it were my office, not theirs.

'Where are the others?'

Baird looked questioningly at Angeloglou.

'Kale's on the phone,' Chris said. 'He'll be along in a minute. Val just popped up for the Super.'

Baird turned to me.

'Satisfied?' he asked with not too much of a hint of sarcasm.

'This isn't some kind of game, Rupert.'

There was a knock at the door, then it opened and a man peered in. He was middle-aged, balding, obviously in charge. He held his hand out to me.

'Dr Laschen,' he said. 'I've been looking forward to meeting you. I'm Bill Day. I'm the head of the Stamford CID. I think we owe you an apology.'

I shook his hand.

'As I was just explaining to Rupert here,' I said, 'I'm not conducting some personal campaign here and I'm not interested in claiming credit. It's just about catching a murderer.'

'Well, that's meant to be our job,' Day said with a laugh that turned into a sort of cough.

'Which is why I'm here.'

'Good, good,' said Day. 'Rupert said you wanted me to be here and that's quite understandable. Unfortunately I've just popped out of a very important meeting and I must pop back. But I can assure you of our full cooperation. If you are dissatisfied in any way, I want you to contact me personally. Here's my . . . er . . .' He rummaged in his pockets and produced a slightly dog-eared business card and handed it to me. 'I'll leave you in Rupert's capable hands. Good to meet you, Dr Laschen.' We shook hands once more and he drifted out, almost bumping into Philip Kale as he did so. The four of us sat down.

'Well?' said Rupert. 'Who is going to start?'

'I was tempted to bring a lawyer with me,' I said.

'Why? Are you planning to confess?' Rupert asked cheerfully.

'No, I thought it might be prudent to make sure that there was some independent record of this meeting.'

'That will be quite unnecessary. We're all on the same side. Now, what was it you wanted to see us about?'

'Jesus, Rupert, what is this charade? All right, if you insist.' I took out my wallet and rummaged in it until I found the blue form. 'Last week I handed in some evidence that in my view justified reopening the Mackenzie murder case. Receipt number SD4071/A. I suggested that the blood type be established. Has that been done?'

'It has,' said Dr Kale.

'What was it?'

Kale didn't even look down at his notes.

'The blood sample derived from the Finn initial on the drawing was type A rhesus D positive.'

'And you have no doubt about the identity of the body in the burning car?'

Kale shook his head.

'The dental records were unambiguous. But just to dispel any doubt, DC Angeloglou has established that over the last couple of years, Fiona Mackenzie was a blood donor.' Kale allowed himself a thin smile. 'A group O blood donor.'

'Just out of interest,' I asked, 'what were the blood groups of the parents?'

Kale rummaged through his file.

'Leopold Mackenzie was B.' He rummaged some more. 'And his wife was A. Nice.'

I gave what must have sounded close to a witch's cackle.

Angeloglou looked puzzled.

'So if we'd only checked, it would have been clear that she couldn't have been their daughter,' he said.

I couldn't help giving a cross sigh.

'No, Chris,' said Kale. 'If one parent is A and the other B, then the children can be any of the four basic blood groups. Which Michael Daley would have known.'

There was a very long silence. I was trembling with excitement and I had to force myself to maintain my composure. I didn't want to speak because I couldn't trust myself not to say 'I told you so' in some form of words. Philip Kale ostentatiously began to put papers in order. Angeloglou and Baird looked uneasy. Finally Baird muttered something.

'What?' I said.

'Why didn't we get a sample of her blood at the scene?'

'The only traces at the scene were those of the parents,' said Kale. 'It didn't occur to me that her blood group was an issue.'

'I had her in my bloody car,' said Baird. 'I had both of them in my bloody car. They'll probably demolish this police station and plough the land. Turn it into a ceremonial park, with Chris and me as park keepers. With all his *scientific skills*,' these last words were stressed viciously, 'Phil there could operate one of those pointy things for picking up litter.'

Angeloglou mouthed an obscenity that I could lip-read from across the room. He was taking immense pains to avoid my gaze. My arms were crossed and I carefully pushed my right hand under the upper left arm and pinched the soft flesh hard, so that there was no chance of a triumphant smile.

'What's your version of events now?' I asked in a studiously sombre tone, trying not to stress the word 'now' too much.

Rupert was drawing an interlocking grid of squares and triangles on a sheet of white paper on the table. These were then filled in with a series of shadings and cross-hatchings. As he spoke, he never once raised his eyes.

'Michael Daley faced a double challenge,' he said. 'He had to murder the entire Mackenzie family and he had to obtain the money. The first was no good without the second. The second was impractical without the first. So he hit on something so simple, so out in the open, that nobody spotted it. He had a collaborator who looked a bit like Finn – only the roughest resemblance was necessary, since she would never meet anybody who had met the real Finn. And, as her doctor, he knew better than anybody that Finn's appearance had changed drastically. Any photograph that was published at the time of the murders would be old and of Finn before her anorexia. The collaborator – I'll call her X – had dark hair and was about the same size, perhaps a little smaller, but that was all to the good. Michael was monitoring the actions of animal rights terrorists, so he knew about the threat to Mackenzie. It's impossible now to establish exactly, but it is to be assumed that the real Finn was abducted and killed and stowed in the boat-house on the day or evening of the seventeenth. Her parents were of course murdered early in the morning of the following day. Fiona Mackenzie was a reasonably gregarious young woman, used to travelling. The Mackenzies wouldn't have been surprised if she was out late. The keys obtained were used to gain entry. The couple were killed and Finn, I mean X, dressed herself in Finn's nightie and Michael made an incision in her throat when the maid was due to arrive. Her face was gagged so the difference in appearance of the similar-looking girl in Finn's clothes, in Finn's bedroom, went unnoticed. That was the situation that we encountered.'

'How could they plan something so risky?' Angeloglou

asked, shaking his head. 'How could they possibly assume that they could get away with it?'

'Some people would be willing to run quite a risk for, what was it, eighteen million or so? Anyway, if you have the nerve to try it, was it all that risky? The girl is under a perceived threat, so she is kept secure. Of course, she had to refuse to see anybody who knew Fiona Mackenzie, but there are no immediate family and anyway, it's an understandable reaction from a traumatized young girl, wouldn't you say, Dr Laschen?'

'I believe that was the professional opinion I expressed at the time,' I said in a hollow tone.

'And the matter of identity is never in question because the trusty family doctor is on hand to talk to her and to offer medical details such as her blood group from a faked version of Finn's medical file.'

'And Finn's, that is, X's hospital file has gone missing,' I added.

'Would it have been possible for Daley to have gained access to the file?' Baird asked.

'*I* did, or would have done, if Daley hadn't got there first.'

'What was necessary was for X to take the role of Finn for long enough to allow her to write a will leaving everything to Daley. The only skill that was required was the rudimentary one of reproducing Fiona Mackenzie's signature. There was one hiccup. The family's cleaner expressed a wish to see Fiona before she returned to Spain. This would have ruined everything.'

'So Mrs Ferrer was murdered,' I interjected. 'Michael went there and suffocated her. Then returned with me. Any signs of struggle, and traces left by him, could be explained by his supposed attempt at reviving her.'

331

Rupert shifted uncomfortably in his seat and continued.

'Then, all that was necessary was to stage a suicide, using the corpse of the real Fiona Mackenzie. That was why it was so important for the car to be set on fire. Daley didn't need an alibi for the Mackenzie killings because he wasn't a suspect. But he arranged to be out of the country when X drove Danny's car up the coast and set it on fire.'

'It was perfect,' I said, in admiration, despite myself. 'The suicide of somebody who was already dead and an alibi created by somebody who nobody knew existed. If there had been any suspicions, they could test Finn's body as much as they wanted. And poor Danny, Danny . . .'

'Rees must have stumbled on the scene when she was pulling out the day you were out.'

I looked down at my coffee. It was filmy, cold. I felt shame burning through my body.

'I kept her in my house, with my child, with my lover. Danny was murdered. I've devoted my professional life to the analysis of psychological states and I've been made to dance like a puppet by this young girl. She mimicked trauma, she mimicked friendship, everything. The more I think about it the worse it gets. She didn't want to go to the funeral. I see it as a symptom. She wants to destroy all of the real Finn's clothes. I see it as therapeutic. She's permanently vague about her past. I see it as a necessary stage. She confides in me that she feels no connection with her earlier, fat self and I see it as a sign of her capacity to recover.'

Rupert finally looked up from his drawing.

'Don't feel bad about it, Sam,' he said. 'You're a doctor, not a detective. Life goes on, such as it does, because most of us assume that the people we're dealing with are not psychopaths or frauds.' He glanced at Chris. 'We're the ones who are supposed to be detectives, unfortunately.'

'But what would have happened?' I asked.

'What do you mean?'

'After the fake suicide of Finn.'

'All very simple,' said Chris. 'Daley gets the money. Then, a year or two later, we would hear rumours which would say something like: poor Daley has checked in with Gamblers Anonymous. Gone off the rails, lost half his money or whatever at the racetrack. In fact, it will have gone in cash to pay off . . .' Chris opened his hands, acknowledging defeat, 'X.'

'Have you any idea at all who this young lady might be?' I asked. 'A patient? An old friend? A previous girlfriend?'

Nobody answered.

'She might have a criminal record,' I ventured.

'Who might?' Rupert asked flatly. 'We only have one link with her.'

'What's that?'

'You.'

'What are you talking about?'

'You knew her better than anybody.'

'Are you mad? I didn't know her at all.'

'All we ask,' said Chris, 'is that you try to think. You don't have to tell us now. Just try to remember anything, anything at all she might have said or done that could give a clue as to her real identity.'

'I can answer you straight away. I've spent days going through every memory, everything she told me, any conversation I can recall. It was all fake. What can I say? She could cook. She could do simple magic tricks. But the more I think, the more she becomes like a nothing. All the things she said, all that she did, were just so much dust thrown in my eyes. When I get beyond it she's not there.

I'm afraid I'm not much help. So what are you going to do now?'

Rupert got up and stretched, his hand touching the polystyrene tiles on the ceiling.

'We'll conduct an investigation.'

'When are you announcing the reopening of the case?'

Was it my imagination or did I see him take a deep breath, steeling himself for what he was about to say?

'We're not announcing it.'

'Why not?'

Rupert cleared his throat.

'After consultations at the highest level we have decided that we might improve our prospects if the murderer doesn't know that we are after her. She has missed out on the money. She might make a mistake.'

'Who might? How would you notice?'

Rupert mumbled something.

'Rupert,' I said sharply. 'Is this a way of burying the case?'

He looked shocked.

'Absolutely not, that accusation is unworthy of you, but I know you've been under stress. It's just the most effective way to proceed and I'm confident it will produce results. Now, I think we've explored everything useful. When are you going to London?'

'Tomorrow.'

'You'll leave your address with us, won't you?'

'Yes.'

'Good. If anything occurs to you, if anything happens, just get in touch.' He held out his hand. 'We're very grateful to you. Sam, for the way in which you have enabled the truth of these tragic events to be arrived at.'

I took his hand.

334

'I'm glad you're grateful, Rupert. And if I ever suspect this case is being hushed up . . .'

'Trust us,' said Rupert. 'Trust us.'

I emerged, blinking, into the pedestrian precinct on the edge of the market square and bumped into an old woman and tipped her wheeled shopping basket over. As I retrieved onions and carrots from the pavement, I felt like a child who had woken from a dream and was surprised to find the world carrying on unaffected. Yet I felt that I was still in my hermetic dream. I still had places to go.

Thirty-Seven

There followed a weekend of boxes, an interested child, a disturbed cat, a large van, flirtatious removal men, mugs of tea, arrangements, bunches of keys, and my own rented storage space, reserving about 5 per cent of my possessions for the temporary flat.

Amid the bustle of obligations there were two things I really needed to do. First of all, I had a sheaf of requests for interviews and I browsed through them and rang a couple of friends who read newspapers and asked their advice, and then on the Monday morning I rang Sally Yates at the *Participant*. Within an hour she was sitting with a mug of coffee, a notebook and a poised pen in the kitchen of a man working in America for a year. Yates was plump, rumpled, sympathetic, very likeable and left long silences which I was presumably meant to fill with confidences about my private life. Don't try to kid a kidder. I was experienced enough in the interviewing of vulnerable people to be able to create a reasonable facsimile of the nobly suffering woman. I wasn't as impressive as Finn, as X, but I was all right. I had decided precisely the unguarded intimacies I would offer – about the pain of losing a lover, about crime and physical fear, about anguish and the irony of a trauma specialist suffering from trauma herself: 'There's a medical maxim that you always get the condition that you specialize in,' I said, but with a sad smile and a sniff, as if I was about to shed a tear.

Then, at the end, came the statement for which I had set up the entire interview.

'So now you've escaped it all . . .' said Sally Yates, sympathetically, her sentence fizzling out so that I could pick up its thread.

'But, Sally,' I said, 'both as a doctor and as a woman, I wonder whether we ever can escape experiences just by running away from them.' I left a long pause, apparently too upset to trust myself to speak without losing control. Sally reached across the kitchen table and put her hand on mine. As if with a great effort, I began to speak again: 'This has been a personal tragedy and – with the new post-traumatic stress unit, a professional falling-out – and at the heart of it are people who were not what they seemed.'

'You mean Dr Michael Daley?' Sally asked, her brow furrowed in deep concern.

'No, I don't,' I said and when she looked quizzical gestured that I could say no more.

As we stood on the landing, saying goodbye, I hugged her.

'Congratulations,' I said. 'You got me to say things I never intended.'

Her cheeks flushed with pleasure, quickly suppressed.

'It was very special to meet you,' she said, holding me even tighter than I was holding her.

The newspaper was clearly eager because less than two hours later a photographer arrived. The young man was disappointed that my daughter was out but placed me next to a vase of flowers instead. I gazed soulfully at them, wondering what sort they were. I was rewarded the next day with a large photograph and a headline: 'Sam Laschen: female heroism and the mystery that will not die.' Not particularly snappy, but it would send a shot across the bows of DI Baird and his merry crew. Next time I would be less mysterious.

I had a second task, a larger and more painful one. A friend had vaguely offered the services of her childminder in an emergency. This was an emergency. I took Elsie round the corner to a chaotic terraced house containing a Spanish teenager and a beetle-browed five-year-old. Elsie stomped in and didn't even turn to say goodbye. I got into my car and headed west. I would be going against the traffic in both directions.

I found Saint Anne's Church, on the Avonmouth side of Bristol, easily, and walked through its gate and into the green quiet of the graveyard holding my bunch of spring flowers. It was easy to tell which grave was Danny's: among all the mossy grey headstones, whose names were scarcely decipherable, his mottled pink slab was starkly new. Someone had put flowers there. I looked at the black lettering: Daniel Rees, Beloved Son and Brother. I grimaced. That shut me out effectively enough. 1956–1996: he'd not made it to the birthday party we'd talked of throwing. I'd grow old, my face would change and wrinkle, my body would develop the aches and pains and fragilities of age, would bend and suffer, and he would be always young, always strong and beautiful in my memory.

I looked down at the six feet of ugly pink marble and shuddered. Under there, his gorgeous body, which I'd held so close when it was warm and full of desire, was charred and now rotting. His face, the lips that had explored me and the mouth that had smiled at me and the eyes that had gazed, was mouldering away. I sat down beside the headstone, put one hand on the grave as if it were a warm flank, stroked it.

'I know you can't hear me, Danny,' I said into the windless silence. Even speaking his name out loud made my chest ache. 'I know you're not there, or anywhere else either. But I needed to come here.'

I looked around. There was no one in the churchyard at all. I couldn't even hear the sound of a bird. Only the cars on the main road a few hundred yards away disturbed the hush. So I took off my jacket, laid aside my bag, took the flowers off the slab and lay down on it myself, cheek to the cold stone. I stretched my length out on top of Danny as I sometimes still did in my dreams.

I cried messily, self-pityingly, in a flood of easy grief, as I lay upon the grave; salt tears puddled on the stone. I cried for my dear life. I allowed myself to remember our first meeting, the first time we went to bed together, outings with Elsie – just the blessed three of us, not knowing how lucky we were. I thought about his death. I knew that I was going to be all right; one day I would probably meet someone else and the whole process of falling in love would begin again, but just now I felt cold and lonely to my bones. The wind sighed through the graveyard; all those dead bones lying under their inscriptions.

So I pulled myself stiffly to my feet. When I spoke I felt absurdly self-conscious, as if I were acting the part of a grieving widow in some stilted amateur dramatic production: 'So this is it. This is my goodbye.' Yet I couldn't stop saying it, melodramatic as it was. I just couldn't bring myself to say it for the very last time. 'Goodbye goodbye goodbye goodbye.'

And then I put on my jacket, picked up my bag, placed the two bunches of flowers back on the stone, just so, walked out of the graveyard and never once looked back through the latch gate at the place where he lay. And if I drove fast enough, I'd be back in time to put Elsie to bed, sing her a song before she slept.

Thirty-Eight

The telephone was ringing as I ran up the stairs, files under one arm and holding two bags full of supper for that evening. I tripped over Anatoly, cursed, dropped the bags and scooped up the phone just as the answering machine clicked on.

'Hold on,' I said breathlessly over my courteous, recorded voice, 'this'll switch off in a bit.'

'Sam, it's Miriam. I'm just checking on tonight. Are you still on?'

'Of course. The film begins at 8.30 and I've told the others to meet at 8.20 outside. I've bought some ready-meals to eat back here afterwards. It'll be lovely to see you again.'

I unpacked the food into the fridge. Elsie and Sophie would probably be back from the park in an hour or so. They'd be surprised to see me here before them. I went through to my bedroom (though personally I thought 'box room' would have been a more precise description of a space in which I had to squeeze past a small chest to get to my single bed) and picked up the pile of dirty clothes in the corner, shoved them into the washing machine.

A pile of bills lay on the kitchen table, a pile of dishes teetered in the small sink, books and CDs were standing in crooked towers along all the skirting boards. The rubbish bin was overflowing. Elsie's bedroom door opened on to a scene of extraordinary chaos. The plants which numerous friends had given to me when I moved here were wilting in their pots. I sloshed water over them recklessly, humming one of Elsie's absurd little ditties as I did so, making lists in my head. Ring the travel agent. Ring the bank. Remember to speak to Elsie's teacher tomorrow. Ring estate agent in the morning. Buy present for Olivia's fortieth birthday. Go through the report on the Harrogate train disaster. Write that promised paper for the *Lancet*. Get someone to come round and fit a cat flap for Anatoly.

The key turned in the lock and Sophie staggered in, laden with Elsie's picnic box and skipping rope.

'Hi,' I said, as I searched through the letters scattered over the table for the note from the ferry company. 'You're back early. But where's Elsie?'

'The most extraordinary thing happened!' She dumped her load on the table and sat down, plump and glossy in her fake-leopard-skin leggings and her tight and shiny T-shirt. 'We met your sister just as we were going into Clissold park. Elsie seemd really pleased to see her, rushed into her arms. She said she'd bring her back in a bit. I last saw them going hand in hand into the park. Bobbie, that's her name, isn't it, was going to buy her an ice-cream.'

'I didn't know she was going to be here,' I said, surprised. 'Did she say what she was doing?'

'Yeah. She said her husband had dropped her off on the way to some meeting or other and she'd been choosing curtains in that really swanky fabric shop along Church Street. Anyway, she can tell you herself later. Do you want me to make you a cup of tea?'

'Coming all the way to London to buy curtains. That's my sister. And then, now that we've got time and no child,

we could make a start on sorting the books and CDs. I
want everything in alphabetical order.'

We'd got as far as G, and I was covered in dust and sweat,
when the phone rang. It was my sister.

'Bobbie, this is a lovely surprise. Where are you? When
will you be here?'

'What?' Bobbie sounded quite bewildered.

'Shall I come and meet you in the park?'

'What park? What are you going on about Sam? I rang
up to see if Mum had rung you, she . . .'

'Hang on.' My mouth had gone strangely dry. 'Where
are you speaking from, Bobbie?'

'Well, from home of course.'

'You're not with Elsie?'

'Of course I'm not with Elsie, I have no idea what . . .'

But I was gone, slamming down the phone on her
bewilderment, yelling to Sophie to call the police *immediately* and tell them that Elsie had been kidnapped,
pounding down the narrow stairs, two at a time, heart
bumping in my chest, please let her be all right, please let
her be all right. I fell through the front door and sprinted,
feet hurting on the hot pavement. Up the street, pushing
past old ladies and women with buggies and young men
with large dogs. Through the slow trudge of people
coming home from work. Across the road as horns blared
and drivers wound down their windows to curse.

Through the iron gates of Clissold park, past the little-
bridge and the overfed ducks, the deer who nosed at the
high fencing with their velvet muzzles, along the avenue
of chestnut trees. I ran and I looked, my eyes scattering
from small shape to small shape. So many children and
none of them mine. I tore into the playground. Boys

and girls in bright anoraks were swinging, sliding, jumping, climbing. I stood between the see-saw and the sand-pit, where last month the park warden had found used syringes scattered, and stared wildly around.

'Elsie!' I yelled. 'Elsie!'

She wasn't there, although I saw her in every child and heard her in every scream. I looked over to where the paddling pond lay turquoise and deserted, then ran on, to the café, to the large ponds at the bottom of the park where we always fed bread to the ducks and the quarrelsome Canada geese. I peered over the fence to where crumbs and bits of litter drifted, as if I would see her little body drifting under the oily water. Then I started to run up the other side of the park. 'Elsie!' I called at intervals, 'Elsie darling, where are you?' but I never expected a reply and I received none. I started to stop people, a woman with a child about her age, a group of teenagers on skateboards, an elderly couple holding hands.

'Have you seen a little girl?' I asked. 'A little girl in a dark blue coat, with blonde hair? With a woman?'

One man thought he had. He waved his hand vaguely towards the circle of rosebushes behind us. A little boy whose mother I accosted said he'd seen a little girl in blue sitting on the bench, that bench, and he pointed towards the empty seat.

She was nowhere. I shut my eyes and played nightmares in my head: Elsie being dragged along, screaming; Elsie being pushed into a car and driven off; Elsie being hurt; Elsie calling and calling for me. This wasn't helping. I ran back towards the park gates again, stumbling, my side hurting, fear burning into my stomach like acid. Every so often I called her name, and crowds parted to let me through, a mad woman.

I raced into the cemetery close by Clissold park, because if someone wanted to drag someone off and harm them, this would be the obvious place. Brambles tore at my clothes. I tripped over old gravestones, saw couples, teenagers in groups, no children. I called and I shouted and I knew that this was futile because the place was huge and full of hidden corners, and even if Elsie was here there was no way I would find her.

So I went home, hope that she'd be waiting for me turning my stomach to water. But she wasn't there. Sophie met me, her face scared and baffled. Two police officers were there also. One of them, a woman, was on the phone. I gasped out what had happened – that it hadn't been my sister in the park – but they'd already had a fragmentary account from Sophie.

'It's my fault,' she was saying, and I could hear hysteria in her normally undemonstrative voice, 'it's all my fault.'

'No', I replied wearily. 'how could you have known?'

'Elsie seemed so happy to go off with her. I don't understand. She doesn't take easily to strangers.'

'This was no stranger.'

No, I didn't have a photograph of Elsie. At least not here. And as I embarked on a detailed description of my daughter, the doorbell rang. I ran down the stairs once more, opened the door. Then my eyes slid down from the smiling face of another uniformed policeman to a little girl in a blue coat who was licking the last of an orange ice-lolly. I sank to my knees on the pavement, and for a moment I thought I was going to throw up all over the policeman's shiny shoes. I put my arms around her body, buried my face into her squashy stomach.

'Careful of my lolly,' she said, a note of concern at last.

I stood up and hoisted her into my arms. The policeman grinned at me.

'A young lady found her wandering around in the park and handed her over to me,' he said. 'And this clever little girl remembered her address.' He chucked Elsie under the chin. 'Keep a better eye on her next time,' he said. He looked round at the other two police officers who were coming down the stairs towards us. 'Little girl wandered off.' The officers nodded at each other. The woman walked past me and began to say something into her radio, cancelling something. The other raised a weary eyebrow at his colleague. Another mad mother.

'Well, not exactly . . .' I started to say and then gave up. 'What did she look like, the woman who "found" her?'

The policeman shrugged.

'Young woman. I said you might want to thank her personally but she said it was nothing.'

With an imitation of effusive thanks, I managed to close the front door and be alone with my daughter.

'Elsie,' I said. 'Who've you been with?'

She looked up at me, her mouth smeared orange. 'You lied,' she said. 'She came back to life. I knew she would.'

Thirty-Nine

My film excursion, all that was cancelled. It was just Elsie and me at home once more and I gave her exactly what she wanted. Tinned rice pudding with golden syrup dripped on to it in the shape of a baby horse.

'It *is* a horse,' I insisted. 'Look, there's the tail and there are the pointy ears.'

It was an overwhelming effort but I made myself be casual.

'And how was Finn?'

'Fine,' said Elsie heedlessly, otherwise engaged in spiralling the golden-syrup pattern in the rice pudding with her spoon.

'That looks lovely, Elsie. Are you going to eat some of it? Good. What did you and Finn do?'

'We saw chickens.'

I manoeuvred Elsie into the bath and I blew bubbles with my fingers.

'That's a giant bubble, Mummy.'

'Shall I try and do an even bigger one? What did you and Finn talk about?'

'We talked and we talked and we talked.'

'There's two little baby bubbles. What did you talk *about*?'

'We talked about our house.'

'That's nice.'

'Can I sleep in your bed, Mummy?'

I carried her through to my bed and I gratefully felt her warm wetness through my shirt. She told me to take off my clothes and I took them off and we lay beneath the sheets together. I found a brush on the bedside table and we brushed each other's hair. We sang some songs and I taught her to clip up, the game in which I turned my big fist and she turned her little fist into a stone, some paper or scissors. Stone blunts scissors, scissors cut paper and paper wraps stone. Each time we did it, she waited for me to show what I was going to do and then made her own decision so that she could win and I accused her of cheating and we both laughed. It was an intensely happy time and I had to stop myself at every moment from running out of the room and howling. I might have done it but I couldn't bear the notion of letting Elsie out of my sight for a moment.

'When can we see Fing again?' she asked, out of nowhere.

I couldn't think what to say.

'It's funny that you talked about our house with ... with Finn,' I said. 'It must be because you played such lovely games there with her.'

'No,' said Elsie firmly.

I couldn't help smiling at her.

'Why not?'

'It wasn't *that* house, Mummy.'

'What do you mean?'

'It was our safe house.'

'How lovely, my darling.' I held Elsie close against my body.

'Ow, you're hurting.'

'Sorry, my love. And did she put things into the safe house?'

'Yes,' said Elsie, who had started to examine my eyebrow. 'There's a white hair there.'

I felt a vertiginous nausea as if I were staring into a black chasm.

'Yes, I know. Funny, isn't it?' Without disturbing Elsie, I felt behind me for the pencil and pad of paper that I had seen next to the phone on the bedside table. 'Shall we go into the safe house?'

'What colour is your eye?'

'Ow!' I howled as an interested finger poked my left eye.

'Sorry, Mummy.'

'It's blue.'

'What's mine?'

'Blue. Elsie, shall we go into the safe house and have a look? Elsie?'

'Oh, all right,' she said like a truculent adolescent.

'All right, my darling, close your eyes. That's right. Let's walk up the path. What's on the door?'

'There's round leaves.'

'Round leaves? That's a funny thing. Let's open the door and see what's down on the doormat.'

'There's a glass of milk.'

I noted it down.

'A glass of milk on a doormat?' I said in my best nursery-school teacher's tone. 'How strange! Let's walk carefully round the glass of milk, without spilling it, and into the kitchen. What's in the kitchen?'

'A drum.'

'A drum in the kitchen? What a mad house! Let's go and see what's on TV, shall we? What's on the television?'

'A pear.'

'That's nice. You like pears, don't you? But let's not

have a bite of the pear yet. Don't touch it. I saw you touch it.' Elsie giggled. 'Let's go upstairs. What's on the stairs?'

'A drum.'

'Another drum. Are you sure?'

'Ye-e-es, Mum,' Elsie said impatiently.

'All right. This is a lovely game, isn't it? Now, I wonder what's in the bath.'

'A ring.'

'That's a funny thing to have in a bath. Maybe it fell off your finger when you were splashing in the bath?'

'It did not!' Elsie shouted.

'Now we'll get out of the bath and go into Elsie's bed. What's in the bed?'

Elsie laughed.

'There's a swan in the bed.'

'A swan in a bed. How is Elsie going to get to sleep if there's a swan in her bed?' Elsie's eyes were starting to flutter, her head wobbling. She would be asleep in a second. 'Now let's go into Mummy's bedroom. Who's in Mummy's bed?'

Now Elsie's voice sounded as if she was drifting away.

'Mummy's in Mummy's bed,' she said softly. 'And Elsie's in Mummy's arms. And their eyes are closed.'

'That's beautiful,' I said. But I saw that Elsie was already asleep. I leaned across and stroked some strands of hair away from her face. Paul, the mysterious absent proprietor of the flat, had a desk in the corner of his bedroom and I tiptoed over to it and sat down with the notebook. I brushed my neck gently with my fingertips and felt the pulse in my carotid artery. It must have been close to 120. Today the murderer of my lover had kidnapped my little daughter. Why hadn't she killed her or done something with her? Suddenly I rushed to the bathroom. I didn't vomit. I took a few deep slow breaths, but it was a close thing. I returned to the desk, switched on the small light and scrutinized my notes.

The murderer, X, had seized my daughter, risking capture, and all so that she could play one of the silly little mind games we used to play together at my house in the country with her. When Elsie told me what they had done, I expected something grisly, but instead there was this stupid collection of mundane objects: round leaves, a glass of milk, a drum, a pear, another drum, a ring, a swan and then Elsie and me in my bed with our eyes closed. What are round leaves? I drew little sketches of them. I took the first letter of each and played around with them uselessly. I tried to make some connection with where each object had been put. Was there something deliberately paradoxical about a swan in a bed, about a glass of milk on the doormat? Perhaps this nameless woman had put random objects into my child's mind as a means of demonstrating her power.

I left the scrawled piece of paper and returned to bed and lay next to Elsie, listening for the sound of her breath, feeling the expansion and contraction of her chest. Just when I was feeling that I had gone a whole night without sleep and wondering how I could possibly get through a whole day, I was woken up by Elsie pulling my eyelids apart. I gave a groan.

'What's happening today, Elsie?'

'Don't know.'

It was the first day at her new school. On the phone my mother had been disapproving. Elsie is not a piece of furniture that can just be moved out of London and then back again whenever you want. She needs stability and a home. Yes, I knew what my mother was saying.

That she needed a father and brothers and sisters and, preferably, a mother as unlike me as possible. I was brisk and cheerful with my mother on the phone and cried when she had rung off and got cross, depressed and then felt better. The primary school was obliged to take Elsie because the flat we were staying in virtually overlooked the playground.

I felt an ache in my stomach as Elsie, in a new yellow dress, with her hair combed flat and tied in a ribbon, walked across the road with me to her new school. I saw small children arriving and greeting each other. How could Elsie survive in this? We went to the office and a middle-aged woman smiled at Elsie and Elsie glared at the middle-aged woman. She led us along to the Reception class, held in an annexe. The teacher was a young woman, with dark hair, and a calm manner that I immediately envied. She came over immediately and hugged Elsie.

'Hello, Elsie. Do you want Mummy to stay for a little bit?'

'No, I don't,' said Elsie with a thunderous brow.

'Well, give her a hug bye-bye, then.'

I held her and felt her small hands on the back of my neck.

'All right?' I asked.

She nodded.

'Elsie, why are the leaves round?'

She smiled.

'*We* had round leaves on our door.'

'When?'

'For Father Christmas.'

Round leaves. She meant a garland. I was unable to speak. I kissed Elsie on her forehead and ran out of the classroom and down the corridor. Emergency, I shouted at a disapproving teacher. I sprinted across the road, up the stairs to the flat. There was a pain in my chest and a bad taste in my mouth. I was unfit. Almost everything was in storage but I had a couple of cardboard boxes full of Elsie's books. I tipped one of them on to the floor and scrambled among them. It wasn't there. I tipped the other one over. There. *The Twelve Days of Christmas Picture Book.* I took it into the bedroom and sat at the desk. That was it. The swans a-swimming. Five gold rings. The drummers drumming. And a par-tri-idge in a pear tree. But what about the glass of milk? I flicked through the book, wondering if I was on the wrong track somehow. No. I allowed myself a half-smile. Eight maids a-milking. So, a contorted reference to a Christmas song. What was the point of it?

I jotted them down in the order Elsie had visited them: eight maids a-milking, nine drummers drumming, a partridge in a pear tree, nine drummers drumming again, five gold rings, seven swans swimming. I stared at the list and then suddenly the objects seemed to recede and the numerals to float free. Eight, nine, one, nine, five, seven. Such a familiar number. I grabbed the phone and dialled. Nothing. Of course. I dialled directory inquiries and got the Otley area code, then dialled again. There was no ring, just a continuous tone. Had it been cut off when I moved out? In confusion I rang Rupert at Stamford CID.

'I was about to call you,' were his first words.

'I wanted to tell you . . .' I stopped myself. 'Why?'

'Nobody's been hurt, there's nothing to worry about, but I'm afraid there's been a fire. Your house burned down last night.' I couldn't speak. 'Are you there, Sam?'

'Yes. How? What happened?'

'I don't know. But it's been so dry and hot. There's

been a rash of fires. Could be some electrical fault. We'll have a careful look. We'll know soon.'

'Yes.'

'Funny thing you should ring just now. What did you want to say?'

I thought of Elsie's words as she had fallen asleep last night.

'Mummy's in Mummy's bed. And Elsie's in Mummy's arms. And their eyes are closed.' Were we asleep and safe or were we dead and cold like the pairs of bodies that X had already looked down on? Leo and Liz Mackenzie. Danny and Finn, brought together in death.

'Nothing really,' I said. 'I just wanted to see how things were going.'

'It's progressing,' he said.

I didn't believe him.

Forty

Mark, the young estate agent, rang me later in the afternoon.

'I hope you've got an alibi,' he said cheerily.

'Now, look here . . .'

'Joke, Dr Laschen. No harm was done.'

'My house was burned down.'

'Nobody was hurt, that's the main thing. But the other thing, not that I'd put it that way myself, but the main thing with a silver lining is that you are insured and some people might at a time like this point out that you will do better by your house burning down than you would have done by selling it.'

'How can that be?'

'It's not that I'd say it myself, but some properties have been slow to move off our books and the sales tend to go to properties that are competitively priced. Very competitively priced.'

'But I thought my house was so extremely saleable.'

'Theoretically speaking, it was.'

'You sound very chipper about the whole thing. Were you insured as well?'

'Inasmuch as we are required to take certain financial precautions.'

'So we both seem to have done rather well out of this disaster.'

'There may be one or two forms to sign on our behalf. Perhaps we could discuss them over a drink.'

'Send them. Bye, Mark.'

I replaced the receiver wondering whether the fire had been a warning or a perverse gift from a woman who knew my pyromaniacal tendencies, or both.

'She's been fine,' said Miss Olds when I went to collect Elsie. 'A bit tired this afternoon, but she sat on my lap and we read a book together. Didn't we, Elsie?'

Elsie, who had given me a casual wave when she saw me, had wandered over to the home corner, where she and another little girl were wordlessly arranging plastic food on plastic plates and pretending to eat it. She looked up at the teacher's words, but only nodded.

'Things have been very, ah, disruptive for her recently,' I said. My heart was still racing in my chest, like a motor car revving up wildly before a race. I clenched my fists together and tried to breathe more slowly.

'I know,' said Miss Olds with a smile. She had read the papers too.

I looked over at my daughter again, stopped myself from running across and picking her up and holding her too tight.

'Yes, so I'm anxious for her to feel safe.'

Miss Olds looked at me sympathetically. She had deep brown eyes and a subtle mole just above her top lip. 'I think she's settling in here.'

'I'm glad,' said. Then: 'Strangers can't easily just get in and wander around here, can they?'

Miss Olds put her hand lightly on my arm. 'No,' she said, 'they can't. Though there are limits to the security

356

you can have at a school where two hundred children arrive every morning.'

I grimaced, nodded. Stinging tears fuzzed my vision.

'Thanks,' I said.

'She's fine.'

'Thanks.'

I called to Elsie, held out my hand, and she plodded over in her buttercup-yellow dress, blue felt-tip in a scar down her flushed cheek.

'Come on, my poppet.'

'Are we going home?'

'Yes, home.'

'At the heart of it are people who were not what they seemed.' That is what I had said, so slyly, to the journalist. It had been intended as a warning to Rupert Baird but it had been read and taken as a warning by X, whoever she was. She had demonstrated once more that nothing was safe. My house was burned down and she had penetrated the mind of my daughter.

When we got home I put Elsie in a bath, to wash everything off her. She was in there pottering and talking to herself while I sat on the stairs outside and stared at the wall, telling a story to myself. I knew nothing about the girl but I knew a bit about Michael Daley. It was possible that if I investigated his life, I might find the shadow from which the girl had emerged. And I thought of the final image in Elsie's safe house. Mummy and Elsie lying asleep in each other's arms. There were two possible ends to the story. Elsie and Mummy dead together. Or Elsie and Mummy living happy ever after. No, that was too much. Living. That was enough. My reverie was interrupted by the ringing of the phone. Baird, of course.

'I hope you've got an alibi,' he said jocularly, as the estate agent had done before him.

'You'll never catch me, copper,' I replied, and he laughed. Then there was a pause. 'Is that it?' I asked.

'We heard that there was an incident yesterday.'

So they were keeping track of me. This was the moment of decision, but I listened to the splashing and knew that I had already made up my mind.

'It was a misunderstanding, Rupert. Elsie wandered off in the park. It was nothing.'

'Are you sure, Sam?'

We were like two chess players testing each other's defences before agreeing a draw and giving up and going home.

'Yes, I'm sure, Rupert.'

I could sense the relief at the other end of the line and he said goodbye warmly, saying that he would be in touch, and I knew that this would be the last conversation we ever had.

I lifted Elsie out of the bath and sat her on the sofa in her dressing gown and put a plate of toast and Marmite on her lap.

'Can I have a video?'

'Later perhaps, after supper.'

'Can you read me a book?'

'Soon I will. First I thought we could play a game together.'

'Can we play musical bumps?'

'That's hard when there's just the two of us, and one of us has to be in charge of the music. I tell you what, it's your birthday in a couple of weeks' time, we'll play that at your party.'

'Party? Am I going to have a party? Can I really have

a party?' Her pale face shone under its smudgy freckles. The tip of her pink tongue licked a smear of Marmite from her lip.

'Listen, that's part of the game, Elsie. We're going to plan your party and we're going to put the most important party things into the safe house.'

'So we don't forget!'

'That's it, so we don't forget. Where do we start?'

'The front door.' Elsie was wriggling happily on the sofa, one Marmite hand in mine.

'Right! Let's take off the garland of leaves. It's way past Christmas. What should we put there instead, if you're having a party?'

'I know, balloons!'

'Balloons: a red one and a green one and a yellow one and a blue one. Maybe they'll have faces on them!' In my mind, I had an image of a line of little girls in their pink and yellow party dresses, all there for Elsie. I remembered the parties I'd been to as a child: sticky chocolate cake and pink-iced biscuits, crisps and fizzy drinks; pin-the-tail-on-the-donkey and pass-the-parcel so that everyone won something, dancing games, Simon Says, and at the end a party bag containing one small pack of Smarties, one plastic thing that would be adored for an hour and forgotten for ever, a whistle, a flat shiny balloon. Elsie should have them all, all those cheap and tacky things. 'And what's next?'

'The doormat, the doormat where Fing put a glass of milk.'

'Yes, well, I think we've knocked over that milk by now.' Elsie giggled. 'What shall we put there instead?'

'Um, what can go on a doormat, Mummy?'

'Well, there's someone we are very fond of who's

creeping nearer to your Marmite all the time so mind out, and he likes to sleep on the doormat.'

'Anatoly!'

'He can be our watch-cat. What shall we put in the kitchen? How about something we've cooked?'

Elsie jumped up and down, so that the plate slithered and I caught the toast stickily on my palm. 'My cake! My cake in the shape of a horse house.'

I remembered. The one at a friend's birthday party with the walls made of chocolate flakes and plastic horses in the middle, and Elsie had been sick half-way through. I hugged her.

'Horse cake. Now, what's on the TV?' She puckered her brow. 'How about my birthday present to you? Something you've wanted for a long time, maybe something that sings.'

Her body went still.

'Really, Mummy, do you promise? Can I really?'

'We'll choose it together this weekend. A canary on top of the TV then, singing away.'

'Can I call him Yellowy?'

'No. Now, what shall we put on the stairs?'

She was firm here: 'I want Thelma and Kirsty and Sarah and Granny and Grandpa, because they're all coming to my party. And that girl I played with today at school. And the other one too, the one you saw me with. I want to send them invitations.'

'All right, all your party guests on the stairs. What's in the bath?'

'That's easy. My red boat with the propeller that never sinks, not even in big waves.'

'Good.' Another boat sailed into my mind, broken and tipping into the crested sea. 'Where next?'

'My bedroom.'

'What shall we put in your bed then, Elsie?'

'Can we put my teddy there? Can we get him out of the packing box so he doesn't miss the party?'

'Of course. I should never have put him there in the first place. And last of all, I know what's in my bed.'

'What?'

'We are. You and me. We're lying in bed together wide awake and the party's over and all your guests have gone and we're talking about all the birthdays you're going to have.'

'Are you very old, Mummy?'

'No, just grown-up, not old.'

'So you're not going to die soon?'

'No, I'm going to live for a long time.'

'When I'm as old as you, will you be dead then?'

'Maybe you will have children then, and I'll be a granny.'

'Can we always live together, Mummy?'

'As long as you want to.'

'And can I watch a video now?'

'Yes.'

I shut the door on *Mary Poppins* and went into the kitchen, where I pulled the window wide open. The sound of London invaded the room: schoolchildren on their way home, giggling or quarrelling, syncopated music from a ghetto-blaster, the roar and impatient rev of car engines, a horn pumping into the stop–start queue, an ignored and insistent alarm, sirens in the distance, overhead a plane. I breathed in the smell of honeysuckle, exhaust fumes, frying garlic, urban heat, the smell of the city.

She was out there somewhere, in that wonderful ungraspable mess, out in the crowd. Perhaps she was close by or perhaps she was gone for ever. I wondered if I would ever see her again. Perhaps one day, across a street, or in a queue at an airport or across a square in a foreign town, I'd glimpse a smooth face tilted upwards in the way I knew so well and stop and shake my head and walk quickly on. I'd see her in my dreams, smiling sweetly at me still. Her freedom was a small price to pay for Elsie's safety. And I'd look at the newspapers. She had escaped but she hadn't escaped with the money, not any of it. What would she do now? I closed my eyes and breathed in, out, in, out, to the roar of London. Danny had died but we – me and Elsie – we had come through. That was something.

The sound of Mary Poppins singing brightly to the children and to my child drifted in from the living room. I pushed open the door. Elsie was sitting back on the sofa, legs tucked up under her knees, glaring at the screen. I knelt beside her and she patted me absent-mindedly on the head.

'Can you watch this with me, Mummy, the way Fing used to?' So I stayed and watched, until the very end.

Read on for a taste of

Killing Me Softly

by
Nicci French

Available in Penguin at £6.99

The following morning, the underground was more than usually crowded. I felt hot inside all my layers of clothing, and I tried to distract myself by thinking about other things as I swayed against the bodies and the train clattered through the darkness. I thought about how my hair needed cutting. I could book it for lunch-time. I tried to remember if there was enough food in the house for tonight, or maybe we could get a takeaway. Or go dancing. I remembered I hadn't taken my pill this morning and must do it as soon as I got to work. The thought of the pill made me think of the IUD and yesterday's meeting, the memory of which had left me more unwilling than usual to get out of bed this morning.

A skinny young woman with a large, red-faced baby squeezed her way down the train. No one stood up for her, and she stood with her child on her angular hip, held in place by the bodies all round her. Only the baby's hot, cross face was exposed. Sure enough, it soon started yelling, hoarse, drawn-out wails that made its red cheeks purple, but the woman ignored it, as if she was beyond noticing. She had a glazed expression on her pallid face. Although her baby was dressed for an expedition to the South Pole, she wore just a thin dress and an unzipped anorak. I tested myself for maternal instinct. Negative. Then I looked round at all the men and women in suits. I leaned down to a man in a lovely cashmere coat, till I was near enough to see his spots, then said softly into his ear: 'Excuse me. Can you make room for this woman?' He looked puzzled, resistant. 'She needs a seat.'

He stood up and the mother shuffled over and wedged herself between two *Guardian*s. The baby continued to wail, and she continued to stare ahead of her. The man could feel virtuous now.

I was glad to get out at my station, though I wasn't looking forward to the day ahead. When I thought about work, a lethargy settled over me, as if all my limbs were heavy and the chambers of my brain musty. It was icy on the streets, and my breath curled into the air. I wrapped my scarf more firmly around my neck. I should have worn a hat. Maybe I could nip out in a coffee-break and buy some boots. All around me people were hurrying to their different offices, heads down. Jake and I should go away somewhere in February, somewhere hot and deserted. Anywhere that wasn't London. I imagined a white beach and a blue sky and me slim and tanned in a bikini. I'd been seeing too many advertisements. I always wore a one-piece. Oh, well. Jake had been on at me about saving money.

I stopped at the zebra crossing. A lorry roared by. A pigeon and I scuttled back in unison. I glimpsed the driver, high up in his cab and blind to all the people below him trudging to work. The next car squeaked to a halt and I stepped out into the road.

A man was crossing from the other side. I noticed he was wearing black jeans and a black leather jacket, and then I looked up at his face. I don't know if he stopped first or I did. We both stood in the road staring at each other. I think I heard a horn blare. I couldn't move. It felt like an age, but it was probably only a second. There was an empty, hungry feeling in my stomach and I couldn't breathe in properly. A horn was sounded once more. Someone shouted something. His eyes were a startling blue. I started walking across the road again, and so did he, and we passed each other, inches away, our eyes locked. If he had reached out and touched me, I think I would have turned and followed him, but he didn't and I reached the pavement alone.

I walked towards the building that contained the Drakon offices, then stopped and looked back. He was still there, watching me. He didn't smile or make any gesture. It was an effort to turn away again, with his gaze on me as if it were pulling me back towards him. When I reached the revolving doors of the Drakon building and pushed through them, I took a last glance back. He was gone, the man with blue eyes. So that was that.

I went at once to the cloakroom, shut myself into a cubicle and leaned against the door. I felt dizzy, my knees trembled and there was a heavy feeling at the back of my eyes, like unshed tears. Maybe I was getting a cold. Maybe my period was about to start. I thought of the man and the way he had stared at me, and I closed my eyes as if that would somehow shut him out. Someone else came into the cloakroom, turned on a tap. I stood very still and quiet, and could hear my heart thudding beneath my blouse. I laid my hand against my burning cheek, put it on my breast.

After a few minutes I could breathe properly again. I splashed cold water on my face, combed my hair, and remembered to remove a tiny pill from its foil calendar and swallow it. The ache in my guts was fading, and now I just felt fragile, jittery. Thank God nobody had seen anything. I bought coffee from the machine on the second floor and a bar of chocolate, for I was suddenly ravenous, and made my way to my office. I picked the wrapper and then the gold foil off the chocolate with shaky, incompetent fingers and ate it in large bites. The working day began. I read through my mail and tossed most of it into the bin, wrote a memo to Mike, then phoned Jake at work.

'How's your day going?' I asked.

'It's only just started.'

I felt as if hours had passed since leaving home. If I leaned back and closed my eyes, I could sleep for hours.

'Last night was nice,' he said, in a low voice. Maybe there were other people around at his end.

'Mmm. I felt a bit odd this morning, though, Jake.'

'Are you all right now?' He sounded concerned. I'm never ill.

'Yes. Fine. Completely fine. Are you all right?'

I'd run out of things to say but I was reluctant to put the phone down. Jake suddenly sounded preoccupied. I heard him say something I couldn't make out to someone else.

'Yes, love. Look, I'd better go. 'Bye.'

The morning passed. I went to another meeting, this time with the marketing department, managed to spill a jug of water over the table and say nothing at all. I read through the research document Giovanna had e-mailed to me. She was coming to see me at three thirty. I phoned up the hairdresser's and made an appointment for one o'clock. I drank lots of bitter, tepid coffee out of polystyrene cups. I watered the plants in my office. I learned to say 'Je voudrais quatre petits pains' and 'Ça fait combien?'

Just before one I picked up my coat, left a message for

my assistant that I would be out for an hour or so, then clattered down the stairs and into the street. It was just beginning to drizzle, and I hadn't got an umbrella. I looked up at the clouds, shrugged, and started to walk quickly along Cardamom Street where I could pick up a taxi to the hairdresser's. I stopped dead in my tracks and the world blurred. My stomach gave a lurch. I felt as if I was about to double up.

He was there, a few feet from me. As if he hadn't moved since this morning. Still in his black jacket and jeans; still not smiling. Just standing and looking at me. I felt then as if no one had ever looked at me properly before and was suddenly and acutely conscious of myself – of the pounding of my heart, the rise and fall of my breath; of the surface of my body, which was prickling with a kind of panic and excitement.

He was my sort of age, early thirties. I suppose he was beautiful, with his pale blue eyes and his tumbled brown hair and his high, flat cheekbones. But then all I knew was that he was so focused on me that I felt I couldn't move out of his gaze. I heard my breath come in a little ragged gasp, but I didn't move and I couldn't turn away.

I don't know who made the first step. Perhaps I stumbled towards him, or perhaps I just waited for him, and when we stood opposite each other, not touching, hands by our sides, he said, in a low voice, 'I've been waiting for you.'

I should have laughed out loud. This wasn't me, this couldn't be happening to me. I was just Alice Loudon, on her way to have her hair cut on a damp day in January. But I couldn't laugh or smile. I could only go on looking at him into his wide-set blue eyes, at his mouth, which was slightly parted, the tender lips. He had white, even teeth, except that the front one was chipped. His chin was stubbly. There was a scratch on his neck. His hair was quite long, and unbrushed. Oh, yes, he was beautiful. I wanted to reach up and touch his mouth, ever so gently, with one thumb. I wanted to feel the scratch of his stubble in the hollow of my neck. I tried to say something, but all that came out of me was a strangled, prim 'Oh.'

'Please,' he said then, still not taking his eyes off my face. 'Will you come with me?'

He could have been a mugger, a rapist, a psychopath. I nodded dumbly at him and he stepped into the road, flagged down a taxi. He held open the door for me, but still didn't touch me. Inside he gave an address to the driver then turned towards me. I saw that under his leather jacket he wore only a dark green T-shirt. There was a leather thong around his neck with a small silver spiral hung on it. His hands were bare. I looked at his long fingers, with their neat, clean nails. A white scar kinked down one thumb. They looked practical hands, strong, dangerous.

'Tell me your name?'

'Alice,' I said. I didn't recognize my own voice.

'Alice,' he repeated. 'Alice.' The word sounded unfamiliar when he said it like that. He lifted his hands and, very gently, careful not to make any contact with my skin, loosened my scarf. He smelt of soap and sweat.

The taxi stopped and, looking out, I saw that we were in Soho. There was a paper shop, a delicatessen, restaurants. I could smell coffee and garlic. He got out and once more held the door open for me. I could feel the blood pulsing in my body. He pushed at a shabby door by the side of a clothes shop and I followed him up a narrow flight of steps. He took a bunch of keys from his pocket and unlocked two locks. Inside, it wasn't just a room but a small flat. I saw shelves, books, pictures, a rug. I hovered on the threshold. It was my last chance. The noise from the street outside filtered through the windows, the rise and fall of voices, the rumble of cars. He closed the door and bolted it from the inside.

I should have been scared, and I was, but not of him, this stranger. I was scared at myself. I didn't know myself any longer. I was dissolving with my desire, as if all the outlines of my body were becoming insubstantial. I started to take off my coat, hands clumsy on the velvet buttons, but he stopped me.

'Wait,' he said. 'Let me.'

First he removed my scarf and hung it carefully on the coat-stand. Next, my coat, taking his time. He knelt on the floor and slipped off my shoes. I put my hand on his shoulder to stop myself toppling. He stood again, and started to unbutton my cardigan, and I saw that his hands were trembling slightly. He undid my skirt and pulled it down over my hips; it rasped against my tights. He tugged off my tights, collecting them into a flimsy ball, which he put beside my shoes. Still, he had hardly made contact with my skin. He took off my camisole and slid down my knickers and I stood naked in that unfamiliar room, shivering slightly.

'Alice,' he said, in a kind of groan. Then, 'Oh, God, you're lovely, Alice.'

I took off his jacket. His arms were strong and brown, and there was another long, puckered scar running from the elbow to the wrist. I copied him and knelt at his feet to pull off his shoes and socks. On his right foot, he had only three toes, and I bent down and kissed the place where the other two had been. He sighed softly. I tugged his shirt free of his jeans and he raised his arms like a little boy while I pulled it over his head. He had a flat stomach with a line of hair running down it. I unzipped his jeans and eased them carefully down over his buttocks. His legs were knotty, quite tanned. I took off his underpants and dropped them on to the floor. Someone moaned, but I don't know if it was him or me. He lifted one hand and tucked a strand of hair behind my ear, then traced my lips with a forefinger, very slowly. I closed my eyes.

'No,' he said. 'Look at me.'

'Please,' I said. 'Please.'

He unhooked my earrings and let them fall. I heard them clink on the wooden boards.

'Kiss me, Alice,' he said.

Nothing like this had ever happened to me before. Sex had never been like this. There had been indifferent sex, embarrassing sex, nasty sex, good sex, great sex. This was more like obliterating sex. We crashed together, trying to get past the barrier of skin and flesh. We held each other as if we were drowning. We tasted each other as if we were starving. And all the time he looked at me. He looked at me as if I were the loveliest thing he had ever seen, and as I lay on the hard dusty floor I felt lovely, shameless, quite done for.

Afterwards, he lifted me to my feet and took me into the shower and washed me down. He soaped my breasts and between my legs. He washed my feet and thighs. He even washed my hair, expertly massaging shampoo into it, tilting my head back so soap wouldn't run into my eyes. Then he dried me, making sure I was dry under my arms, between my toes, and as he dried me he examined me. I felt like a work of art, and like a prostitute.

'I must go back to work,' I said at last. He dressed me, picking up my clothes from the floor, threading my earrings through my lobes, brushing my wet hair back from my face.

'When do you finish work?' he asked. I thought of Jake waiting at home.

'Six.'

'I'll be there,' he said. I should have told him then that I had a partner, a home, a whole other life. Instead I pulled his face towards mine and kissed his bruised lips. I could hardly bring myself to pull my body away from his.

In the taxi, alone, I pictured him, remembered his touch, his taste, his smell. I didn't know his name.

refresh yourself at penguin.co.uk

Visit penguin.co.uk for exclusive information and interviews with
bestselling authors, fantastic give-aways and the
inside track on all our books, from the Penguin Classics
to the latest bestsellers.

BE FIRST

first chapters, first editions, first novels

EXCLUSIVES

author chats, video interviews, biographies, special
features

EVERYONE'S A WINNER

give-aways, competitions, quizzes, ecards

READERS GROUPS

exciting features to support existing groups and
create new ones

NEWS

author events, bestsellers, awards, what's new

EBOOKS

books that click – download an ePenguin today

BROWSE AND BUY

thousands of books to investigate – search, try
and buy the perfect gift online – or treat yourself!

ABOUT US

job vacancies, advice for writers and company
history

Get Closer To Penguin . . . www.penguin.co.uk